RIVERRISE

THE NIGHT WOODS

THE WESTERN WOODS

THE

WOODS

THE NIGHT TRAIL

THE THORN FORESTS

THORN HARBOUR

THE FOUR LAKES

THE NORTHERN REACHES

THE FARROW RIDGES

THE NEEDLES HIGH FARROW

THE WATER CAVERNS

MIDRIDGE

BY PAUL STEWART & CHRIS RIDDELL

THE EDGE CHRONICLES:

The Quint Saga
The Curse of the Gloamglozer
The Winter Knights
Clash of the Sky Galleons

The Twig Saga
Beyond the Deepwoods
Stormchaser
Midnight Over Sanctaphrax

The Rook Saga
The Last of the Sky Pirates
Vox
Freeglader

The Nate Saga
The Immortals

The Cade Saga
The Nameless One
Doombringer
The Descenders

BARNABY GRIMES:

Curse of the Night Wolf
Return of the Emerald Skull
Legion of the Dead
Phantom of Blood Alley

WYRMEWEALD:

Returner's Wealth
Bloodhoney
The Bone Trail

For younger readers:

FAR-FLUNG ADVENTURES:

Fergus Crane
Corby Flood
Hugo Pepper

www.stewartandriddell.co.uk

THE EDGE CHRONICLES

THE DESCENDERS
← BOOK 3 OF THE CADE SAGA ←

STEWART & RIDDELL

CORGI BOOKS

CORGI BOOKS

UK | USA | Canada | Ireland | Australia
India | New Zealand | South Africa

Corgi Books is part of the Penguin Random House group of companies
whose addresses can be found at global.penguinrandomhouse.com.

www.penguin.co.uk
www.puffin.co.uk
www.ladybird.co.uk

Penguin
Random House
UK

First published in hardback by Doubleday and in paperback by Corgi Books 2019

001

Copyright © Paul Stewart and Chris Riddell, 2019
Cover artwork copyright © Jeff Nentrup, 2019

The moral right of the author and illustrators has been asserted

Set in Palatino by Jouve (UK), Milton Keynes
Printed and bound in Great Britain by Clays Ltd, Elcograf S.p.A.

A CIP catalogue record for this book is available from the British Library

ISBN: 978–0–552–56759–6

All correspondence to:
Corgi Books
Penguin Random House Children's
80 Strand, London WC2R 0RL

· INTRODUCTION ·

F ar far away, jutting out into the emptiness beyond,
like the figurehead of a mighty stone ship, is the
Edge. It forms the tip of a vast, sprawling land of rock
and grassland and seemingly endless forest. A river – the
Edgewater River – cuts through it all. Its source lies at
Riverrise, far to the west. From there, it meanders its way
across the shifting landscapes, gathering size and power
as it does so, before pouring over the lip of rock at its
easternmost point in a mighty torrent.

Close to this isolated outcrop, secured to the ground
below it, is the floating city of New Sanctaphrax. In the
First Age of Flight, when the uncharted Deepwoods
were inhabited only by primitive tribes, Sanctaphrax
was the centre of Earth and Sky studies. Later, following
the cutting of the anchor chain that moored it, the city
drifted off into Open Sky, only returning five hundred
years later at the beginning of the Third Age of Flight.

Back then, it was infested with malevolent shapeshifters. But they have gone now, and the city has changed once more.

These days, New Sanctaphrax is vibrant, youthful and growing fast. Ancient, dilapidated buildings are being renovated; magnificent new ones are being built. The city has become renowned throughout the Edge for its liberal values and modern learning. Like weary travellers to a welcoming hearth, the poor, the downtrodden and the oppressed are drawn there; political dissenters and heretical scholars now call it home.

Most prominent among the many newcomers are the Descenders. And although they are revered within the floating city itself, it is because of these brave explorers, who have dedicated their lives to discovering what lies far below the Edge, that the very existence of New Sanctaphrax is now under threat.

From the earliest times, Edge academics have tried to make sense of their world. Earth scholars, cloudwatchers, mistsifters; Professors of Light and Darkness. Theories have come and gone. One century's facts became another century's fables.

Once, for instance, it was believed that those who stepped off the Edge would fall for ever. Now, thanks to the intrepid Descenders and their expeditions down into the depths, this is no longer certain. From beneath the jutting rock, far below the cloud cover and shrouded in permanent darkness, they have brought sightings of land. New, uncharted land. Land unlike any encountered before. Despite the terrible dangers, the Descenders are determined to unlock its secrets. For in doing so, they believe they will discover the origins of life itself.

But not all Edgelanders support this perilous undertaking.

In Riverrise, where the waif elders disapprove of anyone venturing down into the eternal night, descending has been condemned. In Hive, still recovering from years of tyrannical rule, such pursuits are considered pointless at best; at worst, a wicked waste of resources. It is, however, in Great Glade where opposition to the Descenders is strongest.

Like New Sanctaphrax now, the Deepwoods' city of Great Glade was once a magnet for those who wished to live in freedom, peace and harmony. It was founded in the First Age of Flight by the legendary champion of the lost and dispossessed, Maris Verginix, as a safe refuge: a place where everyone was equal. But, like so much else in the Edge, Great Glade has changed over the centuries. Thanks to its power-crazed High Professor of Flight, Quove Lentis, it has become a harsh and brutal place, intolerant of new ideas, leaving its citizens terrified of dissent.

From his sumptuous palace in the Cloud Quarter, and with the support of his mighty skyfleet and powerful army, Quove Lentis rules the city with an iron fist. It is he who decides which academic subjects may or may not be studied. Considering it a threat to his own power, he has decreed that descending must end – and if that means destroying New Sanctaphrax in the process, then so be it.

Opinions differ as to why he hates descending so intensely. Some say that it is because of his allegiance with the waifs of Riverrise, from whom he obtains supplies of the eternal water of life. Others maintain that he fears his stranglehold on skyship-building in this, the Third Age of Flight, might be jeopardized by the new technology the Descenders are using. And then there are those – the majority – who claim simply that his heart has hardened with old age.

Whatever the reason, Quove Lentis has decreed that descending is heresy, and that Descenders and their sympathizers are enemies of Great Glade. They must be wiped out. And it is the most famous Descender of all, Nate Quarter, who is at the top of his list of heretics. Quove Lentis will not be happy until he, and everyone related to him, is dead.

Nate's half-brother, Thadeus Quarter, a talented scholar whose work on phrax crystals had the potential to transform life in the Edge, has already been murdered. And Thadeus's son, Cade, would have been next, had he not managed to flee Great Glade just in time.

Having stowed away on board a passing skytavern, Cade Quarter travelled to the Farrow Ridges, where a tiny outpost was situated on a beautiful lake in a distant corner of the Edge. Here, the former 'city boy' carved out a life for himself, building a cabin, learning to hunt and fish, and forging lifelong friendships.

Cade loves his new home and has no intention of leaving. But he is in great danger. Quove Lentis's influence is spreading to the furthest reaches of the Edgelands. He has already funded an invasion of the Farrow Ridges by ruthless mercenaries; an invasion that Cade and his friends defeated, leaving Quove Lentis more vengeful still. What is more, Drax Adereth, one of Lentis's trusted henchmen – and someone Cade crossed on board the skytavern – is also after him.

Cade Quarter's past, it seems, is impossible to escape.

Now, on a tranquil evening beside the peaceful Farrow Lake, Cade receives an intriguing offer. He must make a decision. But he will have to consider his options carefully, for it is a decision that will change his life – and the lives of all those who call the Edge their home – for ever.

The Edgewater River. Riverrise, Hive and Great Glade. The Farrow Ridges. New Sanctaphrax. Names on a map.

Yet behind each name lie a thousand tales – tales that have been recorded in ancient scrolls, tales that have been passed down the generations by word of mouth – tales which even now are being told.

What follows is but one of those tales.

PART ONE
THE SPYGLASS

· CHAPTER ONE ·

Cade sat in his chair in front of the fire, the brass spyglass in his hands. The yellow metal was tarnished; the two initials engraved into it – N and Q – were clogged with grime.

Over the previous few months, Cade had been so preoccupied with helping to defend the Farrow Lake that he'd neglected his daily chores. His little lakeside cabin grew dirty, while the walled vegetable garden became completely overgrown. Now, with the battle won and Farrow Lake safe once more, Cade decided it was time to put things right.

For two long days he toiled, and though he was tired now, it had been worth it. The floor was spotless. The windows gleamed. The cobwebs were gone. Pots and pans, crockery and cutlery were scrubbed and on the shelves and in the cupboards where they belonged. Outside, a neat pile of newly chopped logs stood at one end of the cabin; at the other, two dozen lakefish hung from hooks on the drying rack. Even the underground storeroom, which had become so depleted, was full once more. Crates of freshly harvested fruits and vegetables rubbed shoulders with boxes of spices and sacks of grain, and a large wooden barrel, where a haunch of tilder was pickling in brine.

Now, all that remained to be done was to polish the brass spyglass. Cade had saved the best till last.

The spyglass, along with the perfume bottle and the four barkscrolls of working drawings, were Cade's most precious possessions. It hadn't been easy, but he'd managed to bring all of them with him when he'd fled Great Glade.

The faint scent of perfume that wafted into the air when Cade removed the glass stopper evoked vague memories of the mother he'd lost to the 'wasters' disease when he was still an infant; the barkscrolls reminded him of his father who, night after night, had worked so hard in his laboratory, unravelling the secrets of phrax – before that evil monster Quove Lentis had had him murdered.

And yet, even though it had belonged to someone he'd never met, it was the spyglass that meant the most to Cade. He carried it with him everywhere he went, and had done ever since his father had given it to him on his seventh birthday. Back then, Thadeus hadn't said much about it. It was only when, eight years later, news reached Great Glade that the Descender Nate Quarter had returned from an epic expedition down the cliff face that Cade learned of its significance.

'N ... Q ...' Cade had whispered softly, tracing his fingers round the familiar letters engraved on the hollow shaft. 'Nate Quarter.' He'd looked up. 'I didn't know you had a brother, Father.'

And Thadeus Quarter had smiled ruefully. 'Neither did I,' came the curious reply.

As Cade turned the spyglass over in his hand, the many sights he'd seen through its lenses came flooding back. His first glimpse of his friend Celestia's tree cabin in the woods that lay to the north of the Farrow Lake. The mighty falls cascading down between East and West Ridge in Hive. The sinister tallow-lit skulls that shrouded the hull of the *Doombringer* . . .

And yet, Cade mused, how many more sights the little spyglass must have revealed to his uncle Nate, the greatest Descender in all the Edge, as he set out on expedition after perilous expedition, climbing ever deeper down the great vertical cliff face. What wonders had he discovered? What dangers had he encountered? What hardships had he endured?

Cade looked down now at the spyglass and frowned. 'If only I could know what you've seen,' he whispered.

Nate Quarter stood on the jutting rock and looked down at the spyglass, his fingers tracing round the engraved *N* and *Q* of his name. It was time for his first descent.

He had felt so honoured when Ambris Hentadile – or the Professor, as he knew him – suggested that the two of them should descend together.

'You and me, Nate,' he'd said. 'We shall discover what lies below the Edge and extend the frontiers of Edge knowledge, so that everyone – *everyone* – will benefit. For ever . . .'

Now the moment for their first descent had arrived, and a mixture of fear and excitement balled in the pit of Nate's stomach, like a drop-weight about to be released.

Pushing any misgivings aside, he checked over his equipment. There wasn't much. Rope coils and rock spikes strapped to his backpack. A pot of mentholated abrasion ointment. Meagre rations. His spyglass . . .

He was ready.

'Tie a knot in your scarf to mark this first descent,' the Professor told him, and smiled. 'The first of many.'

Nate did as he was told, taking the end of his Descender's scarf and carefully knotting it. He pulled it tight, then tighter still, until the knot was as hard as a small stone. And, as he did so, the abrasion ointment on his fingers stained the soft cloth a reddish brown.

He found himself thinking of all he was leaving behind. Eudoxia . . . Sanctaphrax . . .

Sanctaphrax had only recently returned from Open Sky – only recently become *New* Sanctaphrax. The city was still sparsely populated, its inhabitants made up of a motley collection of fettle-leggers, goblins and trolls, and ragged fourthlings like himself who had travelled across the grasslands of the Mire on foot. As for his wife, Eudoxia . . .

'Descend,' said the Professor, his voice breaking into Nate's thoughts.

Nate seized one of the two ropes that had been anchored to the top of the cliff with a rock spike and lowered himself backwards over the jutting ledge. Then, hand over hand, his boots pressed firmly against the cliff face, he began to climb down. Beside him, the Professor did the same. Nate glanced across to see the wild excitement in his friend's eyes.

This is it, Nate realized, his heart hammering inside his chest. I am a Descender.

They made their way down the cliff face in silence. All their thoughts were concentrated on keeping a firm hold on the rope and not slipping, despite the best attempts of the treacherous wind to tug them away from the rock face.

More than an hour had passed before Nate felt his boots land on something solid. He looked down to see that they had reached a jutting outcrop of rock, broad enough for the two of them to stand up on.

'We'll rest here a while,' said the Professor.

While the Professor unshouldered his backpack and rummaged inside for some of the provisions that would sustain them on their expedition, Nate unclipped his spyglass and put it to his eye. He looked up to the top of the cliff, already so far above them, and focused the lens.

Suddenly filling his vision was Eudoxia's face.

Despite everything she'd said the previous evening, she had come to see him off. But it had been a tense, tearful parting, and she had set off back to Sanctaphrax long before he and the Professor had started their descent. But something must have changed her mind. She'd returned and was now staring down at him, as though by holding him in her gaze she might also keep him safe.

Nate swallowed, but the painful lump in his throat remained.

Without a spyglass of her own, Eudoxia couldn't see him that well; but Nate could see her. And the sight of her bleak, tear-stained face, with its red-rimmed eyes and down-turned mouth, was too much to bear. He pulled away sharply and pointed the spyglass downwards, to look at what lay before him rather than torturing himself with the image of the person he had left behind – only to feel the Professor's hand on his arm.

'Don't, Nate,' he said. 'Later, maybe, when there is something specific we wish to see more closely. But not now.'

Nate nodded. The Professor was right. It was all too big; too daunting. The only way to deal with the unknown immensity below was to take it one step at a time. He closed the spyglass and reattached it to the front of his descending jacket, then took the water flask and handful of hard-tack the Professor was holding out to him.

Later, refreshed, but soaked to the skin with the spray blown in from the falls, the Professor inspected the jutting outcrop they'd come to more closely. He made the decision to spend the night there.

'We don't want to overdo it on our first day, Nate,' he said. 'And there's no knowing when we'll come to another suitable resting place.'

They hammered hook spikes into the rock, then attached their tilder-hide bivouacs to them with ropes. It was their first attempt to pitch tent on the cliff face and, hampered by the capricious gusts of wind, took far longer than Nate had hoped. His fingers became numb with cold, and it was only the Professor's quick reactions that prevented one of the groundsheets from flapping off into the void. The sunlight had begun to fade by the time they were finally ready to crawl into their cocoon-like sleepsacks. The Professor was soon snoring and, lulled by the deep regular noise, it wasn't long before Nate too slipped into a deep, if troubled, sleep.

The following morning, it all began again.

That first descent lasted eight days in all – eight long days of hammering in new rock spikes and descending the ropes before setting up their meagre camp once more for another night. Nate found comfort in the routine of it all, but the cold and wet were unrelenting; their rations were fast diminishing and their strength began to ebb.

They had got as far as the High Cliff cleft, a formation of weathered rocks that they immediately named 'the Howler' because of the eerie sound the wind made as it hit the rock face there, when the Professor proposed that they return.

'Are you sure?' Nate asked, looking back down into the seemingly bottomless void beneath them. 'We haven't really come that far.'

'Given the rudimentary nature of our equipment, it has been a remarkable feat nevertheless,' said the Professor. 'And now that we understand the lay of the land down here a little better, we'll be able to make suitable preparations for our next descent.'

Our next descent. The words repeated in Nate's head, setting his heart racing all over again.

Using the ropes they'd left in place, the two of them made good progress as they clambered back up the cliff. As he hauled himself over the lip of rock at the top, Nate had never felt so exhausted – yet when he saw Eudoxia

THE FIRST DESCENT

THE HIGH CLIFF

THE HOWLER

standing there before him, his tiredness instantly melted away.

'How did you know?' he asked, puzzled.

'I've come here every day, Nate,' Eudoxia explained, 'hoping to be able to welcome you both back. And here you are!' she added brightly.

She was putting on a brave face, Nate could see that. And though she praised their efforts enthusiastically, Nate knew that Eudoxia still felt hurt and disappointed by his decision to descend with the Professor in the first place – and to leave her behind.

'I couldn't let him go on his own,' Nate protested. 'Besides, you . . .'

He wanted to tell Eudoxia how much he appreciated her staying behind in New Sanctaphrax; that he understood how difficult it must be for someone who had had so many adventures to settle down; that her hard work organizing the restoration of the floating city was invaluable. But she never gave him a chance. She silenced him, her finger pressed against his lips. Then she stepped into his arms and sobbed uncontrollably, while the white ravens from the stone stacks wheeled overhead, cawing loudly.

'And you're going to descend again,' she said, abruptly pulling away. 'Aren't you?'

Nate did not reply.

Placing the spyglass on the piece of cloth that lay on his lap, Cade reached down for the bowl of polish at his feet. He'd made it earlier, using a formula given to him by his fisher-goblin friend, Thorne Lammergyre. A heaped spoonful of salt dissolved in half a cup of sap-wine vinegar, then thickened with flour. Taking the corner of the soft cloth, Cade dipped it in the bowl, then began wiping the paste carefully over the tarnished metal.

When the entire spyglass was covered with the pungent polish, he leaned forward and snapped off a splinter of wood from a piece of kindling. Then, sitting back in his chair, he began working the point into the crevices of the initials and scraping away at the grime.

'N,' he murmured softly as he did so. 'Nate. Nate . . . Uncle Nate.' Then, a little while later, when the engraved *N* was clean and glinting, 'And Q. Quarter. Nate Quarter. Nate Quarter . . .'

Finally satisfied that both letters were spotless, Cade tossed the little splinter into the flames. It flared for a moment, then turned to ash.

'Nate Quarter,' he murmured softly. 'Who *are* you?'

As he walked across the rock pavement to the cliff edge, Nate tied a second knot in his Descender's scarf. A year had passed since that first tentative exploration of the Edge cliff. Now it was time for him and the Professor – together with twelve other brave volunteers – to undertake a second descent.

This time, Eudoxia was not there to see Nate off. It wasn't that she was still upset – though of course she would miss him – but rather that she was busy supervising the building work in New Undertown and dealing with the flood of new arrivals. Phraxbarges of goods, along with tradesfolk and sympathetic academics from the other cities, arrived daily, bringing a vibrant and optimistic air to the floating city.

She'd done well that first year, the fair-haired mine owner's daughter. During that time her income from the Prade phraxmine and her skyship yard in Great Glade had paid for the restoration of the Knights Academy, as well as half the towers in the High Quarter of the city.

In short, New Sanctaphrax was flourishing.

As for the Professor, he was in his element. Encouraged by the interest shown by the newcomers in what lay beneath the jutting Edge rock, he had turned the refurbished Knights Academy into a centre for the study and pursuit of descending. New equipment had been designed. New descending techniques had been devised.

But, as Nate stood waiting for the Professor to give the call to descend, he was all too well aware that the equipment was untested, while the techniques they were to use were theoretical and untried. Despite the warmth of his fur-lined cliffcoat, Nate shivered.

From the moment the team of Descenders set off, it was clear that this second descent would not be easy. The main challenge they faced was operating the phraxpacks which, ironically, had been designed to make the expedition safer.

Time and again as the descent continued, a phraxchamber would fail, sending a hapless Descender plunging down into the depths, or slamming them against the cliff face with fatal force.

The Professor was distraught. After all, it had been his idea to use phrax crystals to stabilize the backpacks, making it – or so he thought – impossible for the climbers to fall.

'We can harness the innate power of the lightning the crystals are made of,' he'd proposed. 'So long as they're kept blazing inside a phraxchamber, they'll remain buoyant.'

The Professor would never have scheduled the descent if he hadn't been confident that his idea would work and, back in the laboratory of

THE SECOND DESCENT

THE HOWLER

THE HIGH CLIFF

THE CUSP

the refurbished Knights Academy, everything had gone perfectly. But the harsh and unpredictable conditions on the cliffside were another matter.

Gusts of turbulent wind kept causing the blazing shards to gutter and die, and since, in darkness, a crystal of phrax becomes immeasurably heavy, the Descenders wearing them on their backs never stood a chance. And there were other unforeseen problems too. Glister-refraction caused the crystals to pulsate, making the backpacks woefully unstable; while a lightning-ball that strayed too close destroyed two of the crystals completely.

The result was always the same. A long, desperate scream that trailed off into a deathly silence as the ill-fated Descender plummeted down into the yawning void below. Three weeks into the descent, and only half the original team were still alive.

But the survivors kept on, day and night. No one wanted to abandon the descent.

On the twenty-third day, the remaining Descenders split into two groups, and a week after that, the Professor, Nate and two Hive academics – Tulkhusk and Hemp – made it to the bottom of the High Cliff. They set up a temporary base there, and managed to secure mooring rings to the rock that marked the beginning of the Mid Cliff descent.

It was the lowest they were to get on this second descent though. Weather-battered, sleep-deprived, and with their rations running low, they were considering their options for the next stretch when Nate heard something high above him. He grasped his spyglass, put it to his eye and looked up – only to wish that he hadn't.

For there, magnified by the lens, was the panic-stricken face of Perch – a pink-eyed goblin from the second group – as she tumbled, screaming, down through the air. It was a sight and sound that would haunt Nate's nightmares for many years to come.

As Perch's voice faded and disappeared far below them, the Professor turned to the others.

'We'd best head back,' he said, his voice taut and trembling with emotion. 'While we still can.'

With the polish now dry, Cade took the soft cloth and began to rub the spyglass until it gleamed like burnished gold. Outside, the sky was darkening, and through the window he caught sight of the full moon rising over the horizon. He climbed to his feet, crossed the cabin and looked out.

A blustery wind was blowing, and the low yellow moon cast shard-like fragments of light over the choppy waters of the Farrow Lake. A flock of snowbirds, keen to avoid the impending storm, was coming in to land, one after the other, their outstretched webbed feet scudding over the surface of the lake for a few seconds before they folded their wings and bobbed on towards the shallows.

Cade raised the spyglass, admiring the way the polished metal glinted in the moonlight. He put it to his eye and trained it on the lake. Raising it higher, he focused in on the cascades of the Five Falls pouring into it. Then higher still, until he was staring into Open Sky and wondering what might be out there in its awesome, empty vastness.

Catching a flash of light out of the corner of his eye, Cade turned to see a mighty skytavern, its lamps shining brightly as it approached the sky-platform of his friend Gart Ironside. Cade knew that the *Xanth Filatine* was bringing goods to be sold and traded, and maybe also new arrivals from the great cities to swell the swiftly growing population of the Farrow Ridges.

What he didn't yet know was that one of the passengers on board had come especially to see him . . .

The third descent was the most exhilarating to date, but also the most costly. It took place eighteen months after the surviving Descenders of the previous expedition had returned, bone-tired and half starved, and the atmosphere among this new team – ten of New Sanctaphrax's finest – was a mixture of excitement and trepidation.

The floating city itself had continued to flourish, but its success – and particularly its reputation for being the centre of descending – was drawing unwanted attention. And Eudoxia Prade's recent trip to Great Glade had confirmed everyone's worst fears.

'We've been given an ultimatum from Quove Lentis,' she told Nate. 'He wants descending to stop. At once.'

'Or what?' Nate had asked.

'Or he'll prevent the skytaverns visiting New Sanctaphrax,' she'd said. 'And if that isn't enough, he's vowed to put pressure on the merchants of Hive and Riverrise to stop trading with us completely.'

'But why?' Nate had demanded angrily. 'There's so much knowledge to be found down there. Invaluable knowledge. And if New Sanctaphrax stands for anything, it's the pursuit of knowledge. Generations of Earth and Sky scholars have given their lives to acquire and protect learning. We cannot let Quove Lentis control what we are or are not allowed to do. Descending must continue.'

And Eudoxia had smiled. 'I knew you'd say that, Nate. Which is why I have begun making plans . . .'

Eudoxia was as good as her word. She set up the 'Friends of New Sanctaphrax', a network of waifs, goblins and fourthlings in the three great cities, to

counter the influence of Quove Lentis and his cronies. Shipping orders mysteriously started to go astray; requisitions were countermanded, and skytavern routes were subsidized to keep trade and travellers moving.

And the work of the Descenders continued.

Throughout all this, the Professor had also been making plans while waiting to depart on the third major descent. He researched in depth the observations of previous generations of scholars, poring over the barkscrolls of the Great Library. More importantly, he used the time to consolidate the stretch of cliff already explored.

The High Cliff, once so difficult to navigate, had now been mastered, with carefully placed mooring rings and ledge posts hewn into the vertical rock face by teams of quarry trogs from the Northern Reaches. In addition, new spidersilk-rope techniques and phrax-weighted boots had revolutionized this initial part of the descent. Finally – despite the threats coming from Quove Lentis – the time had come for the Descenders to return to the depths, to explore the cliff face further down than anyone had ever gone before.

'All set?' the Professor called, his voice competing with the roar of the mighty Edgewater River as it hurled itself down into the abyss.

A chorus of assent went around the group of intrepid Descenders. Nate fingered the third knot he'd tied on his scarf. His stomach was churning.

'All set,' he breathed.

'Then let us descend,' the Professor. 'And may Earth and Sky protect us.'

With their equipment now tried and tested, and the descending techniques honed through experience, the descent started well. The Descenders made their way down High Cliff quickly and efficiently. That upper section – which had taken a month to complete on the previous descents – was covered in under three days. The mood was optimistic. Spirits were high.

Then they reached the second part of the descent.

This was unknown territory, and any planning could only go so far. The Descenders soon discovered that the Mid Cliff held dangers that would suddenly reveal themselves without warning. Their only protection was vigilance and foresight.

But this was not enough. Despite their experience – and the expertise and advice of the Professor – the climb down the dark, cloud-roiling Mid Cliff proved to be fraught with peril.

Two Descenders were lost to a suspected ravine demon attack at the beginning of the Fluted Decline. A little further on, a young fourthling perished in a freak accident when a dislodged piece of rock struck his head. In spite of these tragic losses, the Professor still had high hopes that they would make it to the Great Overhang, the furthest point yet reached.

But rations were soon starting to run low once again. Provisions were heavy and bulky, and it simply wasn't possible to carry enough to sustain them throughout the slow, dangerous stretches of cliff. Long before their intended destination, most of the surviving Descenders had been forced to turn back.

Nate and the Professor, however, were not about to give up so soon. Together with a waif called Fenebrule, Teep, a grey goblin, and a pair of cloddertrogs, Hackbane and Hitch, they pooled their meagre resources and kept going. Slowly and carefully, they descended in pitch darkness, their phraxlamps dimmed to avoid the attentions of Edge wraiths and ravine demons, until they reached a point where the cliff face curved back on itself in a great grooving arc.

'This, I believe,' the Professor said excitedly, 'is the beginning of the Great Overhang.'

The words had scarcely left his lips when the air around them suddenly filled with countless thousands of tiny pulsating flashes of light. They'd appeared out of nowhere and darted around the Descenders like a swarm of fiery woodmidges.

'A glister storm,' the Professor pronounced, raising his hood, lowering his goggles and fastening the front of his descending jacket.

Nothing, however, was enough to deter the glisters. They had located prey, and now they were attacking it relentlessly. Each one was like a needle stabbing at the senses – the eyes, the ears, the surface of the skin.

And the mind.

Fenebrule was the first to go. Unable to bear this assault on his waif senses, he threw himself screaming

27

into the void. Teep followed him moments later, losing his footing as he tried to protect himself from the vicious onslaught.

With the two of them gone, the others decided to cut their losses and turn back. They set their phraxchambers to maximum, despite the dangers of being seen, and sped up through the darkness as fast as they could, their toecaps scouring the rock as they pressed their boots hard against the cliff to maintain contact.

But then, no more than a hundred strides further up the rock face, a flock of Edge wraiths – attracted by the sparking trails of light and the bright glow from the phrax-lit backpacks – closed in on them. Nate would never forget the look on Hitch's face as a cluster of the papery white creatures enfolded him in a hideous, rustling embrace. As he watched, the Descender was pulled back down into the darkness, to the sound of splintering bone and ripping flesh – and Hackbane, brave but foolish, followed as he tried and failed to help his friend.

Nate and the Professor fled. Everyone else was dead. If *they* were to survive, they had to get out of there, and fast.

They made good progress, soon leaving the glister storm behind them. But the wraiths proved more persistent. They would disappear for a while, their screeches fading to nothing, before returning in increased numbers. Halfway up the Fluted Decline, the Professor abruptly pulled Nate into a cleft in the rock where the two of them cloaked the light of their phraxglobes and crouched down in the darkness to wait for the creatures to give up the search.

Time passed. Occasionally Nate would put his spyglass to his eye and scour the darkness for any trace of the wraiths, hoping the coast was clear. Each time he did so, his vision was filled with the monstrous creatures, with their claw-tipped wings and fang-filled jaws, seemingly staring straight back at him. Then, on the fourth day, there was nothing.

'I think they've gone,' he whispered.

The Professor nodded, and the two of them began the long slow climb back.

Cade turned away from the window. He crossed the cabin to the fireplace, where he set the polished spyglass down on the ironwood mantelpiece above the blazing fire. It was getting late; Cade was hungry, and thinking about preparing himself some supper, when something occurred to him.

The spyglass had been given to him when he was seven years old, getting on for ten years ago, yet Nate Quarter had only returned from his final expedition two years earlier. It meant that, for whatever reason, his uncle could not have had his spyglass with him at the time.

What, Cade mused, *had* happened on that last descent?

· CHAPTER TWO ·

F our years after his first descent, Nate stood at the
cliff edge once more. To his right, the mighty
Edgewater River hurled itself down into the abyss; to his
left, the great floating city of New Sanctaphrax was
silhouetted against the bright sky. Nate didn't look at
either of them. His only concern was what lay far below
the jutting rock.

Once again, Eudoxia hadn't come to see him off. Nate
hadn't taken it personally. She was off doing her best to
deal with the costly consequences of their third descent:
Great Glade and Quove Lentis's increasingly aggressive
moves to bring the upstart city to heel.

Now there was even talk of a blockade . . .

With a thoughtful frown, Nate checked over his
latest equipment, the way the Professor had taught all
the Descenders of the Knights Academy to do. Pockets
of his quarm-fur-lined cliffcoat equipped with

31

drop-weights and spike-floats, flaps securely fastened. *Check.* Copperwood hoops threaded with spidersilk rope on both arms and upper jacket. *Check.* Lufwood hoversack, containing a month's emergency rations of hard-tack, plus pots of wind salve and abrasion ointment. *Check.* The phraxchamber embedded in the side of the pack, steaming coldly; phrax-weighted boots cleat-cleaned and toecaps gleaming . . .

'Ready, Nate?' said a voice.

But where was his spyglass? It wasn't attached to his cliffcoat. Then Nate remembered. He and Eudoxia had been at the top of the Knights Academy a week earlier and, fearing that a distant skycraft might be a spy vessel from Great Glade, she'd asked to borrow it. She hadn't given it back . . .

'Nate?'

It was too late to go back for it now. Not that it really mattered. Where they were headed – a place of permanent darkness – there would be precious little to see . . .

'Nate!'

Nate looked round to see the Professor standing on the cliff edge, booted and kitted, a coil of spidersilk rope in his hand. The familiar feeling of fear and excitement churning in the pit of Nate's stomach intensified. He took the ends of his Descender's scarf and ran his fingers over the three knots tied along it, each one as hard and nubbed as a hull-weight on a skyship. He tied a fourth knot.

'Ready, Professor,' he said.

*

32

It was exhilarating, that first drop to Low Gantry. Nate and the Professor descended smoothly, the cliff face speeding and slowing before them as they controlled their descent, mooring ring to mooring ring. On reaching Low Gantry, with the cloud swirl closing in around them, they were met by a group of apprentice Descenders. And while the two of them drank the sweet hyleroot tea offered them, the apprentices checked over their equipment.

'A fine drop, Nate,' said the Professor. His face glowed with optimism. 'Untold dangers may yet await us, but I'm confident that this fourth descent will lead to the big breakthrough.'

Nate nodded. The 'big breakthrough' was something the Professor was

always talking about. It would lead to what he described as groundfall – where a Descender might finally set foot on land at the very bottom of the Edge cliff.

'We will be able to establish a base there,' he went on. 'Then we can pour the full energies of the Knights Academy into constructing a permanent bastion from which future Descenders can set forth to . . . to . . .' His eyes glazed over. 'To who knows where?'

'Ready?' came a voice.

It was time for the two of them to press on. The apprentices had completed their checks, and the High Cliff sergeant was waiting to see them off.

'Ready,' said Nate, and turned to the Professor.

And the Professor, who had been staring into the mid-distance, abruptly focused. 'Ready,' he confirmed.

The second, third and fourth drops were longer than the first, each one taking an arduous day to complete. Sleeping on the rock ledges quarried into the cliff face at the end of each descent wasn't easy either. The glister-rich rock face caused strange and terrible delusions. To protect themselves from their mind-warping effects, Descenders were advised to wear specially designed sleep-hoods.

And even these weren't foolproof.

A week into the fourth descent, Nate woke suddenly on the ledge. A strange white figure, head bowed and shrouded in white gauze-like rags, was sitting opposite him. Nate flinched. He was staring into a ghostly, flickering face – or rather, a sequence of faces that flashed for a moment, then faded, one after the other. Nate knew them all. They were the faces of every Descender lost on the previous expeditions, coming and going in rapid succession as the figure reached towards him with bony hands. Lodespear, Perch, Sleet Henfur, Hitch, Hackbane, Fenebrule . . .

'Nate! Wake up!'

Abrasion ointment made Nate's nostrils sting and his eyes water as his sleep-hood was torn from his head, and he looked up to see the Professor staring back at him. His heart thumping fit to burst, Nate discovered that he was up on his feet, untethered from the spidersilk safety-rope and teetering on the lip of the narrow ledge. The Professor pulled him back to safety and returned the vial of pungent ointment to his pocket.

'Your sleep-hood, Nate,' he said matter-of-factly, handing him back the conical headpiece with the metal grid embedded in thick fabric. 'The vent's come loose. Repair it while you take next watch.'

The Professor checked that his tether was securely fastened, then pulled down his own hood. He lay down on the ledge, his back pressed against the wall.

'Wake me in three pulses.'

'Will do,' said Nate.

With the Professor sleeping, Nate threaded his rope tether back through the hoops of his cliffcoat. Then he set the pulser and began repairing the vent on the sleep-hood. As he worked, he fretted over his carelessness – and what might happen if he wasn't more careful in future.

In the event, the following day's descent proved easier than Nate had feared. The drop was clean and swift and, though tiring, offered few problems. As he and the Professor reached the Cusp, a towering quarry trog by the name of Dendrock stepped out of the hanging-gantry there to greet them.

Swaying in the unpredictable winds, the gantry looked precarious, but it proved well stocked and neatly ordered inside. Nate and the Professor ate hard-tack and brewed tea, taking the water from the convex condensing shields that collected the swirling mists and spray and funnelled the water into vats that hung like swollen fruit from the underside of the gantry. Then they slept.

The next morning – as grey and misty as the one before – a pair of Mid Cliff class Descenders pulled themselves up onto the gantry. Their faces were drawn and haggard, but Nate recognized them at once. So did the Professor. They were the two who had survived that disastrous second descent, back down beneath the Edge once more: the Hive academics Tulkhusk and Hemp.

'We provisioned the mooring hooks at the Overhang as best we could,' said Tulkhusk, a rangy tusked goblin with one blue eye and one white.

'But the way back up was difficult,' his stocky flathead companion, Hemp, added.

Nate swallowed uneasily. If *he* thought it was difficult . . .

Nate and the Professor began their descent of the Fluted Decline an hour later. Carefully shielded inside their cliffcoats, hoods fastened shut, they descended for three days. Not that days or nights meant much in the pitch black. Time could only be measured in the pulses from their phraxglobes – each pulse the equivalent of two hours.

On the fourth day, they encountered what Descenders called 'cliff-haze'. Notoriously disorientating, this rippling series of whistles and moans was caused by the swirling air currents passing through the ravines that fluted the cliff face. When the wind rose, the Professor speeded up, using the eerie sounds to mask their own. Their presence should not be given away, either by light or by sound, for here, close to the Great Overhang, was the region of scuttling ravine demons and gliding Edge wraiths.

The first ravine demon they came across was small. Its long bony fingers, twice the length of its skeletal body, splayed out on the vertical rock surface on either side of the crevice it had emerged from. Two huge colourless eyes stared out from the blackness, illuminated by the glow of Nate's phraxchamber. Suddenly its mouth sprang open and it spat an arc of pale venom at Nate.

Just below him, the Professor fired a percussion dart. It whistled

37

over Nate's head, struck the ravine demon's shoulder and detonated with a painful high-pitched noise. The creature released its grip on the cliff face and, curling up into a tight ball, fell past the Descenders and down into the depths. In the darkness, other balled-up demons dropped past them, similarly dislodged by the destructive sound-waves the dart had emitted.

'Phraxglow, Nate,' the Professor whispered. 'I think we'd best take this next stretch in full blackout.'

Nate nodded and, as the Professor disappeared below him, he snapped the cover over the phraxchamber on his backpack. Then, with the sound of his anxious breathing loud in his ears, Nate paid out his rope and slowly, silently, dropped through the darkness. The howls and moans of the cliff-haze grew louder as he passed by a deep vertical ravine opening and touched down on a jutting rock.

Click. Click. Click.

Nate started back, his senses on fire. It was another ravine demon. With slow, deliberate movements, he carefully removed a percussion dart.

Click. Click. Click. Click . . .

A huge bony claw scraped down his arm. This ravine demon was far bigger than the first. Nate braced himself.

'Dead drop!' he shouted down to the Professor, and released the rope-catch on his cliffcoat.

He fell just as the claws closed around his left arm, dragging their owner with him. Hurtling down through the blackness, Nate stabbed blindly with the percussion dart. At the third attempt it hit something bony and detonated. The noise was deafening. The hideous ravine demon crashed down into the yawning void.

Then, with a sound like a whipcrack, Nate's rope went taut. His body jolted to a halt, leaving him hanging in the pitch-black air.

Looking up, he saw the glow of a phraxchamber and, illuminated in its pale fuzzy light, the Professor. He was just a short way above Nate, reaching out towards him from the mooring ring he'd tethered himself to. Nate grabbed the Professor's outstretched hand and pulled himself back to the cliff face.

'Excellent dead drop, Nate,' the Professor told him. 'All that practice on the academy tower certainly paid off.' He smiled. 'But let's try not to do that *too* often, eh?'

They were about to resume their descent when Nate noticed something. Beside the ring, scratched into the rock face, were Descenders' marks.

'It's a message from Tulkhusk,' he said.

The Professor nodded, and proceeded to interpret the series of carved lines, dots and squiggles. '*Ravine demons too numerous in the crevices below. Suggest rapid descent on the outer surface of the flute – with wraith precaution.*' He turned to Nate. 'So, what's it to be? Wraiths or demons?'

'I'd prefer the crevices, but Tulkhusk is probably right,' Nate whispered back. 'If they're crawling with ravine demons the size of that last one, we'd never get through.'

'Rapid descent it is, then,' said the Professor calmly.

As Nate twisted the dial to maximum, the phrax-chamber on the side of his backpack whirred into life, the jet of steam suddenly rising up from the funnel illuminated by the chamber's bright glow. Stepping back from the cliff, he released the lock on his rope spool – and dropped like a stone.

Toward the bottom of the crevice-pocked stretch of cliff, Nate pulled on the rope, rapidly slowing himself down. He landed on a fluted ledge and, having shut off the phraxchamber with his free hand, was plunged back into darkness.

Sometimes it was better not to be able to see.

Panting hard, Nate gave another tug on the spidersilk rope for the Professor to follow him down. He reached into a lower pocket of his cliffcoat, took out his phraxpistol and loaded it. Just in case.

'Dead drop!' came the Professor's warning shout from above him.

Nate braced himself. In the blackness, he felt the rush of air as the Professor fell past him. The next moment, feeling the rope spool tighten, he twisted the dial to maximum for a second time. The pack jumped at his back, exerting a counterbalancing force against the rope's pull. The Professor ended up a few strides below him, swinging at the end of the rope. He was smiling.

'We've got to stop doing this,' he muttered as he pulled himself up to where Nate was tethered.

Just then, looming up from the depths, a razor-fanged,

skull-like face appeared, its jaws opening in a horrifying, dislocated yawn. The Edge wraith hovered close by, its breath fetid. Then, with a loud screech and a flash of white papery wings, it swooped back into the darkness and was gone. But around 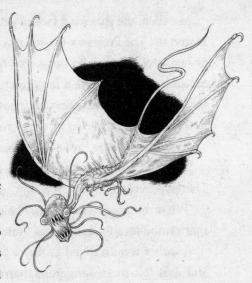 them now the black air was awash with the sounds of rustling wingbeats and sinister calls.

'Now the wraiths have found us, darkness won't help us,' said the Professor grimly. He had his own phraxpistol in his hand. 'Either we make a stand here, or we take our chances in the crevices.'

At the very edges of the light that radiated from their phraxchambers, Nate could make out skeletal shapes as they glided back and forth on the turbulent air currents. Meanwhile, from the cracks and crevices in the cliff face, the scratching sounds of the ravine demons grew louder. It was only a matter of time before one or other of the bloodthirsty creatures attacked.

'There is one thing we could try,' said Nate. 'But you're not going to like it—'

Just then, the shrieking face of yet another Edge wraith reared up. The Professor blasted it with both barrels of his phraxpistol. The wraith burst into flames, blinding them for an instant, then fell, a fiery torch, down into the black abyss – only for three ravine demons to appear from cracks in the rock face, attracted by the stench of burning flesh.

'Try me,' said the Professor, reloading.

'We strap our packs together,' said Nate. 'Back to back. Then we freefall.'

'What, no rope? No tether?' said the Professor. 'But that's unbelievably dangerous, Nate.'

Another wraith dived at them. Nate swivelled round and shot. 'No more dangerous than staying here, waiting to be picked off,' he said. 'And it might just work.'

The Professor nodded solemnly, then clapped Nate on the shoulder. 'Whatever happens, it's been an honour to descend with you, Nate Quarter,' he said. He turned, and the two of them strapped their phraxpacks back to back. 'And to call you my friend.'

'The honour has been all mine,' said Nate.

The wraiths were growing bolder. Ravine demons were emerging in increasing numbers; reaching out and grabbing with extended claws. It was as though they knew the two Descenders were out of ammunition.

'Ready, Professor?' said Nate.

'Ready.'

Slowly, tentatively, Nate untied the spidersilk rope that bound him to the inert body of the Professor. Every part of his own body throbbed with pain. He checked himself over.

No cuts, no broken bones, he concluded.

Wherever they had landed, there seemed to be a light source of some kind that wasn't coming from their two phraxchambers. They were both out of action. Nate squinted into the blue-tinged gloom. Where *was* that light coming from?

But first things first . . .

He turned and examined the Professor. His friend was still breathing but both legs were clearly broken. It occurred to Nate with a pang of guilt that although the two of them had been roped together, back to back, the Professor had come down first and cushioned his fall.

The Professor opened his eyes. 'Nate? We're still alive . . .' He frowned. 'It's the strangest thing . . . I can't feel my legs.'

Nate sat back, trying to clear his head and piece together everything that had happened since they'd decided to freefall to escape the attacking ravine demons and wraiths. He remembered how his fingers had shaken as he released the rope – and then falling, falling . . .

Their phraxchambers had whirred, the buoyancy of the backpacks slowing their descent a little, with the steam from the funnels drawing a crazy interwoven trail behind them as they dropped, spinning round and round in the turbulent wind. At every moment he'd expected them to be slammed into the cliff face, their bodies smashed to a bloody pulp.

Yet, somehow, they had continued to fall.

As they'd fallen, though, so too had Nate's spirits. This descent, their fourth, was pointless. A descent was only meaningful if you could chart your course down the cliff face, attaching mooring rings as you went. Then you could work your way back, scratching useful details of the climb into the rock; enabling others to follow in an endless relay. That was what true descending was.

This was the opposite.

They had tumbled through another glister storm, the tiny needle-sharp points of light plunging through every nerve ending. Nate opened his mouth to scream . . .

Then nothing. He must have lost consciousness – until just a moment ago.

'The phraxchambers ruptured *after* we landed,' the Professor was saying. 'Otherwise we wouldn't have survived. And all these rocks,' he said, looking around. 'It's like . . . like some sort of immense scree field.'

Even after all this, Nate marvelled, despite being broken and unable to move, the Professor was still making detailed observations like the true Descender he was.

'They're covered in some sort of moss-like vegetation,' he went on. 'Dark blue, but luminescent. Dense. Sponge-like . . .' He looked up. 'It probably cushioned our fall.'

Nate surveyed the scene. The Professor was right. They were in the midst of a seemingly endless slope of scree-like rubble, each boulder the size of a phraxbarge. The crevices between them were ink-black and forbidding, though the surface of the rock was springy and lush with the thick lawn of glowing blue vegetation. And then there were the sounds. Nate shuddered. Shrouded in fine mists and caressed by swirling winds, the scree was alive with hissing and whistling and soft howling moans that sounded horribly alive.

Pushing his fears aside, Nate decided to check over their equipment. The phraxchambers were completely destroyed, the crystals of phrax gone. But some things had survived the fall. Nate had his hack-knife and phraxpistol, though no ammunition; the Professor had a couple of rock spikes and the coil of rope.

Beside him, the Professor suddenly groaned with pain as he tried to move.

'I'm so sorry,' Nate said. 'I wasn't thinking. I'll make you more comfortable.'

He pulled the hack-knife from his belt and started cutting away at the dense vegetation. Clouds of sparkling luminescence billowed up and floated off into the inky blackness. Nate checked around warily, hoping he wasn't announcing their presence to an Edge wraith or ravine demon.

Or something worse . . .

He constructed a mattress with the spongy moss fronds and propped the Professor up. Then, having splinted his friend's broken legs with the rock spikes, he returned his attention to the equipment.

The ruined backpacks yielded some useable supplies. A large pack of hard-tack. A stove – which Nate hoped to power up with the phrax crystal from his pistol. A battered pot and two dented copperwood canteens. A coil of wire, needles and a spool of thread. And a mistsifter, to catch and condense the moisture in the air, and ensure they always had enough water.

They ate hard-tack on that, their first day – and, keen to keep an accurate record of the time spent down in the depths, Nate cleared the moss from the surface of a nearby boulder and scratched a Descender's mark into the bare rock with his hack-knife. It was the start of their calendar.

Day one . . .

By the end of the first week, the Professor and Nate had mastered the basic survival routines of living on the scree slope, and Nate began to explore further afield. For his part, the Professor rested up. He was in a bad way. With his legs splinted and the bones beginning to heal, he had begun to regain some feeling – and was suffering terrible pain as a result. Though Nate never once heard him complain.

The first week turned into the first month. Then the second month. Then the third. And as the time passed, Nate was able to assess their situation more accurately.

Wherever they were, it was not the 'groundfall' that the Professor had dreamed of finding on this fourth descent. The scree field descended further – *much* further – down into the darkness. The area of luminous blue vegetation they were stranded upon was relatively small. The rest, as far as Nate dared to venture, was arid and devoid of any obvious life.

It was a harsh, wearisome existence, yet the two of them coped. Just. Sometimes they talked, reminiscing on the past or making tentative plans for the future. But the enforced solitude and constant uncertainty turned them in on themselves, and they remained silent for most of the time, lost in their own thoughts.

When the hard-tack ran out, the two of them faced the prospect of starvation. This, six months in, was when the Professor came into his own. Although restricted, he was now able to move about with the aid of the rock spikes, which Nate had removed from his legs, lashed together and fashioned into a crutch.

The strange vegetation they collected was analysed. Then the Professor began experimenting on himself.

'You observe, Nate,' he instructed. 'There's no point both of us poisoning ourselves.'

The tall swaying fronds of glowing 'plate-moss' proved edible, if rather tasteless. 'Like damp barkscroll,' was Nate's verdict when the Professor had given it the all-clear. There was plenty of the stuff on the boulders, though, and more grew quickly back whenever he chopped it down.

The pungent 'pattern-moss' seemed promising at first but, after a day of extreme sickness, it was agreed never to try it again. There were other, more successful, specimens however. The 'meat-lichen' was delicious, but hard to find, while the 'blue-spore clumps' satisfied their desire for something sweet.

Soon, Nate was foraging successfully, and the Professor was even experimenting with air-drying and smoking the edible moss to create a store. They were surviving, if not thriving. But the routine was as endless as it was mindless. Both of them were starting to wonder – though neither expressed it in words – exactly what they were surviving *for*.

They stopped keeping the rock-surface calendar three years after their freefall. It was too disheartening. From then on, their eerie isolation really began to take its toll. Time lost any meaning, and, increasingly uncertain whether they were awake or asleep, both Nate and the Professor started to have vivid and terrifying dreams.

For Nate, it was usually the looming face of an Edge wraith that haunted his nightmares. Sometimes he'd see Grint Grayle, the mine sergeant who had engineered the 'accident' that killed his father; at other times, the leering face of the black-eared goblin who had pulled a knife on him on board the *Deadbolt Vulpoon* – two characters from his past who had wanted to see him dead. Worst of all, though, were the few occasions when he closed his eyes only to find Eudoxia Prade standing before him, silently weeping.

Nate missed her more than he could say. They had been through so much together; shared so many exciting adventures. Would they ever see each other again?

As time continued to pass – months, years – the dark, sunless days merged into one another to form a single never-ending night. Worse than that, the two Descenders themselves seemed to be disappearing, their minds and bodies melting into the eerie blue light . . .

Then, suddenly, everything changed.

'Nate! Nate!' the Professor cried as he shook him awake. 'Come quickly, you must see this.'

Nate pulled himself up from his moss bed and staggered after the ragged figure of the Professor, trying to remember the last time they'd spoken to each other. Was it days ago? Weeks? Perhaps even years. He'd been dreaming he was a boy again, back in the phraxmines of the Eastern Woods, with his father, Abe. He was ten years old in the dream. But how old was he now? he asked himself, and with mounting horror realized that he had no idea. Thirty? Forty? A hundred?

'Look, Nate. Over there.'

Nate shook himself from his thoughts. The Professor was pointing down towards the edge of what they thought of as their 'moss island'. Thick curling plumes of faintly sparkling mist were spiralling up into the blackness from the crevices of the scree. Then, beneath this billowing mist, one large moss-covered rock began to wobble. Slowly, as the root tendrils of the mossy plants on its surface were prised away, the scree boulder began to rise and gently turn.

There was something familiar about it, Nate thought, and he remembered the curious storm-stones that would sometimes appear up top. Hurtling upwards from beneath the jutting Edge rock, the mysterious objects would arc through the air, hissing and humming, before crashing down in the Stone Gardens or the grasslands of the Mire.

Could *this* be where they originated?

'Take this!' the Professor said urgently, shoving his rock-spike crutch into Nate's hands. He gestured to the boulder. 'You're still strong, Nate. Drive this into the rock and hold on . . .'

He pushed Nate towards the spinning boulder. Nate stepped onto the rock's surface, fell to his knees and drove the spike deep into the surface of the boulder, then clung on tightly.

In front of him, the Professor's face blurred as the mist surge took hold of the rock and suddenly sent it spinning upwards. Nate stared back helplessly.

'Don't forget me . . .' the Professor's voice rang in Nate's ears.

· CHAPTER THREE ·

'**D**on't forget me . . . Don't forget me . . .'

The words echoed in Nate's head as he soared into the air, now quick and high-pitched, like the chirruping of cheepwits; now as slow and sonorous as a tolling bell.

The boulder rose at an impossible speed – faster than freefall, faster than lightning. So fast that Nate felt himself being crushed against the surface of the boulder. His stomach churned and his face slumped. He struggled to breathe. And all the while the boulder spun ever quicker, threatening to hurl him back down into the void. Nate clutched hold of the rock spike, hoping and praying, the dizzying ascent no more than a series of half-glimpsed flashes.

Blue glow . . .

Pitch blackness . . .

The glint of an eye; the flap of a papery wing.

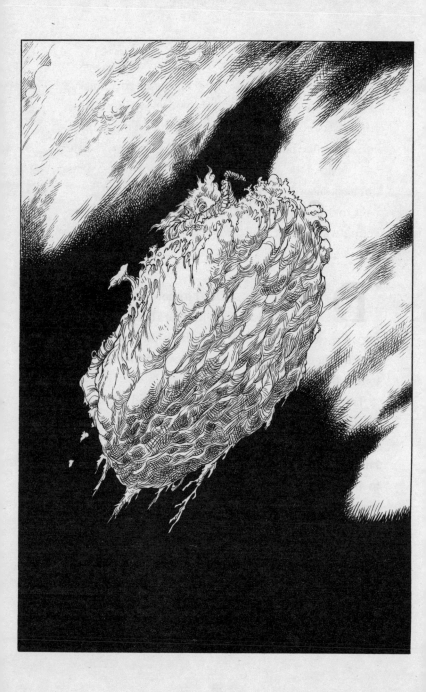

Cracks and crevices . . .

Cloud swirl . . .

Then breaking through the white billowing mass in an instant, back into the light; the sky above him and the cliff face seemingly all around him for a moment, until – with a sound like a cracking whip – he was tossed up over the tip of the jutting rock in a broad arc that projected him back over the land.

At that moment, every thought, every memory, every feeling was driven from his head; everything but those final words he'd heard.

Don't forget me . . .

I won't, Nate promised. I won't forget you, Professor. Ever . . .

The skymarshal came down low and fast over the grasslands, the phraxchamber of his single-seater skycraft, the *Rock Demon*, thrumming. Brocktinius Rolnix raised the visor of his helmet and looked down as he sped past the glowing boulder that had thudded into the soft, oozing Mire soil moments before. Then, using the stirrup bars to control the craft, he circled round, slipping the long-barrelled phraxmusket from his shoulder as he did so.

Brocktinius – or Brock, as he insisted his close friends call him – was young for a skymarshal of the Knights Academy, but he had already made quite a name for himself as a marksman. He could pick off an enemy captain in a wheelhouse at a thousand paces, shooting from the saddle. The eight stormhornets carved into his

wrist armour – each one representing a Great Glade phraxship commander – bore witness to that.

Brock slowed his sky-craft to a hover, slipped out of the saddle and jumped down into the waist-high grass. Gripping the tolley-rope that was attached to the carved rock-demon prow, he pulled the skycraft behind him as he approached the boulder.

It wasn't a Great Glade projectile; that much was clear from the unfamiliar blue-grey moss and lichen that encrusted its sur-face. Reaching out, Brock touched one of the sprout-ing tendrils, only for it to disintegrate into smoky dust.

The boulder had come down out of the broiling clouds and smashed into the Mire grasslands as

Brock was returning from his dawn patrol. Recently, the blockade had grown in vessel numbers, but the skymarshals were holding the line on the outskirts of Undergarden. There was more though, so much more, to being a skymarshal out on patrol.

Brocktinius Rolnix had seen such wondrous things in his short but exciting life as a skymarshal. Flocks of fighting vulpoons and wild tilder stampedes; glister showers in the low sky beyond the Edge falls; blow-holes and grass-slides in the Mire grasslands, when whole pastures would shift, buckle and slide beneath the bubbling soil . . .

Even this – the sudden appearance of a great rock, seemingly out of nowhere – had been sighted before. Storm-stones, they were called. Brock knew that the Earth scholars of old believed these ancient rocks came from the darkest regions of the undercliff. Few ever landed in the inhabited regions of the Edgelands, and when they did, they buried themselves as deep as solidified lightning, yet had none of phrax's immense value.

As Brock watched, this storm-stone was already sinking into the soil. And then he saw it. Some sort of rock spike embedded in the surface of the boulder. He grabbed it and prised it free – just as the last of the immense boulder bubbled down into the earth, and shifting banks of grass slid over it like a green trap door closing.

Brock turned the metal object over in his hand. He saw that it was in fact two rock spikes tightly bound together. One spike had been hammered over at the top and wrapped in moss-like padding that had been secured with coiled spidersilk rope.

'Like a crutch,' he mused.

On the shaft of the second spike was a stamp. It was the tethered-rock symbol of New Sanctaphrax. Brock frowned, wondering what to make of it. But, already late returning from his patrol, he decided he'd examine it more closely later. He strapped the rock-spike crutch to the saddle of his phraxcraft and headed back to the Knights Academy.

Leaving the grasslands behind him, Brock flew low over Undergarden, with its rumble stacks and tumbledown walls overgrown with dense vegetation. He pushed back on the stirrup bars and was about to steer the phraxcraft into a steep ascent that would take him up to the floating city above when, out of the corner of his eye, he caught a flash of white. He leaned forward, backing out of the climb and levelling off, and saw a flock of white ravens circling over the rock stacks of the Stone Gardens, cawing noisily.

Something had agitated these ancient birds. Brocktinius Rolnix decided to discover what.

He flew down through the flock and landed. He looked around – and there, propped up against the base rock of one of the oldest and tallest rock stacks, Brock saw a ghostly apparition.

It was a fourthling dressed in strange ragged clothes – half patched cloth and leather; half woven coverings of vegetation, blue-grey and dusty. The figure's hair was long and tangled and drained of colour, while a grizzled

mane-like beard grew down to the waist. As Brock slowly approached, the figure opened its eyes. They stared back at him, glowing an unnatural luminescent blue, and the young skymarshal wanted nothing more than to draw his long-barrelled musket and keep this ghost at bay.

'Who are you and how did you get here?' Brock demanded, yet even as he spoke the words a nagging thought wormed its way into his head.

He had been five years old when the fourth descent set off from the lip of rock at the edge of the Stone Gardens. In the fourteen years since then, he'd been schooled in the ancient Fountain House and accepted into the Knights Academy. By the age of sixteen, he had risen from junior cadet to the youngest skymarshal of the watch. And throughout that time, his fellow knights academic – the Descenders – had worked tirelessly to consolidate the work of the great Ambris Hentadile and his legendary fellow Descender . . .

'Nate Quarter,' said the ghost, the voice cracked and frail. 'And I have absolutely no idea.'

Sky Sergeant Mudgutt might well dock his pay for returning late from patrol, but Brock knew he had no choice. If this truly was Nate Quarter, High Academe Elect of New Sanctaphrax – mysteriously back after a fourteen-year absence – then there was someone who would want to see him at once.

Brock helped Nate to his feet. 'This way, sir,' he said.

Nate swayed where he stood, but did not move. Realizing that the ghost-like figure could barely remain upright, and was certainly too weak to walk, Brock picked him up in his arms and, shocked by how little he weighed, carried him across to the *Rock Demon*.

Although strong enough, the little skycraft wasn't really designed to carry passengers – particularly one in such a bad way – but Brock knew he would have to try. After all, the High Academe couldn't be left on his own here in the Stone Gardens.

Having secured Nate to the saddle, Brock climbed up behind him and, standing on the stirrup bars, managed to operate the controls. The phraxchamber hummed, a line of white vapour trailed back from the funnel, and the *Rock Demon* took off.

It was an awkward flight back to the floating city. Nate kept slipping in and out of consciousness, and it was all Brock could do to keep him from sliding off the saddle and tumbling to the ground below. Soon, though, he had reached the city and was flying around the spires and towers of the majestic buildings.

As the triple turrets of the renovated Knights Academy loomed up ahead, Brock brought the skyvessel round in a sweeping curve and steered it towards the uppermost storey. It was where the High Academe's living quarters were situated – though with Nate missing and Eudoxia so often away on business, the place was more often than not locked up and empty.

As Brock approached, he saw he might be in luck. The great glass doors that led onto the balcony were open, and there was a figure outside, back towards him, tending to the sapvines that grew over a series of trellised arches. Brock eased back the control lever, causing the phraxchamber's hum to change pitch – and alerting the gardener on the balcony to his presence.

In front of him, he heard Nate give a startled grunt. 'Eudoxia?' he muttered. '*Eudoxia!*'

'Nate!' she called back. 'Nate, is that really you?' She came running towards them, tears streaming down her face. 'Oh, Nate,' she cried. 'I can't believe you're back. After all this time . . .' She wiped away her tears. 'What *happened* to you?'

But Nate Quarter was in no position to answer. As the *Rock Demon* touched down, he finally succumbed to the exhaustion that had gripped him ever since he first stepped onto the spinning boulder. Before Eudoxia could take him in her arms, he fell from the saddle and collapsed at her feet in a deep faint.

Nate Quarter's extraordinary return was soon the main topic of conversation in every corner of New Sanctaphrax. And it wasn't long before the news spread to the other great cities: Hive, Riverrise, Great Glade.

Eudoxia didn't push Nate to do too much too quickly. It was enough that her husband was home at last. Patiently and lovingly, she nursed him back to health; tending to his wounds, spoonfeeding him nourishing broth and leaving him to sleep – sometimes for days at a time – so that he might regain his strength.

And physically, Nate did improve. Mentally, though, he was hard to reach.

He recounted everything he could remember about the long years spent down on the luminous blue scree field with the Professor. He had thought he would die there, he told her, but then the terrible ordeal had come to an abrupt end. Forced to leave the Professor behind, Nate had ridden the storm-stone up from the depths. Alone.

'I promised I would never forget him,' he said, his voice little more than a whisper. 'The Professor . . . It was the last thing I recall.' He shook his head. 'I have no memory of the ascent itself,' he admitted wearily. 'Or how I got to the Stone Gardens.'

'It doesn't matter, Nate,' she assured him, squeezing his hand warmly. 'You're home now. Safe. That's all that matters.'

But to Nate it did matter, and whenever Eudoxia was gone, he racked his brains as to what had taken place. By what buried instinct had he let go of the rock spike to land wherever he had? For even this was uncertain to him. Had he come down in the Mire grasslands, or maybe in the pastures of Undertown on the rock's downward trajectory, then crawled to the stone stacks? Or had he perhaps flung himself down into the Stone Gardens as the hurtling storm-tossed boulder flew up over the Edge cliff?

He couldn't remember. Maybe he never would . . .

As Nate's health continued to improve, Eudoxia allowed others to share his care while she was dealing with the running of the floating city. Gumble and Girolle, a pair of trusted gabtrolls, cooked for him, washed and dressed him; while Strake, a wiry pink-eye, was taken on as his physical therapist. For her part, Eudoxia took it upon herself to inform him – little by little, so as not to trigger any relapse – about what had been happening in New Sanctaphrax while he was gone.

Matters with Quove Lentis and Great Glade had come to a head, Nate learned. The threatened blockade was now in place. The numbers of Edgelanders reaching New Sanctaphrax had dropped dramatically. The upkeep of the beautiful buildings was deteriorating as supplies became harder and harder to obtain. As for the work of the Descenders, Quove Lentis would be delighted to learn that the Knights Academy had suspended all expeditions while resisting the blockade took priority.

It wasn't until months later, when she was sure Nate was up to it, that Eudoxia gave him the most devastating news of all. Stories of a purge in Great Glade's academies had begun to reach New Sanctaphrax – a purge sparked by rumours of Nate's return.

'Because of me?' he said bleakly.

She nodded and patted his hand. 'But don't worry,' she told him. 'It's all going to be all right. Trust me.'

From that moment on, though, Nate sensed a difference in Eudoxia's behaviour. She would listen to him as he tried, again and again, to flesh out the account of his fourth descent, and offer wise counsel. Yet there were occasions when she seemed off-hand. Distracted . . .

Once, he asked her about the whereabouts of his spyglass. He was sure he'd given it to her. But Eudoxia evaded the question, unable to meet his gaze. Nate grew increasingly uneasy. What was it that he could sometimes see in Eudoxia's troubled green eyes?

What was she hiding from him?

Then, before he found out, Eudoxia abruptly left the floating city. It was almost a year after Nate had got back. She told him he was going to be fine; that Strake and the gabtroll couple would take care of him; that the finest healers were at hand; that she would be back soon. But she had to go. All she would say was that she had received important news from the Friends of New Sanctaphrax – that elusive network of hers – and needed to 'deal with matters'.

Now, months after her departure, life had returned to a certain normality, despite the blockade. Most mornings, as High Academe, Nate dealt with the affairs of office; most afternoons, he would withdraw to the Great Library, where he pored over ancient barkscrolls, losing himself for a few hours in the arcane tracts and academic treatises about descending. But his studies offered only temporary relief, for when he left the library and returned to his bedchamber, his heart would sink on finding it still empty.

'Oh, Eudoxia,' he whispered. 'Where *are* you?'

PART TWO
THE VOYAGE

· CHAPTER FOUR ·

'Sanctaphrax.' Cade started back in surprise.

Sanctaphrax . . . The name of the distant city seemed to hang in the moonlit air like a beautiful soap bubble, its delicate surface shimmering with colour. Yet, to the fourthling who had just uttered the word, it seemed less enchanting, for there were tears in her eyes.

For most of that day, Cade had been busy. He'd cleaned his lakeside cabin, cleared his vegetable patch of weeds and harvested fruit and vegetables, which he'd pickled, salted, bottled and boxed, then stored in his underground larder. And when that was all done, he'd sat down and set to work polishing his precious spyglass, thinking as he did so of the famous Descender, Nate Quarter: the uncle he'd never met.

As night had fallen, he'd noticed the *Xanth Filatine* docked at Gart Ironside's lofty sky-platform on the opposite side of the Farrow Lake. He hadn't really given

67

the skytavern much thought – until, noticing the lights of Gart's phraxsloop coming towards his cabin, Cade had stepped out onto the veranda to greet him, only to discover that Gart was not alone.

'You've got a visitor,' Gart called to him.

Standing beside him on the stone jetty was the beautiful stranger who had just uttered that magical word. Sanctaphrax . . .

'Though actually,' she said with a smile, 'we call it New Sanctaphrax these days.'

'New Sanctaphrax,' Cade repeated, abashed to be standing in front of this woman who, it seemed, had come especially to visit him.

She was tall and elegant, with dark eyes and thick blonde hair that was braided and coiled into an intricate plait on top of her head. The long dark cape she wore was well-tailored and expensive-looking. Its hem, though, was frayed and mud-spattered, and beneath it she wore sturdy boots with worn-down heels and scuffed leather. Together, they spoke of the long and arduous journey she'd undertaken.

'Come on then, lad,' said Gart. 'Refreshments for your guest?' He laughed. 'Or are you just going to stand there gawping?'

'I . . . *errm*. Of course,' said Cade, feeling flustered. 'Would you like some hyleroot tea? Or charlock? I've got both, and . . .'

'Hyleroot tea would be lovely,' said the woman, and Cade heard the unmistakable trace of a Great Glade

accent in her voice; refined, lilting, from one of the city's richer districts. 'My name's Eudoxia,' she told him, extending a hand. 'Eudoxia Prade, wife of Nate Quarter . . .'

And Cade felt the hairs on the back of his neck tingle at the sound of his family name on her lips.

'I'll leave you to it then,' said Gart, unhitching the tolley rope and climbing back aboard his little vessel.

While Gart Ironside powered up the phraxchamber and set off back across the lake, Cade led Eudoxia along the jetty, up the wooden stairs to the veranda and inside his cabin. She looked around and, as Cade turned up the tilder-oil lamp, he suddenly saw the place through her eyes: a modest two-room timber dwelling, simply furnished; so much more rustic than what she was used to if her clothes were anything to go by – though at least it was clean.

'I'll put some water on to boil,' he said, and gestured to the fireside chair. 'Do sit down.'

But Eudoxia didn't seem to hear him. She had crossed the cabin and picked up the brass spyglass. With narrowed eyes, she read the letters engraved in the side.

'N Q,' she said. 'Nate Quarter. My husband . . .' She smiled again, and Cade noticed that her eyes, which had looked black in the moonlight, were in fact a new-leaf shade of green. 'And your uncle, Cade.'

Her smile broadened, but it seemed brittle to Cade, and he thought the tears he'd seen before might be about to well up once more. She looked into his face.

'You and I have much to talk about.'

When the pot of hyleroot tea had brewed, Cade poured two mugs, sweetened it with woodhoney, and he and Eudoxia took them out onto the veranda. The pair of them sat opposite one another on stout wicker chairs, a small lufwood table between them. Cade set his mug down. Eudoxia held hers, warming her hands and staring thoughtfully at the steam that swirled over the surface of the tea.

'I was born and raised in the New Lake district of Great Glade,' she began at length.

Cade nodded. That would explain her accent. He knew the area, though not well. It was full of lakeside mansions, owned by some of the wealthiest individuals of the city. Eudoxia's father, it transpired, was one of them. A phraxmine owner, Galston Prade, who had made a fortune in the Twilight Woods. And she went on to explain how she'd met his uncle Nate when the two of them were not much older than Cade was now.

'We had so many adventures together,' she told him, her eyes sparkling at the memory. 'Fighting in the battle of the Midwood Marshes. Journeying to the distant Nightwoods – and to the waif city of Riverrise.' She raised a hand and touched behind her ear lightly. 'I'd been injured. A bullet,' she explained, and then tossed her head as though it was nothing.

Still clasping the hot mug, she leaned forward and took a sip of the hot tea. She smiled appreciatively and drank a little more.

Once she was fully recovered, Eudoxia went on, she and Nate had set forth on an epic voyage back across the vastness of the Deepwoods. They travelled to the very edge of the world, to find that the floating city of Sanctaphrax – which had drifted off into Open Sky centuries earlier – had returned.

'But all was not what it seemed,' she said, her voice laden with doom, 'for the whole place was infested with the most fearsome of all Edge creatures . . .'

'Gloamglozers,' Cade breathed.

'Gloamglozers.' Eudoxia nodded, and Cade's eyes widened as she recounted the pitched battle that had taken place between the legendary fiends and the handful of Edge folk. It was touch and go who would prevail, even tipping in the gloamglozers' favour – until the three Immortals manifested themselves.

'Quint and Twig Verginix,' Eudoxia said. 'And Twig's grandson, Rook Barkwater. Your ancestors, Cade. They defeated the gloamglozer, finally ridding the family of the curse that had plagued it for so long.'

Cade's face broke into a smile.

'And it was there, in Sanctaphrax – *New* Sanctaphrax,' she said, 'that Nate began his career as a Descender.'

As she continued, Cade saw the beautiful stranger's expression change from excitement to . . . to what exactly? Sadness? Regret? She drank the rest of her tea, placed the mug down on the table and, smoothing the creases in her gown with the palms of her hands, explained how Nate had embarked on the first of several expeditions down the Edge cliff.

'With his friend and mentor, Ambris Hentadile,' she added. 'The Professor.'

Her voice cracked as she spoke of watching Nate descend into the darkness with the Professor that first time, leaving her behind to help establish a new society in the floating city. It was a hard and lonely time whenever he was gone, she confessed. Yet the city had flourished.

Cade glanced down at those sturdy boots she was wearing, scuffed and muddy, and so at odds with the fine materials of her gown and cape. Eudoxia was clearly practical and strong. Of course New Sanctaphrax had done well under her guiding hand.

She fell still and, from the expression on her face, Cade knew she was reliving incidents from the past. Then she looked up and gave him that same brittle smile.

'Four descents there were in all, each more perilous than the last,' she told him. 'The fourth was the hardest of all for me to bear.' Her soft lilting voice was suddenly charged with emotion. 'Fourteen years he was away, Cade. Fourteen long years. And during that time, Quove Lentis and his allies grew in strength. They cut off all trade with New Sanctaphrax and made it as difficult as they could for Edgelanders to reach us. But we had friends and supporters, and . . .' She hesitated. 'It was through one of these supporters that I learned Nate had an older brother he wasn't aware of.'

She plucked agitatedly at her cuff, her eyes lowered, then turned and looked in through the open door. Her troubled gaze came to rest on the mantelpiece.

'Nate had forgotten to take it with him on that last descent,' she said. 'His spyglass. So I sent it to your father, and explained the family connection . . .'

Eudoxia fell abruptly silent, the words choking up in her throat. Her eyes glistened in the moonlight, and suddenly the tears that had been threatening for so long spilled over and coursed down her face.

'It was a terrible, terrible mistake,' she said, trying but failing to regain her composure. 'A mistake I will regret for the rest of my life. For by sending the spyglass, together with my message, I believe I must have alerted Quove Lentis and his network of spies. Your father got married, you were born, Cade, and all the while those spies were watching and waiting. Then Nate returned . . .'

Beyond the jetty, the lake had grown still, with the full moon reflected on its mirror-like surface. Only the distant sounds of the forest creatures – fromp barks, weezit squeals and the ghostly hoots of hunting quarms – broke the silence.

Cade staring grimly ahead. 'My father was murdered when news of Nate's return reached Great Glade,' he told her. 'But then I think you know that.'

'Oh, Cade, Cade, I am *so* sorry,' Eudoxia said, leaning forward and clasping his hands in her own. 'I can't undo the damage I have caused. Sky alone knows, I would if I could ... But I have come here in the hope that I can prevent you coming to any worse harm.'

Cade listened, his emotions in turmoil. Eudoxia's one simple act, carried out in all good faith, had had such awful repercussions. What was she about to do now?

'It took me so long to find you,' she said, and smiled weakly. 'I hadn't realized how many tiny settlements there are out here in the Deeplands. Then I heard from one of the Friends of New Sanctaphrax that you'd been seen here, at Farrow Lake. And I came to find you. I didn't trust anyone else to bring the news . . .'

'News?' said Cade.

Eudoxia swallowed. 'There are others who also know of your whereabouts, Cade. Enemy spies, working for those who wish to see you dead. Quove Lentis, back in Great Glade. And one of his paid henchmen, a certain Drox or Drex . . .'

'*Drax*,' said Cade numbly. 'Drax Adereth.'

He remembered only too well the look of scornful amusement on the face of the *Xanth Filatine*'s notorious gangmaster as he'd raised the blowpipe to his lips. If Cade hadn't jumped from the skytavern when he did, then the poisoned dart would have killed him. More than two years ago that had been. He'd hoped Drax Adereth might have forgotten about him by now – but Eudoxia had just dashed those hopes.

'It's no longer safe for you here,' she said, pressing home the point. 'You must leave Farrow Lake.'

'But . . . but where should I go?' he said.

'Back with me, Cade,' she told him simply. 'To New Sanctaphrax.'

They talked some more, swapping information about the floating city and the little settlement by the lake. Cade told Eudoxia about his old life in Great Glade; his new life at the Farrow Lake, spending time describing his closest friends – and also about the barkscrolls she'd noticed pinned to the wall above the mantelpiece; the working drawings on the theoretical harnessing of phrax power that his father, Thadeus, had entrusted to his care. For her part, Eudoxia expanded on the details of the Friends of New Sanctaphrax, and the blockade that was slowly strangling the floating city – and, of course, on his uncle, Nate Quarter.

Cade could have gone on talking for ever, but as the sky began to grow lighter, he saw how tired Eudoxia had become. She rubbed her eyes. She stifled a yawn . . .

'You must be exhausted after your long journey,' Cade ventured, and she readily agreed.

He offered to put her up for the night – what was left of it – and Eudoxia seized the offer gratefully. Leaving the empty mugs on the table, Cade took her back into the cabin and gave up his bed for his aunt to use. For himself, he dragged a hammock outside and hung it from the hooks screwed into the upright posts at the front of the veranda. He removed his jacket, shucked off his boots and climbed into it.

By now, the day creatures had emerged from their roosts and lairs, and the air was full of twittering, screeching and squawking as they saw in the new morning. Cade lay back in the hammock, one arm folded behind his head, and closed his eyes. From inside the cabin, he soon heard the lulling sound of Eudoxia's gentle snoring. As for Cade himself, sleep would not come. He was simply too excited. He rolled onto his side, then over onto the other side, then back again . . .

'Hopeless,' he muttered.

He slipped out of the hammock and, having put his boots back on, descended the stairs and roused his prowlgrin, Rumblix, from his roost beneath the veranda. There, too, was Tug, his friend from the Nightwoods. Tug – born a nameless one, but named by Cade himself – actually had a room of his own in the undercabin. More often than not though, preferring to sleep close to Rumblix, he would curl up in a nest of meadowgrass at the foot of the wooden roost-pole.

Cade looked down at him affectionately. In the short time they had known each other, they had been through a lot together, with Tug ever the true and trusted companion. But he too had a past.

Watching him now, Cade saw how Tug's gigantic claw-tipped hands twitched as he slept. His massive shoulders rose and fell rhythmically, the angry scars that crisscrossed them a testament to the cruelties he had suffered before Cade discovered him. Soft whimpering noises escaped from his fang-studded mouth as he

dreamed of things that Cade could only guess at.

Taking care not to disturb his friend, Cade saddled Rumblix and climbed up.

The pedigree grey prowlgrin that Cade had raised from a hatchling, veteran of Hive city's high-jumping race, purred with keen anticipation. Then, as rose-coloured streaks of light spread out along the horizon, they set off at a gallop, through the woods, then up and across the treetops.

There was a chill to the air, and the leaves were glazed with dew. As Cade reached the forest canopy, the bright sun broke over the jagged mountain tops, making him squint. In the distance, the mighty Five Falls glittered as its great torrents of water fell into the lake below, while stormhornets swooped and fluttered across the rippling surface.

From his lofty position, Cade saw the lights of the Farrow Lake settlement twinkling. On the far shore, the stilt-cabins of the webfoot goblins were clustered together beside their eel-corrals and water gardens. Behind them, lufwood longhouses and thatched lodges circled allotments and glade orchards, where gnokgoblins and mobgnomes were already hard at work. Tree cabins on the forest edge to the west were evidence of the recent arrival of a clan of woodtrolls, while further along the reed-fringed shore, a recently founded slaughterer settlement was growing larger with every passing month. Their communal hammocks crisscrossed the clearing, crimson smoke-pits smouldering below them on the forest floor.

Cade had made many new friends among these newcomers. But he still remembered how it had been before they arrived – when it was just a handful of folk eking out a living around the Farrow Lake. These, the first settlers in the Farrow Ridges, were still his closest friends of all.

To his left, Cade saw the little cabin of Gart Ironside, the skyship platform-keeper, perched high at the top of the towering wooden structure. When Cade had first jumped ship, escaping from the clutches of Drax Adereth, it was Gart Ironside who had found him clinging to a branch of a lufwood tree and saved his life. He had been a good friend to Cade Quarter ever since.

Later, to his right as he galloped on, he passed the tree-cabin where his friend Celestia Helmstoft lived with her father, Blatch. Celestia was a Farrow Laker herself, raised in the untamed woods that fringed the lake's shimmering waters. An excellent prowlgrin rider and able to shoot a phraxmusket from the saddle with deadly accuracy, Celestia also knew more about the healing herbs and plants of the forest than even the most experienced hammerhead goblin healer. She would tease Cade, calling him 'city boy', but her affection for him was obvious, and it was she who had taught him to ride a prowlgrin.

Yes, she had helped him. They all had. Gart. Celestia and Blatch. But of all the settlers Cade had met when he'd first arrived at the Farrow Ridges, it was Thorne Lammergyre who had helped him the most.

Thorne, a grey goblin who lived on the far side of the lake, had shown Cade how to build a cabin, how to fish and how to hunt the deep dark forest. It was thanks to Thorne that Cade had a full larder and a sturdy roof over his head. Thorne was always there for him when he had a problem – and it was to Thorne that Cade was headed now, his head still spinning with the news that Eudoxia had brought him, hoping that he might find the fisher goblin up.

He needn't have worried. As he approached the familiar honey-coloured hive tower, Cade saw his friend in the lake, standing waist-deep in the water, tending to his nets in his eel-corrals.

'Cade,' said Thorne, looking round in surprise. 'Not like you to be up so early. It must be something very important.'

'It is,' said Cade.

'New Sanctaphrax, eh?'

Thorne Lammergyre's eyes widened. They were a dark crystal blue, the colour of the Farrow Lake beneath a stormy sky, and the kindest, wisest eyes of anyone Cade knew.

'As I understand it, the floating city is under blockade,' said the grey goblin, letting go of the eel net he'd been mending and trudging out of the water. 'So your visitor can't have had an easy journey . . .'

'Her name's Eudoxia Prade,' said Cade. 'She arrived last night on the Hive-bound skytavern.

Gart brought her over from his sky-platform as soon as she mentioned my name.'

'You know her?' asked Thorne, taking Cade by the arm and leading him back towards his hive tower.

Cade shook his head. 'We'd never met before,' he said as he followed the grey goblin along the path. Ahead of them, Thorne's hive tower came into view, its wicker gables dark against the brightening sky. 'Though it turns out that we're related.'

'Is that so?' said Thorne.

The two of them went inside.

'She's married to my uncle. Nate Quarter,' Cade said. 'The one I've told you about.'

Thorne, who was forever making improvements to his hive tower, pulled over a couple of newly installed floating sumpwood chairs. The two of them sat down. Then, on releasing the chain locks, they both rose to the first-floor gantry, where carved lufwood beams were festooned with pots, pans and cooking utensils that clinked as they passed by.

'Ah yes, the famous Nate Quarter,' breathed Thorne, clicking the chain lock back into place. The chair hovered beside the gantry. 'As I recall, your illustrious uncle is the reason why you ended up here at the Farrow Lake in the first place.' His face creased up into a leathery smile. 'For which I heartily thank him!'

'Thank him . . . Thank him . . . Thank him . . .' came a voice, and Cade started with surprise as a small furry creature with black and yellow stripes and a twitching nose suddenly landed on his lap.

Thorne chuckled. 'You brought us all together, Cade. Me, Blatch Helmstoft, Celestia, Gart – Tak-Tak here,' he added, nodding at his pet lemkin.

'Tak-Tak here . . . Tak-Tak here . . .' the creature mimicked.

'Not to mention the webfoots, the hammerheads and the white trogs,' Thorne went on. 'Before you arrived, Cade, we were all virtual strangers.'

Cade smiled ruefully. Hearing himself described as someone who had brought the others together only made his news all the more difficult.

Thorne took a long-handled hook from a beam and used it to pull a hanging-stove towards them. Then, reaching up, he grabbed two bowls from one of the many shelves that lined the gantry, and filled them from the pot that was bubbling on the stove. He handed one to Cade, and released the chain lock again.

The sumpwood chair rose some more, past hammocks and a work gantry, and on towards the gabled turret. Cade followed him up, raising the bowl to his lips and taking a sip as he did so.

The breakfast soup was delicious – salted eel, fragrant charlock and succulent lake mushrooms in a clear, aromatic broth. Along with all his other skills, Thorne was an excellent cook.

They came to a halt in front of one of the triangular windows at the top of the hive tower. Thorne opened the shutters and the bright morning sunlight flooded in.

'Just look at what Farrow Lake has become in the short time you've been here,' said Thorne. He was still smiling, but Cade detected a catch in his friend's voice, as if the grey goblin might suspect the reason for this early-morning visit.

Cade looked out of the window – and his gaze fell upon the unassuming timber building on the north shore, directly across the lake from the hive tower. His cabin home. Cade felt a lump in his throat. He took another sip of the broth and swallowed with difficulty.

He wondered whether Eudoxia was still asleep.

The scene became blurred, and Cade realized that his eyes were beginning to fill with tears. He wiped them away on the sleeve of his topcoat and tried to concentrate on the fishy broth. But Thorne, his gaze fixed on Cade, had already noticed how upset his young friend was becoming. Looking away, Thorne took aim and let go of his empty bowl. It dropped to the first-floor gantry, where it landed in a wicker basket with a soft clang.

'You once told me that your uncle Nate Quarter was a Descender, didn't you?' he ventured.

Cade nodded.

'And that Quove Lentis had your father murdered simply for being related to a Descender.' He placed a hand on Cade's arm. 'He wanted you dead for the same reason.' His narrowed gaze intensified. 'That's right, isn't it?'

Cade nodded again, and swallowed hard.

'You were forced to leave Great Glade – and *still* it wasn't over.' Thorne gripped Cade's arm more tightly. 'You had to jump from a skytavern to escape one of Quove's assassins . . . And Gart rescued you from the top of an ironwood pine overlooking this beautiful lake of ours . . .'

'Yes, yes,' said Cade. Thorne wasn't making him feel any better.

'This beautiful lake,' Thorne repeated softly, smiling as he glanced out of the window. 'The past is behind you now, lad. It no longer exists. Only a fool would think otherwise.' He chuckled. 'And you're no fool, Cade,' he added. 'Are you?'

Cade shook his head. He was smiling too, but remained unconvinced. Sometimes, as he was discovering, the past had a horrible way of intruding on the present.

'You're safe now,' Thorne concluded. 'Protected. Here at Farrow Lake, surrounded by friends, and a growing community that you, Cade, have done so much to protect.'

Cade looked down at his soup, the small chunks of smoked eel and thin slivers of lake mushroom floating in the clear broth. He stared into the bowl as if trying to read his fortune in its depths, then drained the dregs of the liquid, took aim and let go. The bowl missed the basket and fell, clanking and clattering through the hanging utensils, before smashing to pieces on the floor far below.

'But . . .' Thorne's expression changed. 'You've come

here to tell me something, haven't you, Cade?' he said gently, his dark blue eyes reflecting back the storm that seemed to be building in Cade's chest.

'Eudoxia has brought me news,' Cade admitted. He couldn't keep it from his friend any longer. 'It's why she travelled so far . . .'

Thorne nodded grimly.

'She says it's no longer safe for me here,' Cade told him. 'Quove Lentis's spies have seen me. I have to leave Farrow Lake.'

The scene outside the window swam before Cade's eyes.

'For ever.'

· CHAPTER FIVE ·

The little skyship dipped then rose in the rain-darkened sky. From the funnel of its phraxchamber, a trail of steam billowed back, stark against the slate-grey clouds.

In the wheelhouse, Captain Gart Ironside stood at the controls. His feet were planted wide apart, one hand gripping the rudder wheel while the other danced over the array of flight levers beside it. Gart's eyes narrowed as he peered through the small circular window in front of him.

'Nothing you can't handle, old girl,' he muttered. 'We've sailed through worse sky squalls than this and lived to tell the tale.'

As if to prove the point, the *New Hoverworm* juddered and leaped forward in the air, like a racing prowlgrin out of the starting-trap.

'That's the way,' Gart said proudly.

Truth was, the *New Hoverworm* was not the most beautiful skycraft to grace the skies. Even Gart recognized that. Cobbled together from his old phraxlighter, which had been badly damaged in a blood-storm, and a battered phraxsloop, once owned by a couple of cut-throat mire-pearlers, it was a curious hybrid. It had an angular prow, crowned with the figurehead of an open-mouthed hoverworm. The stern was blunt, with two sets of bi-rudders fixed on the port and starboard sides, while the phraxchamber, unusually for so large a vessel, had been fitted to the underside of the hull, giving the skycraft a bottom-heavy look.

'Like a low-belly goblin,' Thorne had once teased him.

But Gart hadn't cared. Ugly it might be, but the *New Hoverworm* was strong, fast, stable and utterly dependable – and he loved and trusted her like an old friend.

'Just a touch more phrax power,' he muttered as they headed into low swirling clouds. 'Easy on the aft-weights . . . There we go.'

Strapped into one of the stirrup chairs behind him, Cade Quarter smiled. From beneath his grey crushed funnel cap, a fringe of fair hair flopped over one eye. Cade brushed it back under the brim and pulled the peak down low.

In the time since they'd first met, he and the sky-platform keeper had voyaged far and wide. And during those journeys Cade had often heard Gart talk to his skyship. Usually, when on short ferry trips – loading

goods and supplies on and off the passing skytaverns –
he would be casual and matter of fact.

'Down low on the left ... Watch the cargo doesn't
shift ... That's more like it.'

At other times, such as the year before, when they'd
set off over the treetops in hot pursuit of a renegade
skyvessel, Gart had been terse and abrupt.

'Faster, faster ... That's it ... We've got 'em!'

Now, as the *Hoverworm* bucked and rolled with the
buffeting winds, Gart's voice was soft and coaxing.

'Easy, girl. Easy ... Steady on the hull-weights ...
You're doing just fine ...'

In the chair beside Cade, Celestia Helmstoft tensed
with each dip and rise of the vessel. Her black hair was
pulled back into a tight braided bun and her tilderskin
jacket was buttoned up to the collar. Small tincture
bottles and salve pots festooned the front of the jacket,
with more strapped to the sleeves and hanging in clusters
from her belt. Celestia was a walking apothecary store,
medicinal herbs and soothing ointments always to hand.

Just as listening to Gart cajole the little skyship
reassured Cade, so seeing Celestia – her broad knowledge
of the healing arts so plainly visible on her jacket – made
him feel safe. But Celestia was clearly not so happy.

'It's like riding a prowlgrin,' said Cade, laughing as
the *Hoverworm* suddenly pitched forward.

'Prowlgrins I understand, Cade,' she said, glancing
back at him, her eyes wide with barely suppressed panic
as she gripped the sides of the stirrup chair. 'They're

living, breathing creatures. When they leap with you on their backs, you can trust them. But skyships, with their phraxchambers and flight levers and hull-weights . . .' She shuddered.

'To Gart, the *Hoverworm is* a living, breathing thing,' said Cade. 'Just listen to the way he talks to it.'

The skyship pitched forward again, then rolled violently to one side, its timbers creaking. At the controls, Gart swayed with the movement, his hands a blur over the flight levers as he struggled to bring the little vessel under control again.

'Go with the cross-currents . . .' he crooned softly as the *Hoverworm* righted itself. 'Rise above them . . .'

Suddenly, cutting through his words of encouragement, there came a gruff, guttural voice.

'Tug awake now,' it said. 'Bad dream.'

Behind Cade and Celestia, his great arms looped through mooring rings that were bolted to the cabin walls on either side of him, sat Tug. He was shaking his head from side to side, as though trying to dislodge the memories of the nightmare that had spoiled his sleep.

That morning at dawn – two days after Eudoxia's arrival – Tug had loaded the *New Hoverworm* almost single-handed under Gart's supervision. Moving the heavy crates of provisions as if they were bales of meadowgrass, Tug had skilfully stacked them in the cargo bays fore and aft, making use of every inch of available space.

'He's a strange one, your friend Tug,' Gart had observed to Cade when the loading was complete and they were preparing to set steam from the sky-platform high above the Farrow Lake. 'He looks so huge and cumbersome, and yet it's amazing how he manages to master the most technical of tasks with such ease.'

Cade had had to agree. Ever since he'd first taken the half-starved creature in on that wild and stormy night and decided to share his home with him, Tug had never stopped surprising him. Not only had he continued to grow physically, becoming taller, stronger and more powerfully built than anyone else Cade knew, he also seemed to learn new skills every day.

Creatures like Tug dwelt in the perpetual darkness of the Nightwoods below Riverrise. Edge scholars had studied them in depth for centuries, but had never managed to unlock the secrets of their mysterious origins. That was why they had called them simply 'the nameless ones'. Cade, however, no longer used this term, for this particular nameless one *did* have a name.

Tug. And Tug was his friend.

Cade had told Eudoxia all about him, which was probably the reason why, when she woke up – rested and refreshed after her sleep in Cade's cabin – it was Tug she had first tried to persuade to accompany them back to Sanctaphrax.

'You're his rock,' she told him. 'His anchor. Cade depends on your strength and loyalty more than he could ever explain – perhaps more than he even knows.'

Tug wasn't exactly sure what the stranger in the elegant clothes meant – not least because he found her unfamiliar accent difficult to understand. But he got this much: she and Cade were about to leave the Farrow Lake and head to a city far to the east, and they wanted Tug to go with them.

'Tug come,' he'd told her at once, his great head nodding up and down. 'Tug help Cade. Tug *always* help Cade.'

Eudoxia's conversation with Celestia had not been quite so straightforward. For a start, her father, Blatch Helmstoft, had been there, and he was against the whole venture.

'It sounds utterly foolhardy,' he said. 'Cade would be much safer here, among friends who can look after him. More importantly, I don't want my daughter heading off into unknown dangers.'

Eudoxia had remained calm. Determined and persuasive, she'd pointed out that she and Nate were Cade's closest relatives.

'And as for Celestia,' Eudoxia had said, turning to the girl who so reminded her of herself when she was younger, 'Cade has spoken of you with such affection. And respect. You've become an important part of his life . . .'

She went on – flattering, cajoling, reasoning – and in the end, Celestia was unable to resist. Even Blatch himself found himself falling under Eudoxia's spell. And it was agreed. Celestia would join her, Cade and Tug aboard Gart Ironside's phraxsloop, and – since there was no time to lose – the five of them would set steam from the Farrow Lake the following morning.

As the *Hoverworm* continued to pitch and roll, Tug rubbed his deep-set eyes with the knuckle of a huge clawed hand.

'Tug happy to be with Cade and Celestia,' he said sleepily, and gave that lopsided smile of his.

Celestia smiled back at him, and despite the swaying of the skyship, which she hated so much, she released her grip on the side of the stirrup chair and patted Tug's ridged head.

'And we're happy you're with us,' she said. 'Aren't we, Cade?'

'I'm happy *all* of you are with me,' said Cade. 'Tug, Gart. And you, Celestia,' he said – unaware that, as he'd walked back from Thorne Lammergyre's hive tower the previous morning, his aunt Eudoxia had been out ensuring that the most important individuals in his life *were* travelling with him. 'I'm just sorry I had to leave Rumblix behind.'

'A skyship is no place for a prowlgrin,' said Celestia with feeling. 'Besides, Thorne will take good care of him until we return.'

'That's just it, Celestia,' said Cade sadly. 'I'm not sure I ever *will* return. Not with Quove Lentis's assassins after me. Eudoxia believes New Sanctaphrax is the safest place for me, even with the blockade.'

'Ah, the blockade,' said Gart, glancing over his shoulder at them. 'I don't suppose that fine lady passenger of ours can tell me how we're going to outrun the phraxvessels of the Great Glade fleet.' He shook his head. 'I mean, don't get me wrong, the *Hoverworm*'s a fine little vessel, but she's no match for a thirty-gun phraxfrigate.'

'As a matter of fact, I *can* tell you, Captain Ironside,' came a familiar soft, lilting voice.

Cade turned in his stirrup chair to see that his aunt had entered the cabin. He was surprised. Eudoxia's quarters were below deck at the stern, and ever since they'd set steam that morning, she'd kept to them. But now, with the light failing, she had emerged from her cabin and was standing beside Tug, her grey cape pulled tight about her shoulders and dripping from the driving rain outside.

Holding onto one of the mooring rings, she stooped slightly below the low cabin ceiling and accepted Tug's offer of a steadying hand.

'Thank you, Tug,' she said.

Cade noticed the respect this grand lady of New Sanctaphrax showed his friend, and the effect this had on Tug himself. His misshapen face seemed to soften in her presence, the deep-set eyes looking down bashfully at his feet and that lopsided smile widening.

What was it about Eudoxia Prade that she had such an effect on those around her? Cade wondered.

Even Thorne Lammergyre had been entranced by this visitor from New Sanctaphrax. Eudoxia had gone to see him last of all, and though the grey goblin's heart was close to breaking as she outlined her plans, Thorne had agreed to stay behind.

The Farrow Lake settlement needed a leader, Eudoxia had persuaded him, and there was no one more suited to the task.

That morning, Thorne had ridden Rumblix to Gart's sky-platform to see them all off. Taking Cade aside, he'd pressed a bundle of papers wrapped in oilskin into his hands.

'They're your father's working drawings for the phraxengine, together with some notes of my own,' he'd whispered.

Cade had looked down at the little bundle. Thorne had already worked on his father's blueprints and, turning theory into practice, produced a scale model of a new type of phraxengine. Cade remembered the time when, back in the hive tower, Thorne had demonstrated how the little humming machine worked.

Around a central phraxchamber, four smaller spheres circled at different speeds, hovering just above its surface. And it was these whirring spheres – glowing white, then gold, then red – that had the potential to increase the power of a single phrax crystal a hundredfold, maybe a thousandfold; enough to provide a day's energy for an entire city.

'I've included my workings for that first barkscroll,' Thorne had explained softly and urgently, 'plus my calculations to date on the second and third. It's fascinating stuff.' He glanced round over his shoulder. 'Give them to that uncle of yours, lad. They might well be of some use to him with his descending . . .'

Thorne had looked across at Eudoxia, who was settling herself in her cabin.

'No need to bother your aunt with them, though,' he added. 'From what she's been telling me, she's not as keen on descending as he is.'

Cade had borrowed a needle and thread from Celestia and spent the morning of that first day of their voyage sitting on the aft deck, stitching the papers into the lining of his jacket. When she'd asked, Cade had told Celestia he was just padding it to keep out the cold.

'And the rain, I hope,' she'd said with a laugh as dark clouds had rolled in, blotting out the sun and chilling the air.

That had been at noon. Now, here they all were, the small crew of the *Hoverworm*, sheltering in the wheelhouse from the swirling winds and torrential rain, as night closed in around them. Eudoxia, maintaining her grip on the mooring ring, turned to Gart, who was still fretting about the Great Glade fleet.

'I would never ask you to risk your vessel by trying to break the Great Glade blockade, Captain,' she reassured him gently. 'You've been more than generous even agreeing to embark on this voyage.'

Gart cleared his throat. 'Anything for young Cade, he knows that,' he said gruffly – though when he turned back to the controls, Cade saw he was blushing and that there was a smile on his face.

'No,' Eudoxia went on, seemingly unaware of the effect she was having on the captain, 'what I need is for you to get us safely to Gorgetown in the Northern Reaches. I've arranged for us to be met there by some Friends of New Sanctaphrax,' she added.

The skyvessel shuddered as another crosswind threw it off-course.

'We should outrun this squall by dawn,' Gart announced. 'Then we'll moor up and I'll plot a new route.'

Eudoxia smiled as she carefully made her way across the small cabin to stand beside Gart at the wheel. She

98

placed a hand on his shoulder and spoke quietly to him; he listened intently. Whether Eudoxia was questioning the old skyfarer's abilities or offering advice, Cade couldn't tell, but she clearly wanted to spare his feelings either way.

'Zelphyius Dax?' Gart muttered at last. 'The Midwood Decks? Well, it's an interesting idea . . .'

Eudoxia patted him on the shoulder. Then, gathering her grey cape around her and pulling up the hood, she stepped out of the cabin.

'So, what did she say?' asked Cade after the cabin door closed. 'What's the plan?'

'All in good time,' said Gart, with an enigmatic smile that reminded Cade of Eudoxia's. 'Got a bit of thinking to do,' he added, patting the wheel, 'haven't we, old girl? Sail and steam, eh? The high sky . . .' He shrugged. 'Stranger things have been known, I suppose.'

Gart Ironside, Cade realized, was no longer talking to him.

· CHAPTER SIX ·

The fierce storm that raged throughout that first night of their voyage cleared, just as Gart Ironside had predicted it would. The second day broke, warm and breezy, with a cloudless sky.

The *Hoverworm* made steady progress across the immensity of the Deepwoods. Days of full steam, with the phraxchamber humming as the treetops sped past below them in a blur, were interspersed with nights moored to lonely ironwood pines high above the forest canopy, listening to the booming calls of the night creatures.

Time was of the essence, and they travelled quickly and efficiently. Whenever Eudoxia felt that they were wasting time, or taking too long to pack up or refill their water containers, she would be there, insisting that everyone hurry it along.

'We must press on,' she would say. It was to become a familiar refrain.

Ten days they voyaged like this, under constant pressure to reach their destination as soon as possible. Routine was everything, and soon the crew of the *Hoverworm* became accustomed to life on board the tiny vessel; working as a team to ensure the flight continued with no unwelcome hitches.

Gart stood at the controls, the wheelhouse his constant home. Even when they moored up, he preferred to sleep in one of the stirrup chairs at the wheel rather than take one of the comfortable hammocks below the foredeck.

Celestia and Cade cooked in the tiny galley – no more than a hanging-stove and a battened-down chest full of pots, pans and utensils – on the foredeck itself. Celestia took meals to Gart as they steamed on, while Cade delivered covered trays to Eudoxia in her cabin below the aft deck. There, the two of them would share snowbird stew, or skewers of roast logbait, or other food that he or Tug had managed to forage in flight. And while they ate, they talked.

Cade looked forward to these conversations, enthralled by the unfolding story of his aunt Eudoxia's fascinating life. And no matter how much she recounted, he was always left wanting to hear more.

She told Cade about her early childhood in Great Glade – of her thoroughbred chestnut prowlgrin, Antix; of the little rowing boat she'd sometimes taken out on the lake when the moon was full. And – her gaze unable to meet Cade's, and voice tinged with guilt – of the wealth and privilege she had taken for granted. She moved on to speak of Nate, and how, on their travels together, they had both discovered that there were many in the Edge far less fortunate than themselves.

'In New Sanctaphrax,' Eudoxia explained, 'we tried to do something about that – to provide a safe haven for the weak, the poor, the dispossessed . . . Which is why, with the floating city under threat,' she added, 'we must get back as quickly as we can . . .'

'Then why are we heading for the Midwood Decks?' Cade interrupted. 'Surely the Northern Reaches are in the opposite direction.' He frowned. 'And anyway, who *is* Zelphyius Dax?'

Eudoxia put down her plate, and when Cade looked into her eyes, it was as if, instead of his aunt, he was seeing the girl she had once been.

'Zelphyius Dax is one of the wisest individuals I know,' she told him excitedly. 'And a loyal Friend of New Sanctaphrax. We're going to the Midwood Decks because that's where we'll find him. I believe Zelphyius can help us reach the Northern Reaches in days rather than weeks. I've spoken to Captain Ironside about it, and he has agreed.'

'So we're changing vessels?' Cade asked. 'Leaving Gart and the *Hoverworm*?'

'Not exactly,' Eudoxia replied.

Then she told him, simply and quietly, of her plan.

'And Tug is going to be a great help,' she added. 'Aren't you, Tug?'

Cade looked up, and was surprised to see his friend peering down at them from the aft-deck hatch.

Tug was too big to fit into Eudoxia's tiny quarters, and when away from the wheelhouse he generally kept himself busy on deck, lowering and raising the logs used as bait, and collecting the air-borne creatures that would attach themselves to them. Strange, white, translucent creatures they were, with tentacles and scales, but delicious to eat. And like almost everything else he attempted, Tug had proved to be a fast learner. He soon perfected the art of logbaiting and was now an accomplished cloud angler.

Quick and talented as he was, however, there was one thing Tug could never master, no matter how hard he tried. Singing. Each night, after supper on the foredeck, when the *Hoverworm* was moored safely for the night, Celestia would play the snailskin bagpipes the webfoot goblins had given her, and they would all come together in song.

These were the only times on their long trip when Eudoxia seemed to relax. And since they were moored up anyway, unable to fly during the hours of darkness, she allowed the others to enjoy themselves too, without constantly trying to urge them on.

Gart favoured skytavern shanties, although he blushed crimson whenever Eudoxia gasped with mock shock at the bawdy lyrics. Celestia would sing the strange, sibilant songs the webfoots had taught her, making Cade homesick for the beautiful Farrow Lake he'd left behind. For his part, Cade contributed with the ballads he'd grown up with in Great Glade, which spoke of stirring deeds from the First and Second Ages of Flight – songs like *The Spring of Life* and *The Charge of the Freeglade Lancers* and, his own favourite, *Twig and the Banderbear.*

This was Tug's favourite too, and whenever Cade started singing it, Tug would sway his great head from side to side before drowning out the chorus with his tuneless, rumbling drone.

'They travelled through glades and forests afar,
They yodelled to distant kin.
The tale of Twig and the Banderbear,
Is the ballad of which we sing . . .'

After a few verses, everyone would be helpless with laughter. Everyone, that is, apart from Tug himself, who would smile his lopsided smile and shrug his massive shoulders, and groan on to the very end of the song.

And then, beneath the silver moon, Eudoxia would finally join in. Settling herself at Tug's feet, her eyes half closed, she sang the extraordinary songs of Sanctaphrax: the city of the singing spires.

The songs were wordless, a series of breathy sighs and whistling sounds that corresponded to the different air currents passing through the towers and arches of the ancient academies. To Cade, these gentle songs seemed as mysterious as they were beautiful, and increased his longing to see and hear the fabled floating city for himself.

An hour after they had set steam on the morning of the twelfth day of their voyage – three days ahead of schedule, Eudoxia noted happily – the city of the Midwood Decks abruptly came into view through the rain-swept trees.

Cade shut the lid of the galley chest and closed the vents of the stove, extinguishing the flame, then hurried to the prow. Behind him, Gart stared out of the wheelhouse window, his lips moving as he talked to his vessel.

'Steady now, old girl. That's the way . . .'

Celestia climbed up from the foredeck cabin and joined Cade. Tug dropped the logbaits he'd been checking and lumbered after her, his eyes wide with excitement.

Moments later, Eudoxia, in her grey cape, appeared behind him, a smile on her face. She looked down at the sprawl of buildings in the distance, and nodded.

'The Midwood Decks,' she said, her voice giving nothing away.

As they got nearer, Cade could see that the city was a collection of huge wooden platforms – like the decks of mighty skytaverns – with tall timber-framed constructions clustered around them. The platforms were set at different heights, some low to the marshy ground, others high up, connected by walkways and thoroughfares strung from one to another.

The whole city, Cade thought, seemed to be swaying, the platforms tilting and rotating slowly in different directions. And, on closer inspection, he saw why. Everything was built of buoyant wood – the lightest, most buoyant wood in the Deepwoods.

Sumpwood.

The platforms and the buildings surrounding them were hovering, tethered to the ground by chains and tolley ropes of various designs. Fringing the decks were gantries and jetties, where skyvessels were constantly taking off and landing, like swarms of woodbees pollinating Deepwoods flowers. And in among this endless hustle and bustle were the inhabitants of the Midwood Decks; thronging crowds gathered on the open expanses of the platforms themselves, where carts and market stalls and long trestle tables displayed food and goods of all sorts.

Cade whistled, impressed. 'There must be fifty decks down there,' he said.

'Fifty-five, to be precise,' said Eudoxia. 'The Midwood Marshes have been almost completely covered.'

'It's where you and Uncle Nate fought in that battle, isn't it?' said Cade.

'The Battle of the Midwood Marshes,' said Eudoxia, nodding, and without thinking she raised a hand and stroked the small scar behind her ear. 'Though it seems a lifetime ago to me now.' She hesitated, then smiled. 'It'll be so good to see Zelphyius again.'

'Which deck does he live on?' Celestia asked. She had borrowed Cade's spyglass and was scanning the city below.

Cade saw Eudoxia's gaze fall on the monogrammed *NQ* on the side of the spyglass, and the frown that plucked at her brow. Then she looked away.

'Zelphyius doesn't live on the decks,' she told Celestia. 'But further out, in the sumpwood stands.' She pointed. 'Over there.'

The *Hoverworm* skirted round the bustling city, Gart taking care not to fly too close to the other skyships going about their business. Cade would have loved to land and spend the next few days wandering from deck to deck of this amazing city. But apparently it wasn't possible. Eudoxia had warned him that the Midwood Decks were allied to Great Glade these days, and that the influence of Quove Lentis and the School of Flight was strong here.

Besides, he knew she would want to 'press on'.

As the rain stopped and the midday sun burned off the mist, the skies began to clear. Gripping the safety rail on the starboard side of the little phraxship, Cade looked down at the forest of towering sumpwood trees. He'd seen nothing like them before.

The treetops were broad-branched, with thick clusters of blue sumpneedles pointing skywards. The trunks were squat and bulbous, resembling phraxchambers. But most remarkable of all were the roots. Huge, serpentine and exposed, they were almost three times the height and width of the rest of the tree. Sprawling down from the base of the trunks in great tangled clusters, they buried themselves deep in the swampy, waterlogged mud of the forest floor.

Gart steered the *Hoverworm* in and out of the archways and bridges of the convoluted root system as they went deeper into the sumpwood forest. The light here was

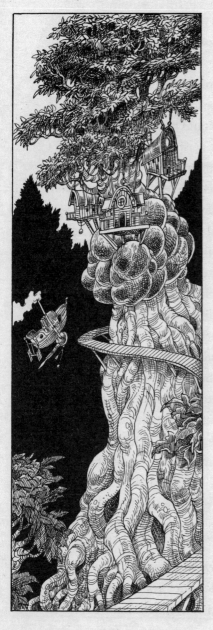

dappled; the air damp and heavy with the slightly acrid odour of wet moss.

Eudoxia had joined Gart in the wheelhouse and was carefully guiding him through this root maze. As they passed, tusked quarms – suspended from the tree roots by their long arms as they warmed themselves in the rare sunshine – stared back at them through manes of purplish hair. Tiny curve-beaked birds fluttered over the skyvessel, sipping at the trail of steam it left in its wake. Then, up ahead, Cade saw a cluster of log cabins attached to the sumpwood trees.

'Woodtrolls!' he said, recognizing the distinctive architecture.

The *Hoverworm* slowed down, then came to a standstill, hovering in the air next to the settlement.

Woodtrolls carrying the tools of their trade – two-handed axes, curved saws and wood callipers – and pulling floating pallets of sumpwood logs, emerged from the surrounding forest and looked up.

Then an elderly fourth-ling in a worn topcoat appeared in the doorway of one of the upper cabins and stepped out onto the jutting gantry. He stared for a moment at the small vessel, then motioned to them – and Gart threw him the *Hoverworm*'s tolley rope, which he secured to a jutting moor-ing peg.

'What a wonderful surprise!' he exclaimed, taking Eudoxia's hand as she stepped down from the *Hoverworm* onto the gantry. 'And welcome to Heartroot. It's been far, far too long, my dear Eudoxia.'

'Zelphyius! It's so good to see you, old friend,' said Eudoxia, embracing him warmly. 'We have much to discuss.'

'Come, come,' said Zelphyius, leading the way to his cabin.

Apart from Tug, who stayed on board the *Hoverworm*, they all followed Zelphyius Dax through the door. Like all woodtroll cabins, it was far larger on the inside than it looked from the outside. The walls curved inwards to a central, ornately carved ceiling boss, from which a constellation of tiny glowing lamps was suspended. The walls were chequered with a lattice of shelves, each one neatly lined with barkscrolls, ledgers and bills of sale, as well as barrels of woodale and shuttered larders.

What was more, Cade noticed, Zelphyius Dax must be some kind of shipwright. There were models of the skycraft he'd designed and built hanging between the tiny lamps and lining the topmost shelves.

Zelphyius gestured towards the cushioned sumpwood benches beneath the lamps, and they all sat down. Then Eudoxia made introductions. They were joined by Zelphyius's chief carpenter and foreman – two woodtrolls with reddish button noses and extravagantly tufted hair – who exchanged looks with each other as Eudoxia explained her plan.

For his part, Zelphyius kept his eyes fixed on Gart Ironside.

'I make no secret of my opinion regarding this Third Age of Flight,' said Zelphyius when Eudoxia had

112

finished. 'The Second Age, when vessels were powered by sail alone, has always been my preference. But I owe Eudoxia a lot. After all, without her help, the Great Glade timber merchants would have wrecked the sumpwood forests here long ago.' He grunted. 'Still might, if they get their way.' He fixed Gart with a penetrating stare. 'This phraxship captain here obviously needs help,' he said, 'so I'll put my best person on to it.'

Eudoxia looked surprised. 'But surely, *you*, Zelphyius, are that person,' she said.

The elderly fourthling shook his head. He glanced over to the shelves in the far corner, and Cade noticed a figure in a quarm-fur forage cap and long-tailed topcoat leaning against a stack of scrolls.

Removing the forage cap to reveal a tumble of flame-red hair, the figure strode across the cabin and stood in front of Gart, before giving a curt bow.

Zelphyius Dax smiled. 'Allow me to introduce my daughter, Delfina.'

· CHAPTER SEVEN ·

'So what does this bit do?' asked Cade, pointing down at a circle with a series of lines radiating off it.

'That's the flux-converter,' said Delfina.

'And that?'

'The array mechanism,' she told him, remaining determinedly patient. 'It connects to the flight levers here, here and here.' Delfina stabbed at the diagram with her forefinger. 'Complete with a heat-modifier for . . .'

Cade shrugged. 'It's no use,' he told her. 'I just can't picture it.'

He and the others were clustered around the barkscroll which Delfina Dax had unfurled and smoothed out on the desk. Drawn on it in smudged charcoal were her sketches for the refurbished *Hoverworm*. They looked impressive, but Cade was at a loss to know what they meant. Gart Ironside's phraxcraft had already been through a major refit; now, it seemed, it was going

to be changed beyond all recognition.

Delfina laughed. 'Trust me,' she said. 'In three days' time the *Hoverworm* is going to fly like never before.' She patted Cade on the arm. 'You'll understand it better when you see the finished vessel.'

Eudoxia was nodding. 'One thing I've got from this is that we're going to be flying at considerable altitude. Is that right?'

'In high sky,' Delfina confirmed.

'So it'll be bitterly cold,' said Eudoxia, 'which means we'll need appropriate clothing.' She looked around at the circle of faces. 'Gart,' she said, 'as pilot, you'll want to know everything about the changes being made, so I propose that you go with Delfina to see the work being done first-hand . . .'

'I'd like that,' said Gart.

'*And* you can help out too,' Delfina broke in, her nose crinkling as she laughed. 'There's no place for spectating in the Dax Skycraft Yard.'

'Tug, you go with them,' Eudoxia added, then turned to Cade and Celestia. 'I'd like you two to sort out the extra equipment we'll need for the extreme cold. Hammelhorn fleeces. Fur-lined gloves. You know the sort of thing.'

Cade nodded. It seemed that he was going to get the chance to look around the Midwood Decks after all.

'There are several places in the city centre,' said Delfina. 'Plus the market. I'll draw you a map.'

'Thanks,' said Cade – although he did wonder whether

her map would make any more sense to him than her working drawings.

'And you, Eudoxia?' asked Celestia. 'What will you be doing?'

Eudoxia's left eyebrow shot upwards as though she was offended by the question – but then her expression softened and she burst out laughing. She turned to Delfina's father, who was standing just outside the small group.

'Zelphyius and I have some serious catching up to do,' she said. 'Don't we, Zelphyius?'

'We do, Eudoxia,' he replied, his weather-beaten features creasing into a smile. 'We certainly do.'

Leaving Eudoxia and Zelphyius sitting on the balcony of his cabin, looking out at the mighty sumpwood stands and discussing old times and future ways to keep the forests safe from over-logging, Cade and Celestia set off into the city.

'Don't talk to anyone unless you have to,' Eudoxia called after them. 'Especially merchants from Great Glade.'

'We won't,' Cade assured her.

'And take umbrellas!' she added.

Outside the cabin, they orientated themselves, then took a walkway that led back to the city. It was raining, but neither of them minded. One of the great conical umbrellas was keeping them dry, and there was some-thing about the misty rainfall that made the Midwood

Decks seem even more exotic. At the end of the walkway, they stepped down onto their first floating platform and, surrounded by tall buildings and jostling crowds, were soon lost in the city's sights and sounds.

'So, this was Eudoxia's hush-hush plan,' said Cade. 'To come to the Midwood Decks to get the *Hoverworm* refitted.' He paused. 'What's the name of the place we're heading for?'

But Celestia was distracted, putting up her own umbrella. They were passing a covered storefront, where a portly red-faced vendor was seated on a stool in the middle of the collection of caged animals he was selling: lemkins, quarms, plus a vicious-looking vulpoon on a leash.

'Celestia?' said Cade.

'Pardon? Oh, sorry, Cade,' she said. 'Gorgetown.'

'Gorgetown,' Cade repeated, and frowned. 'According to Eudoxia, Zelphyius understands the great air currents in high sky better than anyone,' he went on. 'Currents that can knock weeks off our voyage. But the *Hoverworm*'s got to be up to it. And that's where Delfina comes in—'

'Whoa!' Celestia exclaimed as a sudden gust of wind caught her umbrella and almost sent her flying up into the air.

Huge and tent-like, their two umbrellas – like the umbrellas of everyone else on the rain-soaked Midwood Decks – were almost weightless because of the buoyant wood they were made from. High winds could be hazardous, as Celestia had just discovered, so the pair of them stopped and attached to the handles the weights they'd been given. Then on they went.

With only three days in the city, there wasn't enough time to explore all fifty-five of the huge decks, each one the size of a goblin village, but Cade and Celestia were determined to explore as many of them as they could. They headed towards the highest one, situated at the centre of the city. From there, sitting on a gantry platform at its rim, they looked down on the others.

'It's magnificent,' Celestia breathed.

Around the sides of this particular deck were the town's council buildings. Tall timber towers, each of them had decoratively carved lintels of grotesque faces that represented rain spirits and cloud gods. On the deck itself, crowds gathered to listen to open-air disputes being adjudicated, and laws and rules discussed.

As Cade watched, he realized that some kind of protocol was being followed. Umbrellas would go up like sprouting mushrooms when one or another of these proceedings began; then furl and shut with loud *snaps* as they ended – only for another cluster of umbrellas to sprout in a different part of the deck.

The bizarre rituals were intriguing. Cade could have watched them for hours. But, as Celestia reminded him, they hadn't come into the city simply for sightseeing. So they left the council proceedings behind them and, taking walkway after swaying walkway, wandered through the buoyant city in search of a store or market stall where they might buy the goods they needed.

They came to one deck with a bustling fish market. The air was filled with the voices of traders dealing in massive oozefish and cloudshrimps the colour of rainbows, bellowing special offers and never-to-be-repeated deals. On another platform, garment makers displayed their wares on long flapping clotheslines, which were fixed to a tall pillar at the very centre, like the spokes of a colourful wheel.

'Raingear, mainly,' Celestia observed as she flicked through the clothes. 'We need something warmer.'

They kept on searching.

Other decks had similar bustling markets: metalmongers, timber-dealers, fur traders, and one deck devoted to stalls selling delicious-smelling broths and stews, and pastries dripping with delberry jam and woodhoney, where Cade and Celestia stopped for something to eat.

The whole city, it seemed, was devoted to buying and selling goods of all kinds, the traders jostling with one another to attract the attention of passing customers, who peered back at them from beneath their huge umbrellas. But at the end of that first day, with night approaching and the rain torrential once more, they still hadn't found what they were looking for.

'Never mind,' said Eudoxia back at the cabin. 'Tomorrow is another day.' She hesitated. 'You didn't get stopped by any Great Glade traders?'

'No,' said Cade. 'But . . .' He glanced at Celestia.

'What?' said Eudoxia.

'There was one individual,' said Cade. 'A stout goblin matron in a chequerboard rain-cape. I don't know if it was just coincidence, but we kept seeing her. On the fish-market deck. Near the food stalls . . .'

'Ah, yes,' said Eudoxia. 'I forgot to tell you. Zelphyius assigned one of the Friends of New Sanctaphrax to watch out for you. From a discreet distance,' she added, and turned to Zelphyius. 'Though not *that* discreet, by the sound of it.'

Zelphyius shrugged. 'She was there, that's the important thing,' he said.

The following day, Cade and Celestia were making their way to the area of platforms to the north of the Council Deck, when Celestia touched Cade's arm.

'It's her again,' she mouthed.

Cade glanced round. And there she was: the goblin matron with the chequerboard cape and folded umbrella.

'I wonder what she'd actually do if we *were* in danger,' he said. 'I mean, I shouldn't judge, but she doesn't look as though she'd be up to much in a fight.'

'I said the same thing to Zelphyius last night,' said Celestia. 'There's a sword concealed in the handle of that umbrella of hers.' She smiled. 'And she knows how to use it.'

As they continued along the walkways, though, it did seem that Eudoxia might have been unduly cautious. Apart from the goblin matron herself, neither Cade nor Celestia noticed anyone acting suspiciously. The Midwood Deckers were far too intent on commerce to take much notice of them – especially when the two of them made it clear, by lowering their umbrellas in the customary fashion, that they weren't interested in buying anything.

Around midday, they came to a small deck sandwiched between two more grandiose, and much noisier, decks. Thatched workshops stood in clusters, along with dyeing troughs, saw benches, inspection racks and small generators. An assortment of trogs, trolls and goblins were hard at work, but they seemed to be carrying out repairs and alterations rather than selling, and Cade was about to turn back when Celestia took hold of his arm.

'Look,' she said, and led him towards a squat building with a corrugated roof at the back of the deck. Under a striped awning, protected from the rain, was a rail full of bulky-looking clothes. Celestia's face broke into a smile. 'Hammelhorn-fleece jackets. Quilted breeches. Down gloves. And, if I'm not very much mistaken,' she said, unhooking something made of leather and tinted glass and turning it over in her hands, 'these are ice goggles.'

'My father might be old-fashioned, Gart,' said Delfina Dax, 'but what he doesn't know about skycraft isn't worth knowing.'

She stepped back, hands on hips, and surveyed her work on the *Hoverworm*. Her unruly flame-red hair had been tamed, pulled back into a series of braided tufts in the woodtroll fashion, and she wore a timber-apron of tilder hide, with a belt from which woodworking tools hung.

Gart Ironside, in shirt sleeves, wiped his hands on an embroidered kerchief then returned it to the pocket of his expensive-looking breeches.

'He reminds me of a good friend of mine,' he said approvingly. 'A webfoot goblin by the name of Phineal. Phineal Glyfphith. Originally from the Four Lakes.'

The two of them were standing beside a skyship cradle in a clearing in the sumpwood forest, not far from the woodtroll cabins. And beneath a tilder-hide tarpaulin, held secure by chains in the cradle of crisscrossed ironwood slats, sat the *Hoverworm*.

The hull of the vessel had been scraped clean of

mist-floaters and cloud barnacles, and the lufwood timber sanded back to the grain. The fore and aft decks had been similarly cleaned, and the *Hoverworm*'s woodwork now gleamed brightly as the eighth coat of buoyant varnish slowly dried. Zelphyius Dax's team of woodtroll shipwrights had worked tirelessly over the three days since the skyship's arrival, under his daughter Delfina's exacting eye.

'Fine skycrafters, the webfoots,' said Delfina appreciatively. 'Masters at setting sails, by all accounts. It's a dying art in this modern age of ours.'

'Phineal is one of the best,' Gart told her. 'He and his clan-brothers fly messages all over Farrow Lake on their skycraft.' He smiled at the memory. 'Agile as stormhornets they are, and almost as fast.'

Delfina looked puzzled. 'You're a phraxsteamer captain,' she said, 'and yet you sound as though you admire the old ways.'

'I do,' said Gart, and felt his face beginning to redden.

What was it about this female fourthling that made him feel as shy as a sky cadet on his first voyage? he wondered. Was it her straightforward manner; the no-nonsense directness so characteristic of the woodtrolls she worked beside? Or was it the wealth of knowledge gleaned from her father, Zelphyius, that she displayed with such ease and naturalness – as if reciting the forty ingredients of sky varnish was something anyone could do? Maybe it was her flame-red hair and clear blue eyes, and the way her nose crinkled when she laughed . . .

Gart cleared his throat awkwardly.

'I grew up around steam,' he told her, 'and back in Great Glade, phraxships were my life.' He smiled, blushing redder than ever, and stared down at his boots. 'Before I lost everything to a crooked merchant and the gambling tables, that is,' he added sheepishly, 'and buried myself out on that lonely sky-platform in the furthest reaches of the Deepwoods.'

He fell still, embarrassed by how much he was opening up. The sound of the rain pattering down on the tarpaulin above their heads sounded like drums.

'Still, it gave me time to think,' he went on. 'And then Cade came along – and, through him, I got to know my neighbours. Then others arrived . . .' He chuckled. 'Before I knew it, the world I thought I'd left behind had come to me.' He patted the hull of the *Hoverworm*, his hand lingering on the smooth timber. 'Phineal showed me the beauty of the Second Age of Flight,' he said, 'but skycraft under sail, however fast, can only carry one or two. For crew and cargo you need phraxengines and steam.'

'What if I told you that you could have both?' Delfina asked.

She reached out and ran her fingertips over the hull of the *Hoverworm*, testing the dryness of the varnish. And as she did so, her hand and Gart's inadvertently touched. Delfina looked up, and her nose crinkled as she laughed.

'Why, Captain Ironside, you're blushing!'

*

'Wake up, Cade!'

Cade opened his eyes to see Celestia looking down at him.

Sleeping in a sumpwood bunk, swaying gently on the end of a tether chain, felt exactly like sleeping in a hammock aboard the *Hoverworm*, rolling with the motion of the vessel. For a moment, Cade imagined he was back on board, until he saw the cabin shelves behind Celestia, with their neatly stacked barkscrolls of working drawings.

He reached for his jacket, hanging from a hook overhead, and felt for the oilcloth bundle sewn into its lining. It was still there.

'What time is it?' he asked sleepily.

'Two bells,' said Celestia, using Gart Ironside's measure of flight time – the daylight hours divided into six tolls of the bell that hung beside the wheelhouse window. 'Hurry, we're ready to set steam. I mean . . . Oh, you'll see.'

Cade climbed out of the bunk, pulled on his boots and grabbed his jacket and cap. 'Wait for me!' he called as he ran after his friend.

Unlike him, Celestia must have been up at dawn – or first bell – for her black hair was combed back into two neatly constructed woodtroll tufts, and her apothecary jacket was smartly pressed. Outside, Cade followed her down the gantry steps and along the sumpwood walkway that led through the forest to the Dax Skycraft Yard.

A troop of tusked quarms swung up into the branches high in the treetops, their distinctive hooting calls filling the air. Below the walkway, a giant mudworm uncoiled from a sumpwood root and buried itself in the waterlogged forest floor, sending a plume of liquid mud high into the air.

Celestia walked fast, and Cade, struggling into his jacket and trying to button it up, had to jog to catch up.

'What's the big rush?' he protested. 'Can't we get some breakfast at least?'

'I thought you'd appreciate a lie-in more than break-fast,' said Celestia. 'Just wait till you see the *Hoverworm*!'

'They've finished the varnishing?' said Cade.

He stepped through the carved wooden arch that stood at the entrance to the skycraft yard – the clearing in the sumpwood forest with the skyship cradle at its centre – and stopped dead in his tracks. His jaw dropped and his eyes widened as he stared at the refurbished skycraft. Suddenly he understood the barkscroll sketch he'd been shown before.

'Do you like it?' asked Delfina Dax, her nose crinkling as she laughed at the look on Cade's face.

'It's wonderful,' he breathed.

Gart Ironside stood at the wheel of the *Hoverworm* and gazed out of the circular window of the wheelhouse. The row of newly appointed flight levers at his side remained untouched as he concentrated on the rudder wheel in front of him. The phraxchamber below thrummed at maximum propulsion as the little vessel climbed higher and higher into the sky.

127

It looked quite different from the skycraft that had set off from the Farrow Lake – and the gleaming varnished woodwork and renovated figurehead of the open-mouthed hoverworm weren't the only differences. The shape of the vessel itself had changed, as testified to by the shadow scudding over the scrubby landscape below. Set midway between the angular prow and blunt stern, directly above the under-hull phraxchamber, there was now a tall, slender mast, its cross beams concealing the yet-to-be-unfurled sail array.

On the foredeck, securely tethered, Cade stood with Celestia to get the best view possible. Eudoxia was in her cabin, and Tug, leaning in at the aft-deck trap door, was listening intently as she spoke.

'This is as high as I can take her,' came Gart's voice from the wheelhouse.

'Thank you, Captain Ironside,' said Delfina Dax, stepping out of Eudoxia's cabin. 'Tug and I will take it from here.'

Cade smiled at the look on Tug's face as he straightened up and flexed his massive arms. It was a mixture of pride and bashfulness; half smiling, half frowning.

Eudoxia herself emerged from her cabin and stood beside the two of them. She nodded to each in turn.

'Release the aft sails!' Delfina ordered.

Tug gripped the winding mechanism installed in the aft deck and began turning the wheel. In front of Cade and Celestia, there was a sudden flash of white as a sail unfurled from the tall sumpwood mast embedded in the foredeck. On either side of it, as Tug quickly turned the sail crank, an array of dazzling white spidersilk sails billowed out, the wind taking them.

At the controls in the wheelhouse, Gart shut off the phraxchamber and the steam from its funnel wisped to a halt. Then he stepped back to allow Delfina Dax to take over.

In the bitter cold of the high sky, powerful air currents took hold of the *Hoverworm* and sent it speeding across the sky.

'Gorgetown in two days,' said Eudoxia.

Gart Ironside looked at the flame-haired fourthling guiding his ship. Delfina glanced back over her shoulder at him and smiled.

'Here's to steam *and* sail,' she said.

· CHAPTER EIGHT ·

The *Hoverworm* arrived at the Northern Reaches shortly after six bells on the second day. They had made exceptional time.

Throughout the journey, Delfina Dax and Gart Ironside took turns at the wheel, both of them taking care to go with the powerful north-westerly air current that filled the magnificent white spidersilk-sail array. Neither they, nor any of the others on board, had ever travelled at such speed before – or at so high an altitude. Thankfully, wearing the clothes and equipment that Cade and Celestia had purchased back in the Midwood Decks, no one suffered from frostbite or succumbed to ice-blindness.

On their arrival, Gart secured the little vessel to a jutting rock, while Delfina supervised Tug in dismantling the sail array and packing it away in the foredeck hold. They would moor up for the night in this barren land-scape, with its towering escarpment and deep central ravine, then complete the final stretch of their journey the following morning.

'So far as the good folk of Gorgetown are concerned, we're just a small phraxship from a settlement in the Deepwoods,' Delfina told the others, 'in search of some quality streakstone.'

'Well, the first part is true, at least,' Gart said with a laugh.

Cade laughed too. Quite a change had come over the grizzled phraxship captain since they acquired this new member of the crew, he'd noticed. Gart Ironside had started combing and oiling his side-whiskers and moustache, and taken to wearing his best waistcoat underneath his battered topcoat.

It was triple-breasted, with the coiling form of a mythical 'cloudeater' stitched down its front. And at supper later that night, as they sat beneath the stars on the foredeck, Cade noted how the captain took great care to tuck his kerchief in at the neck to protect the waistcoat as he sipped the logbait broth that he and Celestia had prepared.

'This will be the last supper we share together on our voyage,' Eudoxia said softly. 'And on behalf of New Sanctaphrax, I'd like to thank Captain Ironside and Miss Dax for their magnificent efforts.'

In the light of the phraxlamp, Cade could see that Eudoxia's eyes were sparkling.

'Tomorrow,' she continued, 'we will meet up with Lemulis Lope, a stone-master of note *and* a trusted Friend of New Sanctaphrax, in the deep quarry at Gorgetown. Then we shall continue our journey.' She turned to Delfina. 'I promised your father, Miss Dax, that the captain would get you back to the Midwood Decks without delay.'

Delfina and Gart exchanged looks. Then Delfina's nose crinkled and she laughed, while Gart's face grew redder than ever.

'The skycraft yard will do perfectly well without me for a while longer,' she said, reaching out and taking the captain's hand. 'Gart here has promised to show me this Farrow Lake of yours. From the way you all talk about the place, it seems well worth the journey.'

Eudoxia smiled and raised her tumbler of woodtroll ale. 'We all wish the two of you a very happy voyage.'

No one slept particularly well that night. They were too excited about reaching their destination. Before the sun had even risen, they had eaten, packed up and were flying on, the little skyship silhouetted against the pink-tinged dawn sky.

Cade, Celestia and Tug were standing on the deck of the *Hoverworm*, cloaked in the dark blue storm-capes they'd found on a stall on the Midwood Decks, when the hanging-houses of Gorgetown came into view. In the wheelhouse, Gart brought the little vessel in to dock at a stone jetty carved into the side of the towering ravine. It was just one of dozens peppering the glistening rock face, all interconnected by precarious-looking rope bridges and ladders.

Eudoxia emerged from her cabin dressed in her smoke-grey travelling cape, the hood raised. Cade, Celestia and Tug raised their own hoods and followed her as she stepped down silently onto the jetty. They had said their goodbyes the night before, amid laughter and tears, and now, from above him, Cade heard the thrum of the phraxchamber as the *Hoverworm* turned in the air and steamed away, Gart at the wheel and Delfina clutching his arm.

As instructed, he and his friends did not wave to them. Instead, they walked purposefully in single file behind Eudoxia as she made her way through groups of quarry workers and merchants. Cade glanced from side to side from beneath his hood as he walked, trying his best to take everything in without being noticed.

The quarry workers were huge, as big as Tug, who, oddly, in the four stitched-together storm-capes that Cade had made for him, seemed to blend in perfectly. They were the trogs Cade had heard about – Eudoxia had told him how, back at New Sanctaphrax, their rock-cutting skills had proved invaluable in securing the descending trail. But these were the first he'd ever seen.

They were low-browed and broad-nostrilled, with shaved sloping heads and massive, powerful shoulders and arms, coated in thick, bristling fur. They wore baggy breeches, dusty grey aprons and hobnailed boots with metal toecaps, and from their broad belts hung gourds of stone polish and hammer-grease, together with stone-picks and gleaming chisels.

For the most part, they were gathered in groups of ten or more around smaller goblins and fourthlings in distinctive conical hats, with clusters of tiny bark-scrolls hanging from them. These smaller individuals were barking orders and instructions to their quarry teams who, nodding and shrugging their hairy shoulders, were trooping off to whatever part of the ravine they would be quarrying that day.

This same roll call seemed to be taking place on all the other jetties as well. Behind him, Cade heard Tug give an uncomfortable moan, and it occurred to him that this sight must be awakening unpleasant memories for his friend.

In the Nightwoods where Tug came from, his kind were enslaved by tiny red and black dwarves and forced to work the thorn forests, goaded with whips and cudgels, and worse. Tug had escaped, but he still bore the scars of his brutal mistreatment – both physical and mental.

Eudoxia must have heard Tug as well, for she stopped and motioned him over. Tug went to her, stooped low in his patchwork storm-cape, and Eudoxia spoke quietly to him for a few moments in that way that she had. Tug straightened up and nodded, then fell back into line.

'I want to learn how to do that,' whispered Celestia to Cade. 'To allay fears and inspire confidence the way Eudoxia does . . .'

'You heal folk,' Cade told her. 'The sick and the wounded. I've seen you do remarkable things, Celestia. The hammerhead goblins you cared for after the Battle of Farrow Lake, for instance.'

'That was their bodies, Cade,' said Celestia. 'Not their minds.'

'I'll teach you,' said Eudoxia, surprising both Cade and Celestia that she'd overheard their hushed voices. She turned to them. 'In New Sanctaphrax,' she added, and sighed. 'Though we have to get there first.'

They came to the far end of the jetty, where a ladder led down the side of the sheer ravine to what looked like a cave entrance far below. All around them now, the clink and clatter of quarry tools, metal on stone, echoed through the morning air.

'Follow me,' said Eudoxia, and she stepped down onto the first rung of the ladder. 'It's perfectly safe,' she added, turning back, 'built to take a hairy-back trog's weight. And if you fall, the lower nets will catch you . . .' She smiled mischievously. 'Usually.'

The others followed Eudoxia carefully down the swaying ladder. They passed teams of trogs, fastened to the ravine walls by harnesses, who were busy cutting slabs of rock from iridescent-coloured seams.

'We're among friends here,' said Eudoxia as she stepped off the bottom of the ladder and onto the ledge at the cave entrance. 'But keep a sharp lookout. I want to know if you see anything suspicious. Quove Lentis's spies are everywhere these days.'

'Even here?' said Cade, looking around at the bleak mine-scarred landscape.

'Particularly here,' said Eudoxia. 'The trogs are skilled at working stone, and have always made excellent Descenders.' She shook her head unhappily. 'Great Glade has no time for Gorgetown.'

She lowered her hood and, joining her on the ledge, Cade, Celestia and Tug did the same.

A tall thin goblin with heavy-lidded eyes greeted them at the mouth of the cave. He wore a long, glistening robe of green leather, nubbed and grooved and unlike any leather Cade had ever seen.

'Lemulis Lope, how is the blockade-breaking going?' asked Eudoxia, and from the way the goblin bowed to her, low and with great respect, it was clear to Cade that he must be the Friend of New Sanctaphrax that Eudoxia had spoken of.

'The blockade grows more powerful by the day,' Lemulis Lope replied in a thin, reedy voice. 'Getting to the floating city by skycraft has become all but imposs- ible. Fortunately, most of our scuttlebrigs continue to make it through . . .'

Lemulis paused and regarded Cade, Celestia and Tug from beneath his heavy lids.

'I didn't expect you to return so soon,' he said, turning back to Eudoxia. 'I trust you found the person you were looking for?'

'The less you know, the safer for all of us, dear Lemulis,' said Eudoxia, taking the goblin's hand and following him into the cave. 'Do you have scuttlebrigs ready for us?'

'Saddled and provisioned at all times,' he replied. He glanced up at Tug and frowned. 'Though we'll need to arrange something special for the nameless one here.'

'He *has* a name,' Cade said, stepping forward. 'His name is Tug and—' He stopped short. 'What are *those*?'

They were standing in a large cavern, the stone floor polished to a high sheen and pulsating with colours that swirled across its surface. A phraxlamp on a tall tripod stood at the centre, its light playing on the floor creating the effect.

But it wasn't the streakstone, beautiful though it undoubtedly was, that had made Cade stop in his tracks. It was the walls of the cave. They seemed to be moving – until Cade realized that he was looking at roosting creatures of some sort.

They had long tentacle-like antennae, four eyes peering out from beneath prominent brow ridges, and broad leathery bodies the same colour as the rock. Each of them had six legs that ended in broad webbed feet, and that reminded Cade of the umbrellas of the Midwood Decks. They wore collars and neck rings attached to stout-looking tethers that ran down across the floor and were fixed to hooks on the three-legged phraxlamp stand.

'So you've never seen a scuttlebrig before,' said Lemulis Lope dryly. 'I suggest you acquaint yourselves with them quickly, since you'll be riding them all the way to the floating city.'

'*Riding* them?' said Celestia, fascinated. 'Like riding a prowlgrin?'

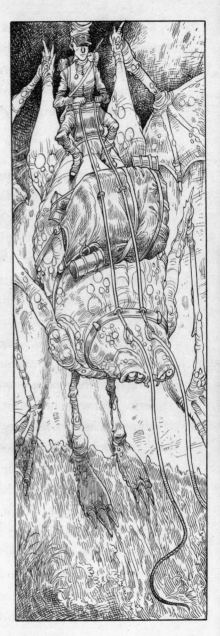

'Not exactly,' said Lemulis. 'They can't climb trees, so branch-hopping is out of the question. Though if you have experience of prowlgrins, I daresay scuttlebrigs won't present too many problems. Now, tell me,' the goblin continued, leaning towards Cade discreetly. 'Does Tug, here, talk?'

'Tug talk,' said Tug softly. 'Tug sail skyships. Tug love prowlgrins.' He gave a lopsided smile. 'Not sure of scuttlebrigs . . . Scuttlebrigs fast?'

'Extremely fast, especially across the grasslands of the Mire,' said Eudoxia, leading Tug and the others over to the phraxlamp. 'They're also perfectly camouflaged, changing their colour to match the land they're crossing,' she explained, 'making it almost impossible for them to be detected from above—'

'Which is just as well,' Lemulis broke in. 'Otherwise *nothing* would have got through the blockade. As it is, judging from the reports coming in, New Sanctaphrax is suffering. But without this lot,' he said, patting one of the creatures on its dark leathery shoulder, 'the place would have been brought to its knees long ago.'

Lemulis shook his head and turned away. He started to select tethers, then gave them out to each of the small group in turn. He paused for a moment before handing an especially broad tether to Tug.

'For Tug here, "Old Scritcher",' he announced. 'The biggest scuttlebrig in the stables.'

From high up on the cave walls, the creatures began to climb down towards them, the phraxlight playing on their bodies. As they approached, Cade saw that they were wearing full harnesses and, on the nubbed tail ridge at the end of their backs, high-backed saddles with circular stirrup rings.

All of them, that is, except for Old Scritcher, who was indeed far bigger than the rest. He had leather traces trailing from his harness and, as the others watched, Lemulis Lope called over three goblin grooms, who were on the far side of the cavern, polishing the floor with round mops.

'The chariot,' he said curtly, and dismissed them.

Moments later, the grooms returned from an inner cave, pulling a floating sumpwood cradle, which Lemulis attached to Old Scritcher.

'It's trickier to handle than a saddle,' Lemulis cautioned. 'Long reins to get the hang of, and without stirrups you need good balance.'

Cade smiled and clapped Tug on the back. 'Something tells me that's not going to be a problem for Tug!'

They set off from Gorgetown shortly before dawn, the lights of the hanging-houses glittering and sparkling like glisters high up at the top of the vertical rock face. The scuttlebrigs moved quickly and smoothly down the steep ravine walls, their umbrella feet peeling off and then sticking to the rock with strange squelching sounds. And as the sun rose, and the land they were crossing grew slowly lighter, so too did the scuttlebrigs' armour-like skin.

Around their shoulders, the riders wore makeshift capes that Lemulis had distributed, fashioned from scuttlebrig hide. They didn't change colour as well as the skin of the living creatures, but they helped conceal them and, as their journey continued, offered protection from the harsh winds and searing sun.

Away from the high escarpment, they came to a ledge that led to another ledge, and then another, and Cade, who was sitting up straight in the saddle on the back of his scuttlebrig, had an excellent view of the rocky landscape ahead. They were moving along a narrow trail, stepping up then down onto the overlapping ledges as they progressed along the ravine. The wind rose and clouds closed in and, after several hours, they emerged from the deep trough onto a vast flat expanse of rock pavement.

'We follow this for the next couple of days,' Eudoxia called back to them above the howling of the wind. 'Until we reach the grasslands.'

Tug and Old Scritcher galloped past her, with Tug swaying from side to side in the sumpwood chariot as it gathered speed.

'Keep to the central pavement,' Eudoxia called after him as she and her own scuttlebrig drew level. She pointed. 'Beyond the ridge line over there is the Edge cliff drop.'

And some way behind, as he watched them galloping on over the barren wilderness of rock slabs and deep fissures, Cade swallowed, his pulse quickening at the thought of tumbling down into the terrible void below . . .

Not only were the scuttlebrigs strong, dependable and supremely well camouflaged – lightening and darkening as day turned to night – but they had incredible stamina and endurance. Back in Gorgetown, Lemulis Lope had fed and watered them, and now they were able to continue on their long journey without ever needing to rest.

While their riders ate and drank in the saddle, the scuttlebrigs maintained an unflagging pace. They followed each other in relays, unbidden, along seemingly well-trodden paths – routes that they alone could sense with their long probing antennae. The colour of their leathery skin changed continuously, a ripple of darkness running the length of their bodies as they crossed a dark crack in the rock; flashes of light or patches of muted green appearing, then disappearing, as they passed over shards of mica or scrubby plants.

Once, as they were passing a cluster of angular boulders, Eudoxia motioned that she'd seen something. The others all looked up – to see a patrol of Great Glade skyvessels far in the distance. They slowed their pace, anxious that the dust they were kicking up might be spotted. But their fears proved unfounded. Camouflaged so well, the scuttlebrigs and their riders were invisible to the enemy fleet, which soon disappeared over the horizon, none the wiser.

For four days they travelled like this. Cade soon got used to the swaying movement of the curious creature he was riding. He would doze in the saddle, wake up, then fall asleep again, sometimes for hours at a stretch.

Then, just as everyone was beginning to think that
the rock pavement might go on for ever, it abruptly
gave way to the grasslands. Suddenly the travellers
found themselves amid a swaying carpet of lush grass
and reeds as tall as they were. And Cade watched,
transfixed, as his scuttlebrig's body turned from the pale
yellow-grey of the bleached rock to a deep verdant shade
of green.

All around the advancing convoy, the air hummed
with clouds of grassland insects. Small animals scurried
for cover as the scuttlebrigs approached; booming marsh-
herons and croaking reed-toads fell silent; huge flocks of
purple and scarlet birds flapped up into the air, chattering
indignantly. The scuttlebrigs never once broke stride, but
ploughed on into the vegetation. Their antennae swished
a path through the long grass in front, which closed
behind them as they went.

As they drew closer to New Sanctaphrax, their journey
changed. Although they were camouflaged, the telltale
movement of the grass threatened to give them away.
And after so long in the saddle, it came as a relief to all of
them when Eudoxia gave the command that, from now
on, they were to travel by night, stopping during the
hours of daylight and hunkering down beneath the green
bodies of their scuttlebrigs.

Cade soon realized that concealing themselves like
this was wise advice for, high in the skies above them, he
saw an increasing number of Great Glade phraxships
weaving a latticework of steam trails in the air as they

patrolled the area. Bristling phraxfrigates the size of skytaverns lumbered past overhead, with skeins of smaller phraxgunships following in arrowhead formations.

It was all too clear to him that, with the blockade in place, no skyvessel could reach the floating city by flying over the Edgelands. The only other way was to circum-navigate the wall of Great Glade vessels, venturing out beyond the Edge and into Open Sky. But this, of course, would have meant flying over the yawning void below, a solution that was deemed far too perilous.

'After all, they call the Descenders mad,' Eudoxia pointed out as they crouched beneath a scuttlebrig in the shifting soil that oozed up around the grass roots, 'but not even *they* would fly a skyvessel without an anchor point below.'

She looked back at the line of resting creatures, and Cade was shocked to see the concern on her face.

'I've been away a long time,' she said. 'When I left New Sanctaphrax, the scuttlebrig trail was a lifeline for the city,' she went on, 'but like all lines, it frays and stretches – and eventually, it will break.'

'And when it breaks?' Cade asked.

Celestia and Tug were asleep on storm-capes spread out on the ground beneath their motionless scuttlebrigs, the chariot concealed beneath a thatch of lush Mire grass. Neither of them stirred as Eudoxia shifted round.

'When it breaks, Quove Lentis's thugs will take over the floating city without even needing to declare a war that the citizens of Great Glade might object to,' said

Eudoxia unhappily as they continued to watch the patrolling vessels. 'Quove Lentis,' she repeated, and snorted with disgust. 'He's seen to it that most of them don't even know what he's doing in their name – while the rest are too busy lining their pockets to care. When that lifeline breaks, Cade, then Quove Lentis will execute all Descenders and force the rest of New Sanctaphrax to accept his terms.'

'Execute?' said Cade, anger boiling up inside him. 'Murder, you mean. Like he had my father murdered – and would have had me murdered too if I hadn't fled.' He shook his head bitterly. 'And now he's forced me to leave the new home I built, and the life I loved, for *this* . . .' He grabbed a handful of Mire soil and flung it across the waving grass.

Eudoxia smiled and took Cade's hand in her own. 'Tomorrow,' she told him, her green eyes flashing, 'we'll be in New Sanctaphrax.'

PART THREE
NEW SANCTAPHRAX

· CHAPTER NINE ·

Nate Quarter, High Academe Elect of New Sanctaphrax, was sitting on a sumpwood chair, halfway up one of the scroll-pillars in the ancient Great Library. It was where he was to be found most afternoons.

When the business of the High Council was concluded, reports on the progress of the blockade assessed and provisions audited, the council leaders went their separate ways. Heldar the fettle-legger, steward of Undergarden, would return to his flocks; Aldus Quodix would hurry back to his workshop; while he, Nate Quarter, would find solace among the roof beams and hanging barkscrolls.

Here, as the shadows lengthened and the turrets and spires sang in the gathering breeze outside, Nate would make himself comfortable on a gantry high in the huge-domed roof, surrounded by ancient treatises and long-forgotten histories. Not that he spent all his time reading. Far from it. Indeed, most often he would sit back in the

carved sumpwood chair, his fingers steepled below the shaggy white beard that Eudoxia had disliked so much, and simply think.

Of the Professor mostly, down there in the depths, and the extraordinary sacrifice his friend had made for him . . .

Almost two years had passed since Brocktinius Rolnix had discovered the High Academe, wild and raving in the Stone Gardens. Throughout that time, Nate had tried to piece together the events of the previous fourteen. Every day, carefully and patiently, he would sift through his memories of those years spent in the depths.

For the most part, it was little more than a blur of tedious routine. Harvesting the mosses that had sustained them; scratching the passing of time onto the face of a boulder – until they'd given up.

What had they talked about in all that time? he wondered. *Had* they talked . . . ?

Then it had all come to an abrupt end – for Nate, at least. He had ridden the storm-stone up from the depths – though he still had absolutely no memory of the ascent. From the moment the Professor had urged him not to forget him to the moment the skymarshal asked him who he was, it was all still a blank.

And so it would remain. Nate would never know what had happened. He accepted that now. What he *did* know, however, and with every fibre of his being, was that he could not leave the Professor alone for ever down there in that infernal blue half-light. One day – when he was completely recovered and New Sanctaphrax was no longer under threat – he would descend once more into the depths to rescue him.

At least, that was what he hoped.

Nate rolled up the barkscroll he'd been reading – a treatise on the sayings of Kobold the Wise – and returned it to its hanging-holder.

Matters with Quove Lentis and Great Glade were coming to a head. The flood of Edgelanders heading for the floating city had fallen to a trickle. With the blockade in place, none were now able to arrive by skyship. Some, it was true, still made it on one of the scuttlebrigs via Gorgetown, while others, having endured the perilous journey across the grasslands, turned up on foot. But over the previous month, Nate could count the number of fresh arrivals on one hand.

And New Sanctaphrax was suffering.

As a new city – or rather, a city that had only recently been newly populated with incomers from various parts of the Edgelands – New Sanctaphrax needed contact with the other great cities. Given time, it would develop its own factories and foundries – workshops, mills and distilleries – but for now it was dependent on trade. And trade had come to a standstill.

Everything was in short supply. From writing ink to woodhoney, from cutlery to clothing, from medical supplies to ammunition. Nothing was getting through. Even the sumpwood chair that Nate was sitting on – a product from the timber yards of the Midwood Decks that had arrived in the early days of New Sanctaphrax – would be impossible to come by today.

And though Undergarden was still able to provide the floating city with an adequate amount of fruit, vegetables and grain, even that was running scarce. As for meat and fish, they had become luxury items, exorbitantly priced and available only from a growing network of black marketeers.

Nate's thoughts switched, as they so often did, to Eudoxia. Almost a year had passed since his wife had abruptly left New Sanctaphrax, yet he still hadn't got used to her not being there at his side. Increasingly, he was plagued by fears that she might never return. After all, since almost no one was managing to make it through the blockade, why should she?

Lost in his bleak reveries, Nate Quarter didn't hear the low creak of the main entrance door as it opened and closed. Nor the sound of the two sets of footsteps that crossed the wooden floor towards him . . .

The basket rose smoothly through the air, swaying in the gentle breeze from the rope that slowly wound itself around the rotating spool above Cade's head. Gripping the side of the basket, Cade waved to Celestia and Tug on the ground below, then called down.

'I'll see you tonight in the . . .' He glanced round at Eudoxia, who was standing beside him. 'Where did you say again?'

'The refectory of the Knights Academy,' she called through cupped hands. 'The basket tenders will show you the way.'

Celestia and Tug waved back in acknowledgement, then led their scuttlebrigs off through the verdant vegetation of Undergarden to the old sewer pipes by the banks of the Edgewater River. As soon as they'd stabled the six-legged creatures – currently as green as the grass they were trudging over – Celestia was intent on exploring the pastures and growing plots of the extraordinary former city.

Once a thriving industrial hub, the place was now an overgrown garden. Plash-ferns with huge plate-like canopies grew in dense, shadow-filled clumps; needle-worts the size of hive towers rose up black against the sky; cascades of flowing dropdaisies swept through long abandoned streets and the ghostly structures of ancient wharfs, down to the verdant banks of the Edgewater River.

'There are herbs and medicinal plants I've never even seen before,' Celestia had told Cade earlier, unable to keep the excitement from her voice. 'And the ones I do recognize are the biggest, lushest specimens I've ever come across.'

Tug had agreed to help Celestia collect some samples. And Cade had smiled, glad to see his two friends happy and relaxed so soon after the tension of their long journey across the Mire grasslands.

High above Undergarden now, the basket carrying Cade and Eudoxia continued up towards the great

Sanctaphrax rock. First the mighty anchor chain came close, then the upside-down forest of ancient weights, hanging from hooks driven into the underside of the rock. Soon they were passing up the side of the rock itself, its surface pitted with cracks and fissures, offering tantalizing glimpses of the stonecomb inside.

Cade was spellbound. He held on tight to the side of the basket and stared intently.

All too soon, the basket came to a gentle halt. A couple of lean-looking basket tenders in threadbare blue-grey robes and peakless hats that bore the New Sanctaphrax emblem appeared. They unbuckled the boarding bridge and ushered Eudoxia and Cade out onto the magnificent West Landing of the floating city.

Cade gasped. It was his first moment on the floating city he'd dreamed about all his life, and already it was exceeding his most feverish expectations.

The ancient mist-shifting towers loomed high above him, and clustered around them were the turrets and spires of the other great academies, each one different in design and construction. Diaphanous wind flags billowed from some; others had roof tiles that rippled as breezes blew through them; and each one was festooned with intricate glass and metal mechanisms whose purposes Cade could only guess at.

And then, as a gust of wind rose, Cade heard the music. He started back in surprise. Soft, discordant, then gathering in rhythm and harmony, the spires and towers were singing all around him. Even the cables from which the West Landing was suspended hummed and thrummed like a mighty, but extraordinarily delicate, harp. Cade found himself thinking of the strange, ethereal-sounding song that Eudoxia had sung on board the *Hoverworm*.

'It's all so beautiful,' he murmured as he followed her down the landing, then out along a broad paved avenue. 'Unlike any other place I've ever seen.'

'I could say that you'll get used to it,' said Eudoxia, smiling at Cade. 'But the truth is, if you're anything like me, you never will. The city is so ancient, and has travelled such distances, there are wonderful new things to be discovered every day.' Her expression hardened. 'And it is this,' she said, her hand sweeping round in a broad arc, 'that Quove Lentis seeks to destroy.'

To their right was the grandest architectural feature of all on the floating rock, the Great Viaduct. Looking up at its broad arches, Cade saw the turrets, minarets and crenulated roofs of the smaller academies that lined the top. Below, thronging with blue-grey robed academics, were the Viaduct Steps.

'In previous times, every academy would have worn robes of a different colour and cut,' Eudoxia explained, her voice calm and lilting once more. 'But since the rock returned to us, we all wear the robes of *New* Sanctaphrax.' She plucked at Cade's jacket sleeve. 'There'll be some robes hanging by your sleeping closet at the Knights Academy, should you wish to wear them.'

'Is that where we're going now?' asked Cade, trying to hide the excitement in his voice.

The academics on the Viaduct Steps looked tired and drawn, yet as Eudoxia made her way past them they smiled and doffed their caps. And she acknowledged them graciously, her expression benevolent and serene. Beside her, Cade felt as awkward as he had on his very first day of school back in Great Glade.

'No, Cade,' said Eudoxia, climbing to the top of a set of empty steps and sitting down. 'It isn't.'

She motioned for Cade to sit beside her.

'I want to tell you about your uncle,' Eudoxia began, her voice quiet and serious. 'He has been through so much . . .' She paused, her face clouding over. 'Nate had already been lost for more than seven years when I first heard that he had a brother – or rather, a half-brother. Thadeus . . .'

'My father,' Cade breathed.

'Your father,' said Eudoxia sadly. 'That was when I sent him the spyglass and the message.' She clasped her hands tightly in her lap. 'You know how guilty I feel about that, Cade.'

Cade nodded.

He knew he should say something like 'you couldn't have known' or 'it wasn't your fault', but could not bring himself to do so. Eudoxia, in any case, continued without missing a beat.

'Nate returned. Quove murdered your father – and, I feared, you too, Cade.' She swallowed awkwardly, and

Cade saw her cheeks colour. 'But then . . . Nate had been home a year, but was still recovering from the descent when I received word of your whereabouts. I couldn't wait until he was strong enough, so I left to find you – to bring you here.'

High above their heads, a flock of small birds – stonefinches or cheepwits – flew from one academy tower to the next, twittering loudly. Cade wondered vaguely what might have disturbed them. Eudoxia hadn't even noticed.

'Nate doesn't yet know he had a half-brother,' she went on. 'And he doesn't know about you either, Cade. I'm going to take you to the Great Library to meet him. But before I do, I want to give you this.'

She reached inside her cape and drew out a bark-scroll.

'One of the Friends of New Sanctaphrax found this in a phraxmine stockade in the Eastern Woods,' she told him. 'I've been saving it, until now. It's a scroll from your grandfather Abe's journal. And I'd like you, Cade, to give it to your uncle.'

Cade unfurled the scroll as the warm breeze stirred again, setting the spires singing all around them. He began to read the yellowed parchment:

Phasia Hexatine was my first true love. I was a young phraxengineer with a promising career in Great Glade. Phasia lived next door to my lodgings in Ambristown. We married soon – perhaps too soon – after we first met.

She was troubled, given to fits of uncontrollable jealousy and dark moods. And I confess, in my youthful arrogance, I did little to help. After a summer of happiness came an autumn of turmoil and despair. We parted. Phasia left me, and Ambristown, and disappeared.

My life since then has been visited by both tragedy and joy. My career flourished. I married Hermia Lentis, despite her brother's opposition to our union, and...

Cade realized his hands were shaking. He stopped reading, unable to follow the florid handwriting as it blurred before his eyes.

Hermia Lentis? Her brother . . . Could this

brother be *Quove* Lentis, High Professor of the Academy of Flight? The monster who'd had his father killed; who wanted him dead as well. Could he, Cade, be related to him? *Could* he? Earth and Sky, that would be such a cruel twist!

'Are you all right, Cade?' he heard Eudoxia ask, and felt a reassuring hand on his arm.

No. No, he was not all right. How could he be? But he nodded, jaw clenched and fighting back the tears, and continued reading his grandfather's words.

. . . we enjoyed a happiness that would never have been possible with Phasia. She gave me a fine son, who I named, at her wish, Nate, only for fever to take her from me. I took my grief, along with my beautiful baby boy, to the Eastern Woods and a new life – but, all these long years later, my old life returned to haunt me.

Phasia too is dead, the circumstances of her passing uncertain, but I now learn from her dying note of an infant son – Thadeus – who was born but a short while after we parted, and abandoned on the steps of the Great Glade Academy School. Nate turns eleven next spring and I yearn to make him a present of a long-lost brother. As soon as the next shipment of phrax is ready, I intend to return to Great Glade with Nate and find this son I never knew I had, bringing forth joy at last from poor Phasia's sorrow.

*

Grent One-Tusk untangled the sleeves of his blue-grey robes. Long hours among the barkscroll stacks – climbing the pillars to the reading gantries, then traversing the roof beams in the library baskets – played havoc with one's robes, he noted.

The sleeves were threadbare and frayed at the cuffs, but the long-haired goblin was rather proud of them. Battered robes told his fellow academics that he was a serious scholar, too busy with his studies to take overdue care of his clothes.

His side-whiskers and forehead tuft were another matter, however. As a proud long-haired goblin, grooming was an important aspect of clan pride. Back in his home city of Hive, well-oiled tufts and plaited side-whiskers

denoted a goblin to be reckoned with. Here in New Sanctaphrax, although his immaculate grooming was seldom mentioned, he liked to maintain the same high personal standards.

Grent climbed down the rungs of the pillar to the floor of the Great Library, a bundle of barkscrolls clamped under one arm. He anticipated another long night back in his rooms at the Loftus Observatory, reading their contents by the light of a phraxlamp. Pausing for a moment, he checked the titles of the scrolls he'd collected – *Storm-Stones: Their Origins and Trajectories; Enquiries into Rock Density*; and *Observations of Samples Recovered at Mire Craters* . . .

Quite enough for one night, he decided.

His own barkscroll treatise was on the desk in his study, still incomplete despite all his efforts. But he lived in hope. You had to if you were an academic of New Sanctaphrax; ostracized by the academies of Great Glade, ignored by the Hive Academy, and positively loathed by the waif professors of Riverrise.

At the bottom of the pillar, Grent paused again.

Perhaps just one or two more barkscrolls, he wondered, looking up into the roof beams – which was when he caught sight of Nate Quarter, High Academe Elect.

The fabled Descender was sitting on a reading gantry halfway up a pillar in the adjacent row. As always, Grent was struck by his leader's appearance. His hair was as white as a raven's plumage; his skin pale, almost translucent. And as for that unkempt beard of his . . .

'Ah, well,' he muttered. 'Each to his own in New Sanctaphrax,' and was turning to leave when he heard footsteps approaching.

Cautious – some might say suspicious – by nature, Grent took a step back and concealed himself behind a pillar. Taking care not be seen, he peered out as the footsteps came closer.

There were two visitors to the Great Library. A youth in a dark blue storm-cape, the type they wore out in the Deepwoods settlements, and . . .

Grent One-Tusk's hand flew to his mouth.

Surely not, he thought. It couldn't be true. After all this time! Yet, there she stood in her storm-grey travel cape, her fair hair wild and wind-tossed, wife of the Most High Academe Elect of New Sanctaphrax: Eudoxia Prade.

As Grent continued to watch, not daring to emerge from his hiding place, Eudoxia and the youth approached the pillar where, high above, Nate was seated. They stopped, their bodies bathed in the shaft of sunlight shining in from one of the library's high latticed windows, and looked up.

'Nate!' Eudoxia called. 'They told me I'd find you here.'

'Eudoxia?' a voice floated down. 'Eudoxia, is that really you?' Nate's pale face appeared high up in the shadows of the gantries. 'Where have you been all this time? And how did you manage to get through the blockade? Wait, wait, I'll be right down—'

'No, Nate,' Eudoxia said, and raised her hand. 'Stay there. I'll explain everything in a short while . . . In the meantime,' she went on, ignoring Nate's sigh, 'there's someone who has travelled a long way to meet you . . .'

'Who?' Nate called down.

Eudoxia turned to Cade and gave him a little nudge. 'Go on, then,' she whispered. 'Climb up.'

Heart thumping in his chest, Cade started up the pegs that were hammered into the sides of the pillar, hand over hand, foot after foot, climbing up to the gaunt figure with the wild white beard and curiously intense blue eyes that he'd seen looking down at him. Could this really be his uncle Nate?

Leaving the two of them to get acquainted, Eudoxia turned and made her way back to one of the adjacent pillars. Seeing the edge of the blue-grey robes sticking out from the side of the pillar, she smiled.

'Grent One-Tusk,' she said quietly. 'How's that treatise of yours coming along?'

The long-haired goblin started, and almost dropped the bundle of barkscrolls he was clutching. He stepped forward.

'Why, Eudoxia!' he exclaimed, smiling broadly. 'I . . . I had no idea you were back. I hope your journey was a success.'

Just then, from above them, there came a gasp of surprise. Eudoxia took the long-hair goblin by the arm and ushered him to the door, leaving Cade and Nate to themselves.

'Thank you,' she said. 'I believe it was.'

*

'To see *me*?' Nate said. 'All the way from the Farrow Ridges. It must be for something very important.'

Cade nodded uncertainly. He'd imagined that Nate would resemble his father, but they couldn't have looked more different. Thadeus Quarter had been stocky, clean-shaven, with a shock of black hair and dark intense eyes. Whereas Nate . . .

'I have this,' said Cade, and he handed his uncle the barkscroll that Eudoxia had given him.

'What is it?' asked Nate.

'Read it,' said Cade, and he sat back in his sumpwood chair.

Nate turned the barkscroll over in his hand. It was different from the others in the Great Library. Smaller, lighter, and tightly laced. He glanced up at Cade, his blue eyes shining an almost unnatural shade of blue. Then, with shaking fingers, he carefully undid the cord bindings and unfurled the scroll. His eyes narrowed as he started to read the contents.

Cade felt his heart hammering inside his chest. What was his uncle thinking? How would he react?

He didn't have to wait long to find out. All at once, eyes flashing and a grin on his face, Nate tossed the scroll aside, jumped to his feet and pulled Cade up from his chair by the hem of his storm-cape. For a moment the two of them stood facing each other. Then Nate flung his arms wide open and Cade fell into his warm, reassuring – and curiously familiar – hug.

Maybe, he thought, his father and his uncle were similar after all.

'Cade, Cade, Cade,' Nate murmured. 'My own flesh and blood . . .' He pulled away and gripped his nephew by both arms. 'Welcome to New Sanctaphrax.'

· CHAPTER TEN ·

As a rule, Grent One-Tusk cooked for himself in the small kitchens below the observatory and took his meals in his room. Every so often, though, he would join the throng in the academy refectory to swap the latest gossip over a slice of snowbird pie. And that evening, after the incident in the Great Library, Grent simply wasn't able to resist attending supper in the vaulted hall.

'Cade Quarter,' he told his dining companions, 'is the High Academe Elect's nephew. Eudoxia Prade, who is back at last,' he added, enjoying the gasps of surprise from his fellow diners, 'told me herself.'

Of course, the mistsifters and raintasters opposite him at the refectory table wanted to know more. And on the benches behind him, a group of Earth scholars pretended to talk among themselves, but Grent could tell that they too were all ears.

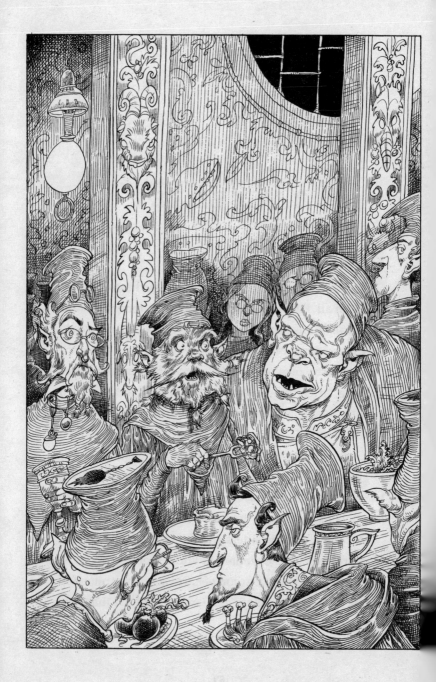

'He was born in Great Glade,' he went on, 'but fled the city after the unfortunate death of his father . . .'

'Unfortunate,' the mistsifters chorused, exchanging looks with the raintasters.

Everyone knew what *that* meant.

'Quove Lentis?' a cloddertrog called Demblick ventured. He worked the bellows in the Knights Academy Armoury, and it was common knowledge that he had lost relatives of his own in the Great Glade purges.

'Who else would it be?' asked Nebulix Fort, a cloud-watcher from the Academy of Drizzle, high up on the Great Viaduct.

Grent wanted to tell them more. He was enjoying being the centre of attention. All too often, he found himself on the fringes of the groups discussing incidents on patrol, or observations in laboratories. But the truth was, his conversation with Eudoxia had been all too short. After their brief exchange, she'd joined the High Academe and his nephew on the reading gantry, and then the three of them had left for their rooms in the Knights Academy soon after.

'He was living in a Deepwoods settlement – one of those new outposts that are springing up on the sky-tavern routes,' Grent told them. 'Farrow Lake, it's called.'

'Never heard of it,' said a raintaster, turning away.

'No reason why you should,' said his companion. 'These settlements. They come, they go, evaporating like mist, most of them.'

The others at the table nodded. Many of them had started out in just such places themselves, before making the long journey to the floating city – back when the skytaverns used to come to New Sanctaphrax. They knew only too well how hard life could be in the mighty Deepwoods.

Not that it was much easier in New Sanctaphrax these days. Not with the Great Glade blockade.

'He has two companions with him,' Grent went on, attempting to hold their attention. 'A fourthling girl and a nameless one, apparently . . .'

Grent continued his story, but his dining companions were losing interest in what he had to say. The conversation turned to politics, the way it frequently did in the current climate.

Although they all wore the blue-grey robes of New Sanctaphrax, there was considerable disagreement between them. Most accepted the decisions of the New Sanctaphrax Council without question. But there were others in the academies – and it was a number that was rapidly growing – who questioned the wisdom of descending the Edge cliff when it provoked such extreme reactions from Great Glade and Riverrise. The mistsifters and Earth scholars were soon in fierce debate, and Grent feared that at any moment goblets would be spilled and platters overturned.

Vulgar and unseemly, he thought, and pushing away his half-eaten tildersteak he got up from the bench and left them to it.

As he made his way out of the refectory, Grent ran into his friend Brocktinius Rolnix, the young skymarshal. The two of them had first met three years earlier, when Grent was just starting out on his research into storm-stones.

'Still working on that treatise, Grent?' Brock asked.

'For my sins,' Grent replied with a rueful smile.

'Well, here's something that might interest you,' Brock told him. 'I caught sight of a couple of mist tornadoes rising from the void while I was out on patrol earlier this evening,' he said. 'If you like, now the *Rock Demon* has been refitted, I can take you stone-spotting tomorrow – so long as you're up early enough.'

And Grent decided to accept his friend's offer.

The following morning, he rose from his bed shortly after sunrise. Yawning sleepily, he climbed out of his wickerwork cot, stretched extravagantly, then crossed his room to the oval mirror. Peering at his reflection, the long-haired goblin reached across to the small table for his trimming shears. Bottles of hair tonic and beard grease clinked as he felt about for them, his eyes still fixed on the mirror.

Finding the shears at last, he began trimming the fringe of his brow tuft, then his side-whiskers, and finally the tips of his ears. Next, he combed his face and applied hyleroot wax to his beard before splitting it into three bunches and plaiting each one in turn. Finally satisfied with his daily grooming routine, Grent turned away from the mirror and got dressed.

As he made his way to the door, he glanced out of his chamber window, high in the tower of the Loftus Observatory. Some of his fellow academics were crossing the square below, already on their way to breakfast in the refectory. But not him. Not today. Today he had something to do that might help him to complete his treatise once and for all.

He met Brock, as arranged, on the East Landing. The skymarshal was sitting on the long-ruddered phraxcraft. As Grent approached, Brock greeted him, and indicated the kitbag behind the saddle.

'Jump up,' he said with a smile. 'And hold on tight!'

Grent was just about to when he caught sight of someone leaning against the parapet of the landing, gazing down below. It was someone he recognized.

'Cade?' he said. 'Cade Quarter? It *is* you, isn't it?'

Cade turned, and was surprised to be faced by a rather well-turned-out long-haired goblin. 'Do I know you?' he asked.

'Grent One-Tusk,' he said. 'We . . . that is, I saw you in the Great Library,' he explained. 'Yesterday afternoon. When Eudoxia introduced you to your long-lost uncle,' he added. 'How did that go, by the way?'

'It was wonderful,' said Cade, happily reliving the moment.

'You must have had so much to talk about,' said Grent, fishing about for something he might entertain his dining companions with later.

And Cade, assuming that this long-hair must know Nate and Eudoxia well, confirmed that he and his uncle had talked for hours. About Abe Quarter. About Quove Lentis. About descending, and the Professor, and the curious storm-stone that had returned his uncle to the floating city after fourteen years spent down in the Depths . . .

'Well, *there's* a coincidence,' Grent said. 'Brock, here, and myself are about to do a little stone-spotting of our own. If you'd care to join us,' he added spontaneously, then turned to the skymarshal. 'Assuming this vessel of yours is strong enough to carry three, Brock.'

'Oh, the *Rock Demon*'s strong enough,' came the reply. 'It's whether there's enough room – though if one of you sits on the cargo rack it should be possible.' He frowned. 'But maybe Cade here has other things to do.' Brock turned to him. 'Would you like to go stone-spotting?'

Cade hesitated. He'd been on his way to the Academy Forge. His uncle had told him about someone there who would be interested in Thadeus's working drawings. If he hadn't been distracted by the magnificent view from the East Landing, he'd be there now. Then again, the chance to see for himself one of the mysterious flying rocks that Nate had ridden was certainly tempting. He decided that the barkscrolls could remain stitched into his jacket for just a little while longer.

'I'd love to,' he said.

Brock clapped his hands together. 'All aboard, then!' he said.

With the skymarshal in the saddle at the front, Grent behind him, and Cade seated on the jutting cargo rack at the back, they were ready to go. Brock raised a gloved hand, signalling that he was all set. Then, as he pushed back on the stirrup bars, the small craft shot up into the sky, leaving Grent's stomach behind – and making the long-haired goblin thankful he'd had no time for breakfast.

Brock took the skycraft into a sharp dive, hurtling down out of the sky, then levelled out abruptly and steered the *Rock Demon* through the Stone Gardens, where he wove a zigzag path between the towering rock stacks at breakneck speed. They swooped and soared; they swerved round stack after stack.

Grent couldn't bear it. He screwed his eyes tightly shut as he clung desperately to the skymarshal's shoulders.

'You're not going to spot any storm-stones with your eyes shut,' laughed Brock, glancing behind him.

The goblin opened one eye and instantly regretted it as they skimmed over the top of the tallest rock stack, sending the roosting white ravens flapping into the air, cawing furiously. He groaned miserably.

'And you, Cade?' Brock called. 'How are you doing back there?'

Cade grinned. For him, the flight was fantastic; every swoop, every swerve, every stomach-churning dive. It reminded him of the time he'd sailed in Phineal's Second-Age skycraft, the *Caterbird*; or when he'd raced Celestia over the forest canopy and up to the Pinnacles on Rumblix's back; or their recent flight, riding the air currents of high sky aboard Gart's *Hoverworm* – except it was better than any of these.

'I'm doing just fine!' he shouted back, then smiled to himself when he heard Grent One-Tusk groan all the louder as they went into another vertical drop.

As the lip of the Edge cliff came up to meet them, the skycraft listed to one side, strong crosswinds rising from below the clifftop buffeting them hard at starboard. Brock brought the phraxcraft round in a tight curving manoeuvre and, ignoring Grent's cries that they were all about to die, pointed below him.

'Down there. Do you see it?' he shouted above the howl of the wind.

Cade looked down. Grent forced himself to do the same.

Far below them was a mist tornado, twisting and swirling up out of the distant darkness. Inside the blurred column, sparks and flashes of fizzing energy crackled. Then, with a noise like a clap of thunder, a glowing blue boulder suddenly shot out of the heart of the storm and came spinning up towards them at incredible speed.

Brock pulled forward in the stirrups as the boulder careered past them, creating a powerful shock wave which sent the *Rock Demon* tumbling away across the sky. Cade shifted his balance, while Grent clung on for dear life, his eyes clamped shut once more. The next moment, he heard the young skymarshal chuckling to himself as they regained their balance and sped off after the glowing trail left behind by the boulder.

'You're actually enjoying this, aren't you?' shouted Grent from behind him.

'Nothing like storm-stone spotting to get the blood coursing through your veins,' Brock shouted back.

Gripping his stubby leadwood pencil in one hand, and holding tightly to Brock's shoulder with the other, Grent made a couple of hurried notes in the scroll cluster that hung from his neck. For his part, Cade stared at the spinning blue boulder in amazement. It was exactly as Nate had described it, though how his uncle had managed to ride the thing without being hurled off into Open Sky he couldn't imagine.

The skymarshal pursued the storm-stone across the sky and down towards Undergarden. For a moment, they lost sight of it, but then, as they got closer to the tangle of dense vegetation, Grent spotted it once more.

'There! There!' he shouted, pointing at the boulder as it crashed harmlessly into an empty pasture, a short distance from one of the ancient sluice gates.

Brock brought the *Rock Demon* down to land beside it, just as the boulder – twice the size of a full-grown hammelhorn – began to sink beneath the sprouting gladegrass. With a cry of dismay, Grent leaped from the saddle and hurried towards it, determined to make whatever observations he could before the mysterious storm-stone vanished into the ground.

But he was too late. Just as he got to it, the boulder disappeared beneath the grassy pasture – only for a trembling *thump* to vibrate back through the ground as it struck a sewer directly below, halting its descent and sending up a great plume of glittering dust.

Standing at the edge of the crater, Grent and Cade peered down into the darkness. They could just make out the outline of the glowing storm-stone, now wedged firmly against the shattered wall of the ancient sluice tunnel.

'Looks like this is one storm-stone you'll be able to study at your leisure, Grent,' said Brock cheerfully as he crouched down beside the pair of them.

The passing fettle-legger botanist was less impressed. Cade looked up as she came sprinting towards them on her

scaly, bird-like feet and trotted around the edge of the hole. He'd heard of the curious folk who lived in the grasslands of course, but this was the first fettle-legger he'd ever encountered.

'Absolutely ruined!' she exclaimed, tugging at the lapels of her blue-grey robes. 'But then what does it matter if Earth scholarship suffers, so long as Sky scholars get their excitement.'

'Grent One-Tusk of the Loftus Observatory,' said Grent politely. 'I don't believe we've met.'

The fettle-legger took a few steps backwards with an angry little snort, then advanced and held out a hand for him to shake.

'Fenda Fulefane, School of Moss,' she said, then turned to Cade. 'And you are?'

'Cade Quarter,' he told her.

'Ah, nephew of the High Academe,' she said, and laughed at the look of surprise on his face. 'News travels fast in New Sanctaphrax,' she observed. 'And do forgive me, all of you,' she said, looking around. 'It's just so frustrating when something falls from the sky and ruins a perfectly good laboratory.'

'Laboratory?' said Grent, peering back down into the sluice tunnel. He saw the instruments and clusters of specimen jars hanging from the dank walls below. 'Oh yes, I see . . . most unfortunate.'

Brock pulled his skycraft towards him with the tether. 'Time for a late breakfast in the academy refectory, I think,' he said, climbing back into the saddle.

Cade joined him, keen to get the barkscrolls to his contact in the Armoury without any further delay. But Grent One-Tusk remained where he was.

'If it's all the same to you,' he said, stroking a well-oiled beard plait thoughtfully, 'I think I might stay here in Undergarden for a little while longer.'

· CHAPTER ELEVEN ·

Quove Lentis stood in the Purple Hall of the Palace
of Phrax, a self-satisfied smile on his bloated
features. The hall had been decorated with chandeliers of
purple crystal, a gleaming tiled floor of purple marble;
purple curtains, purple upholstery and purple rugs –
while in the elegant amethyst-encrusted stove, only
lufwood was ever burned, its flames bathing the room
with deep purple light.

The Purple Hall was every bit as grandiloquent as
Quove had imagined it would be – as was the entire
Palace of Phrax. When Quove Lentis first ordered the
building of the palace, that was the word he'd used to all
those involved in its construction: the architects and
interior designers, the seamstresses, stone masons and
furniture makers . . . Grandiloquent.

Something worthy of his own grandiloquence.

Although maybe, he thought, on this particular afternoon he might have done better to wait for his phrax
commander, Lennius Grex, in the Green Room. Or maybe
the Blue Room. Purple was such a passionate colour and
Quove Lentis needed to remain cool, calm and collected.

'Is he here yet?' he asked, turning to his personal
bodyguard.

Felicia Adereth straightened up. For the last half hour
she'd been standing by the door, hands clasped behind
her back, with precisely that piece of information. Phrax
Commander Lennius Grex was in the High Hall, waiting.

'Yes, sir,' she answered. 'I was told he arrived an hour
ago.'

Quove nodded, then took a tiny sip from the flask the
waifs had sent him as a gift. Water of life, they called it.
Uncertain of its efficacy, Quove nevertheless made sure
to take a couple of drops every day. After all, he reasoned,
it *might* work . . .

'Shall I bring him in, sir?' Felicia asked.

'No, leave him a while longer,' came the reply as
Quove stepped out onto the balcony. 'Let him sweat.'

'Sir,' said Felicia, and she clicked the heels of her
highly polished boots together.

Felicia Adereth had been the High Professor of Flight's
personal bodyguard for more than ten years now. Born
in a slum and raised in a hovel, she had been drafted into
the Freeglade Lancers at the age of thirteen and risen
slowly through the ranks.

A fourthling with waif and cloddertrog blood in her veins, Felicia was both intuitive and prodigiously strong. At the age of twenty she was made mission-sergeant of an assault unit and sent to the district of East Glade to quell a minor uprising. It was there that her particular skills came to the fore: ruthlessness, loyalty and a willingness to shed blood whenever necessary.

She had the ringleaders strung up and executed, and on her return to the Cloud Quarter, Quove Lentis was waiting for her. He pinned a Medal of Valour – Great Glade's highest honour – to her chest. And, meeting her that first time in person, he was so impressed that he took her on as his personal bodyguard. His 'security escort', as he had put it.

A decade later, Felicia Adereth was still in the same post. Her rivals claimed that it was because Quove Lentis saw females as less of a threat to his own power. Felicia couldn't say. Certainly, she'd lasted longer than any of her male predecessors. Certainly, too, she had done better than that wastrel older brother of hers, Drax. *Far* better. And as she watched Quove Lentis pacing to and fro on the balcony, she wondered what her brother was up to now.

Coincidentally, Drax had also been employed by Quove Lentis for a while. Holed up in the bowels of a sky-tavern – the *Xanth Filatine*, if she remembered correctly – he was a gangmaster, getting his band of lackeys to rob, blackmail or swindle the wealthy travellers lodged in the upper decks, as well as dealing with anyone on board whom Quove Lentis wished to see dead.

He'd done well enough, Felicia supposed. But then he'd been arrested for something or other and ended up in a Hive jail for three months, at which point Quove Lentis had cut all links with him.

Felicia couldn't remember the last time she'd seen him, nor did she care. Spiteful and hot-headed, Drax was his own worst enemy – and besides, she'd always hated the horrible habit he had of cutting off the fingers of those who crossed him.

Felicia Adereth was not sentimental. She could not have remained in Quove Lentis's service for so long if she were. But some things were just wrong.

Drax Adereth was doing wrong at that very moment, though that wasn't the way he saw it. So far as Drax was concerned, there was something he wanted to know, and if the individual with the information now roped to the cliff wall in front of him was too stupid to offer it up, then he was asking for everything he got.

'Where is he?' Drax asked for the third time, his voice soft and menacing.

'I . . . I told you,' came the faltering reply. 'I don't know.'

Drax sighed and drew his knife from his belt. 'You're really not doing yourself any favours, Lope,' he purred. He reached up and ran the blade slowly over the goblin's thumb. 'Where *is* he?'

Lemulis Lope had been grading a consignment of freshly mined streakstone when the pale-faced fourth-ling with the shock of white hair had appeared on the

narrow ravine ledge beside him. He'd seemed friendly at first: introduced himself, admired the patterns on the rock, enquired after the price – then, almost as an afterthought, had asked after Cade Quarter.

At first, Lemulis was genuinely puzzled. But then he remembered the youth travelling with Eudoxia. She hadn't said much about him, but Lemulis had gathered that Quove Lentis and his cronies were after him. Maybe the two were unconnected – but there was something about this waif-like fourthling that he didn't trust.

'Never heard of him,' Lemulis Lope said, and turned away, which was when Drax Adereth pounced.

Considerably stronger than he looked, Drax got the wiry goblin in an arm lock. Before he knew it, Lemulis Lope found himself roped to the ironwood rings in the cliff face where, as a rule, scuttlebrigs were tethered. Now, with his arms raised high above his head and his feet dangling over the steep drop, he was totally at the mercy of this pale-eyed villain.

'Let's take this step by step,' Drax said, his voice little more than a whisper. 'I am looking for my old friend, Cade Quarter. I caught sight of him at the Farrow Lake a while back, from the deck of a passing skytavern, but by the time I got back there, he was gone. I asked around. Nobody there seemed to know him either,' he said. 'At first.' He smiled. 'But then a webfoot I came across suddenly remembered that he did know him after all . . .'

Drax's smile grew wider as he played with the necklace of brown, twig-like fingers that hung from a cord around his neck.

'It's amazing how much *can* be remembered,' he murmured. 'With the proper encouragement.'

Lemulis felt the blade of the knife press hard against the base of his thumb.

'What the webfoot told me was that Cade Quarter had left for New Sanctaphrax,' Drax continued. 'Then, during my journey there, and quite by chance, I came across a woodtroll in the Midwood Decks who informed me that he'd changed his plans and come to Gorgetown instead.' He pushed his face closer into the goblin's. 'So where is he?'

Lemulis swallowed. Betray Eudoxia? As a loyal Friend of New Sanctaphrax, he would not. Could not. The knife dug deeper – but then was suddenly removed.

'Fingers no threat, eh?' Drax chuckled, his head cocked to one side. 'How about your eyes, Lope?' he said, and the stone-master felt the point of the knife softly trace his drooping eyelids . . .

'New Sanctaphrax!' he blurted out. 'He and three companions. Yes, they were here. Briefly. But then they continued their journey to New Sanctaphrax. In a scuttlebrig convoy. They set off two weeks ago.' He shuddered, ashamed by his own weakness. 'That's all I know. Believe me.'

Drax Adereth pulled back. 'There, that wasn't so hard, was it?' he said. 'Thank you, Lemulis Lope. I appreciate your honesty.'

He reached up and sliced through the ropes that held the goblin in place. First the left wrist, then the right. Lemulis Lope fell forward, off the narrow ledge, and tumbled down the cliff face to the bottom of the gorge – and certain death.

Drax looked down at the broken body below him, and at the long bloodstained fingers splayed out on the rock.

'Such a terrible waste,' he murmured.

In the High Hall of the Palace of Phrax, two nightprowls sat grooming themselves in the shadows. Their sleek velvety fur, the deepest darkest shade of blue, gleamed in

the dim light. They were purring loudly, their throaty rumble like the thrum of a phraxchamber.

Suddenly the *click-clack* of boots on the polished marble floor caused the great cats to look up. They fell silent, and their pale blue eyes, marsh-gem bright, fixed on the figure that had started pacing back and forward. And, hearing the low grumble of irritation, they growled back menacingly.

Phrax Commander Lennius Grex paused. Maybe it would be best to stay put, after all.

He was dressed for the occasion. His crushed funnel cap was brocaded with plaited gold thread, as was the front of his admiral's frockcoat. Rows of mire-pearl buttons fastened his extravagantly embroidered triple-breasted waistcoat, adding to the air of opulence appropriate for the commander-in-chief of the Great Glade fleet. By contrast, the hooded oilskin storm-cape at his shoulders, from which a cloudmeter and a small phraxlamp hung, was unadorned. It added that all-important common touch, Lennius Grex thought.

'Three hours I've been waiting,' he muttered to himself as a distant bell tolled. 'Three accursed hours!'

He clutched his spyglass tightly in his hand. If he wasn't summoned soon, then the reason for his visit would pass, and the whole afternoon would have been wasted.

If nothing else, the long wait had given him time to reflect on the situation regarding Great Glade and New Sanctaphrax. The blockade of the floating city was not going as well as Lennius Grex had hoped. The Knights Academy was proving to be a resourceful and stubborn opponent. Its skymarshals on their single-seater phraxcraft had taken a high toll on the Great Glade fleet, targeting both the wheelhouses and their crews with those long-barrelled phraxmuskets of theirs. For now at least, his own attacking fleet had been forced back to the relative safety of the grasslands.

The good news was that the blockade was stopping anything getting in or out of the floating city. Supplies there were running low. Lennius could tell that by the way the skymarshals were increasingly careful with their phraxbullets.

It was only a matter of time . . .

The phrax commander grunted angrily. These days it seemed as though he spent his whole life waiting.

Well, he wasn't having it. He'd waited here in this oppressive hall for long enough. Maybe he'd been forgotten. Maybe that idiot gabtroll on the door had neglected to pass on the message that he'd arrived.

Whatever, he thought angrily. He would *not* be treated like this – even by the High Professor of Flight. No. He would go and find Quove Lentis for himself.

Decision made, Lennius Grex hurried past the nightprowls, ignoring their vicious snarls. As he stepped out onto the grand balcony that ran around the palace, he trembled with unease. The Palace of Phrax had always unnerved him. But then, as Lennius Grex knew, that was precisely the point.

Quove Lentis had designed the place as an expression of his own power. Having taken over the other academies, one by one, he had absorbed them into the Academy of Flight, then set about turning the entire academy into a military force. The laboratories and workshops became armouries, developing weapons and phraxships; the academics exchanged their robes for uniforms; while the phraxfleet and city guard were, in rapid succession, also taken over by the now all-powerful Academy of Flight.

Then that Descender Nate Quarter had returned. It had given Quove Lentis the chance to make his power absolute. Lennius remembered it all so well.

The last of the Great Glade academics who had opposed Quove were rounded up by his unit of elite bodyguards, and had not been seen or heard from since. Soon afterwards, the blockade of New Sanctaphrax began – just as the finishing touches were being added to the opulent new Palace of Phrax.

Lennius Grex strode along the grand balcony. He passed the entrances to the various halls, each one decorated with a different colour. Yellow. Green. Blue. Purple . . . Lining the back wall of the balcony were numerous marble statues of the High Professor in various poses – and there, just up ahead, was the High Professor of Flight himself.

He was reclining on a carved sumpwood couch, the tether held by a couple of burly flathead goblins of the phraxmarine. A small albino quarm sat on Quove Lentis's lap, trilling softly as its owner's plump fingers stroked its snow-white fur.

Lennius came to a halt in front of him. He raised a clenched fist, then opening his hand in a crisp movement, gave the academy salute. Quove Lentis eyed him coolly through lowered lids, his small fleshy lips twitching beneath his carefully oiled moustache.

'Ah, there you are,' said Quove Lentis. 'I wondered what had happened to you.' Lennius fought the urge to complain about his being abandoned in the High Hall. 'What have you to report, Phrax Commander Grex?'

Lennius swallowed uneasily. The High Professor of the Academy of Flight's voice was smooth and calm, but his form of address was icily formal. It was not a good sign.

'Report? Erm, well . . .' Lennius Grex was suddenly flustered. 'I haven't come here to report as such. I came for the . . . erm . . .'

The phrax commander nodded towards the edge of the grand balcony. Quove Lentis turned, following his gaze.

The Palace of Phrax towered over the city of Great Glade, and the view from the grand balcony was unrivalled. All twelve districts could be seen, including the oldest district of all, the Free Glades. Here, the ancient Lake Landing Academy still stood, its tower and deck no longer a working academy but a monument to the city's glorious past.

Lennius Grex was looking across the city to the Free Glades district now. A large phraxvessel was hovering over the ancient-looking academy tower at the centre of the lake.

'Ah, yes, of course,' Quove Lentis said, and smiled. 'You're here for . . . the entertainment.'

Lennius Grex nodded, then raised his spyglass. 'Yes, yes, that's it,' he agreed. 'May I?'

'Certainly,' said Quove Lentis, producing a spyglass of his own from his topcoat. 'Let's watch this together.' He smiled again. 'While you give me a detailed report of the blockade . . .' His manner became icy once more. 'Phrax Commander Grex.'

The phraxmarines towed the sumpwood couch over to the edge of the balcony, and Quove Lentis raised his spyglass to one eye. Standing beside the couch, Lennius Grex did the same, but his hands were shaking. From somewhere behind him, he heard the nightprowls' low rumbling growls and snarls, and the sound of huge paws padding across the marble floor as the great cats approached.

'The blockade is going well, High Professor,' said Lennius Grex, focusing his spyglass on the hovering phraxvessel.

On a spar, jutting out from its upper foredeck, stood three figures: a fourthling and two cloddertrogs. They were bloodied and stooped, and their hands and feet were bound tightly together.

'The attacks of the skymarshals have grown less frequent,' Lennius explained, 'now that our fleet is permanently in close hover over the Mire grasslands.'

'So, still no closer to Undergarden and the floating city itself?' Quove Lentis said, his voice still ominously calm.

'It's only a matter of time, High Professor,' Lennius Grex insisted. 'Nothing can get in or out of New Sanctaphrax while our fleet keeps it blockaded—'

'And *while* our phraxfleet is tied up over the grasslands,' Quove Lentis broke in, 'others take advantage.' He nodded to the figures on board the hovering phraxvessel. 'Those three, for example.'

In the distance, the spar abruptly tipped forward, throwing the fourthling and the cloddertrogs headlong down through the air. They crashed into the lake, throwing up plumes of water as they sank, only to bob up to the surface a moment later. Then suddenly, behind them, gleaming shapes rose from the depths, twisting and turning as they leaped from the water and arched their scaly backs, before diving back deep down into the lake.

'Like all true predators, the snaggletooth doesn't wait,' Quove Lentis said, a satisfied smile on his lips. 'It strikes, suddenly – and with deadly effect,' he concluded as the ripples on the surface of the lake died away and the phraxship moved off.

Lennius Grex shuddered.

'Those three were tallow-hats, caught raiding one of our phraxmines in the Eastern Woods,' Quove went on. 'The longer the blockade continues, the bolder these sky pirates become. Do I make myself clear?'

Quove Lentis snapped his spyglass shut, making Lennius Grex jump and almost drop his own. Behind him, the nightprowls snarled more loudly. Lennius Grex looked round to see the two sets of pale blue eyes staring back at him.

'Please, High Professor, we're doing our best,' he said, aware of the pleading tone in his voice. 'We just need a little more time . . .' He was standing at the very edge of the balcony. The nightprowls started padding towards him, their teeth bared. 'I'm begging you, *please* . . .'

'My nightprowls are hungry,' said Quove Lentis evenly. 'They want to be fed . . .' He paused. 'What do *you* think, Captain Adereth?'

Lennius Grex fell to his knees, the hood of his storm-cape pulled up defensively over his head and his eyes clamped shut. Trembling uncontrollably, he clasped his hands together.

'I think the phrax commander deserves one more chance, sir,' said a female voice.

Lennius Grex opened his eyes and looked up. A fourthling in the green uniform of the Freeglade Lancers – Quove Lentis's personal bodyguard – was standing beside the two burly phraxmarines. She had braided hair, pulled back beneath a tall pointed forage cap, large ears, a thin mouth and eyes as pale as the nightprowls'.

'You're right,' said Quove Lentis.

He grabbed the white quarm by the scruff of its neck and tossed it to the nightprowls. Seizing it between them, the two great cats stole back into the shadows, the panicked screams of their victim shattering the quiet, then abruptly ceasing.

Quove Lentis clicked his fat fingers and the phraxmarines towed him back inside the Purple Hall. The Freeglade Lancer captain watched them go, her pale eyes no more than narrow slits. Then she turned to Lennius Grex, who had climbed to his feet and was straightening his fine uniform.

'Thank you, Captain,' he said as he regained his composure. 'Our glorious leader has been known to be somewhat impetuous. Thank Sky that cooler heads like ours have prevailed.'

'So, do you intend to attack New Sanctaphrax?' asked the captain, standing in front of the phrax commander. 'I believe the High Professor made his opinion clear.'

'His opinion concerned the hideous monsters with which he's populated the Freeglade Lake,' said Lennius Grex with all the dignity he could muster. This tall rangy captain with her pale eyes was almost as unnerving as the nightprowls. 'He has left the conduct of the blockade to me. Now, if you'll step aside, Captain . . . ?'

'Adereth,' said the Freeglade Lancer captain. 'Captain Felicia Adereth. And you, Phrax Commander Lennius Grex, have just used up your last chance.'

Reaching out, she gave the phrax commander a gentle shove that unbalanced him.

Flailing wildly, Lennius Grex fell from the grand balcony of the High Hall of the Palace of Phrax, built upon the site of an old loading scaffold, then the highest point in the city. Moments before he hit the ground, its name flashed into his thoughts.

The Forlorn Hope.

· CHAPTER TWELVE ·

As he walked up the grand avenue, with the wind singing through the elegant buildings on both sides, Cade felt for his father's barkscroll of working drawings, his fingertips probing the material of his jacket. They were still there – thank Earth and Sky! – stitched into the lining, where he'd concealed them back on the *Hoverworm*.

It seemed so long ago that his friend Thorne had given them to him. At the time, he'd suggested that Cade should pass them on to the High Academe, Nate Quarter. But when the two of them had finally met up in the Great Library, his uncle had turned them down.

'I'm sure they're fascinating, Cade,' he'd said, 'but leave them where they are. I'm afraid phrax technology really isn't my thing.'

Cade must have looked disappointed, because his uncle had smiled encouragingly and clapped him on the shoulder.

'Seftis Bule is the one you should give them to,' he'd told him. 'New Sanctaphrax's Chief Armourer. He and his Armoury academics will know exactly what to do with them.'

'He's trustworthy?' Cade had asked.

'I'd trust Seftis Bule with my life,' Nate had assured him.

Now, three days after arriving in New Sanctaphrax, Cade was about to meet the armourer at last. As he climbed the broad stone stairs that led up to the Armoury's heavy ironwood doors, with their black studs and elaborate hinges, his body tingled with the thrill of anticipation.

Unlike the reverent hush of the schools and academies Cade had already visited, the entire barrel-shaped building thrummed with the noise of industry. There was the roar of the furnaces, the clank and thud of work tools and, above this background cacophony, the sound of voices bellowing instructions and commands.

Cade raised a fist, hammered loudly on the door and waited. Then, unsure that anyone had heard him, he raised his fist a second time – only for the door to creak open. A brawny cloddertrog wearing a large tilder apron, burn marks from splashes of molten metal staining its shiny leather surface, filled the entrance. He stared down at Cade, his dark eyes narrowed with mistrust.

'Seftis Bule?' said Cade uncertainly.

'What of him?' said the cloddertrog gruffly.

'I'm . . . errm . . . looking for him,' said Cade.

'He's busy,' the cloddertrog grunted. 'The Chief Armourer is always busy,' he added, and went to close the door.

'Nate Quarter sent me,' said Cade quickly. 'The High Academy Elec—'

'I know who Nate Quarter is,' the cloddertrog said. He looked Cade up and down before pulling the door back open and stepping to one side. 'Follow me.'

They went along a broad corridor, both sides lined with mounds of metal objects – suits of armour, antiquated engines and water tanks, gates and metal fencing, rolls of wire netting and heaps of forks and spoons. The air grew warmer and noisier as the cloddertrog led the way to the doors at the far end – then exploded in a wall of searing heat and deafening clamour when he pushed them open.

As they entered the cavernous hall, a dense cloud of glittering smoke billowed up into the air. It startled the ratbirds that, attracted to the Armoury by the heat of the furnace pipes, roosted on the ceiling rafters. Cade looked up to see a large flock of the little creatures flex their leathery wings and take to the air. And as they flitted round and round the high vaults, their high-pitched cries adding to the general din, he was reminded of the forest canopy at dawn in some distant Deepwoods grove.

In every corner of the hall, goblins, trogs and trolls were hard at work, some at benches or cooling troughs, others shifting barrow-loads of raw materials from one part of the Armoury to another. Cade was transfixed.

'He's over there,' the cloddertrog bellowed, and pointed to a blazing furnace at the far side of the Armoury, before turning and stomping back through the doorway.

Suddenly finding himself alone, Cade checked – one last time – that the barkscrolls were still in place, then crossed the oily flagstones towards the furnace. He passed a banderbear who was operating a set of bellows, carefully calibrating the flow of air into the furnace chamber. Ahead of him, standing in front of the blazing forge, was a thin, wiry mottled goblin, the red-hot flames reflected in his sweat-glazed face.

'Are you Seftis Bule?' said Cade.

The mottled goblin stared back at him, his expression blank. Then he cupped a hand to his ear.

'I said, are you Seftis Bule?' Cade shouted.

'Who wants to know?' came the belligerent response.

'My name's Cade. Cade Quarter,' he told him. 'My uncle Nate sent me to see you.' He reached down, tore open the rough stitching in the lining of his jacket and pulled out the sheaf of barkscrolls. 'He said I should give you these.'

Without taking them, Seftis grabbed Cade by the arm and steered him past the forge and into a small room with a desk, a chair and a bank of filing cabinets. He slammed the door shut. Instantly the noise abated.

'Say all that again,' he said.

Cade did so, relieved not to have to shout any more, then handed the chief armourer the barkscrolls. Seftis flicked through them quickly, then looked up.

'I'm going to need some time to look at them more closely,' he said. He frowned thoughtfully. 'Are you at all interested in the Armoury?'

'I think it's incredible,' said Cade. 'Though a bit noisy,' he added with a rueful smile.

'It's not always this loud,' said the goblin. He wiped his sleeve over his sweating brow. 'Or so infernally hot. We've been catching up on an important order. Tell you what, Cade. I'll get Theegum to show you round and we'll meet up again here in an hour.'

Leaving the barkscrolls on the desk, Seftis Bule took Cade back into the forge hall.

'Theegum!' he shouted. 'We got a guest. Cade Quarter. Show him round.'

The banderbear – a huge female with thick

fur and the stubby yellowed stumps of two hacked-off tusks – nodded. Then, without saying a word, she turned and trudged off.

Seftis patted Cade on the back. 'An hour,' he reminded him.

Apart from the odd yodelled grunt, Theegum remained silent as she led the visitor through the Armoury. It was left to Cade to make sense of the things he was seeing.

In the main hall, amid smoke and flames and the smelting of ore, with ratbirds screeching and bellows wheezing, there was the drama of forge work. Beyond the hall were the workshops, where the clink and clatter of the metal workers set up an ever-changing rhythm, and the smell of resin oil and cogwheel polish was heavy in the air. Then, running parallel to the workshops, they came to the arsenal chamber.

For Cade, this was the most interesting part of the tour. There were long shelves of neatly labelled phraxweapons, both arms and ammunition, as well as phraxpacks, protective armour and phraxchambers of every size. Time and again, Cade stopped in front of one of the upright display cases at the ends of the aisles, and peered in at the intricate tools and armaments – ancient and modern – that were stored behind the glass.

One claw-like object in particular caught his eye. It was some kind of metal glove or gauntlet, with small round holes on the knuckles of each finger that looked as though they might fire ammunition of some kind. Though how they worked, Cade couldn't guess.

'Wuh-waah,' Theegum grunted, and swung her arm up in front of her, her clawed paw opening and closing, then darting forward. 'Wuh-wurra-waah!' She stabbed at the air, then repeated the gesture. 'Waah! Waah!'

Suddenly Cade understood. 'Flames,' he said. 'It's some kind of flame-thrower.'

And Theegum nodded, a smile brightening her hairy face. She repeated the whole movement. 'Wuh-wuh.'

As the hour drew to a close, the banderbear indicated – in grunts and gestures that Cade was just about able to interpret – that the two of them should head back to Seftis Bule's office.

Cade realized he was grinning. The previous evening, Tug had asked him what his favourite place was in New Sanctaphrax. At the time, Cade couldn't answer. 'It's all amazing,' he'd said.

Now he had an answer: the Armoury.

For Tug himself, there was no question. It was Undergarden that he loved best; everything about it. The steam allotments that lined the banks of the Edgewater River; the enclosures and pastureland in the western district; the untamed copses and glades amid the ruins to the east. The wildlife and birdsong. The delicious fruits and vegetables, ripe for the picking . . .

Since that first day with Celestia, collecting herbs and plant samples, Tug had found every opportunity in the weeks that followed to leave the confines of the Knights Academy and take the basket down from the West

Landing to Undergarden. There he would spend the day with the Undergardeners – scholars from the Academy of Earth Studies in their blue-grey robes with the distinctive green trim. And for their part, the scholars had welcomed this great hulking 'nameless one' into their midst, finding him chores to do and tasks to complete.

Tug, the Undergardeners soon realized, could turn his hand to anything and was a quick learner. He had a natural affinity with the livestock, shepherding the miniature hammelhorns around in the western enclosures and tending to the elegant blue-backed tilder in the pastures of the palace ruins.

And it was there, amid the lush gladegrass, that he was first brought up short by the sight of a moss-covered stone figure, half buried in the dark soil. Enthralled by the sight of the eerie statue, Tug had taken the time to excavate it carefully with his curved claws and, clamping it beneath one arm, had made his way through the flocks of grazing tilder to the arched entrance to the old sewers. There, he removed all the shrubs and saplings to create a small clearing, and having cleaned the statue, scraping away the soil and moss and returning the carved figure to its original state, had placed it at its centre.

It was to be the first of a growing collection.

On a warm evening some weeks later, Tug was – as usual – down in Undergarden. The low sun dappled the western pastures and was turning the drifting clouds to orange and pink. Tug had already secured the skittish tilder in their pens for the night, and was now making his way back through the enclosures and down the mossy slope towards the banks of the Edgewater River.

Under his arm, he was carrying a particularly fine statue that he'd unearthed that morning. It was a figure of an ancient, long-forgotten Undertown leagues-merchant in a short cape and a high, conical hat. Carefully chiselled and elegantly detailed, it would, Tug had decided, make an excellent addition to his collection.

'*A fellow dweller of the Nightwoods? Why, yes, yes, it is. You must be Tug . . .*'

The soft, sibilant voice seemed to be inside Tug's head. He started with alarm, held the statue out in front of him and stared, furrow-browed, into the impassive stone face. Then, slowly, warily, he brought it closer, until the carved mouth was pressed against his ear.

'*Tug,*' came the soft voice again.

'Wurgh!' Tug grunted in alarm, almost letting the statue slip from his grasp. But then he saw it. The figure of a tiny female waif.

She was standing on the river bank beside a softly rustling dropwillow. Dressed in the blue-grey robes of New Sanctaphrax, she was holding a glass ampoule in her long-fingered hands. As she stepped forward, twenty or so other ampoules chinked in the burlap forage sack that hung from her shoulder.

'Forgive me, Tug,' the waif academic said out loud, the thin barbels on her lower lip quivering as she spoke. 'It was rude of me to intrude on your thoughts like that.'

'Tug startled is all,' said Tug, smiling lopsidedly. 'Tug not heard a waif's voice since Tug was a young'un.'

'There are so few of us out in the world these days.' The waif nodded. 'Especially Nightwoods waifs such as myself. I'm Professor Sentafuce of the Academy of Cloud,' she said, and held up the ampoule. 'I've just been testing the quality of the water . . .' She paused, her large pale eyes widening as they focused on the statue in Tug's hands. 'So it's true what they say about you, young Tug. You're quite the excavator.'

'Tug find in tilder pastures,' he explained. 'In palace ruins. Tug show.'

He turned and took the path that ran along the bank of the Edgewater River towards the sewer entrance. The tiny waif professor followed, dropping quite naturally into step beside him.

'Of course,' she said softly, both inside his head and out loud, 'those ruins are of the Palace of a Thousand Statues. It was where that old tyrant Vox Verlix once ruled all Undertown. You can read about him in the barkscrolls of the Great Library . . . Do you like to read, Tug?' she asked. *'Ah, yes, I can see that you do.'*

Tug smiled again. Having this soft voice inside his head had alarmed him at first, but now he was finding it quite soothing.

'Tug wonder . . .'

'Yes, Tug, I would very much like to see your collection,' said Sentafuce, reading his thoughts. *'What a perfect setting you've created for them.'* She looked up. 'Hasn't he, Demora?'

They had reached the sculpture garden that Tug had created on the river bank above the arched sewer entrance, and in which he had carefully set out the ancient statues. Fifteen to date. They stood in groups of two or three, facing each other, as if in conversation, clumps of gorse-grass and meadowwort already sprouting up around their bases.

Standing in their midst was the towering figure of a quarry trog wearing the robes of the Academy of Earth Studies. Wiping her hands on her robes, she stepped forward.

'I'm Demora Duste,' the quarry trog introduced herself.

She was tall, almost as tall as Tug himself, and when she shook Tug's great clawed hand, her grip was firm and strong.

'I work in the Stone Gardens,' she told him, 'and as a stone scholar, I can certainly appreciate careful, precise excavation like this.'

She ran a hand over the conical hat of the statue that Tug had just brought back.

'*Which is why*,' said Sentafuce's soft voice in Tug's head, '*we would like your help, Tug.*'

Seftis Bule looked up as Cade stepped back inside his small office. His eyes glittered with excitement as he shook the sheaf of barkscrolls in his hand.

'These are exciting, Cade,' he said. '*Very* exciting. I've had my Armoury academics look them over and they've confirmed my initial thoughts. We're looking at improved

phrax technology that could revolutionize life on the Edge.'

Cade smiled, his chest bursting with pride for his father.

'Not only will it mean that a single shard of phrax crystal could produce enough energy – *clean* energy – to power an entire Edgelands city. Lighting, heating, factories and so forth. But – and it's a big but – if that power can be safely controlled, it would also mean that exploration *beneath* the Edge might finally bear the results we've been hoping for. Instead of climbing down the cliff, Descenders would be able to go down in some kind of vessel.'

Warming to his theme, Seftis climbed to his feet and, still clutching the barkscrolls, began pacing around the small office.

'Raw materials should be no problem,' he went on, 'despite the blockade.' Stopping for a moment, he glanced at Cade. 'You'll no doubt have noticed the piles of metal objects near the entrance as you came in,' he said.

Cade nodded.

'It's all part of our defence effort,' he explained. 'Everyone in New Sanctaphrax is doing their bit. Ancient stores have been ransacked, unnecessary decorations have been stripped from the buildings and walkways, while everyone living here has surrendered what they can – all for the common good. It means we have a vast supply of metal objects that we can smelt down to keep the forge running – which, in turn, means that, trade embargo or no, we can continue to produce everything we need.'

The chief armourer paused in front of Cade. He glanced down at the scrolls, then looked up into Cade's face.

'Which brings me to my proposal.'

Cade returned Seftis Bule's intense gaze. 'Proposal?'

'Your father was a genius, Cade,' Seftis told him, 'and we shall certainly make use of his working drawings, endeavouring to turn his theories into something practical. What I propose is that you work alongside us, here, in the Armoury. I know it's not the most exciting place in New Sanctaphrax perhaps—'

'Yes,' Cade said softly.

'But you'll be able to monitor the progress on your father's work and—'

'Yes,' Cade repeated, louder this time. 'I'd love to work in the Armoury. When do I start?'

Seftis Bule looked taken aback, surprised perhaps that Cade hadn't asked for time to think about it. Then a smile spread across his face.

'Excellent,' he said. 'You can start tomorrow morning.'

· CHAPTER THIRTEEN ·

Celestia Helmstoft had been wondering what to do with herself of late. The blockade was still in full force, making the lives of those who lived in New Sanctaphrax more difficult by the day.

Surely, she thought, there was something she could do to help out. After all, her friends were all doing their bit.

Tug, for instance, spent most days down in Undergarden, busy from dawn to dusk with his beloved tilder herd and hammelhorn flock. On occasions, he would also accompany Demora Duste to the Stone Gardens, though why that was, Celestia had no idea.

As for Cade, she'd hardly seen anything of him for weeks. He was in the Armoury every morning, then, if he completed his work early, he would visit his uncle in the Great Library. Most of the time he seemed so lost in thought that, even when they did meet up, they hardly exchanged two words with each other.

Not that Celestia held that against him. She knew that Cade valued having her – and Tug – close by, even if his head was filled with other matters. The trouble was, with her friends off helping the floating city to keep going, Celestia herself was left all the more aware that she too ought to be doing something useful.

Then one evening, several weeks after their arrival in New Sanctaphrax, Eudoxia suggested they take a walk together. They strolled through the great mosaic court-yard of the Knights Academy in companionable silence, ducking their heads as they passed beneath the old tilt-poles where the knights academic in full armour would train their prowlgrins. Suddenly the quiet was broken by the sound of raised voices and some kind of a struggle.

They turned the corner to see a ragtag group of hungry-looking individuals in the middle of a fight. Fists were flying, boots were going in and the air was filled with angry shouts and cries.

'Get off, they're mine!'

'Not now, they're not!'

'Get your filthy hands off . . .'

Then someone spotted Eudoxia – for so long, their acting High Academe Elect – standing watching them, her hands on her hips. The fight stopped at once.

'There is no need for this,' Eudoxia told them calmly. 'Not if we all work together.'

'No, ma'am.'

'Sorry, ma'am.'

Celestia watched, amazed once again by the power of Eudoxia's soothing words, as the protagonists climbed to their feet, shame-faced and apologetic, and one by one shuffled away – leaving the cause of the dispute lying on the ground. It was a basketful of honeybeets and glimmer-onions, the basket now upturned and the vegetables ground to a useless pulp underfoot.

'New Sanctaphrax is approaching crisis point, but we shall remain strong,' said Eudoxia, turning back to Celestia. 'I believe that Cade, Tug *and* you, Celestia, have a role to play in our city's future – and the future of the entire Edgelands, perhaps.'

At the sound of the quiet, reassuring words, Celestia found herself falling under Eudoxia's spell.

'But you must remain patient, my dear,' Eudoxia added, 'and listen carefully to what New Sanctaphrax is saying.'

'The towers, you mean?' Celestia asked. 'The music of the city?'

And Eudoxia nodded.

So it was that Celestia took to walking through the mosaic-tiled streets, courtyards and quadrangles on her own, all the while listening to the strange sounds of the winds that blew through the turrets and spires around her. On stormy days, the music could be deep and sonorous, with fog-filters booming and drizzle-plates spinning, emitting their bright shimmering chimes. In the rain, the pitch would lighten, the mistsifting towers making the air pulse and churn with melodies, while the turrets of the upper viaduct added a thrilling percussion of countless different types.

Loud or soft, the music was never less than mesmerizing. Yet the days Celestia grew to love more than any others were the ones when the wind slowed to a light breeze and gentle, almost imperceptible, breaths of air. On days like these, the towers sang sweetly, filling the streets with the lulling cadence of wistful murmurs and whispered secrets.

It was on one such day, when she was following a delicate sliver of sound down to the clinking cages of the East Landing, that Celestia caught sight of the skymarshals coming in to land. As she watched, standing beside the ancient cages that the scholars of old had used to winch themselves down the side of the floating rock in order to study the sky, the tiny phraxcraft glided towards her like a flock of strange insects.

With their phraxchambers thrumming and their burnished funnels sending thin trails of steam out behind them like woodspider silk, the single-seater vessels came closer. Some two hundred skymarshals in all, she reckoned. They landed in cohorts of ten, smoothly and almost soundlessly, then the pilots jumped down from their saddles, seized the mooring-tethers and led the bobbing phraxcraft back into the floating city.

Celestia couldn't take her eyes off them. Fourthlings, goblins, mobgnomes; all of them dressed in blue-grey topcoats and burnished copperwood helmets, and with long-barrelled phraxmuskets like lances at their shoulders.

As the last cohort came in to land and dismounted, Celestia found herself following them.

The skymarshals talked among themselves, greeting one another and engaging with passing academics anxious for the latest news, as they made their way through the city towards the Knights Academy. They reached the small entrance to the skymarshals' barracks, where the duty marshal ticked off their names on a ledger as they entered, one after the other.

'And last but by no means least, Skymarshal Rolnix,' announced the duty marshal, a portly goblin with tufted ears. 'Perfect score at the cloud range?' he enquired.

'Chance would be a fine thing,' the skymarshal replied with a wry smile. 'But we can't waste ammunition on target practice these days. Just pull the trigger and fly past.' To demonstrate, he raised his phraxmusket in the air and pulled the trigger. There was a dull *click*. The chamber was empty.

'Can we help you, miss?'

The skymarshal had spotted Celestia. She'd been staring at his skycraft, its prow carved into the likeness of what she took to be a rock demon.

'Um . . . I was just wondering what it must be like to fly one of those,' she said, feeling a little bit flustered under the skymarshal's unblinking gaze.

'Best job in the floating city, eh, Mudgutt?' the sky-marshal said, and laughed.

'That's Sky Sergeant Mudgutt to you, Rolnix,' the duty marshal said. 'And I prefer the bench of my sumpwood desk these days. Leave the heroic stuff to you young'uns.' He turned to Celestia. 'Are you interested in flying, miss?

'Yes,' Celestia confessed. 'I've trained and ridden prowlgrins, and that can sometimes feel like flying – though I've never been on anything like these phraxcraft.'

'If you can handle a prowlgrin,' said the skymarshal, 'then you shouldn't have too much trouble with phraxcraft.' He smiled. 'Would you care to see the Tether Hall, where we keep them?' he asked. He stuck out his hand. 'The name's Brocktinius, by the way,' he said. 'Brocktinius Rolnix . . .'

'One of the finest skymarshals I have under my command,' the sky sergeant broke in. 'Eight Great Glade phraxship captains to his credit so far, each one shot through the circular windows of their phraxships—'

'Thanks, Mudgutt . . . *Sky Sergeant* Mudgutt,' Brocktinius muttered as he turned a deep shade of crimson, 'but—'

'Including none other than Admiral Lode Threwlin himself,' Mudgutt went on, undeterred. 'Only the chief of Great Glade's blockade effort. Picked him off from the quarterdeck of his flagship, the *Herald of Wealth*, he did.' He chuckled. 'Later on, that Quove Lentis described his chief henchman's death as "food poisoning while on a trade mission", but *we* knew.' He patted Brocktinius on the shoulders. 'Didn't do your reputation any harm, did it, lad.'

'Take no notice of him, miss,' said the skymarshal, cringing with embarrassment. 'And my friends call me Brock,' he added.

Celestia shook his hand, her green eyes gleaming. 'Celestia Helmstoft,' she said.

Brock's face fell. 'Ah,' he said awkwardly. 'You're the friend of the High Academe Elect's nephew, aren't you? Cade Quarter. I took him stone-spotting a while back and . . . well, maybe he would object to us . . . errm . . .'

Celestia flicked her hair back from her face and laughed. 'Cade and I are just friends,' she said. 'Nothing more. And I'd love to see the Tether Hall,' she added, a smile playing at the corners of her mouth. 'Brock.'

The two of them crossed the courtyard and Brock, still pulling the *Rock Demon* behind him, led Celestia through the great ironwood doors and into a vast hall.

'These used to be the prowlgrin stables,' Brock explained, 'back in the First Age of Flight.'

'Oh, I would so like to have seen them in those days,' said Celestia, staring up at the beams crisscrossing the ceiling vaults of the huge hall. 'There must be roost beams for three hundred prowlgrins—'

'Five hundred and eighty-two actually,' said Brock. 'Old stock prowlgrins. Heavy-set and powerful they were, to take the Knights Academic down into the Twilight Woods on their quest for stormphrax.'

'Stormchasing,' Celestia breathed, her eyes sparkling. 'And now, instead of prowlgrins, there are those.' She nodded up at the clusters of tethered phraxcraft, their carved sumpwood prows bobbing in the warm air. 'Does each one represent a different creature?' she asked.

Brock nodded. 'A different creature, a different name.

Mine's the *Rock Demon*,' he said, 'as I'm sure you already noticed.'

He climbed the pegs of a tall pillar and walked along the horizontal roost beam, then tethered his phraxcraft to a mooring ring. Five other phraxcraft were tethered to the same ring.

'These are waiting to be assigned,' Brock told Celestia, who had followed him up and was balancing expertly on the beam as she watched him. 'Perhaps,' he suggested hesitantly, 'you'd like to take one of them out.'

'I'd *love* to!' said Celestia, and then blushed at the childish enthusiasm she heard in her voice.

But she was excited. Perhaps, she thought, this was what Eudoxia had meant when she told her to listen to what New Sanctaphrax was saying. The beautiful music of the city had led her to the East Landing – and now she was here.

Was this how she was to play her part in helping the besieged floating city?

'I think,' Celestia said slowly, trying to keep her voice calm and neutral-sounding, even though her heart was racing at the prospect, 'it has to be *that* one.'

Brock smiled and nodded his approval. 'The *Storm-hornet*,' he said.

Seated in the saddle of the phraxcraft with the carved stormhornet prow, Celestia raised the spyglass that Cade had lent her and trained it on the horizon. She knew how much the spyglass meant to her friend, but Cade had insisted she take it.

'For luck,' he'd said, tying the tilderleather strap to her flight tunic on the morning of her first patrol.

That had been over a month ago. Before that, Celestia had practised at the end of a tolley rope that was attached to the upper ramparts of the Knights Academy tower – seemingly endless flights on the *Stormhornet* under Brock's watchful eye until, after many weeks, the skymarshal was finally satisfied with her balance and control. Even now, though, Brock still liked to keep a close watch over her when they flew the dawn patrol.

With the chill of the phraxchamber cold on her back as it thrummed behind her, Celestia looked around. The white glow of the combusting phrax crystal cast a beam of light out of the chamber's glass phraxport, while from the funnel above, a thin trail of steam snaked back across the early morning sky. And there was Brock, the steam trail of his *Rock Demon* running parallel with that of the *Stormhornet*, then looping and twisting around it.

Celestia turned back.

Brock accelerated, guiding his phraxcraft round to fly back past her in a protective manoeuvre that would see their steam trails intertwine once more. As he flew by, Celestia noticed that he had slipped the long-barrelled phraxmusket off his shoulder. Moments later, the carved rock-demon prow drew level and, glancing around again, Celestia saw Brock pointing into the distance.

She focused the spyglass. Two phraxfrigates were hovering high above the rolling grasslands of the Mire. Further off, mere specks of black on the horizon, was

the rest of the Great Glade fleet that Quove Lentis had sent to bolster the blockade of New Sancta-phrax. And while Celestia watched, she saw flashes of light as the frig-ates' swivel-mounted guns raked the grasslands below with phraxbullets.

'They must have spot-ted a scuttlebrig convoy bringing in fresh supplies,' Brock called across to her. 'Stay low and cut power when I give the signal.'

Celestia nodded, then lowered the spyglass and took her own phrax-musket off her shoulder.

If the crews of the enemy phraxfrigates had any sense, they would be watching out for any telltale steam trails. She and Brock would have to glide when they approached, to avoid detec-tion. The phraxchamber's thrum rose in pitch as she pushed the flight levers to full power. Then, pushing down on the stirrups, Celestia sent the *Stormhornet* into a steep dive.

The rippling grasslands rose to meet her before turning to a green blur as Celestia pulled back on the stirrups and levelled her phraxcraft off, no more than a couple of strides above the nodding seed heads of the grass. Ahead of her, Brock did the same, then raised a hand. Celestia cut the power to the phraxchamber and the trail of white steam from the funnel abruptly stopped.

They sped on, soundlessly riding the air currents, their stirrups clipping the tops of the tall grass as they closed in on the phraxfrigates. As they drew nearer, Celestia could see figures on the fore and aft decks. They wore green topcoats with distinctive chequerboard collars. Three of them were operating a swivel-gun mounted on the aft deck of each vessel, while at the prow ten more had their phraxmuskets trained on the grasslands below.

Brock indicated that he would take the phraxvessel on the left, which meant that the one on the right was Celestia's. Their phraxcraft slowed as the glide faded, and Celestia brought the *Stormhornet* to a hover some three hundred strides from her target.

Below the phraxfrigates, the grasslands were getting churned up by the phraxguns. Celestia saw a scuttlebrig spring into view from beneath a matted clump of grass. As its rider clung onto the saddle strapped to its tail, the scuttlebrig galloped across the flattened grass in plain sight of the phraxfrigate's swivel-gun.

One, two, three blinding flashes exploded from the

barrel, followed by sharp whip-like cracks that cut through the air. The scuttlebrig reared up, then crashed into the muddy earth of the Mire in a heavy tumbling fall. Its rider, a fourthling in a grey rain-cape and crushed funnel cap, was thrown clear – but before he had a chance to climb to his feet, the phraxmuskets at the prow of the phraxfrigate riddled his body with bullets.

Celestia let out a small anguished cry.

Another brave scuttlebrig rider – trying to break the blockade and bring food and equipment, and maybe also newcomers, to the floating city – had ended up dying for the cause. As a healer, there was nothing she could do for him, but in her new role – a skymarshal out on patrol – she was determined to avenge his death.

Breathing deeply and slowly, she raised her long-barrelled phraxmusket and took aim at the centre of the vessel where, just visible through the circular wheel-house window, a phraxengineer was bent low over the flight controls. Beneath her topcoat, as she focused on the wheelhouse window, Celestia's heart was beating like a ratbird caught in a snare.

Some way further off, two more scuttlebrigs were making a run for it, their riders hunched forward in their saddles as phraxfire rained down around them. Celestia squeezed the trigger . . .

There was a tiny flashing spark as her shot ricocheted off the ironwood panelling of the phraxfrigate's wheel-house. A startled face peered out from the circular window before disappearing again as the phraxfrigate abruptly soared up into the air, forcing the crew on the aft- and foredecks to drop their weapons and cling on for dear life.

The phraxfrigate that Brock was targeting rose steeply too, then sped off after its companion vessel, listing sharply to one side as it did so, its swivel-gun firing blindly behind it. Stray phraxbullets scythed through the tall grass around Celestia, making her flinch. One bullet struck the *Stormhornet*. The phraxcraft spun round, almost throwing her from the saddle.

By the time Celestia had regained control of the vessel, the phraxfrigates were steaming off to join the rest of the fleet on the distant horizon. As for the scuttlebrig convoy, there was no sign of it.

Brock appeared at her side on the *Rock Demon*, his phraxchamber powered up. He was smiling.

'Think I clipped one of their phraxengineers,' he said, and shrugged. 'We scared them off, which is the main thing.' He paused, his expression becoming serious as he reached out a hand to Celestia's shoulder. 'You're bleeding.'

The flight back to Undergarden was hard for Celestia. The pain from the phraxbullet in her shoulder kept hitting her in waves. And each time it did, she gripped the pommel of her saddle and gritted her teeth to avoid crying out.

Forced to land, she cleaned the wound as best she could, applied a dressing of hyleberry compress, then took drops of bitterroot tincture for the pain. Brock assisted her as best he could, untying the appropriate bundles from her topcoat and handing them to her when she requested them. Then he tethered the *Stormhornet* to the *Rock Demon* and the two of them resumed their flight, returning to the floating city at half steam. But with the intense pain continuing to wash over her, Celestia was finding it increasingly difficult to balance her phraxcraft.

'Where are we?' she asked at last, dimly aware that they'd stopped moving.

'Undergarden,' said Brock, helping her out of the saddle.

Through half-open eyes, Celestia saw two figures approach – a fettle-legger in blue-grey robes with a green trim, and . . .

'Tug? Tug, is that you?' she asked weakly.

Then darkness . . .

When Celestia awoke, she imagined for a moment that she was back on board Gart Ironside's *Hoverworm*. She was lying in a hammock in a small room that was cloaked in shadow, with various bits and pieces hanging from overhead hooks.

Except, she realized, reaching out, this couldn't be a skyvessel, because when she touched what she thought was the cabin wall, it was made of stone, not buoyant timber.

The movement made her wince, and the dull throb in her shoulder brought everything back to her. She sat up slowly, then carefully climbed out of the hammock. As her feet touched the cold stone of a paved floor, she shuddered.

Around her, in what appeared to be a vaulted chamber, were hundreds of small pots containing plants that were glowing with a soft blue light. On closer inspection, she discovered that the pots were in fact shards of stone, while the plants that were growing on them were a wide variety of mosses and lichens, the like of which Celestia had never seen before.

Folded neatly in a small alcove in the wall beside the hammock was Celestia's topcoat, along with her boots and backpack. Apart from the ache in her shoulder which, Celestia was pleased to see, had been expertly bandaged, she felt fine.

A figure approached through the glowing plants. It was the fettle-legger.

'I'm Fenda Fulefane from the Academy of Earth Studies,' she announced. 'Tug removed this from your shoulder,' she said, holding up a leadwood bullet between her forefinger and thumb. '*And* dressed your wounds,' she added. 'You taught him well, by all accounts. A talented fellow, your friend Tug.'

Celestia smiled. 'We looked after the wounded together at the Battle of Farrow Lake,' she told the fettle-legger.

'Yes, I know all about that,' said Fenda. She helped Celestia on with her boots and then, taking care not to disturb the dressing, her topcoat. 'Tug and I have become firm friends ourselves.'

'Where is this place?' asked Celestia. 'And what are these plants?'

'This is my laboratory in the sewer chambers of Old Undertown,' said Fenda. 'And as for these mosses, there'll be plenty of time to discuss them. Tug tells me you're quite a herbalist, Miss Helmstoft.'

'Please, call me Celestia,' she said, then added, 'But where's Brock? I need to report back to the Knights Academy . . .'

'There's no hurry,' said Fenda gently. 'You've been asleep here for three days.' She took Celestia by the arm. 'Skymarshal Rolnix returned your phraxcraft and made a report for both of you.' She smiled warmly. 'Now, I promised Tug I'd bring you to see him as soon as you were back on your feet, which, Celestia, it seems to me, you are!'

· CHAPTER FOURTEEN ·

'Cade, lad, what's the hurry?'

Cade looked round.

Sitting at the top of the Viaduct Steps was his uncle, his eyes glowing that weird, almost otherworldly, shade of blue. Cade would have waved if he could, but he had his arms full of barkscrolls. The jumble of notes, calculations and cut-away diagrams they contained seemed to match Cade's thoughts, the inside of his head full of phrax-globes, power conversions and forge calibrations.

'Seftis Bule is waiting for these,' he called up to Nate.

His uncle was looking a lot better than when he had first seen him, Cade noted. The deathly pallor and dusty sheen to his face had gone – though the High Academe Elect's white hair made him look far older than his thirty-four years.

'Ah, yes,' said Nate thoughtfully. 'Our chief armourer is keeping you busy. He clearly found those barkscroll diagrams of your father's interesting. But still, we haven't spoken for – what is it? Days? Weeks? . . .' He shook his head. 'I honestly can't remember the last time.' He patted the step he was seated on, indicating that Cade should sit beside him.

Seftis Bule could wait, Cade decided.

'How's the blockade-running going?' Cade asked as he sat down next to Nate. 'I've been so wrapped up with my work in the Armoury, I'm a little out of touch.'

Nate smiled, but he suddenly looked careworn and tired. 'The scuttlebrig trail is holding,' he said. 'Just. And Undergarden is keeping us fed. But with no raw materials coming in by sky, it's becoming increasingly difficult to replace or repair equipment. And our reserves of phrax and munitions are running dangerously low.' He scowled. 'All thanks to Quove Lentis.'

Cade shuddered. There was something he'd been meaning to ask his uncle, but the time had never seemed right. Until now.

'Nate,' he said slowly. 'Are we related to Quove Lentis? That letter I gave you – the one Aunt Eudoxia showed me – in it Abe wrote that he had married a Hermia Lentis—'

'His sister,' Nate said, his voice flat. 'Yes, Cade, Quove Lentis is my uncle.'

He fell still. Cade didn't press him further. But Nate seemed to feel that he should explain more.

'I went to see him once,' he said quietly. 'After I'd left the phraxmine in the Eastern Woods and gone to Great

Glade. I was fourteen. I hoped he might be able to help me out.' He snorted. 'Fat chance of that. It turned out that Quove was still furious that his sister Hermia had married my father all those years earlier. "A common labourer", he called him. Said Abe had dragged the Lentis family name through the mud.' He paused, his face etched with pain. 'I sometimes wonder whether everything that has happened since is because of Quove's contempt for my father . . .'

He looked down at the yellowed documents in his lap. Realizing that their conversation about Great Glade's tyrannical leader was at an end, Cade followed his uncle's gaze – and saw that the papers contained notes and diagrams of what looked like the cliff face below the Edge. Glancing round, Nate saw him staring.

'Yes, I've been doing a little work of my own – now that I feel my strength returning,' he added. 'These are notes on the descending trail.' He smiled. 'Fourteen years I was gone, but during that time the Descenders of the academy made enormous strides. You can see here, for example . . .'

Nate traced a finger down a leadwood pencil outline of a steep decline.

'This is the central vertical ridge where the Professor and I got into so much trouble on our last descent,' he said. 'Now the route is fully chain-ringed from the Low Gantry to the Cusp, and marked with klaxon poles and flare lamps right the way down to the Great Overhang.'

Cade leaned across and looked closely.

'The High Cliff and Mid Cliff have been conquered,'

Nate continued, his voice full of pride. 'And with the construction of the Keep, just below the Great Overhang, the denizens were on the point of pushing down further into the depths.'

The denizens.

Just hearing the name gave Cade shryke-bumps. He had seen them in the refectory of the Knights Academy. They sat at their own long table on a balcony overlooking the rest. The denizens were the elite of the Descenders, and in their phrax-weighted armour and glister helmets they reminded Cade of the knights academic of the First Age of Flight: the legendary stormchasers.

Instead of prowlgrins, though, the denizens towed sumpwood sleds and wore the phrax-powered gauntlets he'd first seen back in a display case at the Armoury. They were called 'flame claws', and they could incinerate an Edge wraith at a hundred strides. Cade had marvelled at these gloves, and the visored helmets that protected the wearer from the disorientating effects of glister storms. Back in the Armoury, he'd even tried one on when nobody was looking, and imagined himself staking out rows of horizontal phraxlamps and threading them with glowing lightlines as he descended into the inky blackness of the unknown depths.

Not that he would get the chance to do that any time soon. Cade knew that well enough. Descending had been brought to a halt by the blockade, and if Great Glade prevailed, then the descending trail would be abandoned to the ravine demons and Edge wraiths for ever.

'Of course, that was all before the blockade,' Nate was saying, echoing Cade's own thoughts. 'Now Eudoxia is urging me to pull the last of the denizens back from the Keep and assign all the Descenders to the defence of the East and West Landings. It would put at risk all the progress they made in my absence.' He shook his head. 'But Eudoxia fears that an all-out attack is coming.'

'Where *is* Aunt Eudoxia?' Cade asked. 'I haven't seen her around lately.

Nate laughed. 'Your aunt is a remarkable person, Cade,' he said. 'Without her, the city would never have survived for as long as it has. Right now, she's off on one of those missions of hers, trying to get more help for New Sanctaphrax.'

'Who from?' Cade asked.

'I don't know,' he replied with a shrug. 'She doesn't like to bother me with such things. "You concentrate on the future," she told me before she left, "and I'll worry about the present." ' Nate tapped the sheaf of papers he was holding. 'Which is how you come to find me concentrating on the next great descent.'

'To find your friend – Professor Hentadile?' Cade asked, recalling the afternoons he'd spent on the gantry in the Great Library, listening to his uncle reliving every detail of his last descent.

'The Professor? I've almost given up hope of ever finding him,' said Nate bitterly. 'It's anyone's guess how far we fell. It might take years of painstaking descending from Denizens Keep before we find those scree fields again. And even that might only be the start . . .'

Cade frowned. 'I don't understand,' he said. 'If you don't think you'll be able to find the Professor, then why descend at all? Especially with New Sanctaphrax under attack from Great Glade.'

'You're right, Cade,' said Nate, nodding thoughtfully, 'it does seem strange – self-indulgent, even. Yet, if New Sanctaphrax has any purpose at all, it is the pursuit of knowledge. Once we abandon the attempt to deepen our understanding of the way the Edge works, then we may as well all pack up and move to Hive.' He laughed. 'Apart from anything else, it's my own small act of resistance against that monster Quove Lentis.'

Cade thrilled at the words. The more he discovered about his uncle, the more Nate Quarter did remind him of his father.

'What if . . . if you could fall the way you did,' Cade suggested, 'but . . . but control that fall? Charting a free-falling descent,' he said, weighing up each thought. 'If you did that, you could find your way back again, couldn't you?' He looked at his uncle askance. 'Or if you had a ship that—'

'Don't think I haven't thought about it, Cade,' said his uncle, laying a hand on his shoulder, 'but no phraxcraft has ever survived below the High Cliff. The air currents there are just too strong. The vessels end up being smashed against the cliff face.'

'But—' Cade began, only for Nate to interrupt him a second time.

'Seftis got all excited about your father's working drawings when you first arrived, but . . .' He shook his head ruefully. 'Well, you know what happened to the models he built. No, the only way is to descend the cliff face itself, mooring ring by mooring ring, the hard way.'

'The hard way . . .' Cade repeated. He turned to Nate. 'Uncle,' he said, 'what would you say if I told you that one of the models *did* work; that Seftis and I have been working on a full-sized ship – a ship designed especially for you.'

Nate looked at him, hope glowing in his clear blue eyes.

'Is it ready?' he asked.

Cade smiled. 'Almost.'

'Then I'd say, the moment the threat to New Sanctaphrax was over, we'd have to take such a vessel on a test run,' said Nate. He clapped his nephew on the shoulder. 'We would go descending!'

Back at the Armoury at last, Cade noticed that it was quieter than usual, and nowhere near as hot. It would make his work more pleasant, but the reason for the improved conditions was cause for concern. Despite all the sacrifices that had been made by those who now called New Sanctaphrax their home, the materials they'd amassed to be smelted down were rapidly running out.

Theegum looked up the moment Cade stepped into the forge hall, almost as though she'd been waiting for him to get back. Turning away from the bellows, she flung her arms wide. And, grinning, Cade hurried between the piles of phraxchamber cooling plates and hanging nets of ironwood charcoal, and fell into the banderbear's warm embrace.

'Really, Theegum?' came a voice. 'Do we have to endure this performance every time young Quarter enters the Armoury?'

Tutting loudly, the small mottled goblin rolled his eyes, then returned to the molten copperwood alloy he was pouring into the clay mould clamped to the forge bench.

'Theegum's just pleased to see me. Aren't you, Theeg?' laughed Cade. 'How long has it been? Two hours?'

'*Four* hours,' said Seftis Bule sharply. 'Just to pick up a couple of barkscrolls.' He sniffed. 'Still, if it helps us solve this torsion-ratio problem, I suppose it will have been worth it.'

Using long-handled tongs, the chief armourer plunged the ingot into the cooling trough. There was a loud hiss, a cloud of steam, and the metal turned from glowing red to a bright yellow-silver colour. He placed the ingot on the bench and took off his gloves.

'Let's see what you've got, then,' he said, reaching out a hand to take the barkscrolls Cade was clutching – but stopped as Theegum held up a paw, claws raised, before lowering it in a series of fluttering gestures.

'Wuh-wuh, wurgh . . .'

The banderbear's growl was soft and deep in the back of her throat. *'Cade of the far-off lake brings the dust of old learning,'* she said in flowing paw gestures and low growling sounds. *'But new ideas from Sky and Earth also await.'*

She glanced across at Seftis. Cade followed her gaze.

'The little armourer is not good at collaborating with others,' Theegum went on, *'so I, his faithful assistant, have been making arrangements.'* The banderbear gave a tuskless grin. *'When the great fiery ball in the sky reaches its zenith, they will be here . . .'*

'Midday?' said Cade.

'Do you mind not talking about me as if I wasn't here, you infuriating creature,' Seftis huffed, though Cade could see a twinkle in the old goblin's eye. 'And what about "midday"?'

Cade handed the chief armourer the barkscrolls. 'If you spoke banderbear, you'd know.'

'Pah,' said the armourer dismissively. 'All that grunting and flapping about. I'd sooner stick my head in the forge.'

Cade laughed. He knew Seftis didn't really mean it. Ever since he'd first started working in the Armoury, Cade had learned just how close 'the little armourer' and the banderbear were.

'Now, if you'll excuse me,' said Seftis, hurrying off with the barkscrolls, 'I need to take a look at these.'

*

Seftis Bule might have had no interest, but for his part, Cade loved learning banderbear language. It hadn't been easy, but Theegum proved to be an excellent teacher. She was patient and encouraging, and never laughed when he made mistakes. It had taken many weeks, but gradually Cade had picked up the rudiments of the eloquent signing and growled cadences, and as he did so, and learned about Theegum's story, his friendship with her had deepened.

'I was a half-summer cub, newly nested, when the mire-pearlers took me,' the banderbear had told him one afternoon as they sat in the glow of the forge, toasting gladeoak kernels on a long-handled furnace shovel. 'They caged me and taught me to dance at the end of their brazier-heated daggers. I travelled with them across half the mighty woods, in a skyship that carried the scent of death and despair in its belly, dancing that jig of pain and fear.'

Cade had listened with a growing sense of horror.

'But I grew quickly,' she'd continued, 'even on stale rations and regular beatings. Then one day, instead of entertaining the captain with a comic dance on the aft deck, I threw the phraxgunner – my chief tormentor – in the air and gored him with my half-grown tusks. I hardly knew what I was doing, driven half mad by that cruel little blade of his; the woodwasp sting that singed my fur.'

She'd paused, and Cade thought he could hear her heartbeat pounding inside her chest. Then, with low growls and languid body movements, she was off again, narrating the terrible details of her past.

'They beat me till I fell into that blackness that lies beyond sleep, and when I finally found my way back to the realm of light and waking thoughts, I had lost my tusks and was staked to the earth in a mining stockade in the Eastern Woods.

'My new owners were only slightly better than the mire-pearlers, though they sought profit rather than entertainment. I was set to work, hauling heavy lampcrates in their phraxmine . . .'

She had hesitated again, overwhelmed by dark emotions. Cade looked up to see her standing perfectly still, silently reliving that awful time. Then her feathery ears had twitched and, once again, she had resumed her grim tale.

'It was in that underground place of perpetual twilight where I learned from the other slave workers that *there could be another life for the ill-used and downtrodden. One night I summoned what strength I had and tore my chains from the mineshaft wall.'* Her gestures had become short and choppy. *'And I began my long journey to the fabled floating city, like so many others before me.*

'I took the Trail of Ghosts along the very edge of the world, with the Twilight Woods on one side of the rocky pavement and the drop into the eternal void on the other. Hungry, cold, exhausted, I finally reached the grasslands of the Mire. I gathered meadowgrass and constructed a nest from what memories I could recall of my mother, who had taught me as a half-summer cub. Then I lay down to die.'

Cade had listened intently, eyes misting and a lump in his throat that he was unable to swallow away.

'I was happy to be free at last, away from the torments of the fourthling world, and ready to go into those Nightwoods from which no one returns.' She'd looked up, her dark eyes glittering. *'That's when Seftis, the little armourer, found me. I was as weak as the cub I had once been, and so thin that even he could pull me easily on a sumpwood sledge.*

'He took me back to Great Glade first, then brought me, as he had brought others, to the floating city. And here at the Knights Academy, with my head in the clouds, I came back to life.

'My tusks, of course, are lost for ever and will never grow back, but I felt my spirit return, and with it a thirst for life. The Armoury warms me like a sun-drenched glade, the rafters ripple like wind-filled groves, and I can repay the little armourer for restoring me to this world of light . . .'

That conversation had been two months ago or more. And since then, whenever Cade entered or left the Armoury, he had felt himself enveloped in the warmth of a banderbear embrace.

'Well?' said Seftis Bule, impatiently thumbing through the barkscrolls in his hands. 'I'm still waiting to hear what is happening at midday.'

'I don't know,' Cade admitted. 'I think Theegum's arranged for me to meet someone, though she didn't say who.' He turned to her. 'Theegum?' he said.

'*A long wait produces the sweetest fruit,*' she told him cryptically, and returned her attention to the bellows.

'She says I need to be patient,' said Cade. 'I think.'

Seftis rolled his eyes. 'Well, in the meantime,' he said, 'there's something I want to show you.' He took Cade by the arm and steered him back towards his small office. 'We've been making some real progress with the vessel.' He smiled. 'Your father's remarkable working drawings continue to reveal their secrets.'

As they stepped through the doorway, Cade's gaze fell on the miniature engine that the armourer had built. There was something different about it.

'You remember how we incorporated the discoveries your friend made, back at the Farrow Lake?' Seftis said.

Cade nodded. Like Thorne Lammergyre's model, this one also had four satellite chambers that endlessly orbited the main phraxchamber in a smooth blur of movement, whirring and thrumming as it did so. There was a small propulsion pipe emitting a tiny jet of white flame, and a miniature funnel, steam streaming out of it in an unbroken line.

'Well, we've made a couple of extra modifications,' said Seftis, pointing to a series of spoke-like rods, each one topped with a glass disc. 'Mirrors,' he explained. 'Convex and concave. They both diffuse the phraxlight and reflect it back on itself, increasing the energy potential – twentyfold so far, but we're hoping for more.'

Cade inspected the model closely. 'And this is my father's design?' he asked.

'From the third barkscroll,' Seftis said, nodding. 'It's ingenious. We're *so* close now, but there's still one little problem.' He patted the barkscrolls Cade had just brought him. 'Hopefully these will help solve it. Come through to the workshop and I'll show you how it'll work on the vessel itself . . .'

Just then the door opened and Cade and Seftis turned to see Theegum standing in the doorway. Her head inclined to one side, she waved a paw then gestured back behind her.

'They're here,' said Cade.

'Yes, even I could work that one out,' said Seftis. 'Go then, Cade. And while you're having your mysterious meeting,' he added, 'I shall continue our work. Your uncle might still be sceptical that a ship can descend beneath the Edge . . .' He chuckled. 'But I'm not.'

*

Cade emerged through the heavy ironwood doorway of the Armoury to see a phraxlighter hovering in the air above the stairs. He was surprised to see that there was only one academic on board. With his oiled hair, plaited beard and blue-grey robes of New Sanctaphrax, Cade recognized him at once. It was Grent One-Tusk of the Loftus Observatory, the long-hair who had invited him to go stone-spotting. Despite his obvious fear of flying that day, he was piloting the vessel.

'Welcome aboard,' Grent called from the small wheelhouse as Cade jumped up onto the deck. 'We're off to see Tug.'

Cade nodded, then sat down on the seat opposite him. Grent pushed the flight lever forward and the phraxlighter rose slowly and gently up into the air. Then, once they'd flown clear of the great floating rock, it started its descent towards Undergarden.

Cade chuckled. 'Has he found a new statue?' he asked.

Grent looked back at him, puzzled.

'Tug,' said Cade. 'He's always adding to his collection in that sculpture garden of his.'

'Oh, Tug isn't here,' said the long-hair as he turned the wheel slowly round. 'He's in the Stone Gardens.'

'But the Stone Gardens are in the opposite direction,' said Cade. 'Back that way,' he added.

He looked over the side – which was when he caught sight of Celestia.

'Am I glad to see you,' he said as Grent brought the phraxlighter to a hover beside her. 'I heard you'd been injured.'

'It's just a scratch,' said Celestia dismissively. 'Nothing Tug and Fenda couldn't handle.'

She turned to the fettle-legger in the green-trimmed robes at her side and smiled, and Cade recognized her as the Earth scholar he'd met the same day he'd first met Grent. Fenda Fulefane, from the School of Moss.

'Actually, we're on our way to see Tug now,' Celestia added.

'I know,' said Cade, and laughed. 'It seems we're the ones taking you.'

Reaching down, he took Celestia by the arm and pulled her up onto the little vessel. He gave her a hug that made her wince. Cade pulled away.

'Oh, Celestia,' he said apologetically. 'I'm sorry – it's just so good to see you!'

Celestia smiled bravely. 'It's good to see you too, Cade,' she reassured him. 'Oh, and before I forget, thank you for lending me this.' She pulled the spyglass from inside her jacket and handed it to him.

'You keep it for me,' Cade said. 'It's brought you luck once, Celestia, and while I'm busy in the Armoury I like to think of you out here making more use of it.'

The phraxlighter took to the air. Cade and Celestia were sitting next to one another, with Fenda on the bench opposite, her powerful legs tucked back beneath her as, under Grent's expert hand, they flew back over the lush vegetation of Undergarden, past the great floating city, and on towards the boulder stacks of the Stone Gardens.

Three days she'd been asleep, according to Fenda Fulefane. That was all. Yet in that time, Celestia was surprised to learn, the situation in New Sanctaphrax had deteriorated still further.

'The Academy of Mistsifters and half the colleges on the Viaduct have all but given up the struggle,' Cade told her. 'They've had enough of the blockade and want to give in to Great Glade's demands. Which means—'

'The end of descending,' Celestia said.

'Worse than that,' said Cade, his expression grim. 'Quove Lentis has ordered that any skymarshals they capture be taken to Great Glade for trial.'

Celestia snorted. 'Which no doubt means torture,' she said. 'From everything I've heard about that monster, it seems he will do anything and everything he can to discover how he might destroy New Sanctaphrax.'

'Precisely,' said Cade. 'Which is why,' he added, remembering what Nate had told him, 'my Aunt Eudoxia is away at this very moment. She has a meeting with someone she hopes will ensure that never happens.'

· CHAPTER FIFTEEN ·

Outside the light tower, the dense fog swirl was beginning to clear at last. A wind had got up and the jagged pinnacles along the cliff edge were funnelling the air currents. The otherworldly howl it created was music to any tallow-hat's ears. It kept all but the most intrepid Edgelanders well away from this region of fabled ghosts and demons.

Danton Clore, the leader of the tallow-hats, took two dark red candles from the box on the shelf. Then, having trimmed the ends, he pushed them into the holders on either side of the broad-brimmed hat he was holding.

The tallow itself was of the finest quality, carefully extracted and meticulously rendered down from the roots of the bloodoak, the legendary flesh-eating tree found only in the darkest, densest areas of the Deep-woods. When lit, the tallow candles gave off an eerie, misty light and rich, pungent fumes that were believed

both to sharpen the reflexes and give courage. But such candles were rare and highly prized, and the tallow-hats only used them for special occasions.

Clore placed the hat on his head and looked at his reflection in the small copperwood mirror that hung from the cabin wall. The angry scar on his cheek – the result of a dispute with a disreputable shryke trader – was a reminder to Clore to temper courage with caution.

He'd been younger back then, hot-blooded and impatient to make his way in the world. The stilt factories of Great Glade were not for him, never had been. He'd craved adventure – and had known where to find it.

In the First Age of Flight, Danton Clore imagined that he would have been a sky pirate, signing up to one of the legendary crews of a skygalleon and exacting a toll from the fat skyships of the Undertown leagues. In the Second Age of Flight, Clore saw himself as a Freeglade Lancer, serving under General Rook Barkwater himself in the wars of the Goblin Nations. And now, here in this Third Age, far from meddlesome busybodies and surrounded by the unearthly howls of those ghosts and demons, Danton Clore was exactly where he wanted to be.

He looked at his reflection for a moment longer, then, reaching into his topcoat, he took out a pouch of pine-resin matches and struck one on the brim of his hat. He lit the first tallow candle, then the other, and took a long, deep breath.

Several weeks earlier, something had happened. Something that should not have happened. Time and again, Danton Clore had relived the raid that was meant to be routine, but had ended so tragically in Great Glade, always coming to the same conclusion.

The tallow-hats had been betrayed.

But Clore would not be rushed into a hasty decision. He prided himself on his fairness. Pausing for a moment before he left his cabin, he went over the events of that fateful day one last time . . .

Skylancer came in low over the treetops, emerging from the eerie golden glow cast by the distant Twilight Woods. On either side of the four-funnel phraxvessel were two more skyships of a similar distinctive design. *Rainhawk* and *Cloudbreaker*.

With their long 'beaked' prows, their clustered phraxchambers feeding low, curving propulsion ducts, and twin rudders on either side of armoured sterns, these were cloudcruisers, the fastest phraxships in the Edgelands.

At the wheel of *Skylancer*, Danton Clore felt the harness straps bite into his shoulders as he pushed the phraxchambers to full power. Beside him, *Rainhawk* and *Cloudbreaker* did the same.

The slow, cumbersome merchant ship never stood a chance. Not only was it clad with heavy ironwood, but its cargo holds were full of phrax crystals, packed into huge lamp-crates and weighing the vessel down. Phrax-guns peppered its open portholes. Each one was spitting out a steady stream of bullets – but they merely

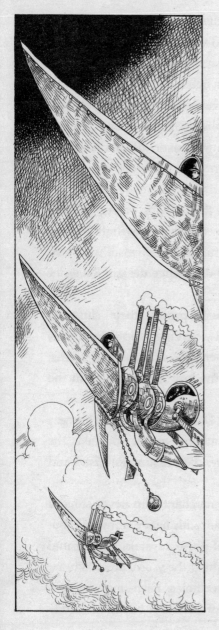

clattered harmlessly off the approaching cloud-cruisers' armoured hulls.

Rainhawk and *Cloud-breaker* abruptly peeled away, flying high and drawing the merchant ship's fire as *Skylancer* dived low for a second time. It was a dangerous manoeuvre, but Danton Clore held his nerve. Gripping the wheel tightly, he braced himself for impact.

A loud *crunch* echoed through the air as the cloudcruiser's beaked prow smashed into the side of the merchant ship's wheelhouse with pinpoint precision, just below the phraxchamber. The wheelhouse disintegrated as *Skylancer* ploughed through it and sped on, then turned in a tight, banking arc and cut its engines. *Rainhawk* and

Cloudbreaker rejoined *Skylancer*, and the three cloud-cruisers closed in on the hapless merchant ship like hungry woodwolves stalking a wounded hammelhorn.

Along the bow of the merchant vessel, portholes were clattering shut, and the silhouettes of fleeing figures, stark against the glowing sky, could be seen clambering up on deck and climbing into small phraxlighters strapped to the stern. One after the other, the phraxlighters took off and steamed away, watched by the three cloudcruisers but not pursued.

Lying among the splintered ruins of the wheelhouse of the merchant ship, now abandoned by its top brass, were the expensively brocaded green topcoats of the captain and senior officers of the Great Glade Academy of Flight. Undamaged, the phraxchamber thrummed, keeping the vessel hovering motionless, if somewhat lopsidedly, in the air.

'Prepare the grappling chains,' Danton Clore called back to his crew in the stern. 'Looks like Great Glade is going to have to pay the tallow tax . . .'

'They did what they always do,' said Danton Clore. 'As soon as we caught up with them, the officers threw off their fancy uniforms and snuck off in phraxlighters, leaving the crew to fight us.' He shook his head. 'Every time . . . The moment I take out the wheelhouse, they simply abandon ship.'

He was standing on the balcony of his light tower, a sturdy timber-frame cabin with a lamp glowing at the

top of its conical roof. The light tower had been built on a platform that was bolted securely to the side of a floating rock. Two other rocks, each with a light tower of their own, floated close by. Chains connected the three of them, one to the other, and then to an anchor ring which was secured to a pinnacle.

Every one of these floating rocks was large enough to have supported the stern and prow of a mighty skygalleon in the First Age of Flight. Now, in these days of phrax-powered skyvessels, they served as a berth for the small, sleek cloud-cruisers of the tallow-hats. *Skylancer*, *Rainhawk* and *Cloudbreaker* were each tethered to their respective rocks. Further along the cliff edge, as far as the eye could see, other clusters of floating rocks swayed in the swirling winds, the lamps of the light towers clamped to them twinkling like a constellation.

'Things have changed, that much is clear,' said the pilot of *Cloudbreaker*, a dour-faced grey goblin called Thane Two-Blades. Behind him, his crew – a gnokgoblin and a hammerhead – nodded grimly. 'Kendius and the others found that out the hard way.'

'Tell me *exactly* what happened,' said Danton Clore, turning to the youngest member of the crew of *Rainhawk*, a fourthling who answered to the name 'Splinters'.

'I already have,' came the reply. 'Nothing's changed.'

'Indulge me,' said Danton Clore, a harsh edge to his voice.

'Well,' said Splinters, with a barely suppressed sigh, 'we towed the merchant ship to the usual glade in the Eastern Woods, just outside the phraxmine stockade. But, like I said, instead of the mine sergeant waiting to pay us our tallow tax, there was a squadron of Freeglade Lancers. They had the whole place staked out and—'

'I'm still having trouble understanding this,' Danton Clore broke in, removing his broad-brimmed hat and examining the blood-red candles, their wicks neatly trimmed. 'Why would the phrax commander double-cross us like this?'

He left the question hanging in the air for a moment before continuing.

'We have a deal,' he said simply. '*We* hijack the cargo of phrax, take it back to be re-stamped at the mine; *he* gets to sell the same cargo twice to the Academy of Flight. We both win. Unless . . .'

Danton Clore's eyes narrowed. The wind had dropped and a damp blanket of fog was settling over the pinnacles like a shroud. He turned back to the young fourthling.

'You piloted *Rainhawk* back here, Splinters, single-handed,' he said.

'That's right, Mr Clore, sir,' the youth replied, breaking into a gap-toothed grin. 'And she flew like a beauty. The Great Gladers couldn't keep up . . .'

'You left Kendius and the cloddertrogs to be taken prisoner,' said Danton Clore quietly, tracing the rim of a candle with a fingernail, 'to be chained and hauled off to Great Glade, where they were fed to those hideous snaggletooths of Quove Lentis.'

'I got lucky,' Splinters said defiantly, although there was a tremor in his voice. He was no longer smiling.

Clore nodded almost imperceptibly. 'Does the name Drax Adereth mean anything to you?' he asked as he examined the second candle.

'Yeah, he ran a gang on the skytavern I used to crew. What of it?' Splinters' eyes were wide, and he was looking to the others for support.

But the other tallow-hats were avoiding his gaze.

'What if I was to tell you that Drax Adereth is one of Quove Lentis's spies?' said Danton Clore slowly. He put his hat back on and fixed the youth with an unblinking stare. 'Are *you* a spy, Splinters?'

'I . . . I . . .'

The fourthling gasped, then stumbled forward, his face contorting with pain. He tumbled to the deck. Thane Two-Blades stepped over the body, wiping the blood from the blade of the stiletto dagger on the sleeve of his topcoat.

'We'd better move our stone harbours somewhere else,' the grey goblin said. 'Somewhere safer. Splinters here has probably led the whole Great Glade phraxfleet to us.'

Danton Clore shrugged. 'I doubt it,' he said. 'The Great Glade phraxfleet has its hands full with the blockade of New Sanctaphrax.' He shook his head thoughtfully. 'But if, as I'm beginning to suspect, Phrax Commander Lennius Grex is no longer in charge, then there'll be no more tallow tax, and the next merchant ship we take on might be a whole lot harder to hijack.'

He prodded Splinters' body with the tip of his boot.

'Everything changes,' he mused. 'Perhaps we should also turn our attention to New Sanctaphrax. I'm about to have a meeting with one of their beleaguered leaders. Eudoxia something or other. It seems she wants our help,' he said and laughed. 'And we tallow-hats are nothing if not helpful.'

Clore pushed the body with his foot, sending it tumbling off the deck and down into the gathering fog. The wind through the pinnacles picked up with an eerie howl.

'Just one more ghost,' he muttered, 'to sing us to sleep.'

Then he turned and went into the light tower, closing the door behind him.

· CHAPTER SIXTEEN ·

A s Grent One-Tusk brought the phraxlighter down low over the Stone Gardens, Cade immediately spotted Tug. His friend was stooped over next to a towering stone stack, his massive shoulder muscles rippling as he delicately scraped at the ground beneath him with his long, curved claws.

With Fenda Fulefane's help, Grent landed the phraxlighter. Celestia climbed shakily to her feet, while Cade jumped down and secured the vessel to a rock with a tolley rope. Then, one after the other, the others followed him off the hovering phraxlighter and onto the rocky ground below.

They were greeted by a small blue waif who was, it seemed, closely monitoring Tug's work. She stared at them intently, her eyes wide, then raised her hands. And in their heads they heard her speaking.

'*Quiet, please,*' she said, her voice low and urgent. '*Twilight is upon us and Tug must work quickly.*'

With the sun low and the light fading, the stacks of buoyant rocks, each boulder larger than the one below it, were casting long shadows across the stone pavement. High above the visitors to the Stone Gardens, white ravens circled, their angular wings outstretched as they glided on swirling up-currents, and their raucous cries filling the air.

Tug clearly hadn't noticed the arrival of his friends, for he continued to scratch away at the stone at his feet, working with painstaking attention. Intrigued, Celestia approached, only to feel a hand on her sleeve.

'*Not yet,*' the voice sounded in her head, and, glancing down, she found herself gazing into the waif's clear blue, and disapproving, eyes.

Celestia turned her attention back to Tug himself. Leaning so far forward now that his nose was almost touching the ground, he was gently blowing the dust away from the small hole he'd been digging in the rocky ground. Then, with obvious care, he reached down into the hole with his talons and removed a glowing pebble, roughly the size of a white raven's egg.

'*A seed-stone,*' the voice in her head informed her. '*And beautifully harvested – like all the rest. Your friend Tug has a great talent indeed . . .*' The waif smiled. '*But then you know that already, Miss Helmstoft.*'

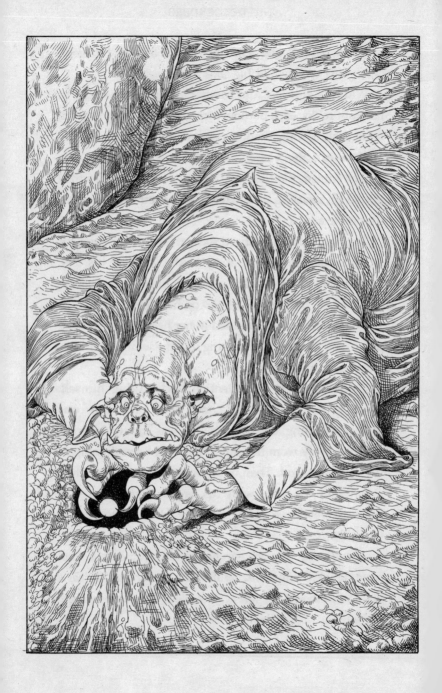

Just then, a tall quarry trog stepped forward, a small casket in her hands. She lifted the lid to reveal a glowing lamp inside, then held it out. Tug placed the seed-stone carefully inside the casket and looked up – and as he caught sight of his friends, a lopsided grin broke across his features. He lumbered over to them and swept Celestia off her feet, enfolding her in an enthusiastic but surprisingly gentle embrace.

'Tug happy you well again,' he crooned. 'Tug did what you teached him. Cleaned and dressed wound with mosswort and hyleberry salve . . .'

'Yes, yes, and you did it very well,' laughed Celestia as Tug placed her back on the ground. 'And it seems that while I've been out patrolling with the skymarshals, you and Cade have made some fine new friends.'

'It's true, isn't it, Tug?' said Cade, smiling. 'We all sit at the same refectory table now,' he explained, and nodded to each of the academics who had gathered round. 'Grent One-Tusk here is an expert on storm-stones and their origins. Fenda has been studying the blue moss spores found on those stones, and—'

'I am Sentafuce,' said the waif, speaking aloud now that Tug's painstaking work was complete. 'Professor Sentafuce. And I am interested in the origin of clouds, while my colleague Demora Duste here has devoted her life to studying these magnificent Stone Gardens.'

The quarry trog nodded and held up the casket.

'Tug has been helping us to harvest seed-stones,' Sentafuce went on. 'The work is difficult. You see, they only reveal themselves at twilight, when their glow can be detected below the surface. Then they must be excavated with extreme precision and at great speed to avoid disintegration.'

Demora laid a hand on Tug's shoulder. 'Tug here has my strength and Sentafuce's delicate touch,' she said, causing Tug himself to turn a bashful red. 'Without him,' the quarry trog went on, 'we would never have made the progress we have.'

'Progress?' said Celestia, looking around at the smiling faces.

'We are all working for the High Academe Elect,' said Fenda Fulefane, lowering the burnished copperwood spyglass she'd been using to scan the horizon. 'It was he who brought us all together in the first place to carry out his plans. Sky willing,' she added, 'we'll have completed those plans before Quove Lentis loses patience and launches his phraxfleet. We've been hearing rumours of an imminent attack.'

Cade nodded. 'We're in an even worse position than you and your skymarshals, Celestia,' he told her with a rueful smile. 'You see, it's Descenders that Great Glade truly hates. And we're all Descenders – or at least, we will be if this blockade ever ends.'

'Come,' said Demora. 'We need to get this seed-stone back to Seftis Bule without further delay.'

They all climbed back aboard the phraxlighter, and when everyone had taken their seats, Grent One-Tusk powered up the phraxchamber and they took off, a trail of steam coiling away behind them. Cade and Celestia fell into conversation about the skymarshals, and how she'd happened to get wounded, with Tug chipping in about how deep the bullet had gone, when suddenly Fenda Fulefane let out a cry of alarm. Standing up now, her spyglass trained on the horizon, she was hopping agitatedly from one taloned foot to the other.

'There! There!' she shouted, pointing.

The others followed the line of her outstretched arm. Sentafuce groaned with dismay, a sound that echoed in all their heads.

The rumours had finally become reality. Quove Lentis's Great Glade phraxfleet was on its way to attack New Sanctaphrax.

His hands a blur of movement, Grent immediately changed course, bringing the phraxlighter round in a broad arc and steering it down towards Undergarden. They'd barely managed to moor up and disembark before the sky above them filled with enemy phraxfrigates and the sound of artillery fire.

'Take cover!' Cade bellowed.

Up in the great floating city of New Sanctaphrax, alarms were sounding. The mist horns boomed from the towers of the Academy of Rain; the wind hammers and hail gongs resonated all along the Upper Viaduct; while the sonorous beat of the barrel drums on the East and West Landings rumbled ominously through the streets.

Academics spilled out from gates and doorways, clasping phraxpistols and muskets, and fastening pieces of armour as they ran. In the courtyard of the Knights Academy, the ranks of skymarshals assembled rapidly and with tidy precision. Then, in groups of ten, they leaped into the saddles of their skycraft, powered up the phraxchambers and took to the air.

High above the bustle of the streets, the sky-marshals formed themselves into three bristling waves, each of them two hundred strong and positioned one above the other. Then, all at once, responding to the raised arm of the pilot at the front of the squad-ron, they gave full power to their phraxchambers, gripped their tillers and soared off fast, flying over

Undergarden and out across the evening sky to confront the enemy fleet.

Advancing towards them in arrowhead formations came the Great Glade phraxvessels. Triple-funnelled phraxlaunches were out in front, flanked by smaller single-funnel attack ships. Then, bringing up the rear of each formation, came a mighty phraxfrigate, towing barges packed with phraxmarines. Spreading across the horizon there were more than two hundred and fifty vessels of different sizes: the entire battle fleet of Quove Lentis's Academy of Flight.

At a safe distance behind the advancing armada was the skyvessel of the new phrax commander. Unlike the armoured, shuttered fighting ships, with their phrax-cannon ports and mounted swivel-guns, the *Progress of Plenty* resembled an ornate skytavern, complete with viewing platforms and pleasure gantries decked out in chequerboard flags and garlands. And on the gleaming aft deck sat Quove Lentis himself, dressed in a simple green uniform and plain crushed funnel hat that was pulled down low over his bloated features.

His former phrax commander, Lennius Grex, had proved useless, and his replacement hadn't fared any better. The recent attack on two of his phraxfrigates had been the last straw. High Professor of Flight Quove Lentis wanted revenge. Putting himself in overall command, he'd finally given the order for the Great Glade fleet to attack. The renegade upstarts of New Sanctaphrax would be destroyed once and for all.

Stationed on either side of Quove Lentis, and looking somewhat uncomfortable, were two phrax admirals, kitted out in all their finery – the brocaded topcoats and plumed bicorne hats making a tempting target for any sharp-eyed skymarshal. Standing behind him was Captain Felicia Adereth. She leaned forward.

'The fleet is closing in as ordered, High Professor,' she whispered in Quove's ear. 'And I made sure to place the captains who are critical of your battle plans in the front rank of the formations.'

'Marvellous,' said Quove Lentis with a low chuckle. 'Let them bear the brunt of the skymarshals' counterattack.' He smiled greedily. 'Then the frigates can finally take control of the floating city.'

Raising a silver spyglass to his eye, Quove looked ahead. His face hardened. What he saw did not please him.

The first wave of skymarshals had levelled their long-barrelled phraxmuskets, and the line of their skycraft glittered like a string of marsh-gems as they fired. The effect was immediate. The first arrowhead formations of the Great Glade fleet buckled as phrax captain after phrax captain collapsed in the wheelhouses, sending their ships careering out of control. Numerous attack ships spiralled to the earth and exploded as they crashed into the verdant pastures of Undergarden below.

Not that the defenders of the floating city were getting it all their own way. As Quove Lentis continued to watch, he saw his Great Glade phraxships return heavy fire, the swivel-guns of the phraxlaunches sending a hail of bullets into the ranks of skymarshals. The sky became crisscrossed with steam trails and yellow tracer fire as the formation broke up and unseated skymarshals toppled to their deaths.

Then, like a great pendulum, the battle swung back in the skymarshals' favour once more.

Rallying their number for a renewed attack, the second and third wave of the skymarshal squadron opened fire. More arrowheads were blunted, with the phraxlaunches losing control, crashing into each other and bursting into flame. Behind them, one of the huge barges snapped its tow rope and plummeted out of the sky, causing the desperate phraxmarines on board to leap over the side in an attempt to save their lives.

Suddenly the booming call of a skyhorn rang out. The phraxfrigates abruptly turned sideways on and set a new course. They flew along the waves of skymarshals at full steam, their gun ports blazing.

For a moment, a dense billowing fog of steam engulfed the lines of battling skycraft, and the pungent odour of burnt almonds filled the air. When it cleared, dozens of individual steam trails were revealed, the white lines leading down through the sky to small explosions on the ground, each one a disintegrating skycraft.

The remaining skymarshals were scattered. Swarming in twos and threes around the larger vessels of the Great Glade fleet, they looked like tackflies buzzing around hammelhorns. More phraxships were toppled, but the phraxmarines in the barges towed by the frigates had by now levelled their phraxmuskets and were steadily picking off the skymarshals, one by one.

'Excellent, excellent.' Quove Lentis smiled from the safe vantage point on the foredeck of the *Progress of Plenty*. 'The skymarshals are falling back at last. Now the phraxmarines can get to work.' He glanced back over his shoulder. 'I trust that my order was made clear to my captains.'

'It was,' Captain Adereth confirmed. She leaned forward again and spoke softly. 'Kill them all. Spare no one.'

'I should be up there with Brock and the others,' said Celestia, her voice trembling with emotion.

Cade nodded, but he was glad that she was standing beside him.

An hour had passed since the sky battle first began, but they were still spectators, staring up at the deadly combat that raged in the skies above their heads. The two of them were standing in Tug's sculpture garden on the banks of the Edgewater River, along with Tug himself. Cade and Celestia held phraxmuskets; Tug was clutching a long-handled scythe. Like the ancient statues around them, all three stood rooted to the spot.

Craters, where skycraft had crashed and their phraxchambers exploded, pock-marked the pastures on the far side of the river, while the wreckage of phraxlaunches and attack ships lay blazing in the gardens below the floating city. High above them, the Great Glade phraxfleet was now closing in on the East and West Landings, both of which had been cleared of defenders by the attackers' relentless phraxfire.

It was looking as though it would all soon be over, with Quove Lentis's phraxfleet victorious.

The skymarshals – or what was now left of them – had brought their skycraft in to hover among the tallest towers of the city. They were returning fire as best they could, but it was not enough. Several academy towers on the Great Viaduct had been hit by phraxcannon and were on fire; the stonework of the Loftus Observatory was peppered with phraxbullet holes.

'It would be suicide to attempt to get up to the city now,' Cade said through gritted teeth. 'We should go down into the sewers and plan a counterattack.'

Grent, Fenda and the others were already down there, barricading the laboratory and stockpiling equipment and supplies. But Celestia couldn't take her eyes off the terrible sky-battle. As she watched, two mighty frigates towing barges full of Great Glade phraxmarines wheeled round and closed in on the East and West Landings.

For a moment, the two sides were locked in conflict, trading fire. It was difficult to tell who had the upper hand. But then, without any warning, the phraxmusket fire from the towers abruptly stopped.

The skymarshals had run out of ammunition.

Celestia trained Cade's spyglass on the East Landing. A group of academics in blue-grey robes – mistsifters by the look of them, and no friends of descending – had emerged from the side streets, their hands up, and were walking in a line across the timber boards. They wanted to surrender. But then, from one of the barges, a volley of phraxmusket fire broke out – followed by another and another . . .

When the steam cleared, the landing was littered with bodies.

Celestia lowered the spyglass. Beside her, Tug's muscles tensed as his grip tightened on the scythe. Cade's face had drained of colour.

'Murderers,' he breathed.

It was over. New Sanctaphrax had been beaten. And so quickly . . .

But then, as Cade and Celestia were on the point of giving up all hope, seemingly out of nowhere, something glinted in the evening sky; something sleek and shiny and very, very fast.

· CHAPTER SEVENTEEN ·

The phrax-powered cloudcruisers sped in across the sky, their armoured prows gleaming in the last glow of twilight. As the vessels went into a steep dive, the low thrum of their phraxchambers turned to a high-pitched whine, and plaited trails of steam stretched out from the multiple funnels like a fisher goblin's net.

Cade, Celestia and Tug watched from below, hearts in their mouths, as the cloudcruisers smashed into the Great Glade fleet that was hovering at the East and West Landings. Their beak-like prows sliced deftly through the aft decks of the phraxfrigates, severing them from the phraxchamber at the heart of each vessel. One after another, the frigates plummeted out of the sky, raining down debris and bodies as they fell.

'Into the tunnels!' Fenda Fulefane shouted from the entrance to her sewer laboratory as the pastures along

the banks of the Edgewater lit up with explosions from the falling phraxchambers. 'All of you! Now!'

High above, blazing buoyant timber from the disintegrating phraxships shot upwards in sparkling constellations, vivid against the darkening sky. A little way off, a swivel-gun crashed into the earth, shattering a group of ancient statues and sending stone shards flying off in all directions.

Tug tossed his scythe aside, swept Cade and Celestia off their feet and ran, head down and shoulders hunched, towards the sewer entrance. Behind them, his sculpture garden was suddenly engulfed in a ball of flame as the swivel-gun's phrax mechanism exploded. Cade glanced back to catch sight of a group of tall-hatted figures, their impassive carved faces staring out from the inferno.

Tug ducked inside the arched opening to the sewer and fell to his knees, releasing his hold on Celestia and Cade, who tumbled gratefully to the stone floor. Celestia sprang to her feet.

'Tug, you're hurt!' she exclaimed, immediately pulling phials and tied-up bundles from her flight tunic.

Cade looked. She was right. Tug's back was peppered with jagged fragments of stone from the shattered statues.

'Tug not hurt,' he said as Celestia began picking the bloody shards out of his shoulders with tweezers and applying a sweet-smelling salve. His small deep-set eyes narrowed, and he shuddered. 'Tug has suffered much worse.'

'*Yes, yes, dear Tug,*' Sentafuce's voice sounded in all their heads. '*But the horrors of the Nightwoods are behind you now.*'

She, Fenda Fulefane, Grent One-Tusk and Demora Duste had gathered together in the darkness of the arched sewer entrance. As Celestia dressed Tug's back, they all looked out on the inferno that gripped Undergarden. The pastures and fields beyond were lit up with countless fires, large and small, that flared then died out as blazing debris from the sky battle continued to fall.

Celestia handed Cade his uncle's spyglass, and Cade trained it on the floating city.

At the West Landing, the cloudcruisers had circled back round. They were hovering in the air now, their prows pointing menacingly at the remaining phraxfrigates and barges, the decks of the Great Glade vessels crowded with phraxmarines. Some sort of dialogue must have been going on, Cade concluded, because, as he watched, Quove Lentis's phraxlaunches and frigates slowly wheeled round and headed back the way they'd come.

The cloudcruisers rose in the sky to let what remained of the Great Glade phraxfleet steam back across the glowing fires in Undergarden. Then, like woodwolves shadowing a tilder herd, they pursued the retreating Great Glade vessels until they entered the grasslands beyond and disappeared into the night.

With the enemy fleet gone, the cloudcruisers – a hundred or so in Cade's estimation – returned to the floating

city they had just rescued. On the West Landing, academics were now crowding the boards, waving and cheering as the vessels began to throw down tolley ropes to dock.

'Who *are* they?' Cade said in awe. 'And where did they come from?'

'Tallow-hats,' said a soft, familiar voice. 'And *I* sent for them.'

Cade and the others turned to see Eudoxia, her storm-grey travelling cape around her shoulders. She was standing at the entrance to one of the sewer tunnels on the far side of the chamber. In the flickering light of the lamp she was holding, her face looked drawn and weary.

'We've been expecting Great Glade to attack for some time now,' she said quietly, her voice amplified by the stone vaults above as she stepped towards them. 'Quove Lentis had grown impatient with his blockade and decided to gamble everything. To have any hope of defeating him, we also had to gamble.'

Cade nodded thoughtfully. The tallow-hats certainly had a reputation for pursuing their own interests. But today they had proved themselves worthy allies – and formidable fighters.

'The Friends of New Sanctaphrax in Gorgetown, Hive and Riverrise – and Great Glade itself – all pooled their resources to buy the services of the tallow-hats,' Eudoxia went on, turning to Cade. 'While you and your friends were working for Nate on his descending plans, I was negotiating to secure outside help.' She gave a little shrug. 'There are plenty in the New Sanctaphrax academies who disapprove of both.'

She took Cade's arm and guided him back across the gallery, motioning to the others to follow.

'Thank Sky I was able to make a deal – *and* that the tallow-hats arrived in time,' she went on. 'Another week or so, and the Academies of Mist and Rain would have caved in and accepted all Quove Lentis's demands.' She turned and looked into Cade's face. 'You must have seen what happened up on the East Landing when the academics tried to surrender.'

Cade nodded dully.

'It's a terrible tragedy that lives were lost,' said Eudoxia, 'but at least now everyone here in New Sanctaphrax understands just how ruthless Quove Lentis truly is.'

They walked on through the tunnel and, at the far end, took a left turn into another. None of them had ever gone this deep into the sewers before.

'Where exactly are we going?' Cade asked.

'You'll see,' said Eudoxia with a smile.

The maze of underground waterways had been constructed centuries earlier – back before the great exodus; back when Undergarden was still Undertown, a bustling industrial city with a population numbering many thousands. A feat of engineering, the vast sewerage system had been maintained by a small army of workers.

Today, it was neglected. Tangles of nethergrass and black fern clogged the walkways, while ferocious creatures were said to lurk in its dark corners – muglumps: huge armoured predators with six thick-set limbs and a whiplash tail that paced the ceilings and sniffed the air for intruders. Bat-like shadowflits and shriekmice were flapping silently through the dank air; sleek oozefish swimming in the filthy water at the bottom of the tunnels, seeking out prey.

Cade turned to Celestia. 'Keep close,' he whispered.

Celestia didn't need to be told twice. She was at home up in the airy light of the forest canopy, not down here in these cold dark tunnels. The ceilings dripped and the walls were slimy, while underfoot the thick mud reduced their progress to a slow trudge. She hated it.

'I wish we'd get to wherever we're going,' she whispered back.

Eudoxia, by contrast, seemed oblivious to their sur-roundings. Striding confidently ahead, she had turned the conversation to descending which, now that the Great Glade phraxfleet of Quove Lentis had been defeated, might finally be resumed.

'I trust Danton Clore,' she told Cade. 'He's proved his worth. With him and his tallow-hats on hand to defend New Sanctaphrax, the denizens can return to their efforts beneath the Edge. Nate will be overjoyed,' she added.

Cade was puzzled. 'But surely Nate won't want to descend now,' he said. 'After all, as High Academe he'll have to oversee the running of New Sanctaphrax—'

'Cade Quarter!' Eudoxia said sharply – causing Cade to turn, wondering what he'd said wrong. 'I managed to "oversee the running of New Sanctaphrax", as you put it, for fourteen years while Nate was away. I daresay I can do it again.'

'I'm sorry . . . I didn't mean . . . I . . .'

His aunt's face melted into a smile and she reached across and squeezed his arm. 'I'm teasing,' she said. 'Nate and I have discussed it. As I always say to him, "You concentrate on the future and I'll worry about the present."'

Cade nodded. He'd heard his uncle say the self-same thing back on the Viaduct Steps.

'I'd assumed he wanted to descend again so that he could find that missing friend of his, the Professor,' said Cade. 'But from what he told me, it's so much more than that . . .'

'I know,' said Eudoxia. 'For Nate, the unknown world that lies beneath the Edge is no less than the final frontier of knowledge, just waiting to be explored. He believes that if its secrets can be unlocked, then the academic endeavours of the last thousand years will finally bear fruit. In short, Cade, that the mystery of life itself in the Edge will be revealed.'

'And ... do *you* believe that as well, Aunt Eudoxia?' Cade asked softly.

Eudoxia laughed, breaking the spell that she had woven. 'It really doesn't matter what I believe,' she said. 'Once Nate sets his heart on achieving something, nothing will deter him.' She hesitated. 'As I'm sure you understand, Cade. After all,' she added, 'you're just like him.'

Cade thrilled at the words. But, like him? Like the great Descender, Nate Quarter? Surely not. Even this short trudge through the sewers was proving an ordeal.

He had completely lost his bearings by now – and was beginning to think that Eudoxia had too. And judging by the long sighs and muttering behind him, the others thought so as well. But then, as they turned yet another bend, there appeared the trace of a yellow glow on the far wall, along with the sound of low voices.

Moments later, they stepped out of the tunnel and into a huge underground chamber. Spanning the vaulted cavern was a magnificent bridge of carved blackwood, as broad as one of the landings in the floating city. And there, waiting beneath it, was Nate.

Cade stared at him. His uncle looked different some-how. Younger. Fitter. He was dressed in full descending

armour and holding a glister-proof helmet under one arm. But that wasn't it . . . Then he realized what had changed in Nate's appearance: his uncle had shaved off his shaggy white beard.

Beside him was the wiry armourer of the Knights Academy, Seftis Bule, and Theegum the banderbear. They too were kitted out in armour and descending gear.

'This is the Blackwood Bridge,' said Nate, 'built in the Second Age by the librarian knights as a refuge from their enemies. When I learned just how far the project had progressed, I told Seftis it would be a suitable place to relocate to in case *our* enemies triumphed.'

He laughed, clapped each of them on the back in turn and embraced them.

'Yet it was us who prevailed.'

He paused in front of Eudoxia for a moment, the look on his face a mixture of excitement and sadness. Then he hugged her too.

'Sentafuce told me that the tallow-hats have defeated the Great Glade fleet,' he said, pulling away at last. 'The blockade is over and our work can resume!'

'Theegum and I have laid out armour for each of you,' Seftis announced.

'You mean . . . it's ready?' Cade could hardly contain his excitement. 'But only yesterday you told me that the stone-band wasn't fully weighted.'

Demora Duste stepped forward and held up the lamp casket containing Tug's harvested seed-stone.

'It will be now,' she said with a smile.

'I don't understand,' said Celestia. 'What is it that you've all been working on, and where are we going?'

Behind Nate, neatly laid out on the black timbers of the bridge, were seven more suits of armour, complete with phraxchambers and glister helmets. He turned to Celestia, his eyes gleaming, and grasped her by the hands.

'I'll show you,' he said. 'But first we have to suit up, Celestia, because we're going to be Descenders!'

PART FOUR
THE DESCENT

· CHAPTER EIGHTEEN ·

U ndertown's ancient central sewer emerged from the Edge cliff and jutted out over the abyss below. There, moored to the great outfall pipe by half a dozen tolley ropes, was an extraordinary-looking vessel. The nightship. Seftis Bule reached out and ran his hand over its metal surface. The black globe was smooth and cold to the touch.

Seftis turned to Nate, a smile on his face. 'We did it,' he said. 'At last.'

'*You* did it, old friend,' Nate said. 'I never thought it was possible.'

The two of them surveyed the vessel that hovered before them – the vessel both of them hoped was not only robust enough to survive freefall, but also powerful enough to return from the depths. It was, as Seftis Bule had maintained throughout the nightship's construction, all about phrax power and control.

Painted pitch black with burnt ironwood-pine resin, the nightship was a curious hybrid, like nothing that had ever been built before. At the front of the black globe was the snub-nosed prow, an armoured carapace with sinew-like cabling leading back to the phraxchamber. It contained the upper deck, where the winch controls, sleeping berths and galley were sited. And below that the descent deck, with its reinforced glass panels, through which rows of sumpwood seats, with descent levers embedded in their sides, could be seen.

The black globe itself formed the outer hull that enclosed the powerful phraxengine. At the core of the chamber was a crystal of stormphrax, kept buoyant by internal lamps, and ready to unleash the latent power of lightning when the torsion-vice tightened around it. Surrounding the core were five smaller phraxchambers, each one containing its own tiny crystal shard. On either side of the main globe were rows of steam funnels that looked curiously like the stubby legs of an insect; while around its middle was a glowing network of pipes, heated from within by phraxlamps: the stone-band.

'I certainly couldn't have done it on my own,' said Seftis as he stared at the finished nightship proudly. 'Everyone played their part.'

His mind recalled the process by which they had finally reached this moment. The first problem he had had to deal with was building a phraxchamber capable of generating enough power to slow the vessel's fall. This long-running problem had, of course, been solved by the

High Academe Elect's nephew Cade – a nephew Nate Quarter hadn't even known he had – who, seemingly out of the blue, had arrived in New Sanctaphrax with Eudoxia and a handful of his father's working drawings.

As Seftis and his team had worked on them, the armourer had become increasingly impressed with the Great Glade academic who had first come up with the designs for the power-efficient phraxchambers. The drawings had detailed innovation after innovation, revealing phraxpower technology far beyond anything seen before.

And just think, Seftis had marvelled, all this was the work of an obscure phraxengineer back in Great Glade. It was hard to take in.

Thadeus Quarter was that scholar's name. Back in the old days, Seftis Bule himself had trained at the Great Glade academy. Who knows? he'd often mused in those past few months. Maybe he had even met this Thadeus Quarter. Not that he could remember. It was a pity, without doubt, but at least he'd now had the privilege of getting to know his son . . .

Finally, after much trial and error, Seftis had constructed a model that did indeed have the power to stop its fall. But it came at a cost, for although the phraxchamber remained intact, coming to such an abrupt halt just above the ground, the casement surrounding the model ship was torn free by the force and broke into a thousand pieces.

Nate had shaken his head in despair as Seftis's sixth model – having dropped from the top of the ancient

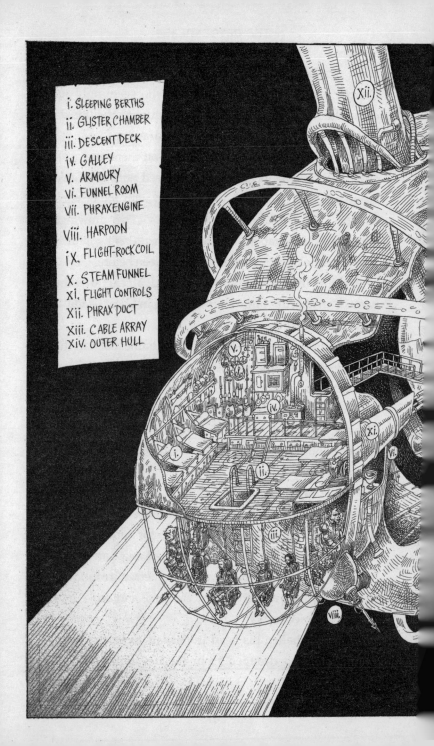

THE NIGHTSHIP
"LINIUS PALLITAX"

Loftus Observatory, the highest point in Sanctaphrax – had suffered the same fate as all the rest.

'The fall is the easy part,' Seftis had muttered. 'Controlling that fall is proving to be impossible.'

But then, just as Cade's arrival in New Sanctaphrax had been a fortuitous coincidence, so too was the chance meeting in the Great Library between Nate and a professor from the newly formed Academy of Earth and Sky Studies. In their subsequent conversation, Nate had recognized the potential importance of the so-called seed-stones that Demora had discovered in the Stone Gardens, and – just as he'd done with his nephew – had put her in contact with Seftis Bule.

In the Armoury, it was discovered that these little stones, when heated and cooled, could soften and stabilize the fall, in much the same way that full-grown flight rocks had once allowed sky galleons to fly.

Cold rock rises, hot rock sinks.

That was the principle by which the fabled stone pilots of the First Age of Flight had, for centuries, flown their skyships. And seed-stones, it was discovered, had a similar power to those flight rocks, but in miniature. By using them, it was hoped that a *fourth* age might be ushered in.

Tug, a friend of Nate's nephew – who had arrived in New Sanctaphrax with Cade – showed an extra-ordinary talent for harvesting these seed-stones. Soon Seftis had enough to carry out more experiments using the newly modified technology. And it worked. The last scale-model skyvessel to be dropped off the Loftus Observatory came to a fast, yet smooth, halt, and the tiny phraxship remained in one piece.

Heartened by this, Seftis had started work on a full-scale version. With Demora Duste's help, he devised what they called the 'stone-band'; a network of pipes encircling the phraxchamber, which contained dozens of the precious seed-stones harvested so carefully by Tug in the Stone Gardens.

'It still seems like a miracle to me,' Nate mused, 'the way everything slipped into place. First Cade. Then Demora – and Tug. Almost as though the building of the nightship was *meant* to happen. And then finding the last seed-stone the very day Great Glade's attempt to crush our beloved floating city was finally thwarted.'

Seftis Bule didn't believe in miracles. He knew only that controlled freefall was possible after all. Now, with the nightship that hovered before them – the last seed-rock in place – he, Nate and the other Descenders were going to test it out for real.

The sound of approaching footsteps broke into their thoughts, and Seftis and Nate turned to see Theegum striding along the sewer walkway towards them. Following close behind her came the seven others, each of them now kitted out in descending armour and equipment.

Celestia's voice, soft and awestruck, spoke for them all as it echoed around the great chamber. 'So this is it,' she gasped. 'The nightship.'

Nate stepped forward to meet them. He was looking more youthful than ever, Cade thought. His back was straight, his stride confident, while his eyes were a more intense shade of blue than he had ever seen them.

'My fellow Descenders,' he said, 'we have worked long and hard. Now, thanks to all our efforts, we are ready to launch. But before we do, there is one last thing to be done.'

Cade turned to Celestia and smiled. 'The naming ceremony,' he mouthed.

As the construction of the nightship had progressed, Nate had thought long and hard about what it should be called. Nothing he came up with seemed quite right. Then, shortly before she'd gone off to negotiate the alliance with the tallow-hats, Eudoxia had made a suggestion.

'With its seed-stone and phrax crystals, Earth and Sky has been combined in this extraordinary vessel,' she'd observed. 'There was once an academic long, long ago who united Earth and Sky scholarship. His name was . . .'

Nate smiled to himself as Seftis handed him a lufwood log with letters carved into its dark bark. Everyone had agreed that it was the perfect name for the nightship.

Pulling a bundle of long resin matches from a jacket pouch, the armourer removed one and struck it on the side of the phraxchamber. It hissed and flared, and he gave it to Nate as well. The High Academe looked down at the log and the blazing match for a moment, his brow furrowed – before turning to Cade, who was standing at his side.

'You do it,' he said simply, passing both the log and the match to his nephew.

'Me?' said Cade. He swallowed, overwhelmed by the honour.

Nate nodded. 'You, Cade.'

His hands trembling, Cade approached the hovering nightship. He knew every bolt and rivet of it from the months of its construction, carried out secretly in the Armoury. Yet now, seeing it hovering over the void, black and sleek against the dawn sky, it didn't seem quite real. For a start, it looked smaller here against the white of the billowing clouds than it had in the Armoury. Back there, it had loomed like a monstrous woodbeetle, suspended from the rafters. Now the nightship awaited them, a tiny world ready to be populated by these Descenders.

Had he, Seftis and Theegum the banderbear *really* made this? he marvelled.

Cade felt the heat of the match as it burned down towards his fingers. He held out the lufwood in front of him and touched the match to it. A purple flame flared, and the log rose from Cade's outstretched hand and flew up into the air. The carved letters blackened as the flames consumed the soaring log. Cade blew out the match.

'I name this vessel the nightship *Linius Pallitax*,' he announced.

*

Cade watched his fellow Descenders fondly as they climbed aboard the night-ship. They were a motley collection. Old friends and new.

Celestia and Tug, from his home in Farrow Lake, he trusted with his life, and of course the same applied to his uncle Nate. But then there were the others. Demora Duste the quarry trog and her friend Sentafuce, the waif professor; Grent One-Tusk the long-hair and Fenda Fulefane the fettle-legger; Seftis and Theegum from the Armoury. Cade had got to know them all so well during his time in New Sanctaphrax. Now, as they were about to head down into the depths beneath the Edge, his heart swelled. Surely there was no finer crew to be travelling with.

Celestia took Tug's hand as she stepped aboard the nightship, and the two of them climbed down through the roof hatch onto the upper deck. There was room for her to stand up, but Tug had to stoop, and even then his skull ridges grazed the ceiling. His descending armour, like that of Demora Duste and Theegum, was far bigger than that of the other crew members, and made him appear much bulkier than usual. And yet, as he guided Celestia to the rear of the deck and inspected the glowing phraxstove and well-provisioned shelves, he moved with a grace and balance at odds with his size.

'Tug happy to cook,' he said, with his lopsided grin. 'But any help is appreciated.'

He turned and ducked through a doorway. Celestia poked her head round the corner of the narrow side cabin, and saw the row of hammocks strung from side to side, and the store lockers below. Tug climbed into the end hammock. His massive arms trailed on either side, knuckles resting on the cabin floor.

'I'll take the one next to you,' Celestia said, and giggled. 'I'm used to your snoring.'

'Tug doesn't snoring,' Tug laughed, and Celestia had to admit that this was true. Her friend slept as quietly as a lemkin – unless, of course, he had one of his Nightwoods dreams. Then he would thrash about, howling and yelping as he relived the torments of his past. But thankfully such troubled nights were rare these days.

Celestia opened a store locker and began to fill it with parcels and bundles taken from the forage bag slung across her shoulder. She looked round.

'If you're ship's cook, Tug,' she said, 'I'll be ship's doctor.' She smiled. 'But any help is appreciated.'

Below them on the descent deck, Grent One-Tusk reached to his shoulder to unbuckle the breastplate of his armour, only for Fenda Fulefane to stretch forward and stay his hand.

'The High Academe . . . I mean, Captain Quarter,' she corrected herself, 'has ordered that armour be worn at all times while we're on duty. After all, we are Descenders now.'

'Indeed we are,' said Grent, and chuckled. 'Sky above, if someone had told me back in my apprentice days at the Sumpwood Bridge Academy in Hive that one day I'd be a Descender, I'd have laughed my whiskers off.' He crossed the deck to the small porthole and peered through it.

'I'd have done the same,' said Fenda, hopping over to join him. She laughed. 'If I had whiskers to laugh off, that is.' Her expression grew serious. 'But here we both are, suited and booted' – she looked down at the phrax-boots, modified to fit her taloned feet – 'about to embark on the greatest adventure of them all. I only wish my mother could see me now . . .'

Grent put an arm round the fettle-legger's shoulder. 'Perhaps she can,' he said, looking out at the swirling clouds. 'Perhaps she can.' He turned to Demora Duste, who had sat down in the sumpwood chair opposite. 'What do you think, Demora?'

The quarry trog laughed. 'I have the feeling that anything and everything is possible on this expedition.'

She reached down and adjusted the height of her chair by cranking the handle in its arm rest. Beside her, Sentafuce the nightwaif did the same, but in the opposite direction, until the two of them were eye to eye with each other.

On the other side of the descent deck, Seftis and Theegum the banderbear made similar adjustments.

'*What a mixed bunch we are,*' Sentafuce observed, her voice in everyone's head. '*I—*'

'Please, my dear Sentafuce, speak out loud,' Demora broke in gently. 'We are descending into regions where thoughts can become complicated, so we must try to think and speak as clearly as possible.'

'Forgive me,' said Sentafuce out loud. Her barbels quivered at the corners of her mouth. 'It's just nerves. Am I alone in feeling nervous?' she asked, and looked around at her fellow Descenders, her enormous eyes widening. 'No, I think not.'

Opposite them, Seftis patted Theegum's paw. 'Thank you, old friend,' he said quietly. 'I know this must be hard for you – bringing back memories . . .' He smiled ruefully. 'But I'm afraid I can't manage the phraxglobe on my own.'

Theegum raised a paw and circled the air with a claw. 'Wurgh . . . wuh-wuh . . . wurrgggh,' she said. *This path that leads to the depths should not be travelled alone.*

Seftis shrugged, baffled by his friend's language.

'And thank *you*, Seftis,' Demora broke in as she checked the stone-band control levers that fringed her seat, 'for believing in my work in the Stone Gardens, when so many called it outdated.'

'The First Age of Flight combining with the Third Age of Flight,' Sentafuce's voice sounded once more in everyone's head. *'Stone and phrax united.'*

'You're doing it again, dear,' said Demora, a little more forcefully this time.

Cade took his seat and strapped himself in. Celestia took her place beside him.

'Everyone ready?' Nate called back from the controls.

There was a ripple of assent and Nate reached forward for the tolley-rope release lever. In the sumpwood seats around him, the Descenders tensed. Below their feet, through the glass panels of the descending deck, they saw the billowing clouds of the white swirl thicken and eddy.

'Phraxengine set at slow descent,' Seftis Bule reported.

'Stone-band at quarter heat,' Demora Duste added.

Nate pushed the release lever forward. 'Tolley rope released,' he announced, and the nightship gave a little jolt.

Sentafuce's voice whispered throughout the *Linius Pallitax*: '*May Earth and Sky protect us all.*'

· CHAPTER NINETEEN ·

The nightship plunged into the roiling clouds of the white swirl, swaying gently at first, then juddering with increasing intensity as the air currents took hold. Cade felt the seat harness strain at his shoulder; the cable attached to his sumpwood chair slackened, then went taut with each dip and roll. Outside, the clouds thinned for a few moments, and through the glass panels of the descent deck he could see the rock face of the high cliff speeding past in a dizzying blur.

At their respective controls, Demora and Seftis worked in tandem to keep the *Linius Pallitax* stable. They regulated the light in the phraxchamber and the heat in the stone-band, causing gusts of dense steam to pour out of the funnels at the sides of the outer hull.

It was going well, but then, all of a sudden, the cliff came rushing up to meet them. Cade flinched, fearing that the winds were about to slam the nightship into the rock face, shattering the glass of the descent deck and sending them hurtling down into the abyss below.

In his sumpwood chair, Nate's jaws clenched as his hands sped over the flight levers, swivelling the funnels and sending jets of cushioning steam blasting against the cliff. The nightship slowed, steadied itself, then abruptly picked up speed again, and Cade felt his stomach do a churning somersault as the vessel resumed its descent.

It was to become a familiar feeling in the voyage ahead. After an hour or so, Cade was just about getting used to it, and he lost himself, staring out through the panelled glass at the mesmerizing white swirl.

For Nate and his two assistants, though, the concentration needed to keep the *Linius Pallitax* from crashing was taking its toll. One moment of inattention or relaxation and the nightship would buck and threaten to spin out of control – only for the phraxchamber to thrum, the stone-band to glow, and fresh clouds of steam to burst forth from the funnels.

'Prepare the tolley ropes!'

Nate's order roused Cade from his reverie. Turning away from the ever-changing patterns of the swirling white mist, he cranked his sumpwood seat up towards the ceiling rung above him. Then, grasping the overhead rungs in turn, he made his way across to the far side of the descent deck. Cade lowered himself, coming down beside the window, the glass pane etched with calibrations that would enable him to take aim.

'Stand by, Cade,' Nate's voice sounded.

Cade shifted in his sumpwood seat. He looked out at the array of mooring rings directly below them, anchored deep in the cliff face on a massive jutting spur called 'the Cusp'.

These had been laid out in an unbroken line by the Descenders who had continued Nate Quarter and Ambris Hentadile's work in the years following their disappearance. No nightship descent for them, though; just the painstaking, arduous manual climb down the cliff face, rock spike by rock spike, as they'd hammered the rings securely into place.

The mooring rings came closer. Cade braced himself.

'When you're ready . . .'

Cade took careful aim, his hand on the harpoon lever in the side of the sumpwood seat. He eased it slowly forward and saw a white flash out of the corner of his eye as the phraxharpoons fired. Below him, through the glass panels, grapples with tolley ropes attached to them spiralled through the air, passed through the mooring rings and spun around them like yarn collecting around a spool.

The tolley ropes, all six of them, sprang taut as the nightship fell past the mooring rings, bringing the vessel to a surprisingly smooth halt. Nate slumped back in his seat, his face bathed in sweat.

'In one short hour, we have made a descent that would have taken many long days on the cliff face,' he said, relief clear in his voice. He unclipped his harness and pulled himself up with the help of a ceiling rung. 'Well

done, everyone. We'll rest up here for a while.' He frowned. 'Then we'll enter the dark swirl.'

He locked the flight levers and looked around at the crew.

'We will take the next part of our descent at a more measured pace,' he said. 'Tug and Theegum, I'm going to need your strength on the winches. Cade, I believe you told me that Celestia is an even better shot than you? I want both of you on the phraxharpoons. Senta-fuce, help them. And Grent and Fenda – could you two relieve Demora and Seftis on the phrax-chamber and stone-band?'

'But what about you, Captain?' said Fenda, rising from her chair.

'Surely you need to rest more than any of us,' added Sentafuce kindly.

'Don't you worry about me,' said Nate. He smiled, but there was a quiet intensity in his manner. 'I've been resting for sixteen years, waiting for this . . .' His voice trailed away, and he shrugged. 'So, Tug, how about some charlock tea?'

Soon they were all gathered around the phraxstove in the galley, drinking the sweet tea that Tug had prepared. Cade was sitting beside him and Theegum, interpreting the banderbear's sign language for his friend. The two of them seemed to have a natural affinity that Cade loved to see.

'The winch will wind our precious vessel to safety,' he told Tug, translating the banderbear's words. 'And we two shall work with gladness in our hearts that will give strength to our arms.'

Tug stroked Theegum's paw. 'Tug has a strong heart,' he told her.

'Are you ready for the dark swirl, Cade?' asked Celestia. She leaned forward, her voice hushed in his ear. 'Ravine demons and Edge wraiths and all . . .'

Cade nodded. 'I think we're both ready,' he said.

They assembled on the descent deck – all apart from Theegum and Tug, who remained on the upper deck. The two of them took up positions at the sally-ports in the nightship's armoured hood, next to winches that were attached to the tolley ropes. Cade and Celestia were situated on the descent deck directly below them, seated in their sumpwood chairs beside the glass aiming panels.

At the flight controls, Nate sounded the bells. This was

305

how they would measure out the rest of the day as they plunged into darkness. Then he released the tolley ropes, and Cade felt the tension rise on the descent deck as the nightship began to descend into the swirling half-light of the grey clouds.

'Fire!' Nate's command rang out as the first of the gale-force winds suddenly buffeted the *Linius Pallitax*.

Cade and Celestia fired the phraxharpoons at the fluted rock formations below them, and not a moment too soon. There were white flashes, puffs of steam, then echoing cracks and thuds as the harpoons struck the rock and held fast. The nightship bucked and rolled, and the crew fought hard to counter the intense swirl of the storm.

From above him, Cade heard the steady whirr of the winch as Tug and Theegum leaped into action, pulling the vessel towards the harpoons now anchored to the rock face somewhere below them in the darkness. As the nightship approached the harpoons, small phrax explosions released yet more of them, and in the rough and tumble that followed, Cade and Celestia fired again at the fleeting glimpse of rock. Then the winches whirred into action once more . . .

Over and over, this procedure was repeated – fire, winch, descend – allowing them to drop down the cliff face safely, and with a remarkable degree of control. They passed jutting spurs and nubbed outcrops, and vertical ravines where Cade caught sight of the glinting eyes of what must have been ravine ghouls peeking out. None of them emerged, though. It was as if they were unwilling to take on this monstrous metal insect that was slowly making its way down the Fluted Decline.

That night, at six bells, the crew slumped gratefully into their hammocks. Moored to the cliff face, the little vessel shuddered and shook, rocking them all to a deep, yet far from dreamless sleep.

As Cade lay there, his breathing soft and deep, the events of the long day played through his head. Finding the barkscrolls that Seftis had requested; talking to his uncle on the Viaduct Steps; flying to the Stone Gardens with the others, where Tug had excavated the final seed-stone. Then Great Glade's sudden aerial attack on New Sanctaphrax – which had been thwarted at the last moment by the arrival of the tallow-hats. And now this, descending in the nightship that had taken so many months to construct; at last—

'Come on, Cade,' said Celestia, shaking him awake. 'Time to get up.'

Three more days passed, and Cade became used to the rhythm of the descent through the darkness: the watchful tension, the moments of juddering chaos, then the steady sway of the winching. To sustain themselves, they ate rich gruel, made from dried compacted bricks of barleymeal dissolved in steam water, and made use of the tiny funnel room when necessary.

Then, on the fourth day, at six bells, with the winches turning, Cade glanced out through the glass panel – and recoiled in his seat.

Something was there.

The others on the descent deck had seen it too – all except for Nate, who continued to work the flight levers, keeping the nightship as steady as possible. Rising up from the cliff face, like some sort of ragged shroud, was an immense fluttering wave of translucent white. As it approached, the wave shimmered and split apart, revealing itself to be made up of a vast armada of pale winged creatures.

'Edge wraiths,' said Nate impassively, even though his eyes were fixed on the flight levers. He'd heard their strange, distinctive calls. Filling the air, low and resonating, they sounded like distant thunder fading to wind howl.

The creatures were huge. And hideous. One after another, they loomed up at the glass of the descent deck, enormous eyes staring, fanged mouths gaping, and skeletal bodies, with their gauze-like wings, scraping against the hull. For a minute or so, as the winches snagged and the vessel jolted, it was like swimming through some childhood nightmare, skittering and fluttering, the monstrous faces flashing close, then disappearing back into the pitch black.

Thankfully, the tolley ropes held as Tug and Theegum kept turning the winches. And slowly the hideous armada vanished back into the black night they had come from, their eerie calls fading away.

Nate continued to work the flight levers. He seemed calm enough, but Cade could tell by the way his jaw clenched and unclenched that what they had all just witnessed had brought back traumatic memories. He and Celestia exchanged troubled looks.

Sentafuce was in an even worse state than Nate. Curled up into a ball in her seat, her hands were pressed against her ears, her eyes clamped tightly shut. Demora reached out and placed a comforting hand on the trembling shoulder of her friend.

'Waifs know only too well the terror and lone-liness of the night,' she explained to the others. 'And Sentafuce here, more than most. Edge wraiths hold thoughts that can sting those minds open to them; that scald them like boiling water . . .'

The winches stopped turning as the nightship reached the tolley-rope

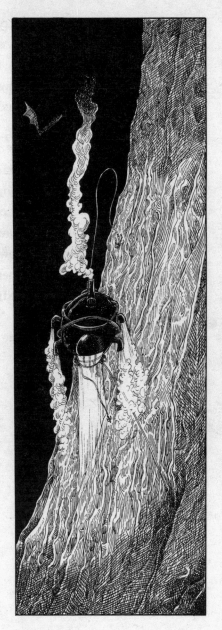

anchors. The now familiar phrax detonations sounded, and the nightship dropped down further, over a great jutting ledge. At the controls, Nate threw the flight levers forward. The funnels billowed steam, the stone-band glowed white hot and the phraxchamber pitched the *Linius Pallitax* forward.

Far in the distance, the cliff wall appeared out of the blackness and, as they raced towards it through the suddenly still and silent air, Cade saw the outline of timber gantries and ribbed cocoon-like huts embedded in the rock face below the Great Overhang.

As they drew nearer, Nate slowed the *Linius Pallitax* down to a steady hover, then closed in to dock at the closest gantry. A light shone from a small round window in the ribbed hut above it.

'Denizens Keep,' said Nate. 'The very furthest point of the Descenders' range.'

· CHAPTER TWENTY ·

Cade stared out through the glass panels of the descent deck. Nate's words were echoing in his head.

Denizens Keep.

Back in New Sanctaphrax, his uncle had spoken of the place with such pride. And there it was, coming towards them – a series of huts and gantries that clung to the underside of the Great Overhang.

Seftis had taken over control of the stone-band and Theegum was now managing the phraxchamber. The nightship approached the nearest gantry smoothly and, when they were close enough, Cade fired the tolley ropes through the mooring rings attached to it. Above him, on the upper deck, he heard Tug begin to winch them in. When they were tethered securely to the rock, the crew unbuckled their seat straps and prepared to disembark.

At least, most of them did . . .

'Anything and everything is possible on this expedition,' Demora had said before they'd set off. But even she hadn't imagined what would happen to her as they descended into the depths.

As she looked through the glass at Denizens Keep, the small huts attached to the wooden gantries suddenly seemed to turn hazy and dissolve – and when the others started to leave, and Cade asked her whether or not she was coming with them, she didn't hear his words.

Maybe it was the breakneck speed of the descent that had confused her. Maybe it was the glister-rich cliff rock affecting her thoughts, or her encounter with the Edge wraiths. Whatever the reason, for Demora Duste, she was no longer sitting in her sumpwood chair on board the *Linius Pallitax*, but instead seemed to have stepped out of time.

Suddenly she was immersed in childhood memories so vibrant – so *real* – she might as well have been plunged back into the past . . .

'. . . *and no lingering at the quarry . . .*'

It was her mother's voice, calling to her from the upper window of their cliff hut.

'I'll come straight home,' Demora promised as she skipped off down the narrow walkway cut into the steep side of the gorge.

She was holding a flask of home-made clusterbean soup in her hand. Her father would welcome the warming broth after his long gruelling shift quarrying whitestone through the night.

All around her, Gorgetown was stirring. The leatherbacked scuttlebrigs and their herders were climbing up from the lower gorge, stones piled high in their side-baskets, while the traders in the hanging-market were busy laying out goods on their sumpwood stalls, ready for the returning quarry workers.

Demora wove her way in and out of the growing traffic on the steep quarry path. Her father and his crew should be finishing soon – so long as their quarry master, a gaunt sour-faced fourthling from Great Glade, played fair with the hourglass. It wouldn't be the first time he'd extended the shift by 'accidentally' failing to turn the glass. Although when it came to their wages, he would always find some excuse or other to delay payment if he could.

As Demora's father never tired of telling her, the life of a quarry trog was perilous and hard. That was why he wanted a better future for his daughter. But the thing was, Demora loved stonework. She always had. Right from the first time she was old enough to pick up a hammer and a chisel, she had felt a certain kinship with it. She could spot a seam of rock, sense the flow of the grain, and understand how to work it just by running her hands across its freshly cut surface.

'You should take your talent to the academies in Great Glade or Hive,' her father had told her more than once, 'not waste them here in Gorgetown working for the quarry masters.'

Demora had reached the lower gantries, the flask grasped in her hand still warm. Below her, the quarry ledges echoed with the steady chink-chink-chink *of hammer on chisel, and the rhythmic work chants of the quarry trogs. She glanced up at the dawn sky. Grey clouds filtered the early morning light as distant thunder rumbled. Except . . .*

Demora froze.

That wasn't thunder. She knew it almost instantly. It was a rock slide, the sound of rocks careening down the steep slope. Heart pounding inside her chest, she looked round to see a thick cloud of white dust rising up from the quarry ledges.

Demora dropped the flask, which broke as it hit the ground, and dashed to the nearest ladder. Climbing up to meet her came a handful of dazed trogs, white with the stone dust, coughing and spluttering. Demora reached the first ledge to find the quarry master surrounded by an angry crowd.

'The second ledge has collapsed,' one of them was shouting, his eyes blazing with rage. 'And it's taken the third with it . . .'

'Dolbin said we were cutting too deep,' cried another trog, stabbing an accusing finger into the quarry master's chest. 'But you wouldn't listen . . .'

Dolbin . . . Her father! Demora swallowed, her face twitching with foreboding.

More trogs were gathering on the ledge, clutching spades and pickaxes and crowding around the quarry master. They were muttering furiously, shaking their heads. The quarry master raised his arms.

'Never mind that now,' he shouted, his voice high and querulous. 'Grab what tools you can find, and dig! You hear me? Dig!'

Demora ran to the tool racks bolted to the gorge wall, seized a pickaxe and shovel, then shouldered her way back through the throng. The quarry trogs all recognized her. Dolbin Duste's

daughter. Tall for her age, and with her father's strength and gift for stone-working. Even the quarry master had been surprised she hadn't begun quarrying several seasons earlier . . .

'My father will have reinforced the cutting site,' Demora told the quarry workers. 'If we can just find it beneath the rubble, we can still save them . . .'

'Follow her!' the quarry master shouted as he backed away along the ledge, heading towards the wooden cabin at the far end, with its account scrolls and wage chests, and the comfortable armchair beside the lufwood stove. 'And do what she says!'

Demora Duste wasn't the only one reliving an incident from her childhood. Beside her, Sentafuce too was finding it impossible to separate the present from the past. And, as she squirmed in her seat, her face contorted with fear and pain, it was clear that the tiny waif was suffering . . .

It wasn't meant to be like this . . .

Imprisoned in the quarry master's hut, Sentafuce pulled her threadbare cape around her small shoulders and gazed into the purple flames of the stove. Inside it, the burning lufwood logs jostled and tumbled in their attempts to break free.

Just like Sentafuce herself.

They had captured her in the Nightwoods, the red dwarf slavers with their clawed feet and sharp beaks – and even sharper metal spikes that they had tortured their captives with. Tortured her *with . . .*

Sentafuce could just about remember the waif clan she'd been born into. The voices in her head. The comfort of communal thoughts in the eternal darkness. She could still recall the touch of her many mothers, fastening her cape and plaiting her hair, and how they would sing to her and her many, many siblings in their minds.

But then she'd been grabbed by a slaver's hook, dragged into one of their cages and taken to the city of night. To Riverrise. She couldn't have been much more than a baby . . .

The red dwarf slavers kept her and the other waifs chained up in their camp on the edge of the Thorn Forest. Sentafuce remembered also the huge nameless ones who had shared their captivity. Reading their thoughts, full of such hurt and bewilderment, overwhelmed her with sadness, and she had tried to keep them out.

Then the merchants came.

She was a nightwaif, wild and delicate. She wasn't worth much, and the red dwarves were happy to throw her in as a job lot with two gigantic nameless ones. The merchants they were sold to were from Gorgetown in the Northern Reaches, in search of sturdy, unprotesting workers for the stone quarries. They agreed to take the nightwaif with them, hardly expecting her to survive long in the daylight world.

Sentafuce read their minds too, learning all she could from them, and from everyone else she encountered on board the skytavern during that long voyage to the distant city. The merchants, it turned out, were kindly. They treated her and the nameless ones well, and were genuinely sorry to hand the three of them over to the quarry master when they got to Gorgetown. But they took their commissions because they had families to support, mouths to feed . . .

The nameless ones were set to work hauling the stone slabs quarried by the trogs up to the masons at the top of the gorge. It was a tough existence, but they were happy to escape the cruelties of the Nightwoods, and grew fit and strong on the nourishing food and decent quarters they were given.

Sentafuce was less happy.

The quarry master was mean-spirited and petty. He resented the wages he had to pay the quarry trogs, and he objected to the kindness and generosity the trogs showed to the nameless ones. So he kept Sentafuce close, locking her up in the wooden hut above the quarry ledges, and forced her to read the minds of his workers. She had to keep him informed of anything – everything,

318

no matter how small and insignificant it might seem – that he could use to dock their pay.

And she hated it.

The minds she had read on the skytavern had opened up to her new worlds which she longed to explore. On board, it was the blue-robed academics' thoughts of the floating city of New Sanctaphrax and Undergarden that were Sentafuce's favourites. They seemed further away than ever now. For here she was in the grey mists of Gorgetown, chained up and huddled beside a lufwood stove.

No, it wasn't meant to be like this.

Just then, from outside, there came a sound like thunder, and Sentafuce heard agonized cries as despairing, panic-filled thoughts suddenly flooded her mind. She leaped to her feet and ran to the window, the ironwood chain at her ankle rattling across the floor and bringing her up just short. She could hear the quarry master's high-pitched, wheedling voice as he scuttled back towards his hut.

'Dig! Dig! Dig!' he was shouting out loud; the thought in his head, Good riddance.

Two individuals. Two sets of memories. But then, as the bewildering influence of the depths grew more intense, something happened.

Just as, in the past, the lives of Demora and Sentafuce had come together, so now, their memories fused . . .

Demora strode to the wooden hut and hammered on the door.

'What is it?' The quarry master sounded exasperated.

'We need help,' Demora said desperately.

The door of the hut opened, and the quarry master peered out. He was holding a loaded phraxpistol.

'The workers are blaming me for this,' he hissed. 'The waif has read their thoughts. I won't put up with it, I'm warning the lot of you.'

'We need to locate my father and the others,' Demora pleaded, 'so that we know where to dig.'

'I can try,' said Sentafuce, her voice sounding in Demora's head, 'but I need to be closer to listen for their thoughts . . .'

'NO!' the quarry master shouted, guessing what was going on. He levelled the phraxpistol at Demora. 'The waif is mine. She goes nowhere.'

Demora's pickaxe struck the pistol, knocking it out of the quarry master's hand and sending it clattering across the floor. Reaching out, she grasped the quarry master by the throat and raised him off his feet.

'The key is in his topcoat pocket,' Sentafuce told Demora silently.

Demora dropped her pickaxe and searched the quarry master's pockets with her free hand. He spluttered and choked and stared back at her with bulging bloodshot eyes. Demora found the key and let go of the quarry master, who fell in a crumpled heap at her feet.

'You'll . . . you'll pay . . . for this . . .' he rasped as Demora unchained Sentafuce, and the two of them hurried from the cabin.

Back at the site of the rock-slide, Sentafuce stood on the great pile of dust-covered rock that filled the lower reaches of the gorge. Trogs towered around the tiny figure of the nightwaif, their pickaxes and shovels raised, waiting to be told what to do next. The barbels at the corner of the waif's mouth quivered as, eyes shut, she stooped and pressed an ear to the rubble.

'There!' She stood up and pointed to an area of scree to her left. 'But hurry,' she added urgently. 'Their thoughts are fading.'

Demora sprang into action. She dug down through the porous white stone with her shovel, pausing only to prise boulders carefully free and toss them aside. All around her, the quarry trogs did the same, working as a unified team.

Two huge creatures in patchwork aprons, ropes hanging from harnesses at their shoulders, lumbered towards them. Both had ridged crests on their heads and leathery, mottled skin. The trogs attached the ropes to the largest of the remaining

boulders and the nameless ones strained at their harnesses, grunting with effort, then hauled them aside.

Beneath the boulders, they uncovered a scaffold of ironwood timbers lashed together. And below it were eight sheltering trogs, huddled closely side by side, their raised arms shielding their heads. Excited murmuring went up as, one after the other, they were helped from the rubble.

'Father!'

Demora fell into the arms of the last quarry trog to be rescued. Tears streamed down her face, streaking the white dust that covered it.

Dolbin Duste embraced her. 'That was fine quarrying, daughter,' he wheezed, sitting down on a boulder. 'One wrong move and the whole pile would have shifted and crushed the lot of us.'

'The quarry master has sent for the militia,' whispered Sentafuce. 'He plans to have you arrested, Demora.'

'I've been meaning to leave Gorgetown for some time now,' said Dolbin, climbing to his feet and shaking the dust from his apron. 'I never wanted this life for Demora, and it's taken a load of rock falling on my head to finally make up my mind.'

'But where shall we go?' Demora asked.

'There is a place,' said Sentafuce's voice in their heads, 'with a great floating city and gardens of stone . . .'

'Demora?' said Cade. 'I asked whether you were coming with us.' He nodded ahead. 'Into Denizens Keep.'

He frowned. The quarry trog looked distracted, her eyes staring into the mid-distance at something only she could see.

'Demora,' he said again, reaching down and shaking her by the arm.

With a sharp intake of breath, Demora suddenly looked up. Her bewildered expression slowly returned to normal as she recognized who was standing in front of her.

'Oh, Cade,' she said quietly. 'I just had the most extraordinary experience. I thought I was—'

Beside her, Sentafuce let out a soft whimper. Demora turned to her.

'Sentafuce,' she said anxiously. 'Are you all right, my dear?'

But it was clear that she was not. The colour had drained from her face, leaving it waxen and slumped, while her entire body was quivering. Whatever it was that had influenced the quarry trog's thoughts, the effect on the tiny waif had been far more intense.

'Sentafuce!' Demora cried out, unbuckling herself and jumping to her feet. She leaned down and stroked the waif's cheek – and was shocked by how cold and clammy it felt. 'You poor thing,' she said. 'Let me help you.'

Demora was still shaky herself, but with Cade's help, she eased the waif from the seat and cradled her in her arms. Rocking backwards and forwards, crooning all the while, she tried her best to soothe her softly groaning friend.

'Come on,' said Cade. 'Let's follow the others. We'll get help for her inside the Keep.'

Demora nodded, but she wasn't so certain. The little body in her arms felt so light, so still . . . She checked that

Sentafuce's heavy glister helmet was secure, then her own, and that the descending armour they were both wearing was buckled into place. Then she took the stairs to the upper deck, and on up through the roof hatch.

'Sentafuce is going to be fine,' Cade said reassuringly – though even he was beginning to have his doubts.

· CHAPTER TWENTY-ONE ·

'*D*emora! Watch out!'

Sentafuce's scream sounded in everyone's head, piercing and urgent. She'd abruptly come round and was sitting bolt upright and rigid in Demora's arms, her eyes wide open.

Nate, who was standing on the gantry, about to enter the hut, let go of the door handle in alarm. Behind him, Cade spun round, his breath fogging his visor. Through the misted glass of their glister helmets they saw a nightmarish sight.

Rising quickly from the underside of the phrax-chamber of the *Linius Pallitax* was a huge spectral creature, bleached white and skeletal. It had been cling-ing to the hull of the nightship with its great splayed talons. Now it lunged at them, propelled by the whiplash of its long prehensile tail.

Two massive pale-yellow eyes swivelled, and its fang-fringed jaws seemed almost to dislocate as they gaped wide open. The glistening translucent body pulsated with muscle ripples and bony clicks as it landed on the gantry and slashed viciously at the quarry trog.

Demora's shoulder armour splintered as a scythe-like talon punctured it, and blood poured down over her breastplate. Still clutching Sentafuce protectively, she stumbled backwards into Celestia, Tug and Theegum. The ravine demon struck out again, this time with its powerful tail. Legs whipped away from under them, Seftis, Fenda and Cade fell to their knees, one after the other.

Through his fogged-up helmet, Cade could just make out the fuzzy outline of the bleached white figure of the ravine demon as it reared up again. With both forelimbs outstretched, it braced its body, ready to strike.

Suddenly, climbing out of Demora's arms, Sentafuce rose, tiny and vulnerable, below the creature's arched body. She tore off her helmet and fixed the hideous demon with an intense stare. The ravine demon's yellow eyes grew wider, the pupils contracting to pinpoints as the nightwaif penetrated what passed for a mind.

It only lasted for a split second. But to Cade that terrible moment seemed to go on for ever.

All at once, behind him, there was a sharp crack and a blinding flash, and the next thing Cade saw was the smoking shaft of a phraxharpoon embedded in the ravine demon's bony chest. An instant later, the

phraxcharges on the harpoon detonated, and the ravine demon exploded in a shower of bone fragments and gelatinous body parts that fell away into the deep night below.

Turning away, Cade saw a figure silhouetted against the open doorway of the ribbed hut, smoking harpoon gun in its hands. It gestured to them.

Cade and the others followed Nate and the figure inside. Theegum and Tug carried Demora between them, while Celestia picked up the quivering body of Sentafuce and clasped her to her chest. Once they were all in the hut, the figure closed the door which, like the walls and ceiling, was heavily padded with a dark quilted material.

Cade unbuckled his glister helmet and took it

off. The others did the same, with Tug kneeling down and removing Demora's helmet for her as she lay moaning quietly on the floor.

The figure removed his own helmet, to reveal the grizzled features of a fourthling with greying hair, oiled side-whiskers and a short white scar that cut one of his eyebrows in two. A look of recognition flashed in his pale eyes.

'Nate Quarter! It's an honour, sir!' he exclaimed, thrusting out a hand. 'Denizen Ulnix Tollinix, last of the fourteenth descending party.'

Nate removed his gauntlet and shook the fourthling's hand. 'Pleased to meet you, Ulnix,' he replied. 'I thought you had all been recalled by the academy when the blockade worsened.'

'The others went back up top, sir,' said Ulnix. 'But I couldn't abandon the Keep. Not after the sacrifices we all went through to get down this far.' He grinned. 'And I suspected it wouldn't be too long before you organized another descent.'

'You know me well,' said Nate, patting the denizen on his shoulder.

'Cade, fetch my backpack from the nightship,' Celestia broke in urgently. 'Quickly!' She grabbed him by the shoulders and pushed him towards the door. 'Tug, help me with Demora. Theegum, you look after Sentafuce . . .'

Cade put his helmet back on and Ulnix opened the padded door, handing him a loaded harpoon gun as he did so.

'Just in case,' he said.

Tug was carrying Demora through to what must be the sleeping quarters at the back of the hut with Theegum and Celestia, Sentafuce in her arms, following close behind as Cade stepped out onto the gantry. With the harpoon gripped in his trembling hands, he hurried back to the nightship, his heart pounding as he searched the black hull for any sign of another ravine demon.

Once on board, Cade grabbed Celestia's backpack from her store locker and slung it over his shoulder. Then, praying that he wouldn't arrive too late, he made his way back to the ribbed hut. Out on the gantry, he glanced down. Below him, the sheer cliff face disappeared into the darkness, and . . .

Cade gasped.

Ripples of light, pulsing and detonating beneath the gleaming surface of the rock, shimmered down the Edge cliff as far as he could see. It was an astonishingly beautiful display, like watching a revolving night sky full of shooting stars and shifting constellations.

'Glisters,' Cade breathed.

These tiny pulses of light embedded within Edge cliff-rock had been observed and studied in the floating city's academies for centuries. They were fine and delicate, sometimes fading away once glimpsed; sometimes lingering for a few moments longer.

But nothing any Sanctaphrax academic had ever seen in a laboratory compared to this. The lights grew in dazzling kaleidoscopic clusters. They mingled and overlapped. They wove in and out of each other, leaving behind shimmering trails that pulsed with their own cold-fire energy.

Mesmerized by the glister display below him, Cade moved towards the edge of the gantry, only to feel a hand on his shoulder. An urgent voice spoke in his ear.

'Look away from the cliff face,' it said. 'Look away *now*, before it's too late.'

Cade glanced round. It was Ulnix Tollinix.

Gently but firmly, the fourthling guided Cade into the hut and closed the padded door. In the back room, Celestia and Tug were tending to Demora and Sentafuce. The air was full of low voices and antiseptic odours. Then Theegum emerged, carrying a bundle of bloody bandages in her hands. She said something to Seftis, who shook his head, unable to understand.

'Celestia has staunched the bleeding and made Demora comfortable,' Cade said, interpreting the banderbear language, 'but the wound will take many weeks to heal. And as for Sentafuce . . .'

'Sentafuce won't wake up,' said Celestia, standing in the doorway. 'Confronting that ravine demon has worsened the damage already done to her by that brush with the Edge wraiths. Her mind seems to have shut down completely. All we can do now is hope that it's repairing itself.'

Grent One-Tusk, who was sitting at the small window beside Fenda Fulefane, looked up. 'Those two have been friends for as long as I can remember,' he said glumly. 'Earth and Sky willing, their story will not end here.'

'They are brave Descenders,' Nate said, with feeling. 'I have known many.'

Grent turned back and looked out of the window. Celestia shuffled her feet and stared down at the floor.

'It was bad luck picking up an unwanted passenger like that,' said Ulnix, breaking into the uncomfortable silence that had followed Nate's words. 'But your ship is mightily impressive, Captain, sir. There were many, even in the Knights Academy, who laughed at your eccentricity – dropping all those strange models from the old observatory . . .' He nodded earnestly. 'But it certainly seems to have paid off.'

'Thanks to everyone here,' said Nate, smiling at last. 'Yet our greatest challenge is still to come.'

Seftis nodded gloomily. 'And with two of our crew members already lost,' he muttered.

'I'll take good care of them,' said Ulnix warmly, 'you can be sure of that. And if the blockade ever ends . . .'

Nate smiled again. 'The blockade *has* ended,' he told the denizen.

'It has?' Ulnix clapped his hands together delightedly. 'Well, then,' he said, 'just as soon as the fifteenth descending party relieves me, I will take your friends back up top myself.'

He crossed to the window and pulled down a shutter, securing it firmly.

'The cliff face is still alight,' he said, turning back to the others. 'It means a glister storm is brewing. But rest assured, the hammelhorn felt will keep the glisters out of the hut – though if you don't want to lose your minds, you must stay inside until it blows over. And try to ignore the voices.'

'Voices?' said Cade.

'You'll see,' said Ulnix grimly.

'How long do these storms last?' asked Nate.

'Hard to say,' said Ulnix. 'The last one' – he reached up and unhooked one of the dozens of barkscrolls that hung from the padded ceiling – 'lasted for three months.'

Nate picked up his glister helmet. 'Thank you

for your hospitality, Ulnix, but we can't risk being delayed for three months.'

'And that was one of the shorter ones,' Ulnix added. 'But, sir, you're taking a terrible risk if you intend flying into a glister storm.'

'Not flying,' said Nate, putting on the helmet. Cade and the others did the same. 'Freefalling.'

They left the denizen shaking his head ruefully. 'Your friends will both be fine in my care,' he reassured Celestia, taking the supplies of bandages and salves from her. 'And Sky watch over and protect you all.'

The depleted crew crossed the gantry and hastily climbed aboard the *Linius Pallitax*, trying not to look at the shimmering cliff face below them. At Nate's suggestion, Grent and Fenda took to their hammocks on the upper deck to rest up until they reached the bottom of the breakneck descent.

'You'll be more use to us there,' he said.

The others went down to the descent deck, strapped themselves into their seat harnesses and buckled their glister helmets. Nate reached for the flight controls and locked them into position. He turned to Seftis.

'On my order,' he told him, 'shut down the phraxlamps in the phraxchamber.'

Cade looked across at Celestia. In darkness, storm-phrax becomes immensely heavy. They both knew that.

Nate turned to Theegum. 'And turn the heat to maximum in the stone-band.'

Hot rock sinks . . .

Cade gripped the arm rests of his sumpwood seat as Nate turned back.

'Release the tolley ropes, Cade,' Nate ordered. Then, leaning back in his own seat, he gave the order to Seftis and Theegum. 'Freefall!'

· CHAPTER TWENTY-TWO ·

'Whatever happens, keep your glister helmets on
at all times!'

Nate's voice was muffled, but Cade could hear the
urgency in his uncle's voice well enough. Through his
visor, and the glass panels of the descent deck, he could
see explosions of light outside. They sparked and
shimmered, rippled and coalesced, in an ever-changing
display. Transfixed, Cade stared unblinking at the lights
as they seemed almost to dissolve, then reassembled,
showing him different scenes, other places . . .

He saw his veranda on the Farrow Lake. He heard a
voice calling to him – Thorne Lammergyre, who was at
the end of the stone jetty beckoning to him.

'Come swimming, Cade. Take your cap off and dive
in . . .'

Cade reached for the buckle of his glister helmet, only
for Celestia's hand to close over his.

'It's the glister storm!' she shouted from inside her own helmet. 'Don't listen to the voices.'

Beside her, Tug strained at his seat harness, then fell back, breathing heavily and misting his dark-tinted visor. Theegum was swaying from side to side, and Cade tried hard to focus on her through the spellbinding explosions of crystallized light.

'Cade, come and see this . . .'

Cade's heart leaped. It was his father's voice now, calling him into his workshop in the academy tower. He was only little – no more than four years old – and the workshop was a magical place for him. Cade wanted so much to see inside. He struggled to get to his feet – but the seat harness was holding him back . . .

In their hammocks on the upper deck, Grent One-Tusk and Fenda Fulefane stared up at the ceiling through the glass panels of their glister helmets. The air seemed to be sparkling. Grent pushed himself up on one elbow and looked round.

'Are you asleep, Fenda?' he asked.

Fenda shrugged. 'I'm not sure,' she admitted. 'I don't think so – but maybe I'm dreaming. I keep hearing someone calling me . . .'

'Calling *you*?' said Grent. He shook his head. 'You're mistaken, my dear. It's someone calling *me*.' He paused. 'Listen. There it is again . . .'

'Welcome to the Sumpwood Bridge archives of Earth Studies. Please step inside.'

It was Durldew the archivist's voice; warm, measured, full of wisdom. Grent loved that voice.

Grent One-Tusk, a long-haired goblin from a prominent Hive family, lived up in Mid Town, in a grand mansion with a spectacular view. The window of his bedchamber looked down on the Sumpwood Bridge and along the banks of the Edgewater River, and at the profusion of clan huts, stilthouses and goblin hive towers competing with each other for a place in Low Town. Further upriver, he could see the waters of the Hive Falls that thundered down from the lofty palaces of High Town, past the terraced mansions of Mid Town, through the span of the bridge and out into the rich farmlands beyond.

Famously warrior-like and fearless, long-hairs in Hive had become the most prominent goblin clan, ruling over the others in the Goblin Nations and, when called to, leading them bravely into battle. Grent himself had worn a tailored militia topcoat from the moment he could walk, and could dismantle and reassemble a phraxpistol by his fifth birthday. He first rode a prowlgrin down the high jump of the Hive Falls at the age of ten, and fought his first duel at twelve – a trifling dispute with another cadet about the role their fathers had played in the Battle of the Midwood Marshes. Grent still bore the axe scar that proved honour had been upheld.

His was a world of barked commands, drills and chilly obedience. But then, one warm yet blustery day, all that changed.

Out on an errand, Grent found himself crossing the Sumpwood Bridge between the ornately carved academy buildings that lined both sides, their timbers glowing in the midday sun. Pausing beside an exceptionally elegant stairway, he looked up and noticed the carved head of a flathead goblin, a great metal hoop gripped in its mouth, fixed to the door at the top.

Later, Grent would never know what had possessed him, but that morning he climbed the stairs, grasped the hoop and rapped it hard against the burnished panel.

From inside, there came the echoing sound of footsteps, accompanied by the tap-tap-tap *of a stick, and the door swung open. Grent took a step backwards, his hands clasped behind his back. An archivist stepped out of the shadows.*

He was immensely tall, almost three strides, but stooped. Beneath his fur-lined cap, the great dome of his forehead, mottled and furrowed, gave way to bushy eyebrows, each of them plaited above heavy-lidded grey eyes. At either side of his tusked underbite, extravagant side-whiskers sprouted like grey storm clouds. He wore long, greenish-blue robes festooned with carefully rolled notes, and leaned on a bloodoak staff.

'Well, well, what have we here?' It was that voice again, its tone so gentle, so kindly.

Durldew's grey eyes had looked Grent up and down, then focused on the copperwood helmet he wore; 1ST HIVE CADETS *carved into its polished surface.*

'Let me take that from you.'

The voice was comforting, reassuring, as if it knew the weight of expectation and unflinching discipline that this particular copperwood helmet represented.

Grent reached up and unbuckled the helmet, and took it off.

Suddenly it was as though the golden timbers of the Sump-wood Bridge Academy were glowing even more brightly. Grent was filled with a delicious feeling of release. This, he realized, was the world he wanted – the world of knowledge and enquiry; the world of questioning and freedom, rather than blind obedience.

The world of academic study, not war.

'Welcome to the Sump-wood Bridge Archives of Earth Studies,' Durldew's voice sounded again. The archivist was standing right in front of Grent, his green-blue robes shimmering with light. 'Please step inside.'

'Grent?' Fenda called. 'Grent, are you all right?'

Grent did not reply, and for a moment Fenda was concerned. But then she heard the soft voice calling her name once again, and her concerns melted away.

'Just wait a second, Grent,' Fenda told her

friend, her voice soft and dreamy. 'Someone wants me. I'll be right back . . .'

'Fenda, darling, are you ready? We're about to set off.'

Fenda Fulefane stretched out her legs, flexing the muscles and warming her joints as she prepared to run.

'Coming, Mother,' she said softly.

Fettle-leggers were good at running. Their legs were powerful, their stride was long; they were sure-footed and agile. Every year, when spring arrived, everyone in the nine villages – old and young – would run together from the high forest, down to the loom huts on Weavers Lake.

It was a joyful occasion. As they ran, each family would trail banners, intricately patterned and finely woven, to show off their weaving skills. Down the forest trails, fringed by brooding ferns and dark gorse, they would run, then nine times around the lake, leaping from white stone to white stone. It felt so good to stretch your legs after a winter spent weaving at the great looms.

Merchants from far and wide used to come to view the banners the fettle-leggers trailed. Then they would bid high prices for those materials they thought the fine folks in the great cities would buy.

But Fenda remembered how the hard times had come. The steam factories of Great Glade copied the fettle-leggers' designs on their phraxlooms, mimicking the basket-cable and henchpike-bone stitches they had perfected, and producing the finished products for a fraction of the cost. Fewer and fewer merchants made the long journey to the fettle-leggers' part of the Deepwoods.

And then the forest fires had struck . . .

No one knew how they started, though there were plenty of rumours. What was not in doubt was the high number of loom huts that were burned to the ground, causing the fettle-leggers to abandon their white stone cottages and return to a wild existence foraging in the forests.

The Deepwoods were dark and dangerous, but also full of wonders. Fenda's mother taught her about the plants around them, how even the humblest, most insignificant among them could contain hidden wonders.

'Just like you, my little sapling,' her mother told her, her voice tear-soaked but urgent. 'You have such potential, Fenda. When we get to the floating city, you'll see . . . But first we must cross the grasslands.' She frowned. 'Take off your bonnet, Fenda.'

343

Fenda undid the bonnet. It was heavy and stifling, and it felt good to take it off.

Around her the grasslands rippled with iridescent light. Her mother stood in front of her, and Fenda felt as if her heart was about to explode. Fenda reached out towards her, but her mother had already begun to run, taking great powerful strides as she raced off across the shimmering grasslands.

Her voice floated back to her. 'Run! Fenda, run!'

'Grent? Are you still there?' Fenda asked.

'I'm still here,' he said, though his voice sounded distant. 'But we really must go now. Leave your bonnet. You won't need it. Just as I don't need my helmet any more. Not where we're going . . .'

'Where *are* we going?' said Fenda.

'It's a secret,' he said. 'But there's still something I want to show you.'

Fenda laughed. 'There's something *I* want to show *you*, Grent.'

She took his hand, and together they set off. Neither of them looked back . . .

Down on the descent deck a cry went up.

'Seftis!' It was Nate, his voice cutting through the shimmering lights. 'On my order . . .'

Outside, the glister storm seemed to be fading now, the lights glowing more faintly above them as the nightship hurtled down into the endless darkness. Cade's head began to clear.

He was still strapped into his seat; still wearing his protective glister helmet. They all were. Celestia and Tug were on either side of him. Seftis and Theegum were across the deck, their hands poised over the controls to the phraxchamber and stone-band. And there were four empty seats . . .

Cade frowned, puzzled. But then, as his thoughts continued to come back to him, he nodded. Of course. Sentafuce and Demora were back at Denizens Keep, being tended to by Ulnix Tollinix, while Grent and Fenda were asleep in their hammocks.

As for Nate, Cade saw that his uncle was slumped forward over the flight levers, his eyes fixed on the blackness below.

'There!' Nate turned to the others. 'Can you see it?'

Cade peered down through the glass. Far, far below, specks of blue light had begun to appear, and were rapidly growing larger as the nightship hurtled towards them.

'That's the place where I left the Professor,' Nate said excitedly. 'I'm sure of it . . .' He twisted round. 'Seftis?'

'I'm ready, Captain.' The wiry armourer tensed in his seat.

'Now we'll see what the *Linius Pallitax* is really made of,' Nate muttered through gritted teeth. His hand hovered over the flight levers. 'Fire up the phraxchamber!' he ordered. 'Cool the stone-band!'

Seftis pulled back the chamber levers, and powerful steam jets shot out of the funnels as the phraxchamber thrummed. The glow of the stone-band began to fade and, as it did so, an immense force pushed all of them back in their seats.

Cade felt as though an iron fist had closed around his chest and was steadily squeezing all the air out of his lungs. Inside his glister helmet, he gulped at the air like a beached oozefish. Only when the nightship's freefall came under control did the pressure ease off, and Cade was able to breathe freely again. He looked down through the panels of glass.

The nightship, he saw, was hovering above a vast sloping landscape of huge boulders that descended into the darkness below. In the distance were the patches of glowing blue light which, unlike the treacherous glister storm they had gone through, were pale and constant.

Slowly and carefully, Nate guided the nightship down the scree slope towards the blue light. He was navigating his way through a narrow gulch studded with outsized boulders when they saw them.

Two bodies.

Their arms were entwined and their heads thrown back, as if they were reclining on a bed rather than draped over the hard surface of a scree boulder. A long-haired goblin and a fettle-legger, the two of them kitted out in descending armour – but without their glister helmets. Their necks and backs were broken, and their eyes stared up into the blackness, unseeing.

Swallowing hard, Cade unbuckled his harness and climbed the steps to the upper deck. The roof hatch was wide open, and there they were, the two glister helmets that had been removed and discarded, lying on the floor beneath it.

Coming up behind him, Celestia began to sob gently. 'Grent,' she murmured. 'Fenda . . .'

· CHAPTER TWENTY-THREE ·

The crew of the *Linius Pallitax* stood on the lip of the giant scree boulder, the nightship moored above them. Heads bowed, they looked down at the two hammocks that lay, stitched shut, at their feet.

Theegum and Seftis had dismantled two of the sump-wood seats, painfully aware that they were no longer necessary, and used the panels to construct a pallet. Then they had laid the sealed hammocks containing the bodies of Grent One-Tusk and Fenda Fulefane upon it.

The air was still and cold; the inky blackness beyond the lamps of the nightship silent and impenetrable. It was like staring into nothing.

Nate Quarter knelt down and lit the buoyant sump-wood with a pine-resin match. The flames flared bright green, and the pallet trembled and lurched, then ascended smoothly into the blackness above.

'We commit our comrades Grent and Fenda to Open Sky,' said Nate solemnly, 'that they might return to the clouds from which all life comes.'

'Sky take their spirits,' the others replied in unison.

As they watched, the flaming sumpwood became a twinkling green star far in the distance. Then it disappeared.

Cade looked away. He heard Celestia sniff and, turning, saw her wipe away a tear. Tug reached out and took her hand in his, while Theegum – still staring up into the darkness – moved her arm in a graceful rising spiral, her long claws seeming to caress the air as she bade a silent farewell to her fallen companions.

No one spoke as they returned to the nightship and resumed the slow downward journey over the scree fields. Cade looked around the descent deck, his heart heavy. They had begun their voyage with a crew of ten: ten comrades united in their commitment to descending. Four crew members had been lost already – and there appeared to be no end in sight.

The scree fields sloped down into the blackness, lit only by the occasional cluster of blue moss-covered rocks. And as the nightship descended ever further, the phraxchamber thrumming and the stone-band glowing bright and fading in turn, Cade, Tug and Celestia took it in shifts to search the rocky landscape for the Professor, while Nate, Seftis and Theegum flew the vessel.

The time was measured out by the chimed bells; the nights, indistinguishable from the days, spent sleeping

fitfully inside their glister helmets. Meal times became the highlight of the day, a chance to huddle around the phraxstove eating the nutrient-rich gruel and sharing stories from their past. After the experience of the glister storm, it seemed important that they should hear each other's memories, spoken out loud and shared.

Cade and Celestia talked of Farrow Lake and their adventures there, while Seftis spoke of rescuing Theegum, and their twinned careers; first in Great Glade and later in the floating city. For his part, Nate told them all about his childhood in the phraxmines of the Eastern Woods, and how, later, he and Eudoxia had met for the first time in Great Glade.

One memorable meal time, Nate even spoke of the astonishing events that had occurred at the return of the Sanctaphrax rock. As Cade and the others sat spellbound, he described the appearance from the heart of a great storm of three legendary Edge figures – Quintinius Verginix and his son Twig, and Twig's grandson, Rook Barkwater, the famous Freeglade Lancer.

The Immortals, he called them.

'The barkscrolls recount how Quint witnessed Linius Pallitax create – or rather, resurrect – the shapeshifting gloamglozer out of glisters,' Nate went on. 'And I once stood in the very same laboratory he worked in, right at the heart of the Sanctaphrax rock. More than that . . .' He paused, enjoying the rapt attention of his listeners. 'I myself came face to face with one such evil creation.'

'You saw a gloam-glozer?' Cade breathed. He remembered what Eudoxia had told him back at the Farrow Lake, but hearing the events direct from his uncle's mouth was so much more intense.

Nate nodded. 'A whole army of them,' he said, his voice low and hushed. 'They were infesting the floating rock that had just returned. The Immortals defeated them, of course, and Sanctaphrax was restored. But ever since then I've known that I cannot rest until I discover just how Earth and Sky are connected.'

Nate looked away, lost in his memories. And as the others watched him, his unfocused gaze staring into the mid-distance, they saw how that strange, otherworldly shade of blue had returned to his eyes.

'Glisters from the Edge cliff,' he murmured. 'The Immortals appearing from the storm. Stormphrax and flight rocks . . . The Deepwoods and Open Sky . . .' Nate turned and stared into the glowing stove. 'I'm certain that the answer to it all lies at the bottom of the Edge cliff itself,' he told them. 'At groundfall.'

Cade nodded, enthused by his uncle's words – but Celestia had gone silent. Though no one else seemed to have noticed, *she* had been all too aware of the name of that ancient academic who had unleashed the power of the gloamglozer. Linius Pallitax. The same name that had been given to the nightship.

She hoped it wasn't an omen.

Time passed. The crew continued to search the scree fields. They discovered more islands of blue moss, which they harvested, to supplement their meals with the edible lichens and glowing fronds. Tug, Cade and Celestia became accomplished scree explorers. Wearing phraxpacks, boots and full armour, they clambered over the boulders in search of any sign of the missing Professor, while the *Linius Pallitax* hovered overhead, lighting their path with its powerful phraxlamps.

It seemed a hopeless task, looking for one lone Descender in this endless sloping desolation. But then, one day at four bells, as yet another glowing blue scree island came into view, Nate's hands tightened around the flight levers.

'I really do feel I know this place,' he said slowly, and Cade could have sworn his uncle's eyes looked even bluer than they had done moments before; the bluest he had *ever* seen them.

'Seftis, take over the flight levers,' Nate ordered. 'I'm suiting up and going down with Cade, Tug and Celestia.'

'We'll hold her nice and steady, won't we, Theegum?' the armourer reassured him.

The four Descenders climbed through the hatch and down the side of the nightship before stepping onto the glowing, moss-covered scree. As they did so, Cade straightened up, then took a step back.

There was something approaching, floating towards them out of the darkness. Up the rock-strewn slope it came, heading for the island of moss where they were standing. It was huge, twice the size of the

354

nightship at least; white and translucent – almost transparent – and there were small, glister-like pulses running across its surface. It was dome-shaped, fringed below by thousands of feathery tendrils, and with a tangled mass of what appeared to be eyestalks sprouting from the top.

Nate held up a gloved hand, indicating that they should fall back behind the cover of the blue moss fronds. Cade and the others crouched low as the creature moved closer. Above them, the nightship dimmed its lamps and climbed higher – though as a precaution, the tolley-rope harpoons swivelled round and took aim.

The creature reached the scree island and moved slowly over the surface of the moss, the glowing tendrils below it sending flickering pulses radiating over its surface. The eyestalks swayed in the night air, lighting up in turns and emitting beams of cold throbbing light that illuminated the surrounding blackness. Ethereal and diaphanous, it looked so beautiful . . .

As the creature moved on, Cade saw that behind it the scree boulder had been stripped of every trace of moss. It turned its attention to another boulder in the cluster, then another; moving with seeming purpose over one island of light after the other, until the entire archipelago had been reduced to a single clump of glowing blue moss – the place where Cade and the others were crouching.

Nate stood up, phraxharpoon in hand. Above him, the *Linius Pallitax* switched on its phraxlamps full beam.

The creature instantly went dark, reacting in what must have been shock. It shrank back, then quickly retreated, the eyestalks disappearing into its dome-like surface and the tendrils beneath shooting out to an incredible length, propelling the creature high into the blackness above, where it disappeared from view.

'What *was* that?' said Celestia.

Nate was looking thoughtful. 'I've seen creatures like it clinging to the logbaits let down into the clouds by skytaverns,' he said. 'Though they were no bigger than an oak-apple . . .'

Cade peered down at one of the stripped boulders in front of them. 'Uncle Nate,' he said, 'are these what I think they are?'

Nate followed his gaze. The surface of the freshly revealed rock was covered in a pattern of intricately chiselled symbols. He nodded.

'Descenders' marks,' he said.

· CHAPTER TWENTY-FOUR ·

The *Linius Pallitax* hung in the air overhead, the yellow beams of light from its phraxlamps illuminating the scoured rock below. Nate knelt down and ran his hand over the marks carved into the bare surface. Cade and Celestia crouched down beside him.

Cade knew all about Descenders' marks, though these were the first he'd seen up close. This was how Descenders on different descents communicated with each other. A combination of lines and dots chiselled into the rock, they logged times and distance, creatures encountered, routes taken; they warned of dangers and advised on courses of action.

No one, though, apart from his uncle and his companion, had ever been this far down in the depths before. Cade knew that it could mean only one thing.

'The Professor made these marks,' Nate breathed.

Cade nodded. 'What do they say?'

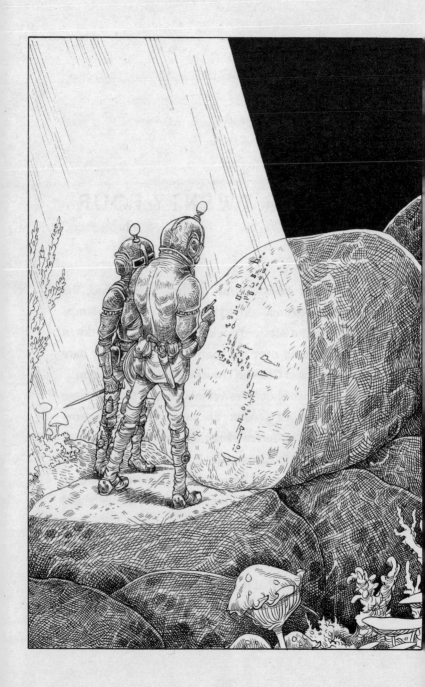

Nate pointed to a series of thin arrows underscored with spiky symbols and bisected by curved waves. 'This is a record of air currents cross-referenced with a timeline, but—' He took a sharp breath and shook his head in disbelief. 'It looks like the work of many years. Thousands of meticulous observations. See here . . .'

He pointed again, this time to a complex series of interconnecting circles and parallel lines.

'Quite remarkable,' he said, his face rapt with excitement. 'Based on his observations, the Professor has worked out a route down through the maze of air currents.'

Nate ran his fingers along a furrowed groove.

'Still air here,' he continued. 'Then evacuation points, here, here and here, where updraughts erupt.' He looked up, his eyes shining. 'This is invaluable information. It tells the Descenders when they should descend and when they should anchor themselves to the scree.'

He pulled out a leadwood pencil and a notebook, and started to copy the markings carefully down.

'This is the way the Professor intended to continue his descent,' he said, tracing a finger along a chiselled line. His brow furrowed. 'The trouble is, we have no way of knowing how far he got, or even whether he's still alive. And yet . . .' He looked around, his otherworldly blue eyes glowing intensely. 'You *are* here, aren't you?' he whispered softly. 'Somewhere . . .'

Just then, everything was abruptly plunged into darkness as the nightship moved away. Cade gripped Nate and Celestia's shoulders.

'Look,' he whispered.

One of the huge, luminescent creatures had returned. The sweeping beams from the nightship had picked it out, then shut off. They weren't needed.

Glowing brightly, the creature glided silently through the dark air. Unlike the one they'd seen before, feeding on the blue moss, it wasn't alone; merely one in a shifting constellation of hundreds. Each of them would glow intensely for a moment, then dim. Together, the entire airborne multitude created an endless rippling array of prismatic light pulses.

Standing on the boulder, Cade, Celestia and Nate stared up in astonishment, transfixed by the evershifting display. None of them knew what the creatures were, yet none of them were afraid. The mood felt tranquil, almost benevolent; as though the overwhelming sense of calm was emanating from the creatures themselves.

But then, all around them, the scree suddenly began to clink and rattle. Soft sighs rose from the crevices between the boulders as powerful currents of air stirred.

'A wind storm is coming,' said Nate. 'Quickly, both of you. Back to the nightship.'

Celestia and Cade followed him to the *Linius Pallitax*, where Tug extended a massive arm to help the three of them up. As they scrambled aboard, Tug pulled down the hatch and secured it.

Back in their sumpwood seats once more, they watched the creatures moving slowly down the sloping scree and into the depths. Nate took out his notebook and consulted the Descenders' marks he'd copied.

'To be safe, we ought to anchor up until the storm passes and the air currents drop.' He frowned. 'The thing is, though, I've got a hunch that these sky creatures know where they're going.' He looked round. 'Power up the phraxchamber, Seftis.'

With the chamber thrumming, Cade released the tolley ropes and the nightship began to descend, gathering speed as it headed after the great glowing shoal of translucent creatures. Below the glass panels of the descent deck, the massive boulders of the scree fields became a foggy blur.

'Where *are* you, Professor?' Nate whispered.

*

Ambris Hentadile. I am Ambris Hentadile. I am Ambris Hentadile.

Academic.

Ambris Hentadile. Academic . . . Along with my dear brother, Ifflix, I was the brightest talent in the Academy of Great Glade. But then the Society of Descenders was shut down, together with the School of Edge Cliff Studies. That was my cue. I abandoned my academic life, lured by the promise of easy riches at the gambling tables of the skytaverns, while Ifflix continued his search for knowledge by descending . . .

Yet here am I now, in a wilderness of scree far beneath the Edge, surrounded by endless night, marooned on this island of glowing blue.

How long has it been since Nate left . . . ?

Concentrate, Ambris. Concentrate!

Time has no meaning here. Only the intervals of time make any sense – when the storms rise; when the scree ripples; when the air currents eddy around this blue island of mine, then fade away to stillness. There are patterns to it all. Times of stillness, times of turbulence. They are constantly changing, but recur in loops.

I will map these loops. What else is there to do?

The surface of this rock is rapidly filling with my observations. I scrape away the glowing lichen to make more room for my marks. And one day Descenders who follow after me might find this record . . .

How long have I been down here?

Those skytavern years, how futile they were, full of fights and intrigues, drunken nights and meaningless affairs. My life had no purpose – until young Nate needed rescuing and our fates became intertwined, leading me back to my dear brother Ifflix, and . . . and . . .

Concentrate, Ambris! Concentrate! . . .

The air currents are beginning to swirl once more, rising up through the scree, howling and sighing. This is the start of another of the big storms. It will rage and bluster, with hurricane-force winds, thunder and lightning. But then it will pass, just like every other storm has passed, and the stillness will return . . .

Time is as time does.

I have mapped the weather of this place now; the pulses, the ripples, the stirrings . . .

And the violent eruptions.

I know when they are about to begin. I know how long they, and the periods of stillness between them, will last.

But I have spent too long down here, alone on this glowing blue island. My hair and my beard have grown long. My descending armour is in tatters. Mapping is all I have to anchor my mind; to stop myself wandering off into the endless night. But even this cannot hold me much longer. I feel myself . . . how to describe it? Thinning. Becoming insubstantial. Turning translucent, like the sky creatures that loom up from the silent depths . . .

But who is this?

A pale figure in a tall hood is standing on the edge of the carpet of glowing blue lichen. It is as pale and see-through as I feel.

I move towards it . . . Or perhaps I am dreaming. I didn't think I could dream any more, but how can I tell?

The figure reaches up and undoes the clasps that hold the hood in place, then takes the hood off. Bright orange hair cascades over slender shoulders. It is a young girl in the antique costume of a stone pilot – fire apron, gauntlets, belt with rock callipers and cooling spikes hanging from it. She looks back at me, her eyes wide, then smiles.

'You're fading,' she observes, 'as all must do.'

I hold up my hands. I can see through them. I nod.

'Are you ready to find out what is below?'

I nod again.

'Then follow me.'

The nightship continued down, dropping swiftly into the blackness, surrounded on all sides by the glowing sky creatures. At the controls, Nate kept the flight levers aligned, while Theegum and Seftis tended to the phraxchamber and flight-rock coils. Cade and Celestia sat forward in their seats, hands poised over the tolley-rope harpoons, while above them, on the upper deck, Tug stood ready at the winch.

They were dropping smoothly, silently, in perfect time with the sky creatures. Nate glanced down at the Professor's descending marks again.

'It's as if we're passing through the holes in a net,' he said. 'We're surrounded by a mesh of air currents, with erupting storms swirling all around us, yet we're falling through still air.'

He closed the notebook and put it back in his jacket pocket. His gaze returned to the scene beyond the glass panels.

'Descending over the scree, anchoring during storms,' said Nate, 'it must have taken the Professor many long months to descend so far.'

Cade glanced up from the tolley-rope lever. Nate's eyes were wide and bright, and there was a smile playing on his lips. He was looking younger and younger, as though all the cares and tribulations of his descending years were falling away as the nightship continued to drop.

'Perhaps this is it,' Nate said, looking around at the crew of the *Linius Pallitax*. 'The time when we'll finally make groundfall.'

We're falling, falling, falling . . .

Yet somehow it doesn't feel as though I'm falling at all. No, it's more like floating. I can feel the swirls and eddies and ripples of the air currents as we pass over the near-vertical scree and continue down into the inky darkness.

My guide and companion, this young stone pilot from another age, is beside me but, when I reach out, my hand passes through hers like a glove through mist. Or maybe it is her hand passing through mine. It's difficult to be sure. She is glowing, the outline of her body growing misty and diffuse. And I feel the same sense of blurring from within myself – yet as we fall, I am also overcome by an intoxicating sense of joy. One by one, the burdens of my past life are falling away, even as I fall through the blackness . . .

Except it isn't blackness. Not any more. All around me, it is becoming lighter. Slowly at first, but growing in intensity. I can see the scree boulders far below. They seem to smudge as we fall past them towards the ever-growing brightness, while the stone pilot herself is now just a glowing pulse of light, shimmering against swirling, gold-tinged clouds.

'We are here,' she says at last, and her voice seems to have a thousand whispering echoes.

My heart is hammering inside my chest. Suddenly it seems as if my entire life, with its countless twists and turns, has been leading up to this single moment.

'Where?' I say. 'Groundfall?'

*'Not groundfall,' thousands upon thousands of whispers respond as the clouds swirl around and through me. 'Ground*rise.*'*

Cade's hands on the tolley levers felt cold and clammy. He looked around at his companions.

Theegum was standing stock-still, her muzzle pressed up against the glass panel in front of her. Celestia had taken off her glister helmet and was smiling back at Cade, her face radiant. Seftis was slumped in his sumpwood seat, his hands no longer on the phraxchamber controls, but shielding his eyes as he peered outside.

Only Tug was not there with them. He was on the upper deck at the winch, Cade remembered, waiting for Nate's signal to turn the ironwood handle and bring them to rest.

Except that this was not what Tug was doing . . .

From the moment of his birth, life had treated the nameless one harshly, punctuating his days with pain and hunger; separation and loss as he'd wandered, frightened and alone, through the mighty Deepwoods. True, his lot had improved when he met Cade and his friends at the Farrow Lake. Half-starved and delirious with fever, Tug was hardly even aware of the gentle hands that dressed his wounds and fed him succulent gladegrass.

Slowly, light had come into Tug's dark, nightmarish world.

But now there was this, the never-ending descent into the depths. It was proving to be the most testing trial of all. Tug felt his mind closing down again, the terrors of his past returning with ever more vivid intensity the further they went. The crew had endured many terrible trials and tragic losses before this latest part of their long journey, travelling down through the scree fields. Yet for

Tug, this was the worst. Here. Now. Despite the glowing armada of sky creatures surrounding the nightship, he felt a darkness growing within him.

Down, down, down the nightship went and, beside the winch, Tug dropped trembling to the floor. He curled up in a tight ball.

He was back in the Nightwoods of his birth once again. Back in the endless cold night. Panic rose from the pit of his stomach and he fought the urge to throw open the hatch and end it all, the way Grent and Fenda had. At least that would be quick. And final. No more memories crawling out of the darkness to torment him . . .

But then the light began to grow more intense. Tug sensed it through eyelids clenched shut. He opened one eye, and then the other.

Light was flooding in through the hatch which, to his surprise, he saw was open after all. The nightship had come to rest now and Tug felt a strange energy suddenly coursing through his body. His muscles relaxed, his heart swelled and his head cleared. A figure was standing over him.

Tug climbed to his feet.

'You are a creature of the Nightwoods,' said the figure, transparent and glowing, glisters dancing around its outline. 'The newest, most primitive life to be seeded in the Edgelands. Others of your kind will grow and evolve in time, and move out from the darkness. But you, Tug, have taken a faster path . . .'

The figure was wearing a crushed funnel hat and battered descending armour, and was as glowing and translucent as one of the sky creatures outside. This, Tug suddenly realized, must be Nate's long-lost descending companion – Ambris Hentadile, the Professor.

'What has happened to you?' Tug asked, and was surprised by the sound of his own voice. It was no longer deep and rumbling, but sounded clear, almost lilting.

'The same thing that is happening to you, Tug,' said the Professor, in a voice with a thousand whispered echoes. 'We are evolving . . .' He reached out a pale hand and showered Tug in sparkling, sparking glisters. 'And now we have to tell the others that their journey ends here. But we must hurry, Tug, for there isn't much time . . .'

On the descent deck, Nate climbed out of his seat and stood looking out from the nightship. He unbuckled his glister helmet and let it clatter to the glass panelled floor. Cade did the same – and gasped.

They had stopped falling and were now floating in a dazzling, cloud-filled sky. It was almost as though they'd gone so far down into the depths that they had emerged on the other side, into an astonishing world where every known scientific law – meticulously calculated and tested by Edge academics down the centuries – had suddenly been turned upside down and inside out.

No one on board the *Linius Pallitax* had ever seen anything like the spectacle that lay before them. How could they? The wonders unfolding outside the confines of the tiny nightship were beyond their imagination.

Sky creatures of every description floated past in vast shoals – some winged and fluttering; some sinuous and writhing; some with tendrils, some with crests; others, huge and diaphanous, coiling and flexing as they floated off into the distance. And all the while, far below them in the constantly churning clouds, countless tiny glisters rose in glittering plumes.

At first, it was impossible to tell what was happening, but as they watched, they discerned a pattern – if not logic – to what was taking place.

From minute specks, the glisters grew in size and intensity, coalescing to form bright pebbles. The pebbles clustered together to form rocks, then boulders, then great columns of scree that rose higher and higher, up towards the nightship, and on into the darkness far beyond . . .

'We're here,' came a voice, and looking round Cade saw Tug climbing down from the upper deck.

He looked younger than before, fresh-faced and bright-eyed. The scars on his shoulders had faded to nothing, and when he smiled his teeth were no longer jumbled and fang-like, but evenly spaced and regular.

And he wasn't alone. Behind Tug came a pale shimmering figure dressed in a crushed funnel hat and worn, tattered descending armour.

Nate turned from the glass, his eyes wet with tears. 'Professor,' he breathed.

· CHAPTER TWENTY-FIVE ·

The crew of the *Linius Pallitax* stood staring out from the descent deck.

'So this is it,' said Nate Quarter, his voice breathless with awe. 'The place we've spent so long attempting to reach. And at such a cost,' he added.

The Professor, pale and glowing beside him, nodded. 'This,' he said, 'is groundrise.'

Cade pressed his nose up against the glass panel. It was an extraordinary sight. The swirling clouds sparked and glittered with glisters, countless millions of them.

'Glisters are the building blocks of all life in the Edgelands,' the Professor explained, his body glowing more brightly as he spoke. 'The clouds of Open Sky around us carry them over the jutting rock in great storms – Mother Storms – seeding the Edgeworld with life.'

The Professor pointed to the long trails of glittering

specks. The others watched spellbound as the marvel of creation continued before their eyes.

'The glisters are also the building blocks of the Edge cliff itself,' he said, 'forming scree, then solid rock.'

He paused for a moment, his expression one of intense concentration. It was as though he was finding it difficult to speak, to find the right words.

'The densest formations of all emerge as flight rocks in the Stone Gardens,' he continued at last. 'But there are others that are propelled upwards by air currents; sporadic eruptions that send them hurtling into the skies above the Edge.'

Nate Quarter turned to the Professor. 'So the Edge cliff itself is floating in Open Sky?'

'It is,' said the Professor, 'but more than that, Nate. So much more. You see, it is all part of the eternal cycle of Earth and Sky. Just as the ancient scholars of old Sanctaphrax always suspected.'

Nate nodded, struggling to make sense of the Professor's words.

'The glisters form the Edgelands, but they also form the clouds of Open Sky,' the Professor went on slowly, patiently. 'These clouds turn into storms above the Edgelands and deliver lightning. The lightning solidifies into stormphrax, buries itself, and sinks back down to groundrise. Then, back here, the stormphrax disintegrates in the light, releasing its innate energy and creating fresh clouds that are seeded with yet more glisters. And this cycle is repeated endlessly.'

'For ever and ever,' Nate murmured.

Celestia looked over at Cade, and frowned. 'You seem to be glowing,' she said.

Cade frowned back at her. 'So do you,' he said. 'In fact, we all are . . .'

The Professor nodded. 'The forces at groundrise are immensely powerful,' he cautioned gravely. 'Here, things return to what they are made of. What they originally came from. It is a wonderful feeling, and I welcome returning to Open Sky.' He shook his head. 'But none of you are ready for that. Not yet. You must leave this place now.'

Tug took a step forward and solemnly bowed his head to the Professor. 'I am glad to have made this journey,' he said, 'and also glad that we found you, Professor.'

Accustomed to his friend's guttural grunts, Cade was taken aback. Tug's voice sounded clear and measured now, while the words themselves were as formal as those used by any well-bred fourthling.

'Groundrise has been good for you, Tug,' said the Professor, 'but now you and your friends must return in this wonderful vessel of yours. Already the phrax crystals are becoming unstable, and the seed-stones of the flight-rock coil might fail at any moment . . .'

'And you, old friend,' said Nate. 'What will become of *you*?'

The Professor smiled. 'I will fade, until I am a collection of the glisters that made me,' he said. 'But before I do, let me help you.'

The Professor stepped forward, passing through the glass panel of the descent deck and outside. And without any warning, as Nate, Cade and the others watched, he transformed into a rippling, translucent sky creature.

'Prepare to ascend!' Nate's order cut through the silence on the deck.

Cade fell into his sumpwood seat and fastened the harness. He felt light-headed; elated, yet strangely calm. Theegum was at the flight-rock controls, her gestures puzzled and concerned.

Seftis nodded. 'My controls aren't responding either,' he told Nate.

Nate pushed the flight levers forward, then pulled them back again – once, twice, three times – before slumping back in his seat.

'We have no power,' he said.

Just then, a ripple of light passed across the glass panels of the descent deck, and Cade felt a slight lurch as the nightship began to rise. Slowly at first, then gathering speed, they ascended between the twisting columns of glisters.

Outside, the sky creature that had been the Professor seemed to be towing the nightship up towards the beginnings of the scree fields. As their speed increased though, the energy of the task was obviously taking its toll. Time and again, the sky creature flickered and faded, then grew bright, only to fade again moments later.

The air around the nightship pulsed in waves, and the sky began to darken. The scree fields were just above them.

All at once, the sky creature glowed a dazzling white and an explosive air current erupted from the scree, flinging the nightship upwards. Then, far behind them as they rapidly rose, the sky creature seemed to vaporize into a glittering array of glisters.

'Goodbye, old friend,' said Nate, looking back as they sped on. 'And thank you.'

· CHAPTER TWENTY-SIX ·

'The flight-rock coils are back in action,' Theegum reported with a tuskless smile. 'Phraxlamps on low heat . . .'

'Phraxchamber not responding!' Seftis called out. There was unmistakable panic in his voice. 'Unless we can turn up the phraxlamps in the chamber, we risk the phraxchamber going dark.'

Cade swallowed uneasily. In darkness the phrax crystals would become immeasurably heavy and send the nightship hurtling back down in freefall. At the flight levers, Nate was battling to keep the *Linius Pallitax* stable as the powerful air currents continued to propel the vessel upwards.

'I'll go and check,' said Cade, unbuckling his harness. 'The connecting rods might have jolted loose when the chamber became unstable back at groundrise.'

'I'll go with you,' said Celestia, leaping from her seat.

Outside, the scree fields were indistinct as the night-ship hurtled past them. At this rate, they would reach the beginning of the glister face in a few minutes. If the air current dropped, though, they would be dependent on the power from the phraxchamber. Time was running out. They had to get the phraxlamps working, and fast.

Otherwise they would be trapped here in the depths. For ever.

Cade and Celestia scrambled onto the upper deck, where Tug had already opened the panel that led into the phraxchamber. Cade peered in through the opening. He knew the inner workings of the chamber from the months of patient construction in the Armoury of the Knights Academy. And he knew the dangers.

Ahead of him was a narrow walkway that passed through a thicket of cooling pistons and stabilizing rods. At the far end was the inner chamber, around which the phraxengines were whirring in orbit. It was bitterly cold and, despite his descending armour, Cade realized he was shivering.

'Be careful,' said Celestia as she handed him a long-handled ratchet.

'I will,' he reassured her.

He felt Tug pat him on the back. 'Duck your head, Cade, or one of those phraxengines will take it off,' he said in that clear voice he had so recently acquired.

Cade stepped out onto the walkway and inched his way forward, stepping over cooling pistons and squeezing carefully past the thick stabilizing rods that

led to the steam funnels. One touch, he knew, and he would be fused to the freezing metal.

As he got closer to the central chamber, the nightship juddered, and Cade was almost thrown off his feet – but not before he had to duck as one of the spherical phraxengines shot past his right ear. He hesitated for a moment, looking around cautiously. Then, straightening up, he began to check the connecting rods that controlled the phraxlamps in the central chamber.

Numbers four and five were solid, but number one looked loose, and two others had come adrift completely. The nightship juddered again.

All too aware of how quickly he needed to work, Cade reached out with the ratchet, only for another of the phraxengines to dash it from his hand as it whirred past. The ratchet bounced off the walkway with a loud *clang* and clattered down through a steam funnel vent.

'Cade? Are you all right?' Celestia called into the chamber from the opening. Her voice, strident with alarm, echoed around Cade's head.

'Lost the ratchet,' he called back. 'I'll have to tighten it by hand.'

To do that would mean going to the very edge of the walkway, then leaning down as far as he dared to reach the disconnected joint, all the while dodging those orbiting phraxengines. It wouldn't be easy. Was this how it was going to end? Cade wondered. His brains dashed out by his own father's brilliant invention . . .

Cade pushed the thought from his head as he reached

the end of the walkway.

Thrum! Thrum! Thrum!

The phraxengines whirred past again and again, missing him by inches. Lying on his front, his body pressed against the sumpwood slats of the walkway, Cade stretched out one hand, then the other. He slotted the first joint, then the second, into place, and twisted the rods until he felt them click.

Thrum!

The hair at the back of his head was parted as a phraxengine hurtled past, grazing it.

'Cade!' Celestia called. 'Cade! Get out of there. Seftis has to power up the chamber . . .'

Cade turned and scrambled back as, sure enough, the chamber began to hum loudly and ice-cold steam shot out from the stabilizing rods. Tug reached in through the opening, grasped Cade by the shoulders, and pulled him back out onto the upper deck. Celestia slammed the panel into place.

'Thank Earth and Sky,' she murmured.

The nightship bucked and rolled, then righted itself as the phraxchamber returned to full power. The steam funnels billowed out great white vapour clouds, and the nightship continued to rise.

Cade and Celestia clambered down to the descent deck and buckled themselves back into their seats.

'Good work, Cade,' said Seftis approvingly. 'I hope I didn't give you too much of a scare.'

The *Linius Pallitax* was rising at a considerable

speed now, no longer dependent on the air current, but flying with the smooth buoyancy afforded by the phraxchamber and the flight-rock coils. Looking out through the glass panel beside him, Cade saw the flickering lights of the glister cliff face, and pulled on his protective helmet. They passed on rapidly, and as the time sped past, Cade found his thoughts wandering . . .

They had descended to the very bottom of the Edge cliff to discover where life began and ended; to a place where both Sky and Earth were born, only to find that they couldn't stay there. They, the Descenders, had reached the end, but also the beginning.

Cade looked up at his friend, Tug. What was it

the Professor had said? *Groundrise has been good for you.*
He had certainly been right.

Smiling down at him from his sumpwood seat, it was
as if Tug – the *real* Tug, who Cade had come to know so
well – was now visible. His jawline was tighter, the hunch
had gone, and the contours of his face seemed to have
meshed together to reveal a sensitive and intelligent
nature.

'My thoughts are so much clearer,' said Tug, as if in
answer to a question Cade had not quite formed. 'It's as
though my mind has been released, up into the light.'

He smiled with a trace of that lopsided grin. Cade
smiled back.

'I'm glad, Tug,' he said. 'And glad to be heading home.'

The nightship travelled up past Denizens Keep – where
Demora and Sentafuce came aboard, fully recovered
from their injuries, although appalled by the news
of the loss of Fenda and Grent; up the Fluted Decline,
with eerie Edge wraiths gliding past and ravine
demons scuttling through the shadows; and beyond.
Nate steered an even course, flying wide of the cliff
face as he kept on upwards through the dark swirl,
confident that the combined power of the phraxchamber
and the flight-rock coil would combat the unpredictable
gusting winds.

Above the Cusp, they made short work of the High Cliff,
rising swiftly through the white swirl, and continued past
the Low Gantry. Soon, the great cascade of the Edgewater

falls was washing the nightship clean with its fine spray. Then, moments later, the *Linius Pallitax* abruptly broke cloud cover and, leaving the eternal darkness behind, soared up over the jutting lip of rock and on towards the floating city itself.

Cade stared down at the Stone Gardens and, once again, found himself thinking about the cycle of life on the Edge that they had learned about from the Professor. As they approached New Sanctaphrax, Nate steered the nightship round the Loftus Observatory and, looking across at the East and West Landings, Cade was surprised to see that they were crowded with the sleek cloudcruisers of the tallow-hats.

So was Celestia. 'How long have we been gone?' she asked. 'Two weeks, is it? Three?'

'Longer,' said Cade.

'Hmm,' said Celestia. 'Well, the tallow-hats certainly seem to have made themselves at home in that time,' she murmured, then looked up at Cade. 'And *that's* odd . . .'

'What is?' asked Cade.

'No skymarshals on patrol.'

Nate didn't say anything as they came in to land in the central square below the Great Viaduct. Cade released the tolley ropes. They were taken up by a group of tallow-hats, each of them festooned with phraxpistols, muskets and sabres.

'And no academics around either,' said Cade to Celestia.

The crew of the *Linius Pallitax* climbed out of the hatch and stepped down onto the mosaic tiles of the square. Tallow-hats, dozens of them, rose from the Viaduct Steps and came clattering down to meet them. Orders were barked, messengers dispatched, and the tallow-hats levelled their weapons at the Descenders.

'This is a fine greeting,' said Nate, stepping forward. 'Where is Eudoxia?'

A tallow-hat strode towards them, the others stepping aside to let him through.

'You'll find Eudoxia Prade waiting for you soon enough,' the tallow-hat said with a nonchalant smile. He nodded to his comrades. 'Seize them!'

PART FIVE
THE FOURTH AGE

· CHAPTER TWENTY-SEVEN ·

With a bony finger, Danton Clore traced the nubbed ridge of the scar that ran down his right cheek.

'Be sure to include this,' he told the portrait painter, a short, angular gnokgoblin academic from one of the Viaduct Schools.

The goblin nodded, his feathery brush dabbing away at the wooden panel on the easel in front of him.

'Certainly, your . . . erm . . .' he replied uncertainly.

'Knight-General of New Sanctaphrax,' Danton Clore said, his voice clipped and clear as he stressed each word. 'No more High Academes and Professors of this, that and the other for the floating city, but instead the Knights of the Tallow and the Company of the Willing.'

Danton Clore sat back in the high-backed sumpwood chair. He clasped his hands behind his head and gazed up at the vaulted ceiling of the Great Hall of the ancient Knights Academy.

Willing Companions, he mused. As well they should be.

At the easel, the painter stiffened, his brush poised, and tutted softly. 'If the Knight-General doesn't hold his pose,' he said, 'I can't guarantee the portrait will be finished for the Launch Ceremony.'

'You have taken the Oath of Loyalty, I trust,' said Danton, sitting up and turning his head back to its original position.

The portrait painter plucked at his black robes, the front emblazoned with a white bloodoak.

Danton smiled to himself. Restructuring the upper echelons of New Sanctaphrax hadn't been easy, but he was finally beginning to make real progress. One by one, his tallow-hats had forced the academics of the floating city – willing or unwilling – to pledge their allegiance to the new order. And it was a nice touch, he thought, to have made them give up their blue-grey robes for something altogether darker.

'I have sworn to serve the Knights of the Tallow,' the gnokgoblin confirmed, without enthusiasm.

'Then my portrait *will* be finished, even if you have to stay awake for the next three nights to get it done,' said Danton, his voice soft but edged with menace. He fixed the portrait painter with an unblinking stare. 'Scar and all.'

The gnokgoblin dipped his brush into red, then ochre paint, and returned to dabbing at the wooden panel.

He, along with his fellow scholars, had been ambivalent about the presence of the newcomers in the floating city at first. Long discussions and heated debate had ensued, weighing up the pros and cons. Now that the tallow-hats had established themselves permanently, though, he had learned to keep his mouth shut. It wasn't wise to question the decisions made by the new Knight-General.

In stark contrast to the scholars in the small viaduct schools, many New Sanctaphrax academics had welcomed the tallow-hats with open arms. After all, Danton Clore and his comrades had saved the floating city from the phraxships of Quove Lentis, just as they'd promised they would . . .

Danton Clore himself had relived that day a hundred times or more, and the sequence of events that had led up to it. Even now, his heartbeat quickened as he remembered Eudoxia Prade in that smoke-grey cloak of hers, stepping down from the scuttlebrig onto the Edgeland pavement. She'd looked so vulnerable, yet so determined. Then she had lowered her hood, and the moment Danton had looked into her clear green eyes, he knew that he would follow her anywhere in the world.

'I need your help,' she'd said simply, her voice soft and lilting.

She sounded shy, nervous even, but those green eyes of hers had spoken to Danton of the inner strength she possessed. Back then, though, with the phraxfleet of Quove Lentis threatening to attack, that was not enough – she needed strength of a more practical kind.

'Can you help me, Danton Clore?' she asked, then smiled. '*Will* you help me?'

And Danton had been powerless to say no.

The other tallow-hats were less sure. Danton had sent out ratbirds summoning the cloudcruisers, and they had come in their hundreds. Gathered together in the desolate fringes of the Edgelands, where the barren pavement fell away into the abyss, they had listened to Eudoxia appealing to them for their help.

'If New Sanctaphrax should fall to Quove Lentis,' she'd argued, 'then his fleet of phraxships will come after you next. And with all their might. The tallow-hats will be destroyed.'

Her words had failed to impress them. The tallow-hats were used to a life on the run; used to hiding out in these barren wastelands, fighting and fleeing. They were not afraid to die. Scornful and dismissive of this elegant young woman, they were preparing to leave when Eudoxia made them an offer that had captured Danton Clore's attention.

'New Sanctaphrax,' she said, that beguiling smile playing on her lips, 'has something new and important to trade.'

She explained how the academics of the floating city had made a great breakthrough in phrax technology, enabling them to produce an almost limitless supply of energy from a single phrax crystal. It was, she went on, an advance that would not only produce clean power for the great cities, but would also make all phraxships faster and more powerful than ever before – introducing a *fourth* age of flight that, in the right hands, could spread peace and prosperity throughout the Edgelands.

'And in return for your cloudcruisers coming to our aid,' she told the tallow-hats, 'I, as acting High Academe and representative of the Descenders of New Sanctaphrax, am prepared to share that great breakthrough with you.'

It was an offer she would live to regret. At the time, though, Eudoxia had been sure that Nate would have approved. After all, during his long absence before, she had made many decisions on his behalf – and certainly it got Danton Clore's attention.

He saw all the possibilities at once. While the grizzled captains of the tallow-hat fleet remained unimpressed, shaking their heads and muttering among themselves, Danton Clore had taken Eudoxia aside.

'Leave them to me,' he'd whispered. 'You shall have our help.'

How he treasured the look she had given him at that moment, one of trust and gratitude. It was a look he received from her a second time when, days later, he had climbed down from his cloudcruiser onto the West Landing, victorious after the great battle with the phraxfleet from Great Glade.

But no longer.

Danton abruptly stood up and, ignoring the painter's protests, strode across the hall to the great circular window and looked out. There, by the West Landing, in a specially constructed skyship cradle, was a cloudcruiser. He nodded appreciatively. Eudoxia had certainly been right about the advances in phrax technology.

With its sleek beaked prow and burnished ironwood bows gleaming in the sun, the phrax-vessel looked magnificent. Danton admired the curved phraxchamber, with its encircling flight-rock coil, full of latent power; and the sinuous lines of the steam vents that arched so elegantly from the twin-ruddered stern. A flight across the Edgelands that would once have taken weeks to complete should soon be possible in hours.

As Danton watched, a black-robed team of the newly created Companions were carefully painting letters on the polished hull of the vessel. The *Herald of the Fourth Age*. It had been a difficult journey but, after weeks of intense and careful planning, Danton could feel the prize almost within his grasp.

And the hardest part of that journey?

Danton turned from the window. 'Enough!' he barked. 'Take your sketches and studies, and finish the work in your studio,' he told the portrait painter as he marched past him and out of the hall.

Gripping the banister, Danton climbed the stairway to his sumptuous apartments on the upper floor of the Knights Academy – or rather the Tallow Hall, as it had been renamed. Knights of the Tallow, in their crisp black tunics and gleaming helmets with side candles, saluted as Danton passed quickly by. Most were former academics who had taken the Oath and renounced their robes of Sanctaphrax blue. Some, though, were former tallow-hats. No longer dandified sky pirates, they had become harder and smarter, and with a new sense of purpose.

Danton Clore's purpose.

That *had* been hard, Danton acknowledged as he stepped inside his chambers: dealing with those difficult tallow-hats who had not shared his vision. Some of them had been unable to see the advantages of seizing control of the floating city; others were reluctant to abandon their old ways – while a significant few were actively resentful that Danton Clore himself had become so powerful. None of them guessed that his takeover of New Sanctaphrax was only the beginning . . .

As he entered his high chamber, two black-robed Companions bowed low before him, obsequious smiles on their faces. Danton washed his face and hands in the copperwood bowl of scented water that one of them held out, then dried them with the soft linen towel offered by the other. Once High Professors of the School of Mistsifters, the two of them were now his personal servants.

The thought pleased Danton.

He unbuttoned his black topcoat and let it drop to the floor. One of the servants snatched it up and hurried off to hang it in the wardrobe, while the other held up a loose black robe with a chequerboard collar; Danton slipped it on.

'Leave me now,' he told the two Companions as he crossed the chamber.

When they had gone, Danton pulled a key on a gold chain from inside his tunic, unlocked the door in front of him and stepped into the room beyond. It was immense, with a great domed ceiling of leadwood struts and panes of crystal above, and a broad curved floor of polished lufwood below.

Danton stood on one of the elegant balconies and looked up into the space in the centre of the dome. There, sitting at a sumpwood lectern, surrounded by other floating lecterns, was Eudoxia Prade.

This, the old Hall of High Cloud in the former Knights Academy, was where renowned professors had once lectured their students. Now it acted as Eudoxia's prison cell.

Danton pulled a lectern down towards the balcony, climbed on to it and allowed it to float back up to where Eudoxia was sitting. Above his head, clouds billowed up

and scudded past the glass, which was etched with ancient cloudwatching calculations.

Eudoxia put down the barkscroll she'd been reading and looked up at him.

This was the hardest part, thought Danton as he looked back into those clear green eyes and saw the rage and resentment in them. She was furious with him for abusing her trust – and even more furious with herself for having trusted him in the first place.

It had started when Danton had put the first part of his plan into action, just after the battle. The tallow-hat captains had wanted to be paid off, happy to take flight rocks, phrax concessions and mire pearls, and return to the wilderness of the Edgeland's margins. But

Danton couldn't allow that; not if his dream of being Knight-General was to become reality. So he had dealt with the leading captains – the would-be troublemakers – in the Stone Gardens one moonless night.

Those tallow-hats who had helped him, though, Danton promoted, making them Knights of the Tallow. Then, with these loyal reinforcements at his side, he'd moved against the Sanctaphrax Academy itself. He imprisoned Eudoxia and, with their acting High Academe gone, it wasn't long before the academics caved in and took the Oath.

All, that is, except for the skymarshals.

The majority of them had been killed defending New Sanctaphrax, but a stubborn few had fled into the sewers beneath Undergarden. And while the rest of the academics became black-tunicked knights if they supported Danton Clore, Knight-General, or were forced to join the Company of the Willing and exchange their blue-grey robes for sombre black, this small group of skymarshals watched and waited.

Swiftly and ruthlessly, Danton took over the Knights Academy and plundered the Armoury for its secrets. Then the work had begun. Although not easy, with co-operation from the new 'knights', it hadn't taken long to construct first a phraxengine, and then flight-rock coils like those used in the now infamous nightship the *Linius Pallitax*.

And throughout all this, as he was systematically taking absolute control, Danton had had to suffer the

silent fury and growing contempt of Eudoxia Prade. It
was like a dagger to his heart, but Danton would not
give up.

With the skies free of Great Glade phraxships for the
time being, and New Sanctaphrax now in his grip, Danton
intended to re-equip his cloudcruisers and build a fleet,
the like of which had never been seen before – and which
would travel to the furthest corners of the Edgelands . . .

There had remained, however, one possible scenario
that threatened to scupper his plans. The return of Nate
Quarter. If the High Academe himself were to rally the
skymarshals still loyal to the old order of the floating city,
then everything might still fall apart.

Then, like a gift from the sky itself, the *Linius Pallitax*
had returned.

The crew was arrested. And so simply. It had been like
spearing fish in a barrel. Danton couldn't help but smile
as he recalled the looks on their faces – so bewildered
and helpless – as the cry had rung out to 'seize them!'

'What is this?' Nate Quarter had demanded, reaching
for the phraxpistol at his belt – only to have it snatched
from his hand and turned against him by the tallow-hat
at his back.

'Celestia!' the youth beside him had cried out, turning
and shielding a dark-haired girl protectively. But another
of the tallow-hats had prodded him viciously in the side
with a long lance and dragged her away.

The nameless one hadn't liked that. With a ferocious
roar, he'd barrelled through three more of the tallow-hats

standing in his way, sending them sprawling, and struck Celestia's captor hard with the flat of his hand. The tallow-hat had stumbled backwards and crashed to the ground, and the nameless one had reached out for Celestia . . .

'Be careful, Tug!' she'd cried out – but too late, as a large net came down over him, and he was wrestled roughly to the ground.

The banderbear had suffered the same fate. Except it took even more of the tallow-hats to pin her down. Time and again, one, then another of her attackers was sent flying as the furious, snarling creature lashed out through the netting with her taloned paws. But with an ever-increasing number of tallow-hats joining in to overpower her, slowly, inevitably, the net was tightened and her struggle came to an end.

Meanwhile, the trog and the waif had tried – and failed – to make a run for it. And when the little goblin armourer put his hands up, it was all over.

Disarmed, exhausted after their time in the depths and completely outnumbered, there was nothing any of them could have done. As the last member of the crew was taken prisoner, a loud cheer had gone up from the Viaduct Steps, the crowd of tallow-hats roaring their approval. Any there among them who were uneasy at seeing their brave High Academe and his Descender friends being treated so shamefully remained silent.

Danton Clore had stepped forward and issued commands.

Seftis Bule and his banderbear were put to work in the Armoury, where, against their will, they immediately helped to speed up the work on the new tallow-hat fleet. Demora and Sentafuce were confined to a laboratory and forced to reveal everything they knew about phrax technology. Nate's nephew and his Deepwoods friends, meanwhile, were taken to Undergarden and locked up in a prison where they would remain until they could be persuaded to take the Oath of Loyalty. As for Nate Quarter, former High Academe of New Sanctaphrax . . . well, he was going to be the most useful one of all.

'Have you thought about my offer?' Danton asked, meeting Eudoxia's gaze. 'I think it is a generous one.' He smiled. 'The launch is three days away. If you become my partner in Sky and Earth, then I shall release Nate Quarter and his nephew to live out their days in exile, anywhere they choose. So long as it is away from the great cities,' he added. 'And if you refuse . . .'

The look came into Eudoxia's eyes that always made Danton flinch. Hatred. Pure hatred. But he was helpless. Just as he had been when he first laid eyes on her. She would be his, even if he had to destroy everything she held dear to keep her with him.

If he couldn't have her love, then he'd settle for her hate. But she *would* be his.

'. . . I will sell them to Quove Lentis.'

· CHAPTER TWENTY-EIGHT ·

Brocktinius Rolnix looked up at the great floating city, far above his head. It was ten weeks since Quove Lentis's phraxfleet had come so close to defeating its defenders. Brock knew he should have been happy with the way events turned out – but even back then he'd been uneasy.

By rights, of course, he shouldn't be here now. During the sky battle, his phraxcraft, the *Rock Demon*, had taken a direct hit, sending Brock himself hurtling to the ground; his fall broken by the thick wind-chime netting strung out between two low towers of the School of Squalls in the old quarter. But since he *had* survived, Brock vowed to serve and defend New Sanctaphrax until his last breath.

After all, he thought, reliving that heroic last-ditch charge of the skymarshals, it was as though he'd been given a second chance.

When he had finally come to his senses after the crash-landing, the first thing Brock noticed was how silent it had become. The battle was over. The Great Glade phrax-fleet of Quove Lentis had been routed by the tallow-hats he'd seen speeding in from the far horizon, and his heart soared – until he saw the number of sharp-prowed cloudcruisers already docked at the twin landings of New Sanctaphrax.

Not that anyone else seemed that bothered.

Brock's misgivings, however, had proved well founded. Rumours began to spread through the floating city like wildfire: the water had been poisoned, the Professor of Glister Studies had been arrested, Quove Lentis was planning another strike . . . And, with the city in disarray, the tallow-hats had made their move.

Brock himself went to ground in Undergarden to await developments. Holed up in the overgrown ruins of an ancient foundry, he bided his time, hoping and praying that something might thwart the tallow-hats' complete takeover of the floating city.

What remained of the skymarshals – about forty or so – soon abandoned the sewers and returned to New Sanctaphrax to join the so-called Company of the Willing. But, although they'd put on the black robes with the bloodoak insignia, they remained loyal to Brock, becoming his eyes and ears in the stricken city . . .

Danton Clore. This was the name that Brock would hear increasingly often from his spies. He was, it was said, driven. He was cold and calculating. Vain. He would brook no dissent; stop at nothing. He was utterly, utterly ruthless . . .

As for Brock, although he was learning much about the self-appointed Knight-General from his spies, he himself had had no direct contact with Danton Clore since that brief glimpse of him when the tallow-hats first arrived. But then came that moonless night in the Stone Gardens.

Brock would never forget it.

He'd been out scouting near the Edgewater Falls, half hoping to pick up signs that the nightship with Nate Quarter, High Academe Elect, on board was returning. Brock found the Descender post deserted, and was about to return to his hideout when he heard raised voices. He ducked behind a stone stack, its topmost boulder crowded with roosting white ravens.

Close by, standing near the jutting lip of the Edge cliff, was Danton Clore. Brock had recognized him at once. The leader of the tallow-hats was wearing a splendid black topcoat edged in silver braid, and on his head a gleaming helmet with two tallow candles, burning blood red, attached to its sides. Danton was not alone. Flanking him on either side was a phalanx of black-uniformed figures. Their phraxpistols were aimed at a small group standing on the cliff edge.

Brock couldn't quite believe what he was seeing.

The group were tallow-hat captains, twenty at least, dressed in gaudy waistcoats and crushed funnel hats – the leaders of the tallow-hat armada that had 'rescued'

405

New Sanctaphrax. Danton Clore hadn't wasted any time grabbing power, though this latest twist puzzled Brock.

Then one of the tallow-hat captains stepped forward.

'Danton, please,' he said, 'you stay here if you must, but we just want to take our crews and head back to the wilderness. Old Thane Two-Blades here has always had your back, you know that, but you've changed, Danton. This place has got to you . . . *She* has got to you . . .'

Behind the tallow-hat captain, the other captains bristled, their fists clenched and narrowed eyes glaring at Danton Clore. He smiled back at them, the scar on his cheek flexing in the light of the tallow candles like a rivulet of blood.

'Take one pace back,' he said coolly as the black-uniformed guards beside him cocked their phrax-muskets. 'And another . . . And another . . .'

Staring grimly back at him, the tallow-hat captains disappeared in a rippling wave as they stepped back into the void. Their despairing oaths rang out as they fell.

'Sky curse you, Clore . . .'

And, just like that, Danton Clore had taken absolute control. He was now ruler of New Sanctaphrax.

Shaken by what he'd just witnessed, Brock returned to his secret hideout in Undergarden. Everything he'd heard about Danton Clore was true – and it strengthened his resolve to rid the floating city of this tyrannical usurper, once and for all.

His infiltrators in the Company of the Willing kept him informed of the latest events up in New Sanctaphrax, while Brock, for his part, continued to bide his time in Undergarden. But it hadn't been easy. Especially when, almost four weeks after it had descended, word reached him that the nightship finally *had* returned.

That was when Brock and the resistance to the Knights of the Tallow began to get truly organized. There would, though, be no acts of sabotage; no eye-catching stunts or demonstrations. Instead, Brock chose to remain hidden and concentrate his energy on spreading his contacts throughout the Company of the Willing. Quietly. Covertly. Danton Clore must have no idea of the resistance until Brock was ready to strike.

Now, that moment was close. Prompted by three, superficially unconnected, incidents, Brocktinius Rolnix was making final plans . . .

The first was news he'd received from one of his undercover skymarshals about a curious meeting that had taken place between Danton Clore and Nate Quarter, up in the Loftus Observatory, where Nate was being held captive. The Knight-General, it was reported, had made the former High Academe an offer. According to Brock's sources, he'd wheedled, cajoled, threatened and shouted abuse, but Nate Quarter had refused to be bullied. In fact, he'd refused to utter a single word to his captor.

The second incident occurred several days later. Another of Brock's spies had intercepted a ratbird that was carrying a message addressed to Quove Lentis in Great Glade. Reluctant to trust anyone else to deliver it,

the black-robed 'Companion' – a skymarshal by the name of Stark – had brought it to Brock in person.

'I thought you should see this,' he said gruffly as he handed over the small creature, its wings held tight against its body.

Brock looked down at the ratbird, and at the rolled-up message secured to its leg. The words *High Professor of Flight* were clearly visible on the piece of yellow parchment. He undid it and read it through:

Dear Quove,

This is to confirm that, as arranged, Nate Quarter and his nephew, Cade, are about to be dispatched.

Expect delivery in three days.

Yours, Danton C.

Brock nodded grimly. 'You did well, Stark,' he said. 'This changes everything.'

The message, he realized, tied in with the third piece of information that Brock had recently received: that Danton Clore was about to launch the first of his newly upgraded cloudcruisers. Now Brock knew where that maiden voyage was bound.

The weeks of patient watching and waiting were finally over. It was time for Brock to act.

But he couldn't do it all on his own . . .

As the moon set and, one by one, the stars flickered and dissolved into the lightening sky, Brocktinius Rolnix crept closer to the rusting hulk. It was the wreck of a phraxship from the Great Glade fleet, brought down in the battle over Undergarden.

Its cavernous upended hull, embedded in the earth, had been turned into a makeshift prison. The entrance was a walkway which led up to the jagged remains of the wheelhouse. The phraxchamber had been removed and replaced with a timber stockade, from which gantries led off to cell doors cut into the port and starboard bows.

Six black-uniformed guards – Knights of the Tallow – were lounging around by the phraxgun emplacement on the foredeck, their faces glowing in the light of a blazing brazier. By the smell of it, they were roasting hammelhorn steaks. Brock recognized quite a few of them: mistsifters, raintasters and fogprobers from the academies of Sky Studies.

His lip curled with contempt as he unclipped his long-barrelled phraxmusket.

These were, and always had been, the most awkward academics at the refectory tables. They had loudly opposed descending and were always out for whatever personal power they could gain. During the sky battle, they had been ready to surrender the floating city to Great Glade – and some of them had even been killed doing just that. Not that the others had learned their lesson. Since the victory of the tallow-hats, they had eagerly joined Danton Clore's Knights of the Tallow.

Right now, the six of them were concentrating on little else but filling their bellies before the dawn guard came to relieve them. A faint pink glow was already streaking the eastern horizon. Brock didn't have much time.

He would have to make every shot count.

'Six weeks,' Cade called out as he scratched yet another line into the metal hull of his prison cell. He tossed the fragment of stone away. 'Six wasted weeks! How long do you think we're going to be held here?'

'Until we swear the Oath of Loyalty,' came Tug's deep voice from the cell to his left.

'Which means we'll be here for ever,' said Celestia from the cell on his other side. 'Because I, for one, am never going to do that. As I said to that ridiculous black-robed hammerhead oaf again last night, "I remain loyal to the true High Academe of New Sanctaphrax, Nate Quarter." That's what I told him. "Not to some

jumped-up sky pirate with a candle on his hat." And I meant it.'

Cade smiled to himself. He'd heard every word Celestia had said at the time. After all, with their three prison cells next to each other, it would have been impossible not to.

Every evening the hammerhead came, delivering meagre portions of food and demanding to know whether they were ready to swear the Oath – and every evening, the defiant answer he got back was the same. It was all so predictable, and would have been laughable if it wasn't so serious. Cade was beginning to fear that they might never be released.

How much longer, he wondered, would Danton Clore be prepared to wait? Or would he simply give up and leave them to rot?

With night receding, Cade climbed off the metal cot at the back of his cell, crossed the floor and looked out through the small window in the door, his hands gripping the bars so tightly his knuckles turned white. After everything they'd achieved down in the depths, to return to New Sanctaphrax and be imprisoned like this; it was so frustrating. More than that, with the floating city now at the mercy of Danton Clore and his bunch of cut-throats, and Cade himself unable to do anything about it, he was left bursting with impotent rage.

They had all attempted to escape. Celestia had tried using a hairclip to tease the lock open. Tug had hurled himself at the door of his cell time and again, in the hope that brute force might work. For his part, Cade had endeavoured to bribe the hammerhead, promising him that his uncle would make him his own personal bodyguard when he regained control of the city – and when that failed, he'd attempted to break the hinges of the door using a metal bar that he'd snapped off the cot.

Nothing had worked.

The time passed, one day merging into the next. Occasionally, the three of them would talk, or rather shout, to one another through the walls of their cells – reminiscing about their lives at Farrow Lake; reassuring one another that everything would be all right and making plans for a future they all still hoped for. Most of the time, though, they sat on their cots, lost in their own thoughts, or listening to the cries and whimpers of the other poor wretches Danton Clore had imprisoned.

Cade had tried to keep his spirits up but, as he watched yet another day dawning outside, his heart sank. Even if any of them did manage to break out of their cell, then what? The six armed guards on permanent watch outside would soon deal with them. Cade was losing hope, and he knew that Celestia and Tug were feeling the same way.

'Are you awake, Cade?' It was Celestia, calling from the adjacent cell.

'I am,' he called back, and sighed.

'Look over by that sallowdrop tree,' she hissed, her voice hushed and urgent. 'I thought I saw something . . .'

Brock took aim at the guard hunkering down by the phraxcannon, a hammelhorn steak on a platter in his hands. He squeezed the trigger.

P-pithhh-ickk!

The long-barrelled phraxmusket jumped in his grasp. The guard slumped forward, unnoticed by his comrades.

P-pithhh-ickk!

With a sound like the low whine of a glade mosquito, the phraxmusket discharged another bullet. A second guard seemingly stumbled, fell forward and disappeared into the shadows behind the cannon.

The others looked up from their breakfasts.

P-pithhh-ickk! P-pithhh-ickk! P-pithhh-ickk!

The third, fourth and fifth guard fell twitching to the deck. The sixth was up and running, heading for the cover of the timber stockade, his faltering breath pluming in the frosty air.

P-pithhh-ickk!

His legs went from under him.

P-pithhh-ickk!

Face down, he fell still. A trickle of blood seeped from under his gleaming helmet.

Brock sprinted across the spongy turf, reached the body and unclipped a bunch of keys from the belt. The sky was growing lighter. Any moment now, the guards of the dawn watch would be here. Brock clattered along the upper gantry of the wrecked phraxship, stopping first at one cell door, then another, and another, unlocking them all and throwing them open.

The High Academe's nephew, Cade Quarter, stumbled out into the early morning light, dazed and dishevelled. Then his friend Tug emerged from the adjacent cell. And, finally, Celestia.

'Brock? Brock, it that you?' she cried. 'It is! It *is*!' And she flung her arms around him.

'No time for that right now, Skymarshal Helmstoft,' said Brock, easing her arms from around his shoulders and placing a phraxpistol in her hand. 'We've got to get up to the West Landing.'

· CHAPTER TWENTY-NINE ·

The West Landing was clear, though the central
avenue leading to it was thronging. Knights of the
Tallow lined the route from the Tallow Hall, standing
to attention, phraxmuskets at their shoulders. Behind
them, crowding the Viaduct Steps, were the black-robed
Companions of the Willing, hundreds of them, muttering
excitedly and jostling to get the best view.

The cloudcruiser, the *Herald of the Fourth Age*, sat in its
sky-cradle, towering over the gawping crowd.

High above, the towers of the floating city chimed and
sang as a gentle breeze passed through revolving sky
instruments. Then, from the turrets of the Academy of
Rain at the far end of the avenue, there came the sonorous
booming of the mist horns, and Danton Clore, Knight-
General of New Sanctaphrax, stooping low as he emerged
from the Gate of Humility of the Tallow Hall, marched
forward.

Eudoxia Prade followed him, the hood of her grey cape raised and her face bathed in shadow. Behind her came Seftis Bule, the chief armourer, followed by Theegum the banderbear, and . . .

A gasp went up from the watching crowd as Nate Quarter, the erstwhile Most High Academe, appeared. He looked tired and drawn, with dark rings around his eyes and a sunken look to his cheeks. In deference to his former status, he was wearing a cloak with a chequerboard collar and, behind the rows of impassive Knights of the Tallow, the Companions bowed their heads as he passed.

While the small group made its way up the grand avenue towards the West Landing, the wind grew in intensity and, all around, the music of the towers became louder and more insistent. Both the paving stones of the avenue and the masonry of the buildings lining it started to shimmer and glitter with millions of tiny fossilized glisters, causing further ripples of excitement to pass through the watching crowds.

Danton Clore and Eudoxia reached the end of the avenue first. They stepped up onto the timber boards of the West Landing, Eudoxia holding onto the hem of her cloak as the wind grew stronger still. Nate Quarter followed them onto the landing. He paused and looked up into the swirling clouds high above the towers and, as his eyes seemed to glow unnaturally blue, another murmur passed through the captivated crowd.

'Knights of the Tallow, and Companions of the Willing,' Danton Clore called out, his voice rising above the song of the towers. 'I have important news . . .'

He surveyed his audience and, as his gaze swept from one side of the crowd to the other, his heart swelled with pride. Born into a poor family in the Copperwood district of Great Glade, he was expected to become nothing more than a labourer in one of its stilt factories; little more than a slave. From his earliest years, he'd had dreams of a different life, a better life – yet even in the wildest of those dreams Danton Clore had never imagined that he might one day become Knight-General of New Sanctaphrax. Now there was just one more thing he had to do, and then his power would be unassailable.

'Nate Quarter has grown weary of our great city and wishes to retire to the Deepwoods,' he announced. 'And on the launch of *the Herald of the Fourth Age*, I myself shall escort him to his destination, then return to New Sanctaphrax to be united with Eudoxia Prade, who has, I am pleased to announce, taken the Oath of Loyalty—'

'It's a lie!' a black-caped figure shouted out from the teeming viaduct steps.

Danton fell silent. Everyone turned to see who had dared to interrupt the Knight-General. Pulling back the heavy hood to reveal his face, Brocktinius Rolnix stared back at Danton Clore.

'This tallow-hat sky pirate is going to betray our most High Academe and deliver him to Quove Lentis,' he

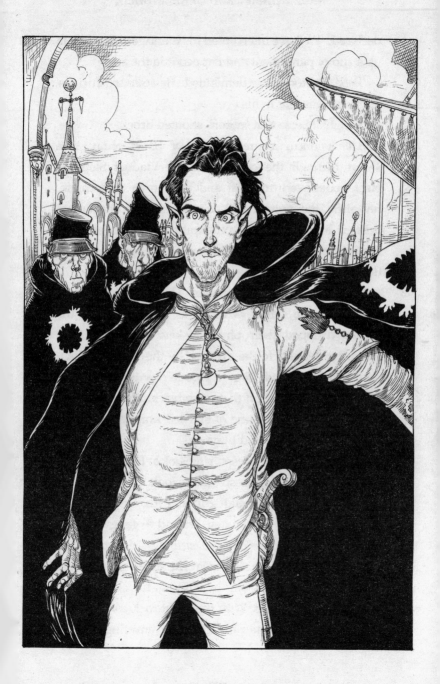

declared. 'We have intercepted his messages.' Brock held up a slip of parchment and flapped it in the air.

'*We?*' Danton Clore demanded. He sounded furious, but there was fear in his eyes.

'Knights! Seize that traitor!' shouted Brock.

All at once, a great wave of Sanctaphrax blue swept through the crowds on the Viaduct Steps as black robes were torn off and thrown to the ground, revealing the gowns still worn beneath. The crowd bristled as hundreds of phraxpistols were raised and levelled at the startled knights, who were turning to face the steps.

For a moment, no one moved. Then the air abruptly filled with the clatter of metal as the Knights of the Tallow dropped their phraxmuskets and flung their gleaming helmets to the ground. By the West Landing, Cade, Celestia and Tug – together with Seftis and Theegum – had cast off their own black robes, and were pushing through the line of startled knights to form a cordon around Nate and Eudoxia.

Danton Clore cast a despairing look at Eudoxia, before his face took on an impassive stony look.

'So be it,' he said through gritted teeth.

Turning away, he vaulted onto the gangway and leaped aboard the *Herald of the Fourth Age*. Moments later, with an icy billowing blast from the steam funnels that blotted out the view from the landing, the cloudcruiser soared up into the air. With the flight-rock coils hissing and glowing, and the phraxchamber emitting a high-pitched whine, the vessel wheeled round in the sky and flew off over Undergarden at colossal speed.

'He's leaving!' said Cade, astonished.

Behind them, the academics, in their blue-grey robes once more, continued to round up the protesting knights, accusations and excuses ringing in the air.

'Wait!'

It was Eudoxia. She was gripping Nate's hand and staring up into the sky.

The cloudcruiser had turned in a wide arc, a streak of white steam trailing behind it as it sped back towards them. On either side of the sleek beak-like prow, twin phraxcannons swivelled as they took aim. Then, with a stuttering *crack-crack-crack*, two lines of dazzling yellow phraxfire sliced through the air, the bullets striking the Loftus Observatory and one of the Mistsifting Towers, pockmarking the walls and sending shards of masonry flying.

Breaking free of the cordon, Eudoxia ran across the boards of the West Landing, her arms spread wide and the smoke-grey cloak billowing out from her shoulders as the cruiser closed in.

'Kill me, if you must,' she shouted. 'But spare the city! Leave us in—'

'*NO!*' bellowed Brock, throwing himself in front of Eudoxia as more phraxfire strafed the landing. The bullets cut a bloody line across his chest and the skymarshal slumped to the wooden boards.

'Brock!' Celestia screamed.

Dropping to her knees at his side, she tore back his robes and ripped open the shirt beneath it, exposing the angry ragged wounds. Tears streamed down her face as she fumbled blindly for the bottles and bundles pinned to her chest, desperate to stem the bleeding; to make him all right.

'Brock, Brock, Brock,' she moaned as the skymarshal stared up at her, his eyes wide with shock and pain, his lips mouthing words she could not hear.

'Take these,' said Tug, handing her a roll of bandage and a vial of astringent salve.

But it was already too late. Before Celestia had even removed the stopper from the little glass bottle, Brock's face contorted, his back arched, and from the back of his throat came a soft rattling sigh as he breathed his last.

'No,' Celestia gasped as Brock's body went limp. 'You can't be dead, Brock,' she groaned. 'You *can't* be . . .'

She stroked his cheek, then fell forward onto him, her body racked with sobs – until Tug gently lifted her away.

Cade was there to comfort her. He wrapped his arms around her and held her close. 'I'm so sorry, Celestia,' he whispered. 'But . . . but I'm here for you. Always.'

He felt the tension in her body relax slightly. She pulled away and held his troubled gaze.

'I know, Cade,' she said quietly. 'And thank you. I— *Watch out!*' she shrieked.

Far above them, the cloudcruiser had turned in the sky again and was swooping back down towards the city, its phraxguns blazing. There was chaos on the twin landings and the broad avenue beyond, with everyone screaming and shouting, dashing in all directions or falling to the ground, desperate to get out of the way of the attacking vessel.

Cade grabbed Celestia by the arm. Head down, the two of them started running for cover when, all at once, soaring up from the depths and speeding over the towers of New Sanctaphrax, a huge boulder appeared, glowing blue. With a deafening *crunch*, it crashed headlong into the cloudcruiser, shattering the skyvessel into thousands of flaming

shards that rained down over Undergarden as the storm-stone continued on its trajectory over the Mire grasslands.

As Cade watched, scarcely daring to believe what had just happened, the vapour trails streaming from the falling boulder seemed to detach themselves and twist upwards and away – looking, for a moment, almost like one of the sky creatures from the depths – before disappearing into the shimmering atmosphere.

'The Professor?' he murmured.

Beside him, Celestia nodded numbly. 'I was thinking the exact same thing.'

· CHAPTER THIRTY ·

The acceleration of the refurbished cloudcruiser was phenomenal. As Nate pushed the phraxengine to full power, Cade grunted, the straps of the seat harness biting into his shoulder armour.

'Seftis and Theegum have surpassed themselves,' said Nate approvingly. 'The *Beacon of Hope* here is faster even than the *Linius Pallitax* in freefall.'

Cade looked across at his uncle. He looked well, no longer gaunt and bowed by his imprisonment at the hands of Danton Clore, who had kept him in chains at the top of Loftus Observatory. Locked up in the tele-scope chamber of the long-forgotten Professors of Light and Darkness, Nate had eked out the long weeks of confinement by cloudwatching and stargazing through the ancient instrument. Apart from that one occasion when Danton Clore had visited him, Nate had seen no one but his jailers.

'Yet I sensed Ambris's presence many times,' Nate had told his nephew after the fatal crash of the *Herald of the Fourth Age*. 'Watching over us all. Perhaps whatever it is that the Professor has become *did* guide the storm-stone's path . . .'

And Cade, for one, liked to think that it had.

From his seat in the glass-panelled flight pit, Cade looked down at the Deepwoods, now little more than a smudge of green. Nate pulled back on the twin rudders, and the cloudcruiser rose steeply through the thin air and on into the icy vastness of high sky.

So much had happened since that fateful day when Danton Clore was removed from power, Cade mused.

Despite their initial enthusiasm for the tallow-hat general, most of the floating city's academics had been only too happy to swap the black tunics and polished helmets of the Knights of the Tallow for their old robes of Sancta-phrax blue. It hadn't taken them long to tire of the Knight-General's despotic ways. A few, though, had left the floating city with the remnants of the original tallow-hat gangs, all of whom had been granted amnesty by the reinstated High Academe Elect. They'd set off together for the Edgeland wilderness in fewer than twenty of the old cruisers, leaving hundreds more of the vessels behind to be refurbished.

With the prototype cloudcruiser – *Herald of the Fourth Age* – smashed to smithereens by the mysterious storm-stone, work on the other cloudcruisers had resumed in earnest.

'Soon, New Sanctaphrax will have a fleet worthy of it,' Nate had said, looking around appreciatively as Seftis and Theegum organized the refitting of the cloudcruisers moored at the East and West Landings.

Along with Tug, the two of them worked steadily and methodically, harvesting seed-stones in the Stone Gardens for the rock coils and forging new phraxengines and thrust funnels in the city's foundries. And when, four weeks later, and way ahead of schedule, the first two cloudcruisers were pronounced ready for flight, Nate had immediately summoned Cade.

'We have unfinished business, you and I,' he'd said, laying a hand on his nephew's shoulder.

In his descending armour, newly re-equipped for sky flight with harness buckles and shoulder armour, and tilderskin gloves rather than heavy gauntlets, Nate looked ready for business. Especially with the two gleaming phraxpistols holstered at his side.

Cade had nodded. He knew only too well what this unfinished business was – and how it might be resolved – and he had changed out of his blue-grey robes at the Knights Academy and put on the clothes specially laid out for him.

'Quove Lentis will be expecting us,' Nate had said, opening the cage at his feet and taking out the little ratbird hunkered down on the perch inside. He checked that the newly written message wrapped around its leg was secure, and smiled. 'We mustn't disappoint him.'

Raising his arm, Nate released the ratbird. In a blurred hum of flapping wings, the little creature launched itself into the air, and he and Cade watched as it grew smaller, then disappeared in the darkness of the sky.

The *Beacon of Hope* had set steam at daybreak. Now, with Nate operating the thrust control, the airy whine from its phraxengine rose several octaves. Ice-white flame shot out of the thrusters, and steam from the sloping funnel became a pencil-thin line as the skyvessel rapidly picked up speed. Its beak-like prow sliced through the air, while the flight-rock coils around the phraxchamber heated and cooled, smoothing and cushioning the immense power being generated. Behind the flight pit, the phraxengine whined as the cloudcruiser sped on through the high sky.

'New Sanctaphrax to Great Glade in less than a day,' Nate Quarter breathed. 'This truly is the dawning of the Fourth Age of Flight.'

The second cloudcruiser to launch from New Sancta-phrax had set steam the previous evening. The *Spirit of Light*. Already, only two days later, its crew could see the distant lights of Riverrise – the waifs' city of night – twinkling in the eternal darkness.

With Brock gone, Celestia herself had agreed to pilot the new vessel and, as they came closer to their destination, she eased down the phraxengines and dimmed the lamps in the flight pit. Beside the aft deck, Tug, who had been working at the phraxcannon, charging the barrels with leadwood bullets, stepped back. From the observation port in the bow came Eudoxia's voice, clear and calm.

'The Thorn Gate is directly below us,' she reported. 'I can see lamp trails and campfires.'

'That'll be their main camp,' Tug replied with a shudder and, glancing across at him, Celestia could see the pain in her friend's face. 'The slave corrals will be in the darkness beyond,' he said, 'together with the nightwaif pens.'

'Stand by,' she called out. 'We're going in.'

The cloudcruiser slowed, the phraxengines' whine deepening to a familiar thrum as it did so. Celestia dropped the beaked prow down towards the dense forest of thorns below and squeezed the firing trigger.

The twin phraxcannons sprang to life, spitting out a trail of glowing phraxbullets that burst into two dazzling lines of orange as they hit the thorns. At the end of the fiery trail, the phraxcannon ammunition hit a stockade of blackthorn wood, which exploded, disintegrating into a mass of blazing splinters.

As the cloudcruiser swooped down lower still, tiny beaked creatures with wide startled eyes could be seen, leaping from the ornate lamphouses of the compound beyond the burning stockade and scuttling for safety on their thin claw-like feet. The cruiser sped past them, its rear phraxcannon swivelling round and drilling the lamphouses with further volleys of the explosive bullets.

Celestia brought the cruiser about in a broad arc and came down to a low hover in the middle of the compound, where hundreds of the red and black dwarves were huddled close together in a terrified crowd. The light from the blazing lamphouses cast an eerie flickering glow on the thornwood pens and corrals beyond. There, shackled by yokes and chains, thousands of stooped nameless ones raised their heads and stared up from the muddy pits they were crouching in.

'Oh, those poor wretched creatures,' Celestia breathed.

Beside her, Tug trembled as the dam broke inside his head, and memories – memories he didn't even know he had – came flooding back.

Tug's earliest memory was of being cradled by his mother. Huge arms enfolding him; the warmth of her skin; the steady beating of her heart; and the soft lilting lullaby, wordless but comforting, that made him so drowsy he could never keep his eyes open.

After that came memories of the Nightwoods. Moving, always moving, at the centre of a herd of mountainous bodies as they tramped through the forests of milkthorn and spike-briar.

And then, in the darkness, there was also the memory of tastes. The bitterness of the pungent bark; the meaty flavour of succulent grubs, and those soft juicy berries whose sweetness exploded on the tongue. Also the biting cold, the mist that seemed to seep through his skin – and pausing to lap at the earthy water that had collected in pools between tree roots as they tramped on and on in the endless darkness . . .

Where were they going?

Back then, Tug didn't have the words to ask his mother or the others. His mind was as dark and cloaked as the Nightwoods

themselves. It was only later that he started to understand. They were moving towards the silence, away from the scritching, chattering voices of the nightwaifs.

The waifs' voices pierced his head, and the heads of the others, if they came too close. They hurt like ice-cold thorn barbs and drove the herd away in panic-filled stampedes.

Tug still awoke some nights, his heart thundering in his chest at the memory of those headlong dashes into the darkness. It was in one such stampede that he lost his mother – for ever – her great clawed hand slipping from his grasp.

He didn't know it at the time, but it was a tactic of the black and red dwarves of the Nightwoods to use nightwaifs' thoughts to scatter the nameless ones. It made the great lumbering creatures easier targets if they could be separated from the herd, especially the infants. Once netted, these vulnerable young ones would be shackled, then whipped and beaten into obedience.

That was Tug's fate. And those were the memories that were the hardest to bear. His master's lacerating voice in his ear; the bitter sting of his whip, and the sharp glinting spikes that were jabbed so painfully into the soft sensitive places behind his ears and the tender membrane in his nose. There was no time to think, no time to order his thoughts or mourn the loss of his mother. Just the beatings and the endless hauling of thorn bundles out of the forest and into the embankments of the Thorn Gate.

Beyond the Thorn Gate, Tug had glimpsed the flickering lights of Riverrise, and had even heard the distant whispers of the waifs who ruled there. But he had needed to be careful. The other nameless slaves of the red dwarf had been broken. They had no thoughts left, and simply responded to the whip of their brutal master, not even flinching any more.

This, he told himself, would not be his fate.

To spare himself extra beatings, Tug learned to conceal his intelligence. He copied the others, swaying back and forth dementedly like they did when at rest; grunting and moaning like they did when at work. And he waited, at the end of his shackles in the darkness of the slave camp, for the red dwarf with the shiny key at his belt, and the cruel whip, to make a mistake – to come one step too close when he dealt out the daily flogging.

This was a memory that made Tug flinch, but it had needed to be done. He'd taken no joy in it, except perhaps for the quickness of the act.

The red dwarf had stepped up to add force to his whiplash, only for Tug to trip him with an outstretched claw, then drag him into his grasp. Now, like everything else, the sound of the red dwarf's spine snapping like a dead branch was just another memory that haunted Tug's dreams.

He'd taken the key from the red dwarf and unlocked his shackles, along with those of the other slaves, though they had been too cowed and broken to follow him as he made his escape . . .

And now he was back at the Thorn Gate once again, and below him were more of the nameless ones, all of them as cowed and broken as the ones he'd left behind before. He would not make the same mistake again.

With a deep mournful cry, Tug leaped down from the *Spirit of Light*, a phraxpistol gripped in each hand. He rounded on the dwarf slavers.

'Release them!' he roared.

'On whose authority?' a tiny crimson-skinned dwarf hooted, clacking its beak in agitation. 'We are licensed by Great Glade to maintain the Thorn Gate, and to collect tolls. The Waif Council has agreed to this.'

Tug levelled his pistols at the quaking creature. 'Justice and freedom,' he said, cocking each pistol in turn. 'Unless, of course, you'd like to argue . . .'

*

The *Beacon of Hope* powered down its phrax-engine and slowed to a steady pace. It kept level with the Great Glade phraxfrigate that had been sent out to escort it. At the wheelhouse and along the fore and aft decks of the older vessel, green-tunicked phraxmarines trained their spyglasses on the remarkable stream-lined skycraft that was flying alongside them.

Next to the sleek cloudcruiser, the frigate looked squat and cumbersome, like an old hammelhorn following a fleet-footed tilder. The deck-mounted phrax-cannons it carried were awkward and exposed in comparison with the cruiser's embedded phrax-cannon, while the great clouds of steam billow-ing from the frigate's tall

funnel looked almost comical beside the thin wisp streaking from the cloudcruiser's elegantly sloping one.

Up ahead, high above the teeming city of Great Glade itself, and getting steadily closer, was the magnificent Palace of Phrax. The cruiser eased ahead of the frigate, then dropped down until it was level with the upper balcony of the towering building, where it hovered next to the high pillars of its balustrade. With a click and a hiss, tolley-rope grappling harpoons shot out from the cloudcruiser, coiled round the pillars and secured the vessel smoothly and efficiently.

Nate turned to Cade. 'All set?' he checked. 'We're only going to get one chance at this.'

· CHAPTER THIRTY-ONE ·

The hovering cloudcruiser trembled as the glass-panelled canopy over the flight pit slid back, and two figures emerged on deck. Cade Quarter adjusted the chinstrap of the helmet he wore and straightened his robes. It felt strange to be wearing the black uniform of a New Sanctaphrax Companion. He reached out, took his uncle by the arm and pushed him roughly ahead.

'That's the way,' Nate muttered under his breath. 'This has got to look real.'

Stepping down onto the balcony, the two of them were greeted by a young female fourthling, dressed in the uniform of the Freeglade Lancers. A smile played on her lips as she reached for the long-barrelled phraxpistol at her belt.

'Felicia Adereth,' she said, addressing the young tallow-hat. 'We received word that you were coming.'

The tallow-hat merely nodded, then, head lowered, he shoved Nate forward. Felicia looked him up and down.

'Paid for,' she said, training her phraxpistol on Nate. 'And now delivered. My compliments to your master.'

The young tallow-hat nodded again. 'Danton Clore doesn't like to keep his customers waiting,' he said.

Felicia grunted appreciatively. 'Danton Clore is clearly someone Great Glade can do business with,' she commented, before grabbing Nate by the shoulder, twisting him round and shoving the phraxpistol into his back. 'Move,' she told him gruffly. 'Quove Lentis has already waited far too long for this meeting.' She glanced round at the tallow-hat. 'You come too.'

The three of them headed across the paved balcony, the marble slabs gleaming in the sunlight. As they passed a darkened chamber to their left, Nate glimpsed a pair of ferocious-looking nightprowls through the glass doors, their pale blue eyes shining as intensely as his own.

'Keep going,' said Felicia, her grip tightening on the handle of the phraxpistol. Her hands were sweating and she silently cursed this sign of her own anxiety.

Felicia Adereth was painfully aware of how precarious her position had become. The defeat at the hands of the tallow-hats had been a great setback. Quove Lentis was notoriously unforgiving of failure, and now Felicia was living on borrowed time, her own life in danger. When he'd ordered her to deliver Nate Quarter into his clutches, she'd known she would have to come up with the goods.

She had done well.

She'd made direct contact with the new leader of the floating city. Danton Clore had named his terms and they had reached an agreement. Now, after their intricate secret dealings, here was this young tallow-hat handing over the great Nate Quarter to Quove Lentis, the ruler of Great Glade.

Nate Quarter was valuable, though. Far too valuable for the fate that Felicia knew Quove Lentis had planned for him: sacrificed to the snaggletooths to satisfy his lust for blood. A more far-sighted leader would use such an eminent prisoner to unpick the secrets of the floating city, turn its strength against itself and conquer it once and for all. But Quove Lentis was not far-sighted. He was petty, vindictive and unpredictable.

She was armed with her phraxpistol, but Felicia wasn't about to take any chances . . .

High above the lofty balcony, with its intricate mosaics, its glazed pots of topiaried woodbay and black-sage trees, and its ornately carved sumpwood furniture, puffs of white cloud scudded across the sky. A pair of caged lyre-doves cooed longingly as a skein of snowbirds flapped overhead, while curled up in one of the doorways at the end of a silver chain, a vulpoon was sleeping.

At the far end of the balcony, reclining on his couch, Quove Lentis was also asleep. A rhythmic wheezing came from his moist flapping lips as his chest went up and down. Felicia smiled. This would make things that little bit easier.

As Nate Quarter and the tallow-hat came to a halt beside the couch, Felicia stepped forward and, turning away, picked up the decanter of ruby-red sapwine and refilled the corpulent High Professor's goblet. Turning back, she set the decanter down on the low table. Noisily.

Quove Lentis gave a spluttered snort, and his small eyes snapped open. He barely acknowledged his captain standing beside him – but then this was nothing new.

As Quove Lentis's gaze fell on the two visitors to the Palace of Phrax, his eyebrows shot upwards and a smile plucked at the corners of his mouth. He swivelled round on the couch.

'Is this who I think it is, Captain?' he asked, his voice plummy but indistinct, as though he was talking with a mouthful of pebbles.

'Indeed it is, sir,' said Captain Felicia Adereth crisply. 'Just as I promised.'

Meanwhile, with the enslaved nameless ones now free, the *Spirit of Light* had left the Thorn Gate and continued over the Nightwoods to Riverrise. Before they returned to New Sanctaphrax, there was something that needed to be done if the floating city was to survive and prosper.

With Eudoxia's help, Celestia brought the cloudcruiser down near the bottom of the waifs' city, and Tug tethered it securely to a mooring post. Then the three of them made their way to Kobold's Steps, the ancient stairway cut into the rock that led all the way up the Riverrise mountain, out of the darkness and on to the Gardens of Life at the very top.

'It's so *noisy*,' said Celestia as she and Tug followed Eudoxia. 'In here,' she added, tapping a finger to her temple.

They were passing by the city of night itself, its glass houses festooned with lamps that turned the steep streets into glittering clusters of lights. Thousands of whispered thoughts created a constant babble of sound as the waif inhabitants read each other's minds. Occasionally, a chorus of voices would rise up as an entire neighbourhood joined into a single unified thought, before ebbing away and returning to the soft feathery murmuring.

Trying their best to ignore it, the three visitors climbed higher. And, as they finally left the city below them, it was a relief for them all to put some distance between themselves and the never-ending chatter.

Peace and quiet, thought Celestia gratefully.

Ahead of her, Eudoxia turned back and smiled, almost as though she herself had acquired a waif's uncanny ability to mind-read. Tug, in contrast, was grim-faced. Sleeker, more upright, and able to articulate his thoughts clearly since their descent to groundrise, he was looking troubled.

Of course, Celestia realized, despite the way things had turned out for her friend, this return to the region of his birth must be difficult for him. She reached out and took his hand, and squeezed it reassuringly.

Big and muscular though it undoubtedly still was, even Tug's hand now seemed less gnarled and claw-like than before. And in the robes of Sanctaphrax blue he was wearing, he could have passed for a prosperous cloddertrog, or perhaps a refined quarry trog from the Northern Reaches.

They passed beneath a stone arch, then stepped out onto a wide escarpment. Celestia looked up, and gasped. So this was it. Nestling in a broad hollow below the Riverrise spring, the fabled Gardens of Life.

Before them, towering high above the darkness, was the mighty stone spike, which incoming Mother Storms from Open Sky would strike, unleashing their life-giving power.

Up here in these gardens of verdant vegetation and leafy trees, there was daylight; clouds swirling in a blue sky. Disconcerted to find herself so suddenly out of the permanent night, Celestia looked back down the steps they had ascended, to see that it was still pitch black below.

'Welcome, emissaries from the floating city.' Soft voices were speaking in unison in each of their heads. *'We have had ample time to sift through your minds on your journey up the steps to the Gardens of Life . . .'*

Celestia turned. Three white-robed waifs were sitting side by side on a rock which jutted out over the curved bowl of the Riverrise lake. Two females and one male, they were; all with huge milky eyes – sightless and unfocused – and fluttering translucent ears that seemed to turn in towards Celestia, Tug and Eudoxia as they approached.

'So you know everything,' said Eudoxia simply, lowering the hood of her storm-grey cloak.

The blind waif elders nodded.

'You come in peace to offer friendship and support,' the waifs' voices sounded, though their lips remained still. *'Tug and Celestia descended to a region hitherto unknown, and have returned with an understanding of its mysterious properties—'*

'But we believe that this place, groundrise, must be protected from any further intrusion,' Tug broke in. 'For nothing must risk interrupting the cycle of Earth to Sky and Sky to Earth.'

The waifs nodded. *'This we also believe.'*

One of the female waifs stood up and approached Tug directly.

'Descending will go no further than the upper scree fields,' Eudoxia promised. 'And our two cities – one where the sky seeds life; the other where stones are born – will protect this cycle.'

The waifs nodded again.

'*You, Tug, have done the city of Riverrise a special service,*' the female waif told him, staring up into his face with her milky white eyes. '*You have broken the stranglehold the dwarf slavers held over our city through their control of the Thorn Gate. Great Glade was behind their efforts, holding Riverrise to ransom, but you and your skyvessel have put them to flight.*'

Tug bowed, and Celestia could see that his face was wet with tears.

'*Yes,*' said the waif, in answer to Tug's unspoken thoughts. '*We* shall *protect and nurture the former slaves. Henceforth, they will be known as the New Nations, and they will be welcomed into our city.*'

'And Great Glade?' asked Eudoxia.

The waifs' ears twitched. '*Now that descending has been curbed, you will have the support of the Waif Council of Riverrise in your dealings with that city,*' they assured her silently. '*Riverrise and New Sanctaphrax will, from this day forth, have a special relationship that will benefit us all.*'

With a soft grunt, Quove Lentis climbed off the couch. He plucked at his sleeves and gathered his robes about him fussily.

'Captain Felicia has delivered on her promise and brought you to me, Quarter,' he said, taking a long thin

dagger from within his robes. 'Now it is time to settle old scores.' He turned to the tallow-hat. 'The money barge is in the Mire grasslands waiting for your master,' he said. 'I trust Danton Clore appreciates it. But' – he hesitated, amusement flickering on his lips – 'unfortunately for you, your journey ends here. My phraxengineers will seize your ship and dismantle it to learn its secrets.'

Quove turned to his captain. 'Adereth,' he barked. 'Kill this tallow-hat.'

Captain Felicia Adereth raised her long-barrelled phraxpistol – but not at the tallow-hat. Instead, she pointed it at Quove Lentis.

'I'm sorry, your Eminence,' she said, 'but the days of my taking orders from you are over. Great Glade needs a new leader. Someone with vision. The phraxengineers might indeed learn something from dismantling the cloudcruiser, but the secrets that Nate Quarter holds are far more valuable. And what's more, Quove' – she smiled unpleasantly – 'I, as new leader of Great Glade, shall discover what they are.'

She pulled the trigger – only for the pistol to click emptily. The smile froze on her lips.

With a sneering laugh, Quove Lentis flung his arm out. The dagger flew from his hand and embedded itself in the Freeglade Lancer captain's chest.

Felicia Adereth stared down at the hilt of the knife, a look of disbelief on her face, then pitched backwards and landed heavily on the marble floor. Quove Lentis reached down and pulled the dagger from her body. He turned to Nate Quarter.

'If I've learned anything as High Professor of Flight,' he said, smiling as he opened his clenched fist and let a handful of phraxbullets drop onto the table, 'it is not to trust anybody.'

He picked up the goblet of wine.

'I have a company of lancers waiting outside this chamber,' he told the tallow-hat as he took a sip of the wine. 'They will take Nate Quarter to Lake Landing, where I will watch his execution. As for you, you may as well go. I wanted to test my captain's loyalty, that's all. You're of no further use to me—'

'But you are, to me,' said the tallow-hat, unbuckling his helmet and dropping it on the floor. 'You don't know me,' said Cade Quarter, 'but I know you. You had my father murdered and forced me to flee for my life. But I'm back now, and you will answer for your crimes, Quove Lentis.'

Cade stopped. The High Professor's face had turned a deep, dark shade of purple. His bloodshot eyes were bulging and, as he began to tremble and choke, his stubby fingers clawed at the fromp-fur collar at his throat.

'The wine,' Nate murmured as Quove Lentis fell back onto the couch, the heavy impact snapping its anchor chain.

As Nate and Cade watched, the sumpwood couch floated up into the cool air. It rose above the Palace of Phrax, where the wind took it, sending Quove Lentis's lifeless body, now beyond the help of the waifs' tincture, floating away from the city he had spent his entire life attempting to control.

Nate looked down at the upturned goblet. The poisoned sapwine was dripping down onto the marble floor beneath the table and mingling with Felicia Adereth's blood.

· CHAPTER THIRTY-TWO ·

The skytavern, the *Xanth Filatine*, moved slowly across the sky above Great Glade. The huge vessel was tethered by long chains to sleek cloudcruisers, which were deftly guiding it into the waiting sky-cage.

All at once, there was a great grinding sound like the death cry of a Deepwoods creature, followed by a booming *clunk* as the snub-nosed prow met the bars of the cage and was held tight. As the skytavern came to rest, flakes of rust fell from the empty phraxchamber at its centre, while the lattice of timber at the bow, where the ornate upper decks had been stripped for salvage, stuck up like a scavenger-picked ribcage. Below, in the depths of the vessel, however, the hull was intact.

Standing in the shadows of an alleyway in the Ambristown District, Drax Adereth looked up at the obsolete vessel, his jaw clenching and unclenching. This skytavern had been his world for longer than he cared to remember. Throughout that time, he had served his master, Quove Lentis, loyally – luring unsuspecting academics who had displeased the High Professor of Flight down into his lair in the depths of the hull, and disposing of them.

Of course, he'd had the run of the tavern too, skimming off his share of the takings from the gaming tables and the pickpocket gangs. The skytavern owners had put up with it because they knew he was Quove Lentis's servant. Anything for a quiet life . . .

But that was all before a certain young fourthling had crossed his path. Afterwards, everything had seemed to go wrong for Drax Adereth, which was particularly galling since, at the same time, his twin sister had prospered.

Drax removed his tinted spectacles and rubbed his pale eyes, so sensitive to the glare of daylight. They might have shared the same master, but there was no love lost between him and Felicia. He had no time for her airs and graces. Never had done, even when they were children back in the slums of Ambristown.

And now, here he was, back where he'd started.

Above him, those new cloudcruisers had released the ropes tethering them to the skytavern, and phraxcharges were being detonated. The tiny explosions were tearing the *Xanth Filatine* apart, bit by bit, causing the debris of timber, fittings, decking and phraxchamber-plates to fall into vast nets strung out below the cradle.

It reminded Drax of the time he'd watched, from one of the viewing baskets that used to be lowered from the skytavern for the city tourists, a pack of wig-wigs devour a hammelhorn. Drax sighed. Those days were over and done with now. He put his spectacles back on and slouched off down the alley as the explosions continued above.

Nowadays, the new skycarriers – sleek and efficient, and with no depths to hide in – were taking increasing numbers of passengers between the far-off settlements and the main cities of the Edgelands in comfort and safety. It made Drax Adereth sick to the stomach when he thought about it.

Everything, it seemed, had changed. Quove Lentis had been overthrown. Drax's sister had been reported 'killed in the line of duty'. And here, the last of the skytaverns – *his* skytavern – had been decommissioned, cleared out and was being broken up for scrap.

What really made Drax Adereth's blood boil, though, were the stories doing the rounds in the inns and alehouses of Great Glade.

They were stories of descending, embroidered with descriptions of some miraculous new phrax technology which had heralded a new age of flight. And with all these stories, there was one name that kept cropping up. It was a name Drax Adereth recognized: a name that meant a lot to him personally . . .

Keeping to the shadows, Drax headed towards the Ledges District of the city, absentmindedly touching the curious necklace he kept hidden from view below the collar of his topcoat. In the old days, the skytavern days – the *good* old days – if you didn't pay Drax Adereth his due, he would take your fingers, one by one.

Drax crossed a busy avenue and approached the new office of the Great Glade Line, an open-fronted building of ironwood timber and fluted pillars. A row of gaudily feathered shrykes were sitting behind glazed windows etched with destinations. Goblins, trogs and trolls, mobgnomes and fourthlings, were standing in lines in front of each window, waiting patiently to purchase tickets.

Outside, at the high platforms, the skycarriers were landing and taking off, the now familiar whine of their phraxengines powering up filling the air. Drax pulled up the collar of his topcoat and waited in the queue until his turn came.

'Where to?' clacked the yellow-and-blue-plumed bird-creature behind the glass.

Despite himself, Drax Adereth felt himself smiling. Cade Quarter. That was the name on the lips of every bleary-eyed goblin drunk, every slouching fourthling sapwine drinker, every cloddertrog ale-trough guzzler. Cade Quarter – who had not only slipped through Drax's clutches, but had subsequently caused his world to come crashing down around him.

Cade Quarter.

Drax Adereth had never abandoned his search for him. After that goblin stone-master in Gorgetown had given him the information, he'd headed to New Sanctaphrax. And Earth and Sky, *that* hadn't been easy,

FOUR Lakes
New Sanctaphra
Hive
Gorgetown
Riverrise
Midwood Decks
Eastern Woo
Cloud Falls
Stonecleft
Mire Town
Foundry Glade
High Peak Ridge
Farrow Lake
Low Haven

what with the blockade and all. He'd arrived to find that the slippery little eel had gone descending. Was that *it*? he'd wondered at the time. But then, some weeks later, he'd glimpsed Cade in a makeshift prison down in Undergarden – though the six-strong guard had proved impenetrable . . .

Drax still hadn't given up, though. He'd kept his ear to the ground, and finally his patient determination had paid off. Word was that the High Academe's nephew was leaving the floating city – though not to return to the city of his childhood. No, apparently he was going into the Deepwoods, the rumours maintained, though Sky alone knew where . . .

But Drax Adereth knew.

As for himself, Drax intended to travel to the wilderness of the Edgeland pavement. He would try his hand at sky piracy with the tallow-hats, or what remained of them; build up a crew of his own, perhaps. Start all over again . . .

But before any of that, there was something Drax Adereth had to do.

'Where to?' the shryke demanded a second time, drumming her talons on the counter in front of her impatiently.

Drax Adereth smiled. 'Farrow Lake,' he said.

· CHAPTER THIRTY-THREE ·

Leaving New Sanctaphrax was hard. Cade had grown to think of the magnificent floating city as his second home and, in the time that had passed since he and the other Descenders returned from the depths, he often thought that he might stay for ever.

He loved to stroll down the mosaic-tiled great avenue, sifting through the wares on the stalls that would spring up on market days; spending time with his friends in one of the many taverns and listening in on the blue-robed academics gossiping on the Viaduct Steps. And he never tired of the music of the city – the sounds of wind chimes, mist horns and rain cascades that filled the streets with their soft yet eerie laments. Evenings on the West Landing, watching the cloudcruisers weave lattices of steam over the skies above Undergarden. Nights out beneath the stars in the Stone Gardens, walking hand in hand with Celestia . . .

Yes, New Sanctaphrax was his second home. But Cade was restless. He could feel his first home calling to him. Farrow Lake. And now that Quove Lentis was dead, there was no reason for him not to return to it.

'I feel it too,' Celestia told him a few weeks after her return from Riverrise. 'The Five Falls and the Western Woods . . . I dream of them almost every night.'

Cade nodded thoughtfully. 'When we left Farrow Lake, I feared I might never see it again. I'll tell you what, though,' he added with a shake of his head, 'I think Tug misses the place more than either of us. Just the other day, I found him in the Great Library, reading a barkscroll all about prowlgrins. He said he was afraid that Rumblix might have forgotten him.'

Celestia reached out and took his hand. 'It's time to go home, Cade,' she said.

And so, the following morning, they prepared to leave New Sanctaphrax, quietly and without fuss.

Following the poisoning of Quove Lentis, the tyrannical Academy of Flight had been disbanded. Scholars now moved freely between the two cities, working together to develop phrax technology still further in this new Fourth Age. As for the Great Glade Council, it had been completely restructured. Its members were all now elected and met daily in the old Palace of Phrax which, following a unanimous vote, had been renamed the House of the Districts. And in addition to New Sanctaphrax, Great Glade had also forged new links with Riverrise and Hive.

The many changes gladdened Cade's heart, and he wished so much that his father could have lived to see them. As for himself, though, the memories were still too raw. Great Glade could never be his home.

On that morning of their departure, Cade, Celestia and Tug stood on the West Landing as Eudoxia and Nate embraced the three of them in turn, and Eudoxia gave each of them a storm-grey travel cape with a chequerboard collar.

'As you wear them, think of us,' Eudoxia said, her voice solemn and eyes bright with tears.

'And travel back to us often,' Nate added. 'For this is the Fourth Age of Flight, after all.' He smiled, and despite the sorrow of their parting, Cade thought he had never seen his uncle look happier.

Just then, there came the sound of footsteps, and the five of them turned to see Seftis Bule running towards them over the wooden boards.

'So glad we caught you!' he exclaimed breathlessly. 'We couldn't let you leave without wishing you well.'

Behind the wiry goblin armourer were Theegum the banderbear, Demora Duste and, held in her arms, Sentafuce the waif. And soon there were more tears and embraces as they made their farewells.

'Wuh-wuh wurra,' Theegum told Cade, her long arms moving gracefully as she spoke. *I shall think of you in those distant woods and remember both the good times we shared and the dangers we faced together.*

'I shall think of you too, Theegum, old friend,' Cade told her.

Celestia looked up at the sky. 'And I shall also think of you, Grent and Fenda. Absent friends. Your souls belong to the clouds now,' she said softly. 'Mine to the forests.'

'Earth and Sky united,' said Nate, his blue eyes gleaming. 'As it always was and always will be.' He took Cade and Celestia by the hand. 'We learned that on our descent, didn't we? It's something I shall never forget.'

'And nor shall we,' Cade and Celestia answered together.

'*The Descenders are parting,*' Sentafuce's words sounded in all their heads. '*But we will reunite each year at our refectory table in the Knights Academy. I want your promises on that.*'

And, 'By Earth and Sky', they had all sworn on it.

Finally, it was time for Cade, Celestia and Tug to leave the floating city – before one, or all of them, changed their minds. They climbed into the flight pit of a gleaming cloudcruiser and took their places. Cade released a ratbird with a message to Gart Ironside, informing him of their imminent arrival, then Celestia powered up the phraxchamber and, without any further delay, they set steam for the Deepwoods, the refurbished craft flying as fast and smoothly as only a skyvessel of the Fourth Age of Flight could.

By the time dawn rose on the following day, they had reached Hive. Celestia eased off on the power, and the cloudcruiser dropped down out of the high sky to fly slowly over the thronging streets of the city.

'To think,' said Cade, 'when Gart, Thorne and I made the voyage here all that time ago, it took us weeks, yet now— Look!' he cried. 'The Hive Towers! And the Sumpwood Bridge Academy!' He called out landmark after landmark to the others excitedly. 'And there!' he announced, pointing towards a jutting structure at the head of the gorge where the river cascaded down. 'That's the gantry at the top of the high-jumping course! Sky above, I'll never forget how Rumblix jumped that day!'

Beside him in the flight pit, Tug's face creased into a smile. 'Rumblix!' he exclaimed. 'Rumblix will be so pleased to see us all again!'

Celestia smiled back at him. 'He will, Tug. Now, Cade,' she said, turning to him, 'if you can show me the docking gantries, I'll bring us in to land.'

Tillman Spoke, owner of the finest prowlgrin stables in all of Hive, was delighted to see them. He and Cade had first met years earlier on board the *Xanth Filatine* – and Rumblix himself had hatched from a consignment of pedigree-grey prowlgrin eggs that Tillman Spoke was transporting.

'It's been a long time, young Cade,' he said warmly. 'The High Council has been buzzing with news of your exploits. And here you are with two of your fellow Descenders!'

The grey-haired fourthling shook Tug and Celestia by the hand, then took them all through the roost-house, past perches full of thoroughbred prowlgrins. Time and again, Tug stopped to pet one of the pedigree greys, and smile as they nuzzled up to him, purring loudly.

'Just like Rumblix,' he murmured softly.

'Of course,' Tillman Spoke was saying, 'when you sent word that you were coming, Cade, I kept it quiet. Otherwise the stables would have been overrun with well-wishers.'

They crossed a square, and Cade's gaze fell on a wooden contraption with horizontal wheels and a water spout at its centre. His stomach churned. It was where he and Rumblix had spent so many long hours practising for the high-jumping contest.

'Ever since the changes that have taken place in Great Glade, Hive has been enjoying a boost in trade.' Tillman's words broke into Cade's thoughts. 'And as for those new-fangled skyships,' he said, 'or cloudcruisers, I believe they're called; well, we've never seen anything like them! And they say that New Sanctaphrax and Great Glade are building upgraded skytaverns as well. Can this be true?'

Cade smiled, amused by his old friend's obvious enthusiasm. 'It can and it is,' he told him.

They'd reached Tillman Spoke's quarters, a lufwood cabin at the top of a rickety staircase. A bevy of cheepwits chattering on the wood-shingled roof took flight as they approached.

'But we call them skycarriers,' Cade explained. 'The bad old days of the skytavern gangs are over.'

At the top of the stairs, Tillman opened the cabin door and ushered them inside. 'Glad to hear it,' he said with a shudder. His brow furrowed. 'You had direct experience of those gangs, didn't you, Cade?'

Cade didn't reply. He'd been distracted again. For there in the lufwood cabin, sitting by a stove with a bundle in her lap, was a short, snub-nosed fourthling with thick fair hair plaited in a rope-like braid.

'Whisp, it's you!' Cade exclaimed.

The fourthling put down the bundle and leaped to her feet. Cade rushed over and embraced her tightly, before stepping back and turning to the others.

'May I present Feldia Dace.' He smiled. 'Or Whisp, as she's known. High-jumping champion of Hive!'

462

'With a little help from Dominix,' said Whisp, blushing crimson.

'Whisp works for Tillman,' Cade explained, 'and back when I was here with Gart and Thorne, trying to buy weapons to defend Farrow Lake against the mire-pearlers, she and I once raced against one another for the prize. Me on Rumblix; Whisp here on Dominix. And it was a close thing,' he added with a laugh. 'Though Whisp won . . .'

'But only by a whisker,' Whisp said quietly.

Turning away, she stooped and gathered up the bundle at her feet, then shyly held it out.

'I always hoped you'd come back, Cade,' she said. 'This is for you. With all my love.'

Back on board the cloudcruiser, it was full steam to the Farrow Lake, the familiar whine of the phraxengine high-pitched and loud. As they sped on towards their destination, Cade realized his breathing quickened each time they passed over a landmark he recognized. And when the Five Falls suddenly came into view, his heart leaped into his mouth and his eyes welled up. He wiped them on his sleeve and, glancing round, saw Celestia doing the same – while for his part, Tug made no effort to stem the tears running down his cheeks.

'Home,' he said, in a soft voice choked with emotion.

'Home,' Cade repeated, and he and his two friends embraced one another tightly.

The cloudcruiser soared above the Needles and High Farrow, then skirted round the town of Farrow Lake, strung out along the western shore. Webfoot goblin stilt cabins, hammerhead hive towers and timber-walled long-huts clustered around a central square that was lined with silver-leafed sallowdrop trees.

Despite the length of time they'd been gone, on the opposite side of the lake, the wilder eastern shore still had far fewer dwellings, and Cade was able to pick out Thorne Lammergyre's hive tower with ease. Behind it in the forest, Gart Ironside's sky-platform towered high above the trees, wisps of smoke rising from the modest cabin at the far corner telling Cade his friend was at home.

Celestia brought the cloudcruiser in low over the glittering waters of the lake. She eased down the

power to the phraxengine, while the flight-rock coil glowed white hot. Some way ahead, coming up to meet them at the northern edge of the Farrow Lake, was a simple timber cabin.

Cade's eyes welled up again as he stared at the home that he – with a little help from his friends – had constructed. And this time he made no effort to wipe away his tears.

'I'll drop the two of you off here,' Celestia told them, bringing the cloudcruiser to a thrumming hover just above the stone jetty. 'If you don't mind, I can't wait to see my father and the hanging-cabin.' She laughed. 'To think I'm going to sleep in my own bed tonight . . . !'

Tug was already unbuckling his seat harness. He climbed to his feet and pushed open the hatch in the glass canopy, then he and Cade jumped down onto the jetty.

'Give your father my best, Celestia,' Cade called above the rising whirr of the phraxengine. 'We'll all meet up tomorrow.'

The cloudcruiser turned in the air and sped off across the glittering waters of the Farrow Lake.

· CHAPTER THIRTY-FOUR ·

Cade waved goodbye to the cloudcruiser as he stood at the end of the stone jetty, the late afternoon sun warm on his back. A happy smile spread across his face. He could scarcely believe he was back.

'Look at it, Tug,' he said. His arm swept round in a broad arc that encompassed the glinting Needles, the cascading Five Falls, the red- and green-tinged marshes of the Levels, the towering trees of the Western Woods, and the Farrow Lake itself, glittering like a million shards of mirrored glass as a soft breeze ruffled its surface. 'It's all so beautiful,' he breathed. 'And it's my home.' He turned to his friend. '*Our* home.'

'And home to plenty of others since we were last here,' Tug observed. 'See how many more buildings there are now lining the shore.'

Cade surveyed the recently constructed settlements and nodded. 'New friends,' he said, then frowned. 'I

wonder how our *old* friends are doing? I'm so looking forward to seeing them again.' He paused. 'I hope our message got to Gart. Do you think anybody saw us arriving?'

Gart Ironside, for one, certainly had. Hearing the high-pitched whine of a phraxengine, he'd laid the wooden spoon aside, returned the lid to the stewpot, then crossed the cabin to the window. He looked out.

Skycarriers appeared every other day now, with fifty or sixty passengers at most on board, rather than the hundreds there had been on the old skytaverns. It had all been different in the old days. Back then, the passengers had stayed on the skytaverns, staring down at Gart from the viewing platforms, and wouldn't have dreamed of setting foot in the dangerous Deepwoods themselves. But these days, passengers would often disembark – and stay.

Farrow Lake was growing bigger every day.

Gart scanned the sky, trying to see what type of vessel was approaching. He was an old 'steamer' – always would be – and still could not differentiate between the sound of these new phraxvessels with their whining phraxengines and hissing rock coils. Was this another skycarrier arriving – or might it just be a cloudcruiser with his returning friends on board.

On the far side of the room, Delfina Dax put another log into the belly of the stove and sat back. Her flame-red hair gleamed in the flickering light.

'Your cooking's getting better and better, Captain, my love,' she said, looking up with a contented smile. Her eyes narrowed as she looked past Gart and out through the window. 'But wait – is that what I think it is?'

'It is!' said Gart as his gaze fell on the sleek new cloudcruiser passing by overhead. 'I reckon that must be them now,' he said excitedly, 'all the way from New Sanctaphrax in the blink of an eye.'

Delfina joined Gart at the cabin window. She had loved her old life as a sky-vessel engineer. But she loved everything about her new life out here in Farrow Lake even more: flying with the webfoots in their skycraft; hunting with the hammerheads in the Western Woods; exploring the glittering caverns below the Five Falls with the white trogs . . .

Most of all, though, she loved this old sky-platform keeper, and his cooking.

Far below the cosy cabin, the cloudcruiser had come down low and was gliding over the still waters of the Farrow Lake. The whine of its phraxengine changed as it came to a hover beside the stone jetty of the little timber cabin on the north shore.

'Cade, Tug and Celestia!' Gart exclaimed delightedly, hugging his wife. 'It *is* them. They're home!'

Delfina laughed. 'And not a moment too soon,' she said. 'The preparations in Sallowdrop Square have all been made. The webfoots have rigged up that silkwood banner right across the square, and all the lanterns have been strung up, ready to be lit at dusk. It's going to look so beautiful.'

'I'll go and tell them all about it!' said Gart, reaching for his flight hat and jacket.

Delfina placed a hand on his arm. 'Leave them for now, my dear,' she said. 'They've had a long journey. They'll want to unpack and settle in. Thorne was over at Cade's cabin yesterday, making sure that it was all stocked up – and returning Rumblix to his roost-perch.'

'You're right,' said Gart. 'Oh, but it'll be so good to see them this evening and hear all their news.' He smiled and took her by the hand. 'And we'll be able to give them *our* news.'

'If you want to make yourself useful,' Delfina added, 'why don't you head across to Sallowdrop Square and see if they need any help there.'

Gart Ironside wasn't the only one to have noticed the phraxvessel returning. On the far side of the Farrow

Lake, Thorne Lammergyre was sitting on a tree-stump in front of his hive tower, mending his eel nets. His pet lemkin, Tak-Tak, sat on his shoulder, purring softly.

'Cade?' the fisher goblin murmured as the sound of a phraxengine passed overhead.

Dropping his work, he jumped up and, with a raised hand shielding his eyes from the low sun, looked out across the water. A cloudcruiser was powering down its phraxengine and gliding over the Farrow Lake like a huge glittering stormhornet.

'So, they've arrived!' he exclaimed. 'And in plenty of time.'

'In plenty of time . . . In plenty of time . . .' Tak-Tak, his pet lemkin, mimicked, before jumping down from the old fisher goblin's shoulder and scurrying off into the trees.

'And no wonder,' Thorne breathed as, spyglass raised to his eye, he recognized Cade and the others on board. 'That's one of them new-fangled phraxvessels if I'm not mistaken.'

In the distance, the cloudcruiser had come to a hover over the stone jetty. Thorne couldn't take his eyes off it.

To think that the little model he'd engineered from Cade's father's drawings had led to this. It was incredible. The start of a new age: the Fourth Age of Flight. Thorne had never even dreamed that he would live to see it – but that was before his friends had left on their epic journey. Now they were back.

Rumblix would be so happy to see Cade and Tug, he

thought. The celebrations weren't till nightfall, so he'd give them time to get reacquainted before he picked them up. In the meantime, there was that batch of smoked eels he'd promised to deliver to Phineal.

In Sallowdrop Square, webfoot goblin Phineal Glyfphith had also seen the approaching cloudcruiser. He was standing at the top of a ladder, securing one end of a billowing spidersilk banner to a gable end with a double-hitch skycraft knot.

He smiled as they flew low over the far side of the lake, relieved that they hadn't spotted the banner. That would have spoiled the surprise. The fettle-legger weavers had done a wonderful job with the lettering:

Phineal was looking forward to raising a glass of finest sapwine to them all . . . Which reminded him: they still had the barrels to set up, as well as the trestles and benches. Not to mention the hammelhorn spit-roast the slaughterers of the Southern Pastures had promised . . .

The webfoot smiled. At sunset, Thorne Lammergyre was going to the little cabin to bring Cade and Tug over for a 'quiet' supper at the Winesap Tavern. Celestia's father, Blatch, was doing the same. Then they would all spring the surprise! The crest on Phineal's head rippled orange then red with pleasure at the thought of it.

'Anything we can do to help?' came a voice.

'And where do you want these smoked eels?'

Phineal looked down to see his friends Gart Ironside and Thorne Lammergyre standing at the foot of the ladder. He climbed down to greet them.

'Everything's coming along nicely here,' he said. 'How about the cabin?'

'I've opened the shutters to air it,' said Thorne, 'restocked his larder, and I fed and watered Rumblix and left him in his stable below the cabin.' He smiled. 'What a magnificent creature that prowlgrin is.'

'Indeed,' said Gart. 'And Cade trained him well. Not bad for a "city boy", as Celestia's always calling him,' he added with a chuckle.

'Everything the lad turns his hand to, he does well,' said Thorne, his heart swelling with pride. 'Fishing. Hunting . . .'

'Sailing a skycraft,' Phineal broke in. 'I still remember that first flight we took when he was showing me around the Farrow Lake.' He sighed. 'How long ago that now seems.'

'There are so many Farrow Lakers who will be pleased to see him back,' said Gart. 'Blatch Helmstoft, for a start. And I know the hammerheads are planning a special surprise – Chert still hasn't forgotten how he rescued his son, Teeg, from that bloodoak. And there are rumours that the white trog queen herself is preparing to leave her caverns behind the falls to greet him in person . . .'

'It isn't just Farrow Lakers either,' said Phineal. 'Only the other day, I met someone who was asking about him. A stranger.' He frowned, recalling the encounter. 'I was mending my aft-sail when he walked past. A fourthling. Thin, slightly stooped, with large waif-like eyes behind dark tinted spectacles.'

He told the others how the stranger had stopped to admire the carved prows of his old-fashioned skycraft tethered at the shore. He'd chatted briefly to the webfoot, enquiring about the celebrations for the returning travellers which the whole town was so excited about.

'You didn't find out who he was?' Thorne asked.

'No,' said Phineal, shaking his head. 'I told him he'd be welcome to join us in Sallowdrop Square, and he thanked me and left. I thought no more about it. Until now,' he added thoughtfully.

As the cloudcruiser had disappeared off into the forest, Cade turned to Tug.

'Our little cabin,' he said. 'Just like we left it. It's as though we'd never been away.'

His gaze fell upon a folded piece of barkscroll, anchored by a stone at the end of the jetty, the corners fluttering in the breeze.

Tug reached down and handed it to him.

'It's from Thorne,' said Cade. 'He says he's fed and watered Rumblix, and settled him on his roost-perch.' The two of them headed along the stone jetty. 'He's also stocked up the storeroom – though knowing Thorne,' he laughed, 'that probably means the place is full of smoked eels . . .'

'Rumblix *loves* smoked eels!' Tug exclaimed. 'You check the storeroom and I'll go and fetch him!'

'Oh, and Thorne's invited us for supper at the tavern in the square,' Cade added. 'He'll call for us at sundown.'

He smiled. It was just what he felt like – a quiet supper with his friends.

The two of them had reached the wooden steps that led up to the cabin. Cade reached into the inside pocket of his jacket and pulled out the little bundle that Whisp had given him back in Hive.

'Show Rumblix this, Tug,' he said. 'But make sure you keep it warm,' he cautioned.

'I shall.' Tug smiled lopsidedly. 'Rumblix is going to be so happy to find out about his future friend.'

With that, he headed down to the undercabin, his broad shoulders swaying from side to side. Cade turned away and started up the steps.

With the precious prowlgrin egg that Cade had just given him cupped in one massive hand, Tug opened the door to the room below the cabin. It was where he and Rumblix had always slept and, as he stepped into the timber-walled undercabin, he was struck by the familiar sweet fragrance of the gladegrass carpeting the floor. He walked through the dark room, the sound of footsteps echoing around him as Cade crossed the timber boards of the veranda above his head.

'Rumblix?' Tug said softly. 'Rumblix ... *There* you are,' he said happily, spotting the pale grey fur of his prowlgrin friend curled up in the corner. 'Rumblix, it's me, Tug. I'm back.'

But the little creature made no move, and Tug felt a sudden fierce pang of alarm. Something was wrong. He put the egg bundle carefully down and, reaching out, laid a hand on his friend's shoulder.

It was cold.

Tug turned Rumblix over, gently, anxiously. And it was then that he saw the phraxbullet wound in the side of the prowlgrin's head, deep and dark and encrusted with dried blood ...

Up on the veranda, Cade had stooped down and picked up the strange shrivelled root that lay outside the door of his cabin. He turned it over in his hands, to find a curved fingernail on the other side.

'No,' Cade gasped.

It was like a punch to the gut. Suddenly before him was the image of the glass bowl full of severed fingers, brown and desiccated, that he'd seen in the gangmaster's quarters, deep down in the bowels of the *Xanth Filatine*. But it had all been so long ago. Surely that evil monster Drax Adereth couldn't still be looking for him.

With a shudder of revulsion, Cade dropped the dismembered finger to the floor – just as Tug's agonizing howl of grief rang out:

'NOOOOOOO!'

Cade instinctively reached for his phrax-pistol. Gripping it tightly, he kicked open the cabin door – to be confronted by Drax Adereth himself staring back at him, his own phraxpistols pointed at Cade's chest.

'We meet again at last,' Drax said softly. 'I've been looking all over for you, Cade Quarter. Drax Adereth never forgets a debt.'

He kicked the shrivelled finger across the veranda as he stepped forward, the necklace of bony trophies around his neck tapping together as he did so.

'I trust you appreciated my little present,' he said. 'A little present from me to you, to remind you of the old days.' With a sneer, he jerked the weapons in his hands at Cade. 'Drop the pistol.'

Cade let his phraxpistol clatter to the floor. Behind him, he heard Tug's heavy footsteps thundering up the stairs.

'He's killed Rumblix!' Tug roared as he reached the veranda and, overwhelmed by rage and grief, he threw himself at the smirking murderer before him.

'Tug! No!' screamed Cade as Drax Adereth fired, both phraxpistols flaring.

Tug toppled back, crashed through the copperwood balustrade of the veranda and hit the ground below with a heavy thud.

Cade threw himself down onto the wooden boards, grasped his own phraxpistol and came up firing. Once, twice, three times . . .

Drax Adereth staggered backwards and fell heavily, the green-tinted goggles dislodged from his face as his head struck the floor. A line of blood trickled from the corner of his mouth and pooled on the timbered boards. The smirk was frozen on his lifeless face.

Cade leaped to his feet and raced down the steps. Kneeling beside Tug, he cradled his friend's great head in his arms.

'Tug,' he sobbed, tears streaming down his burning cheeks as he rocked slowly back and forwards. 'Tug. Tug. Tug . . .'

In the sky above, clouds had rolled in, shutting out the sun and darkening the waters of the lake. A solitary black heron stood stock-still amid the spiky reeds, its mournful cry carried away on the rising wind.

· EPILOGUE ·

Cade Quarter, Councillor-Elect of Farrow Lake, stood on the veranda of his beautiful house on the north shore. A gentle wind stirred the surface of the lake.

To the west, the stilt factories of the silk weavers steamed, their phraxlooms busier than ever while, all along the jetties, webfoot skycraft were taking to the air in a fluttering armada. They joined the skycarriers, arriving at and departing from the sky-platforms, along with the elegant blond-timbered sky yachts out on pleasure cruises above the Western Woods.

So much had already changed in the Edgelands since the ushering in of the Fourth Age of Flight, and perhaps nowhere more so than in Farrow Lake, the small outpost at the furthest reaches of the Deepwoods. Numerous stilt factories and workshops had sprung up, all of them powered by a single crystal of phrax, using the latest technology to produce an endless supply of clean energy.

The streets were lit, the houses were heated and, by channelling the warm steam the phraxengines gave off into vast glass-framed domes, prodigious quantities of fruit, vegetables and herbs were produced, enough for the ever-swelling population.

As Cade leaned forward on the balustrade that enclosed the veranda, and surveyed the lake, the doors behind him opened, and he turned to see his wife, Celestia, stepping out from the lakeside gallery. In her arms she cradled their new-born baby.

'Celestia,' he said softly, and his eyes lit up as his gaze fell upon the swaddled infant. 'And you too, little one.'

Nearly five years had passed since the two of them had first met. Almost immediately they'd become the closest of friends – although, if Cade was honest, he'd always felt that he liked Celestia just a little bit more than she liked him. Together, they'd had so many adventures – riding over the treetops on their prowlgrins; falling into the clutches of the hammerhead goblins in the Western Woods; fighting side by side at the battle for Farrow Lake; descending the Edge cliff, all the way down to groundrise . . .

And yet, during all that time, although they had trusted each other with their lives time and again, they had never been *more* than good friends.

All that had changed in New Sanctaphrax. Celestia had been distraught when Brock had died and, as always when she needed to be comforted, Cade was there for her. Good old dependable 'city boy'; never giving too little or demanding too much. Suddenly Celestia had realized that Cade was *more* than a friend to her after all, and always had been – and Cade, for his part, had been overjoyed to discover that his feelings for her were finally being returned.

'It's a beautiful morning,' Celestia said, smiling wistfully.

From the prowlgrin stables below, they heard a whinnying cry, and a young prowlgrin came bounding up the stairs to join them.

'Ruffix!' Cade laughed, tickling the prowlgrin between his nostrils. 'You grow bigger every day!'

'Let's take our little one down to the lake,' said Celestia. She nodded thoughtfully. 'Almost a week has passed since he was born. It's time he had a name.'

Cade and Celestia descended the stairs and walked along the stone jetty. Next to the mooring ring at the far end, a figure turned to greet them.

'Tug,' said Celestia. 'Would you like to hold our new arrival?'

'Oh, yes,' said Tug, and Celestia carefully placed the little bundle in his huge arms.

Tug looked down into the round pink face staring back up at him. Cade saw the two pale scars above his brow ridges crinkle as Tug smiled. And, not for the first time, Cade marvelled at Celestia's healing skills. After Drax Adereth had shot Tug, there had been long, harrowing hours of painstaking surgery, followed by days of potions, poultices and prayers as his friend hovered between life and death.

How many times had he almost given up hope? thought Cade. But not Celestia. His Celestia. She had refused to let Tug go. Cade could never thank her enough for that. Slowly and surely, the wounds had healed, Tug's strength had returned and the scars faded.

Cade put an arm round his friend's massive shoulders.

'We'd like *you* to name him,' he said.

Tug looked suddenly serious. His head cocked to one side, and then a smile broke once more across his face. He looked out across the lake, glittering in the morning sunlight, then back at the tiny baby in his arms, and when he spoke, his voice was soft and gentle.

'By Earth and Sky, I name you . . . Twig.'

ABOUT THE AUTHORS

STEWART & RIDDELL are the co-creators of the
bestselling Edge Chronicles, which now boasts sales
of over three million books and has been published
in over thirty languages around the world. They
also created the award-winning series Far-Flung
Adventures, and the fantastic Barnaby Grimes.

PAUL STEWART is a highly regarded and award-
winning author of books for young readers –
everything from picture books to football stories,
fantasy and horror. Before turning his hand to
writing for children, he worked as an English
teacher in Germany and Sri Lanka. He met Chris
Riddell when their children attended the same
nursery school.

CHRIS RIDDELL is an accomplished illustrator and
author. He has illustrated many books for children,
including *The Sleeper and the Spindle* and *Coraline* by
Neil Gaiman, Russell Brand's retelling of *The Pied
Piper of Hamelin*, and *The Tales of Beedle the Bard* by
J. K. Rowling, and he writes and illustrates the
Ottoline and Goth Girl series. Chris has won the
Kate Greenaway Medal three times, and his book
Goth Girl and the Ghost of a Mouse won the Costa
Children's Book Award. He was the UK Children's
Laureate from 2015 to 2017.